Roma Invicta Est

Alfonso Solís

To my father Adrian and my nephew Ángel.
They are helping from heaven for this dream to come true.

CONTENTS

In the 7th century BC. after a hazardous and adventurous life, Romulus and Remus, the grandsons of Numitor, the king of Alba Longa, decided to found a city and establish their kingdom on its solid foundations. Romulus proposed to erect it next to the river Tiberis, on the Palatine Hill, while Remus suggested to doing it on the Aventine Hill. Impulsive and stubborn young man, they didn't reach an agreement and turned to an augur to guide them in their decision. The soothsay recommended that they ascend the hill that each had chosen and wait there for a sign from the gods.

After several weeks of waiting, Remus saw six eagles flying overhead. Confused by such a strange event, he went in search of his brother Romulus who told him that he had seen twelve eagles soar the skies of the Palatine Hill that same day.

Convinced that the gods had sent them a sign, they visited the soothsayer again to interpret the meaning of the message. The augur, after meditating for a few minutes, said:

"You are right young brothers, the flight of the eagles has been an omen sent by the gods and this is his message: if your city is founded on the Aventine Hill, it will be blessed by six centuries of glory and splendor, but, if it stands on the Palatine Hill, it will survive for twelve centuries and its memory will never be forgotten. This has been his word."

Romulus, who was convinced that he was the chosen one of the gods, began to trace the outline of Rome, as he decided to call the city, with a plow, and threatened to kill anyone who dared to cross it. Remo didn't accept the designs of the soothsayer and crossed the imaginary border in order to challenge him, convinced that he would not have enough courage to carry out his threat.

But Romulus, a slave of his words, killed his brother remaining as the sole sovereign. The blood of Remus watered the land where the most powerful city in the world was built.

In the 5th century AD, twelve centuries after its founding, Rome is surrounded by dozens of barbarian tribes and threatened by the hosts of Attila, God's scourge. Dark omens loom over the Empire. Will the augur's prophecy come true?

CHAPTER I

Attila, or the war of the worlds.

Attila vivo, Romani in magno discrimine semper versati sunt.[1]

Several hours had elapsed since the sun leaned out the horizon, announcing a warm day in mid-June. We Roman soldiers remained in formation, oblivious to anything that was not the attentive vigilance of our enemies. Due to the unbearable heat and suffocating hours, we had been in training, both my cuirass and my helmet had heated up, scorching my body as if it had been thrown into a pyre filled with incandescent ashes.

Thirst was burning my throat while fear fiercely bit my gut. I was hardly a young and inexperienced recruit who observed with horror the thousands of standards, flags and banners that waved threateningly in the clear sky, swayed by the capricious wind, as if they were the waves of a rough and dark sea, eager to fall against the coast, leaving not only a trail of destruction in its path, but also a serious warning to those who dare to stand in its way. My heart was beating in my chest with the fury of a thousand titans and threatened to flee down my throat and escape from that fateful place that presaged nothing but misery and death. I could barely bear the weight of my *scutum* and my *spiculum*, since my

---

[1] *While Attila lived, the Romans were always in great danger (phrase extracted and adapted from the Latin Grammar book by Santiago Segura Munguía).*

arms were trembling with fear as I contemplated those beings fleeing from the deepest hell.

I was in my early twenties and was facing my first match. And the fates saw fit that at my baptism of blood I participated in the most formidable battle that history had ever witnessed: The war of Christianity against paganism, of civilization against barbarism, of order against chaos. In short, of the world that until that moment we had known against the world of darkness and the unknown: the world of Attila.

"Look, we're surrounded by barbarians," a soldier began to say. "To our right we have the Alans of Sangiban and the Visigoths of Theodoric and, protecting our rear-guard and keeping a close eye on the supposed allegiance of the Alans, the Franks of Meroveo." And with a snort he added. "Supported by these barbarians we will confront the Huns of Attila, the Ostrogoths of Valamir and dozens of foreign tribes..."

"Don't be unfair to our *foederati*," another legionary replied, "they are in a hurry to stop the insatiable Huns."

"As much as we are..." I interrupted.

The first who spoked was called Sextilius Arcadius, a good comrade in arms. We met in the fortress of Tarraco and he was a Hispanic from the Tarraconense region. He was my age but much heftier. With bushy eyebrows, his body was practically covered in hair and his arms were powerful as oak logs. His prominent forehead made him look tough and fierce, but he was a noble and kind person incapable of hurting someone who had not done enough merit to deserve it. The one who answered him was called Lucius Calerus, and we also met at the training camp. He was younger than us and came from a good family in the Hispanic region of Segobriga. Calerus was tall, with a slim build and a carefully shaved face. Young, cultured and restless, he had read the fables of Phaedrus, the poetry of Valerius Catus and, of course, the works of the famous Virgil, as well as other writers and poets, which had given him a certain ascendancy over the *circitores* and *centenarii* and the hundreds who came to him to ask for advice or to transcribe a document. Like most of us, he was a Christian and professed his faith with utter devotion.

"Think whatever you want, I don't trust the Visigoths, as I don't trust any barbarian," Sextilius Arcadius declared. "Or do I have to remind you that it was the Visigoths who sacked Rome forty years ago?"

"I don't like the Visigoths either, they are still Arian heretics, but of all the barbarians they are the ones who most resemble us," Lucius Calerus replied.

The sun was beating hard on my exhausted body and I lacked the courage to participate in the debate, rather it was a feat not to have fainted. We were grouped in centuries and prepared for combat, standing firm on an infinite esplanade dotted with small low hills near the city of Maurica. A small stream, which would not hinder the maneuvers of the *vexillationes*, separated the battlefield into two almost symmetrical halves. Ahead was the most powerful army that ever lived. It was commanded by the invincible Attila: the feared *Dei flagellum...* God's scourge The Hun king, allied with Ostrogoths, Heruli, Gepids, Burgundians and other barbarian peoples, raised a great army and crossed the borders of the Empire. He plundered and razed every city he encountered in his path and directed his hosts toward his true goal: Rome. But we were there to prevent it. Allied with other barbarians, but, as Calerus would say, more civilized, we had proposed to prevent the advance of the savage Huns. For this purpose, we had required the help of the Visigoths, Franks, Alans, and Lycenes *foederati* and several other tribes which for being unknown for me or due to the small number of supplied troops, I have forgotten their names.

The military training in Tarraco had lasted four months and it had been very hard. There were not few recruits who had given up or who had been expelled from the army for different reasons. Now I was supposed to be a real *miles*: a Roman soldier ready to go into battle when required. But the truth was quite different. I was terrified due to the infinite image of thousands of barbarian warriors. The sound of their war drums ripped through my mind and I had to make strenuous efforts not to throw my *scutum* to the ground and rush out from the hell that loomed.

I don't know why, but suddenly the memory of my family came to my mind, as if sensing the approach of death, my last thoughts were with them in a vain attempt to appease my martyred spirit. I remembered my old house near the port of Saguntum and my father's exhausting working days to be able to bring just a crust of bread and some fish to our table. My origins were humble. I was the youngest of five children and my father earned his living as a longshoreman on the docks. Due to the barbarian incursions, trade had fallen dramatically, and few were the merchants who ventured to sail the Mediterranean in search of a good deal. No, it was no longer profitable to trade for the Empire, and the amount of ships that loaded or unloaded goods in the once important port dwindled until they practically disappeared, and with them my family's livelihood. They were years of famine and scarcity, until I made the determination to leave my home and enlist in the army. My father gladly accepted my decision, more for having one less mouth to feed than for enjoying the pride of having a soldier in the family. That was how one day, I said goodbye to them, possibly forever, and left, taking the Via Augusta north, towards Tarraco, hoping to be able to fill my bowl every day with something that was more or less edible.

And now, I was drenched in sweat against the invincible hosts of Attila, God's scourge, the son of the devil, the invincible... Of all the attributes, names and nicknames that were granted to him, the one that infused me more fear was that of "invincible," It meant that he had won each and every one of the battles in which he had participated, and there were not few the battles that the barbarian had fought in his long life as a soldier. "Invincible, Attila is invincible," this thought tortured me over and over again. "I am going to die; soon I will meet the Almighty," this was the other thought that floated my head, even more disturbing and disheartening.

"I think I'm going to faint," I whispered in a small voice.

"What are you saying, man? Hold on a bit, the party will start soon," Sextilius Arcadius said.

"Are you fine, Adriano?" Lucius Calerus asked me.

"I'm terrified," I replied.

The *centenarius* asked Arcadius to behave properly when he broke into a raucous laugh.

"We are all afraid, dear friend, but take into account that this battle will go down in history and you possibly with it," Arcadius said.

"Have faith in God and, if His will is for you to die in this combat, your sacrifice will not be in vain and you will be received in Paradise," Calerus intervened.

"I'd rather not have to check if Paradise exists," I said, a little more animated.

"You can wait for me too," Arcadius added with a smile.

We had just finished our training at Tarraco fortress, and our unit of *limitanei* was summoned by Aetius: «the bravest of the Roman generals.» He had exhorted all the legions, *numeri, foederati,* auxiliaries and all those soldiers who, Roman or not, were faithful to the Empire, to defend Rome from the greatest danger that loomed over it since the Visigoth king Alaric sacked it in 410 of Our Lord. And there we were Arcadius, Calerus and I, the three friends, the three companions, the three *milites* ready to sacrifice our lives for Rome and for the Empire, since we had been instructed to do so.

"When is this going to start?" I asked rhetorically.

"I suppose when one of the two armies launches itself over the other," Arcadius replied mockingly.

"This heat is going to kill me," I said.

"Be patient, it won't be long now," Calerus pointed out.

"How do you know?" I asked for.

"The sun has been shinning during many hours and we are two powerful armies that are facing each other and neither of us is interested in it getting dark," he answered.

"You're right," Arcadius confirmed with a nod.

Suddenly, a clamor of cheers and salutes directed my attention to a horseman who had positioned himself in front of the Roman column, riding on a beautiful war chestnut. Despite the cuirass and the plumed helmet that covered his head, I could make out in this man the noble and handsome features of our general Aetius. The *centenarii* asked to maintain order and the acclamation shouts ceased. Our *magister utriusque militiae* was speaking with one of the tribunes who led the troops and for a brief moment, or so I want to remember it, from his reddish mount he directed his gaze towards me, and, not only that, but I am also convinced that smiled at me. Almost instinctively I stood up firmly and stuck my chest out like a presumptuous rooster trying to attract the attention of the rest of the henhouse. His powerful, crystalline gaze infused me an unknown courage. General Aetius had smiled at me! I felt exultant, blissful, triumphant, and a confident smile spread across my face. Fear and fatigue disappeared, as if I was suddenly protected by the aegis of Mars, our ancient God of War, being now invulnerable to enemy arrows and swords. Now I only had the restlessness of someone who yearns for something with impatience and cannot wait to get it. I needed the fight to start as soon as possible. I was in dire need of showing my general that I was worthy to serve under his command. Arcadius noticed my smile and, with a frown, asked me:

"Now what are you laughing at?"

"I believe that the victory will be ours," I answered totally convinced.

"You're weird," he replied, shaking his head.

A noise of drums and trumpets halted the conversation, flooding the battlefield with the sound that precedes screams of fury, fear and pain. From the Huns troops, several horsemen broke ranks and, at full gallop, headed towards a small knoll on our left flank. They wore felt pants and protected their heads with a leather helmet embroidered with animal skin. From their small but fast horses, they uttered terrifying howls with the purpose of intimidating us. And by God… ¡they were getting it! Beside me, a young legionary couldn't contain his sphincters and a stream of urine slid down his thighs. His face was contracted because of fear and he clung to the *spiculum* with the vigor that comes from panic. I realized that there were not a few Romans who were in an equally dire situation: terrified, driven by fear to defend our lives convinced that the battle was lost. But we were *milites*, imperial soldiers, we had sworn to defend Rome from her enemies, and we could do little more than offer our lives in sacrifice.

If the Huns managed to conquer the hill, they would dominate an important part of the esplanade and would lead the fight on that flank. But a dust cloud from our right wing revealed that we would not let the Huns conquer it so easily. I recognized Visigoth prince Turismund uttering fierce war shouts as he led his soldiers into the inevitable confrontation with the invincible Huns. Aetius ordered two *vexillationes* to come in support of the federated and hundreds of horsemen rode swiftly in pursuit of the same goal: successfully reaching the top of the hill before the enemy. The Huns mounted on their small but strong horses, the Visigoths riding their chestnuts, much larger and faster, but more sensitive to fatigue. From our positions, Visigoths, Romans, Alans, Franks and other barbarians and allies shouted, haranguing the young prince to successfully conquer the hill before the enemy. Attila, flanked by his generals and commanders, was watching the mad race attentively, obviously hoping otherwise. But it was the Visigoths and our *vexillationes* who reached the top first, and the Huns, who were still climbing it, were showered with darts, spears, stones, rolling rocks, and all kinds of throwing elements. The Hun horsemen fell with their mounts downhill, overwhelming those behind, causing panic and disorder in the entire troop. When Turismund ran out of arrows and rocks to roll down the slope, he launched himself, raising his terrible pike, on the disorganized Huns, who died pierced by spears or trampled on by horse hooves. Hundreds of Huns died, managing to survive a few who fled taking refuge behind the ranks of the barbarian army.

Our joy shouts reached Attila's ears, which, goaded by such an affront, sent the Ostrogoths led by their king, Valamir, against the Visigoth and Roman horsemen with the purpose of taking the hill from us, but the *foederati* and our *equites* fought with resolute courage to defend

17

it, unleashing a ruthless carnage that sowed the mountainside with hundreds of deaths from both sides. Meanwhile, Attila had sent his troops against the Sangiban Alans who could hardly withstand the thrust of the Hun enraged by his small defeat. We, the bulk of Aetius' army, stood expectantly, away from the front line of combat, watching the barbarians kill each other. Meanwhile, Attila had sent his troops against the Alans of Sangiban who could hardly withstand the thrust of the Hun enraged by their small defeat. We, the bulk of Aetius' army, stood expectantly, away from the front line of combat, watching the barbarians kill each other.

Attila had no difficulty in getting rid of the Alans, and thanks to a storm of arrows and the courage of thousands of Franks soldiers he was unable to reach our rear-guard and destroy our camp, which, no doubt, would have been disastrous. The Huns, forced by such a colossal defensive barrier, had to retreat and, realizing the problems in which their Ostrogoth allies found themselves, rode diligently to their aid, as they could hardly withstand the onslaught of the hosts of Turismund and our *equites.*

Finally, Aetius ordered us to attack the right wing of the Huns where Ardaric, the Gepids king, was. We gave a good account of them and we managed to put many to flight, not a few barbarians tasted the cold of my spatha. It was even better for Arcadius, who enjoyed punishing our enemies with his broadsword at will... I saw him with his face splattered by the vermilion liquid and he winked at me boldly while he pierced from part to part, a Gepid with his sword. I looked for Calerus who already during the training had shown to have serious difficulties when it came to using the sword. He was brave and didn't shy away from combat, but he was not excessively skilled. Much to my regret, I quickly understood that he would never be a great legionary. I saw him fighting with serious difficulties against a giant with long red hair. I went to meet him and, with my spatha, pierced the back of the burly barbarian, who fell inert to on ground with the reflection of surprise in his eyes.

But Ardaric rebuilt his ranks and stirred like a cornered and wounded animal, hurling his Gepid hordes at us with the fierce determination to inflict as much damage as possible before being skewered by our swords. The battle escalated into a fierce mob of screams, the cracking of swords, and the crunching of bones. The barbarians managed to isolate and surround Mansueto, the *comes Hispaniarum*, and he defended himself with valiant courage against the Gepid attacks, but a spear struck the side of his horse that fell to the ground between heartbreaking neighs of pain, dragging his master in his drop. I ran towards him, getting rid of every Gepid that I found on my way, and I managed to avoid his death just at the moment when a barbarian was about to skewer him with his pike. With a certain movement of my *spatha*, I mortally wounded him in the neck and his blood splattered my face staining it with blood. I helped the shocked *comes* and he asked me:

"What's your name, soldier?"

"Salvio Adriano, *domine*."

He nodded with puckered lips and said:

"I'll never forget that you saved my life." And he added. "Now let's kill a few more bastards and water this land of Gaul with their dirty blood. Today will be a glorious day for Rome." And, uttering a terrifying cry, he attacked a Gepid, plunging its sharp spatha into his stomach.

Of the circumstances that occurred during the combat, I can only speak of what I saw and heard, but much information that I still keep in my memory was provided to me by soldiers who actively participated in the fight. The truth is that during the battle Attila was in serious trouble. The Visigoths put the Ostrogoths to flight, who only managed to reorganize when the Hun king came to his aid. Aetius and we Romans, we surpassed the Gepids and we dominated the right flank of the Huns. The Meroveo Franks supported their Visigoth cousins by forcing the Huns and Valamir's troops into the center of the formation.

So, Meroveo with his Franks and Theodoric with his Visigoths controlled the left flank of the Huns and we controlled the right one. Both armies formed an indestructible pincer on the hosts of Attila and his allies, who clustered in a disorganized way in the center of the battlefield. But the king of the Huns was not a man who was daunted by the first obstacle that came across his path, but quite the opposite. He felt like a trapped animal and as such he behaved, fighting fiercely to defend his life and haranguing his soldiers so that they would not lose heart and prove in battle that the Huns were the best warriors in the world. The victory, which seemed ours, was diluted like water between our hands and both armies fought with renewed vigor with the intention of putting an end as soon as possible to that holocaust of blood and destruction.

The heat was unbearable and the fight seemed endless. Immersed in the maelstrom of combat, I hadn't realized how thirsty I was and, accompanied by Arcadius, Calerus, and several other legionaries, I went to the small watercourse that ran through the battlefield. I looked at my companions and we smiled. We were completely dehydrated and the image of the stream lifted our morale a bit. But when we knelt to quench our thirst, we noticed with horror how the water was dyed red by the spilled blood. I was repulsed and refused to drink, but one of the Romans, even more thirsty than I, or at least with much less apprehension, pushed a corpse away from the stream and drank greedily, staining his face and hands the color of blood. Impelled by thirst, we advanced towards the enemy, leaving behind the rest of the army, which had withdrawn, leaving us alone with a few Roman soldiers with the sole company of several Visigoth equites. A group of Hun horsemen who noticed our disadvantage, rushed at us brandishing their swords and spears. We took cover behind shields while Visigoth horsemen protected our flanks. We repelled the incessant barbaric onslaught, gutting horses and finishing off riders in a confused whirlwind of screams, cries of pain, and animal neighing.

Dirty with dust and blood and impregnated with the acrid smell of death, I began to give orders to Visigoths and Romans who, perhaps surprised by the authority that my words emanated or by the logic of them, obeyed without opposition. There I suffered my first serious injury. A Hun horseman attacked me with his sword piercing my coat of mail. Luckily, it only brushed me wounding my rib which caused a terrible pain. I was bleeding profusely, but the wound was not serious. The Visigoth King Theodoric, noticing the harassment to which we were subjected, came to help us and, spear at the ready, went to meet the Huns accompanied by his *spatharii*. The Visigoth troops were received by a shower of arrows and javelins from a regiment of Ostrogoths that came in support of their allies, with such a bad luck that one of the arrows seriously wounded the Visigoth king himself, causing him to fall to the ground and be trampled by the horsemen who followed him and who, due to the confusion had not noticed his fall. The fighting was fierce and hundreds of soldiers from both sides perished, but the Visigoths were superior and forced both Ostrogoths and Huns to retreat.

When Turismund knew about the death of his father, he went angrily against the Hun troops who, unable to stop the prince's attack, withdrew in disarray towards his camp. Aetius advanced on the few Gepids and Burgundians who were still alive, engaging in fierce skirmishes.

The battle was won, and now our aim was to get out as whole as possible from that field infested with dead and mutilated limbs. Attila, who was protected by his personal guard, watched helplessly as Turismund fought bravely, getting rid of the Huns and how the Romans advanced inexorably, finishing off the wounded and exterminating the stragglers who had not had the common sense to flee when they had the chance to do so.

The great Attila arrived dejected at the Hun camp, where several hundred horsemen were already waiting for him and managed to escape. We continued to finish off the wounded and fight against some indomitable who refused to surrender until twilight announced the end of the fight. Completely exhausted, I fell on my knees and it took the help of my companions to get up. I put my hand on my side and noticed that it was still bleeding. Carried almost in flight by Calerus and Arcadius, we arrived at the *valetudinarium*, where the physician didn't lack work. The hospital was embalmed with the acrid smell of blood and death. The cries of pain were confused with the heartbreaking cries of the mutilated and with the pleas of the wounded, imploring someone to release them from their agony. I was sure that hell wasn't much different from that dark and terrible *valetudinarium*. They undressed me and I observed that, from the wound, between a layer of dust, sweat and dry scabs, a thread of blood flowed.

"Your first war wound!" exclaimed Arcadius who looked exhausted. "We can be proud, we have defeated the almighty army of Attila," he added, collapsing on a footstool. Before long he was sleeping peacefully, like a child sleeping exhausted on his pallet, after having enjoyed his favorite game for hours.

"Paradise will have to wait, right?" Calerus asked with a smile.

"It will have to wait…"

Those were my last words. Deaf at the heartbreaking wailing and plaintive screams that filled the field hospital, I fell into a deep, restful sleep. Despite having seen so much suffering, so much death, so much destruction, I had one of the most pleasant dreams of my life. Had I become a bloodthirsty savage warrior, or was I just mere miles doing his job well? The battle against the barbarians of Attila was my baptism of blood and, I don't know if unfortunately or fortunately, I felt no remorse for the lives I had taken. War turns men into beasts, awakening in them their most cruel and soulless side.

I woke up just before dawn and realized that the physicians had done their job very well. My wound was clean and well stitched. I freshened up and dressed in my ripped coat of mail. I looked at the crack between two metal bands that had wreaked the barbarian's sword and could not help but smile at my prodigious fortune. I was about to leave that hospital full of misery and pain, when Calerus and Arcadius made an appearance.

"How are you feeling?" Calerus asked smiling, handing me a jug of water and a piece of bread.

"I slept like a child. The truth is that I feel completely new, the wound hardly hurts," I replied, eating quickly the delicious piece of bread like a starving. "Didn't they hurt you?"

"Bah!" Arcadius exclaimed. "Some minor scratch, unfortunately my body remains virgin of war wounds. I hope I will have better luck next time," he replied with a laugh.

Being wounded during battle and that such a wound caused an indelible scar, was an honor for any *miles*. It meant that you had defied the Grim Reaper and that you had won, it meant that you had fought in the front row and that you had not stayed in the rear-guard guarding the provisions and supplies. A wound is a memory of the combat and the possibility to count the moment it happened and, of course and not least... to be able to tell it! Sextilius Arcadius contemplated my scar with envy until a few months later a barbarian produced a similar one. But this is another history.

"I have a cut on my arm," Calerus said, touching a bulky bandage on his left arm. "I still haven't thanked you for saving me from the red-haired giant."

"You don't have to give them to me, my friend."

"I hope that whatever happens, we will never part and be always together. At least as long as we stay in the legion," Calerus wished.

We both smiled and joining our hands we made an oath. I'm happy to say that for years we kept it. I have never had more faithful friends than those I met in Tarraco and with whom I fought the invincible Huns of Attila.

"You should see the battlefield, it is full of the dead," Arcadius said.

"It's a devastating sight," Calerus muttered, with a sad face.

"It's war, friend," replied a pragmatic Arcadius.

"Let's go," I said eager to see the damage caused by our troops.

Our camp was waking up with the *milites* reluctantly beginning to leave the tents. The sound of trumpets would be heard soon and the soldiers would form ready for breakfast. A long and hard day awaited us, for Attila had not yet been defeated.

The call for breakfast surprised us on our horses, watching an endless sea of corpses. Tens of thousands of men lay inert beyond where the eye could reach. Our horses could not avoid trampling the mortal remains whether they were friends or enemies. Strung out with spears, swords, arrows, mutilated, beheaded or dismembered, thousands of human and animal remains greeted the new dawn with a tragic gesture. In the sky, the most skilled vultures flew eager for a great feast, and crows, foxes and several abandoned dogs roamed the wasteland, devouring the spoils with carelessness and indifference, persuaded that there was food for all. But what I remember most about that ghastly scene was the smell. Many years have passed, and I remember that smell as if only a few hours had passed. I breathed that fetid air that penetrated my mind leaving an indelible mark. Some call it the smell of war, others of death; I simply consider it to be the smell of human misery. It was a mixture of blood, vomit, urine, feces, sweat, fear... Yes, fear. Fear can be perceived and smelled, and there, in that field, hidden under the sinister shadow of desolation, there were huge numbers.

"It's hell on Earth," Calerus observed, moved, as we were all due to the devastating spectacle.

"It would be hell if the Huns had won," Arcadius said.

"We must return to the *castrum*," I said, wanting to leave that field strewn with death and destruction as soon as possible.

Suddenly, we heard a deafening scream. We looked at each other and, without a word, drew our *spatha* and galloped at full speed towards the *castrum*. Our hearts were pounding, as we concluded that our camp was under attack. But when we arrived, we realized that the shouts were not of war, but of jubilation. A Visigoth delegation had informed general Aetius that Attila had protected himself in his camp behind a wall of chariots and belongings. The Visigoths and Romans embraced each other and drank wine toasting victory. Attila was in our hands, and his annihilation looked very near. It was then that I saw Aetius and prince Turismund enter the tent of our *magister utriusque militiae*.

Little has transpired from the conversation between such powerful generals, but I remember that, at the end of it, both of them left the *praetorium* with serious faces and frowns. Turismund rushed to his camp where he was proclaimed *rex Gothorum* by the Visigoth nobles. Soon after, our allies launched a solo attack on the Hun camp. It was a disaster, a shower of arrows fell on them causing a large number of casualties and preventing them from approaching, not even, the first of the palisades. Aetius watched the senseless attack from a distance, possibly pleased by the large number of Visigoths who died in the ill-fated attempt to storm the Hun defenses.

That same night a colossal bonfire was observed burning inside the Hun camp. As I well knew later, in the absence of wood, Attila had piled up a mountain of saddles and set them on fire, simulating a makeshift funeral pyre. He himself considered that this would be the last night he would remain among the living. But there were no more attacks. The siege lasted for two days until one morning, just after dawn, we noticed that the Visigoths had abandoned the siege and were returning to Tolosa. I will not deny that the withdrawal of our allies was a complete setback, but even so, we had enough forces to maintain the siege of the Huns and kill them with hunger and thirst, or to force them out of their mousetrap and fight. However, we were far outnumbered, and our morale soared to the skies after the overwhelming victory. But the gesture of the *milites* changed in surprise when Aetius, incomprehensibly, ordered that the fence be lifted and we return to the *castrum* of Lugdunum, in Transalpine Gaul. We had the lion caged and ready to be slaughtered, but not only did we leave him alive, we also opened the cage.

For confusing reasons, Aetius and Turismund allowed the Hun to escape the insurmountable siege. I didn't know why his capture was not ordered when he was defeated and humiliated, but the truth is that, after the battle of Maurica, Attila fled to Pannonia persuaded of his fate and brooding his revenge, while the Roman army, Tarraco *limitanei* included, was heading to the Lugdunum barracks awaiting his presumed return.

CHAPTER II

Mansueto's embassy.

Et Roma misit legatos Gallaeciam pacem petentes.[2]

Summer had not breathed for last, but a gentle, refreshing breeze caressed our sweaty bodies as we exercised with the *spatha*. I practiced with Arcadius, while Calerus did the same with a Gaul named Vedio Quirico Nabor, but whom we called Ajax, because of his extraordinary resemblance to the mythical Achaean warrior described by the ineffable Homer in the Iliad. In order not to inflict more serious injuries than what a simple training warrants, we used wooden swords. I had never beaten Arcadius in combat, which was much more skillful and skilled than I was, and that cool afternoon it was not going to be different. He practiced with considerable momentum and sweated more than usual, but once again, I ended up on the ground with Arcadius's wooden sword threatening my neck. When I got up, I noticed that we were surrounded by legionaries who, once our combat was over, broke into cheers, cheering Sextilius Arcadius, who raised his arms in triumph, enjoying the moment of glory from him. Calerus, who had long since concluded his particular duel, approached us with a big smile.

"What a fight!" He exclaimed excitedly. "We have all abandoned our training sessions to observe you."

I smiled at my friend and said:

"You must be talking about Arcadius style; I have simply tried to defend myself from his attack."

"Ha, ha, ha!" Arcadius laughed. "Don't be modest; I've sweated to beat you. If you keep training like this, maybe one day you can beat me."

"Yeah, but I can boast about this," I said sarcastically, lifting my camisole and showing him the scar on my side, like an indelible memory of the battle of Maurica.

He looked at it and smiled.

---

[2] *And Rome sent ambassadors to Gallaecia to ask for peace (phrase extracted and adapted from the Latin Grammar book by Santiago Segura Munguía).*

"Someday I will have not one but dozens of scars like that across my body and they will remind me of the battles I have participated in and all the enemies I have killed," he replied.

"Those are just cravings to have your body riven by horrible scars," I mumbled, patting him on the shoulder. "How about you with the Gaul?" I asked Calerus, pointing at my scar with the wooden sword.

"Look," he replied, lifting his shirt sleeve and showing a huge bruise on his left arm.

"Ugh, that must hurt."

"Only when they touch me," Calerus said with a smile.

Several *milites* approached to congratulate us for the fight by patting us on the back and squeezing our forearms. Arcadius was highly esteemed in the *castrum*. He had proven to be strong as a horse and elusive as an eel. Calerus was also known in the barracks for his ability to recite the classics or for solving certain accounting issues of one or another *centenarius*. On the other hand, in the few weeks that I had been in Aetius's camp, I had gone completely unnoticed and was simply known as the one who accompanied the wise man Lucius Calerus or the brave man Sextilius Arcadius. For this reason, I was surprised to be summoned by the *circitor* of my regiment as soon as I arrived at my tent, since the general required my presence. I still remember with pleasure the expression of surprise, and perhaps envy, that the faces of my friends sketched.

"The *magister utriusque militiae* wants to talk to me, not to you second class legionaries," I told them, swollen because of the pride, as I searched for a basin to wash me.

"Why the hell does he want to talk to you?" Arcadius asked, scratching his head.

"As soon as you leave the meeting, you can come here immediately and tell us everything," Calerus said, following me from one side of the store to the other.

But I wasn't listening to them. I didn't even remember where my bed was since I was very nervous. I quickly took the jug, poured some water into a basin, and wiped the sweat off my body. Then I girded my tunic with the *cingulum militare* and protected my chest with the torn coat of mail. I put on my helmet and, saying goodbye to my friends, I went to the *praetorium*. I rubbed my sweaty hands, which were shaking due to the impending meeting with the general. Meeting with the *magister utriusque militiae* was an honor to which very few *pedes* were called. But a deep unease, like an ominous omen, turned happiness into uncertainty. Immersed in my thoughts, I reached the entrance to the *praetorium*. I identified myself to the *circitor* and after a brief wait he led me into an anteroom where I was greeted by a Gallic officer belonging to the general's personal guard, whose name was Traustila.

"Are you Salvio Adriano?" he asked me.

"Yes, *domine*," I replied.

"Come with me," he ordered.

I followed the officer of Aetius's personal guard, a stocky man, battle-tested, with the neck of a bull and his arms as broad as legs. He wore a plumed helmet on his left arm revealing his dark hair, very short and slightly gray. He had tanned skin, eyes pale as honey, and a broad, worn forehead. A scar on his neck attested how close he had come to death. I looked at the scar, and I thought Arcadius would have loved to have one just like it. My lips formed a smile and the officer looked at me: my smile faded with the same speed with which it had appeared. I calculated that he would be in his early forties and dozens of deaths behind him. And those that still had to be reaped.

We went through a long corridor until we came to a large wooden door. Traustila opened it and ordered me to enter, and then he entered, closing the door as he passed. The room was bright and spacious. It was soberly decorated with several wooden chairs, a large table in the center, and the marble bust of an emperor that I couldn't recognize. Aetius was absently contemplating the castrum through one of the large windows that illuminated the room. He wore a military uniform and a *paludamentum* covered his shoulders. I noticed that he was wearing the characteristic long leather boots of the Huns. Beside him was the *comes Hispaniarum* Mansueto. He was a mature man, with strong features and a sharp jaw. Like Aetius, he wore a military tunic with chain mail and the distinctive *paludamentum* of his high rank hung on his shoulders. Last rays of sunlight illuminated his armor and the metal slats glowed, providing them unreal, almost divine features.

"I greet you, legionary," Aetius said, picking up a glass and pouring himself some wine.

"I greet you, Salvio Adriano," Mansueto intervened. I was surprised that he still remembered my name.

I had a lump in my throat that prevented me from speaking. I was overwhelmed by the presence of these men, and I limited to position myself in a martial gesture.

"Have some rest. Would you like a glass of wine?" The *magister utriusque militiae* asked.

I was surprised by his offer, since I was nothing more than simple and vulgar *pedes*. His kind gesture instead of reassuring worried me: the prerogatives granted by the powerful are never gratuitous. Aetius looked at me and smiling asked me:

"Don't you know how to speak?"

"No, *domine,* I mean yes, *domine,*" I stammered.

My body was shaking in convulsions and my mind was so dull that I was afraid of breaking into some other folly.

Laughers from one of the corners of the room caught my attention. Until that moment, I had been so spellbound, so absorbed by the imposing presence of such egregious *dignitates,* that I had not noticed that another person was in the room. I was embarrassed by the laughter of the stranger.

"Optila, don't offend our guest," the general said aloud, feigning anger.

"I'm sorry," said the stranger through tears, heading toward the table with the intention of pouring himself a glass of wine. "If you don't want to, I do."

"Thank you, *domine;* I would gladly accept the glass of wine."

My words came out of my lips in an uncontrolled way, but with an authority and a confidence that left those present astonished.

Optila burst out laughing again and served me the wine. As he approached, I could identify him as another Gallic officer of Aetius's personal guard.

"Take this, legionary, and rest, you are among friends," he said, handing me the glass of wine with a smile.

He was possibly the same age as Traustila and would be somewhat younger than Aetius. He had short blond hair, and his frizzy beard hid a sharp-featured face. Strongly built, his eyes revealed steadfast loyalty and unshakable dignity. The ideal soldier to entrust the most delicate and dangerous missions.

I took the glass and drank.

"It's not as sweet as Hispanic wines, but it's not bad at all," Optila said.

"No, *domine,* but compared to Betic wines, any other is nothing more than water mixed with grape juice," I replied, with excessive audacity.

"It's true," Mansueto intervened. "But we haven't made you come to talk about the virtues of Hispanic wines, friend Adriano."

The four men took their seats by the table and the *Hispaniarum comes*, with a gesture, invited me to do the same. I swallowed hard and my insides turned watery, like I'd drunk vinegar. For a few moments no one spoke, and we fell into an awkward silence. I was puzzled and somewhat scared. I looked around the room without daring to meet their eyes. I didn't know what I was doing there, sitting in front of those brave soldiers with their hard and deep eyes. I linked my fingers to prevent the trembling of my hands from betraying my restless mood.

"You saved my life in Maurica," Mansueto began, breaking the thick silence for which I thanked him by releasing a soft snort. "I told you I would never forget it, and I'm a man who usually keeps his promises." He picked up a glass and took a long swallow of wine. "I have spoken to Aetius," He said, looking at the *magister utriusque militiae*. "And we have agreed that your feat deserves to be rewarded."

"Your behavior on the battlefield didn't go unnoticed," Aetius intervened. "And I'm not just referring to the fact, not least important, of saving the life of the Hispaniarum *comes*."

"*Domine*," I said, bewildered. "I did what I had to do, what any thousands would have done."

"Weren't you aware of what happened?" Optila asked me, and I denied with my head. A smile arose on the lips of the four men.

"I remember that we fought against the barbarians and supported by the Visigoths..."

"No, no, no, you definitely haven't realized what really happened during that battle," Aetius interrupted, rising from his chair.

I looked at him puzzled, not being able to understand his words.

"After saving Mansueto's life," he continued. "You advanced to meet the Hun troops accompanied by a handful of *milites*. I still don't know if it was a brave or foolish gesture, but the truth is that you faced the barbarians supported by the Visigoth horsemen. The Huns saw a magnificent occasion to annihilate you and hundreds of horsemen with slanted eyes, straight hair and the smell of sewer charged you. Then a Roman legionary devoid of rank and command appeared, and he began to lead both the Romans and the Visigoths. The Huns attacked you fiercely not once, but several times and you repelled each of the raids causing them numerous casualties. The legionary seemed to sense where the enemy was going to attack and moved the few troops he had with speed and sanity. When we were about to intervene, we noticed that Theodoric was going to help you with his spatharii, so I ordered my troops to stop." the general's bright eyes were veiled. "with the intention that the barbarians would kill each other, that the Huns would fight with the *spatharii* and inflicted relentless carnage on each other. For the sake of Rome, and with our hearts in our hands, we had to sacrifice you. But you survived God lives!" He exclaimed, raising his fist high. "Theodoric died, but you saved the honor of the Roman legions."

Then he put his hand on my shoulder and said:

"That legionary was you."

My mind conjured up the battle. Until that moment I had not remembered that Aetius didn't come to our aid when we needed him most, when we were harassed by hundreds of Huns. But I had nothing to reproach him for, since I would have sacrificed my life for the good of Rome without much trouble. The audacity of young people is as impetuous as it is foolish, and in their ignorance it is difficult to rationally order certain priorities. It is true that I remember how I gave orders to each other, and how everyone obeyed them without question. But I didn't attach importance to it. I simply did what I thought was most appropriate and said so to Aetius, who nodded and said:

"During battle, the courage of heroes or fear of cowards shines with all its brilliance. It is when we reveal who we are and what feelings inhabit our hearts." He paused slightly so that his words settled in my mind like solid mortar, and continued: "There are only two ways to confront the Grim Reaper: by throwing oneself decisively towards her without taking our eyes off their empty sockets or fleeing like a fearful man, shedding one's sword and shield."

"Is this the reason why I'm here now?" I asked for.

"It's one of the reasons," Mansueto answered. "As I have commented before, your behavior towards the Huns deserves to be rewarded. With your promotion, the *milites* will understand that Rome rewards heroes who risk their lives to defend our *limes*."

"My... my promotion?" I stammered.

"For your demonstrated courage in combat and for saving Mansueto's life, *perfectissimus comes Hispaniarum,* I have promoted you to *centenarius,*" said Aetius.

For a moment I was absorbed by the words of *the magister utriusque militiae.* A few months ago I was a simple *tiro* that was receiving training in the Tarraco limits, and now I had become an officer with a hundred soldiers under my command. I shook my head, unable to assume such a position. I was just *pedes*, a lowly legionary with only one battle behind him. I didn't deserve such a distinction, and I manifested it.

"*Domini*, I thank you for your high esteem towards me," I began to look into the eyes of those brave officers. "but I don't think that I'm the right person to lead a *hundred milites*. I lack the necessary leadership experience and skills. I would be responsible for the lives of a hundred men and their deaths would fall on my conscience like a heavy slab."

"That is more or less the amount of soldiers that you lead without being aware of it, in Maurica," Traustila intervened. "And how many died despite the Huns outnumbering you? You are perfectly suited to command a hundred legionaries, even two hundred if you hurry me. Have confidence in yourself, because we have it."

The Gaul's words gave me new courage. I was aware of the deference that those officers were showing me, because it was not easy in the legion to reach the rank of *centenarius*. There were only three ways for a *miles* to get promoted: after serving fifteen years as a legionary; after ten years of service as an imperial guard in the *palatinae scholae*; and by direct appointment for having served as a magistrate, coming from an illustrious family or having achieved military merits.

"However, don't consider us foolish enough to throw you into a horde of barbarians commanding a hundred *milites*. Soldiers are not exactly what we have in abundance," said Aetius with a smile. "We trust that your first mission will be placid and calm."

"My first mission?" I asked for.

The *Hispaniarum comes* took a drink of wine and said:

"Two years ago, the Suevian and the Visigoths formed an alliance to counter the pact signed between the Empire and the Vandals. To reaffirm this agreement, Theodoric offered the king of the Suevian the hand of one of his daughters in marriage. Requiario went to meet his fiancée and, on the way to Tolosa, razed the Tarraconense region subjecting it to looting and predation. But on his return and allied with a *Bagaudae* named Basilio, he attacked Turiasso ending the life of Leo, the bishop of the city. Not satisfied with this, they seized Ilerda, and captured hundreds of Hispano- Romans, condemning them to slavery."

"The emperor has entrusted us with the mission of making peace with the Suevian in order for them to leave our territory and return to Gallaecia, since after the battle against Attila's hosts our armies have

32

been quite depleted and won't be able to cover and defend all our provinces," Aetius claimed.

"The territories of the Empire are vast and our troops limited," Optila interjected. "The emperor has considered that it is preferable to reach an agreement with Requiario than to have to move our legions from Gaul, where they are undoubtedly essential to deter the northern barbarian."

The raids of the Suevian king through our lands were known, as well as his excessive greed. Hispania, without Roman legions to protect it, was at the mercy of the barbarian hosts, who looted our defenseless cities causing great devastation and suffering.

"A diplomatic delegation will depart soon to Bracara Augusta," Aetius said. "It will be headed by Mansueto and will be escorted by Optila, Traustila and you, Adriano, since Mansueto has requested it that way."

"My safety couldn't be in better hands," the *Hispaniarum comes* put in, lifting his glass.

I nodded gratefully, without really knowing what to say and overwhelmed by events that were happening in a hurry confusing my exhausted mind. Then, I remembered my friends Arcadius and Calerus. Together with them I felt more secure and confident, and with a trembling voice I said:

"I would like to request permission for my comrades in arms Sextilius Arcadius and Lucius Calerus to accompany me on this mission."

Aetius looked at Mansueto demanding his approval, and he just raised his hand indifferently.

"No problem. You will go with your friends if that makes you feel better."

"Thank you, *domine*."

"It is vital that the negotiations with Requiario be successful and conclude with the signing of a stable peace," Aetius continued, dismissing banal requests. "For this reason and so that Requiario understands that Visigoths, despite their alliance, are still *foederati* of the Empire, in this embassy you will be accompanied by prince Euric, brother of King Turismund. As I have agreed with the *rex Gothorum*, the prince will act in the interests of Rome, putting the foedus signed with the Empire before the pact agreed with the Suevian."

33

"We will go to Tolosa where Euric will join our delegation; from there we will cross Hispania to Bracara Augusta, the capital of the Suevian," Mansueto concluded.

"You are welcome, Salvio Adriano, *centenarius* of Rome," said Optila, lifting his glass.

And the officers and generals raised their glasses and toasted the success of the embassy. I barely took a small sip, my throat was dry and blocked because of the whirlwind of emotions. My hands were still trembling at the imposing presence of those illustrious men. I exhaled a long sigh assuming my new condition and begged the Almighty to live up to what the circumstances demanded.

Optila suggested that I go to the warehouses as soon as possible and requested the *biarchus* the uniform of my new rank. I accepted his proposal and returned to the barracks dressed in the coat of mail and a military tunic that identified me as a *centenarius*. My friends blinked confusedly as soon as they noticed my presence, to later harass me with questions about the reasons why I had reached such a high rank in such a short time. After giving the appropriate explanations, I made them aware that they would accompany me to Bracara Augusta, news that they received with satisfaction since their blood was young and boiled at the prospect of enjoying new adventures.

In two days, we headed our steps towards Bracara Augusta, in Gallaecia. The delegation was protected by a detachment of one hundred legionaries among which was the giant Ajax and several Sarmatian cataphracts, who rode on their mighty horses protected to the forehead by metal scales. Several *milites* some of them *semissalis*, looked at me with distrust and without hiding a certain animosity. These were veteran soldiers with long years of service behind them, who despite having shed their blood for the Empire the only thing they had achieved was to earn a salary slightly higher than that of a simple soldier being relegated from any kind of promotion. Among all of them there was one named Demetrius Tancinus, who kept giving me furtive sidelong glances charged with anger. He was a strong man of about thirty-five years old, with angular features and a thick beard. He sported several scars on his face and arms. He was skilled with the sword and with the javelin, which he threw with precision and forcefulness.

Despite being a great soldier, his irascible and quarrelsome character, had closed the doors of promotion on many occasions. As I knew later, he had recently requested a promotion again, but his request was rejected. Demetrius Tancinus considered that he deserved the recognition of his superiors, but when he was denied his anger clouded his reason and he lost all understanding. According to what they told me, that same day he went to a brothel and wounded in his pride, he poured out his anger on a prostitute until he almost left her dead. And now he suffered the derision of serving under a newcomer who had been promoted directly by Aetius himself. I suppose his guts were churning restlessly wondering what the bitter injustice was due to.

We were close to the city of Tolosa, it was getting dark and we camped in an esplanade near a frozen stream. After organizing the guards, Optila had sat alone by one of the many fires we lit to prepare dinner. Traustila chatted with various *milites* in a relaxed way, since they didn't stop laughing. I saw an excellent opportunity to speak alone with Optila, with whom I had gained certain sympathy during the march. So, I left my friends heating pieces of meat on the fire and headed towards the blond Gallic officer.

"I salute you, *domine*," I said, pounding my chest with my fist.

"Relax, boy, we're not in the camp," said Optila, waving his hand.

"Can I sit?"

"Of course," the Gaul conceded.

I took a seat next to him and he offered me a piece of meat that he had put on the fire. He wasn't hungry, but it would have been rude to turn him down. It was a cool moonless night and the stars accompanied us with their faint glow, giving our weary souls a moment of peace and quiet. But Optila was not resting. The responsibility of this trip was immeasurable, and although he was a jovial and cheerful man, the lines on his forehead revealed an unbearable concern. He gently struck the fire with a branch and small twinkling embers lit up his eyes, warning me that his mind was far away from that meadow. So, I decided to break the silence.

"There are many dangers that threaten the Empire," I said, without taking my eyes off the fire. "But if our *magister utriusque militiae* has defeated the Huns, I'm convinced that he will also defeat the Suevian if they don't accept the peace treaty."

A harsh smile broke out on the Gaul's lips and he said:

"Make no mistake, the Visigoths won in Maurica, not us." His eyes shone reflecting the flames of the bonfire. "Aetius devised a proverbial stratagem that allowed us to defeat Attila's hosts with hardly any losses in our ranks, bearing the weight of the battle on the Visigoths' backs. It was they who faced the disciplined troops of the Ostrogoth King Valamir and the hosts of Attila, enduring enormous casualties. Instead, we fought against the exhausted Gepids and Burgundians, who were little more than somewhat organized highwaymen."

He raised his eyes and, looking into my eyes, continued:

"When you and your companions found themselves on enemy terrain supported by a handful of Visigoth horsemen, Theodoric came to our aid accompanied by his *spatharii,* and Aetius saw an excellent opportunity to dispose of a good number of elite Visigoth soldiers, leaving them at the mercy of the Huns and Ostrogoths. What Aetius didn't count on was that Theodoric, Rome's loyal ally, would die in the attack. Then, Turismund, eager to avenge the death of his father, threw himself against the Ostrogoths and other barbarians while we limited ourselves to finishing off the wounded or chasing one or another Gepid, lagging behind. At the end of the day the victory had been ours, both Visigoths and Romans, but the losses of the former were infinitely higher than ours. The historic battle of Maurica was a fierce and merciless fight of barbarians against barbarians, just as wolves bite into each other to win the favor of a female or the remaining of a dead lamb."

I reflected on his words, and I realized that Optila had accurately described the course of the battle: we returned almost unscathed to our *castrum* in Lugdunum, while the Visigoths sacrificed thousands of men, including their own king. But a long, forgotten doubt resurfaced in my mind, and throwing a branch into the fire I asked:

"But why didn't we capture Attila when we had the best opportunity to do so?"

The Gaul stroked his beard thoughtfully, as if searching his mind for the right answer, and after a few moments he said:

"Turismund was not exactly enthusiastic about the *foedus* that his father Theodoric signed with the Empire. For him, Rome is not an ally, but huge loot, an easy prey to seize and devour. He is aware of the fragility of the Empire and senses that a sovereign with sufficient courage and troops could destroy it simply by trying. But first he has to exterminate the pesky Huns. They are the enemy, and really dangerous.

They came from distant steppes with their long, straight hair and fine black mustaches, mounted on their small, swift horses, sowing terror and chaos wherever their steeds rode. Aetius was convinced that if the Huns disappeared, Rome's days would be numbered and Turismund wouldn't lack time to organize his troops and cross the *limes* of the Empire, violating the alliance signed by his father. Curiously, *the magister utriusque militiae* needed the king of the Huns alive and for this reason he refused to launch a direct attack on his camp on the pretext that it would cause heavy casualties and that it would be preferable to besiege the Huns and force their surrender out of hunger and thirst. As you know," he continued. "Turismund refused, and sent his troops to the assault on the barbarian stockade, but they were massacred by the Hun archers. After his failed attack, the new *Gothorum rex* came to his senses and accepted the plan proposed by our general."

The Gaul gave a big smile and, shaking his head, continued:

"Aetius is cunning as a fox and sent an emissary to Turismund reporting that Theodoric, his younger brother, had left the camp for Tolosa. Turismund, suspicious and distrustful as he was, feared that his brother had marched towards the capital of *regnum Gothorum* with the purpose of proclaiming himself king and dismantled the siege by marching swiftly towards Tolosa. But the truth is that Theodoric was at *the praetorium* invited by our general. When the young prince knew about Turismund's departure, he was enraged for not being warned and Aetius persuaded him to remain in the castrum where, no doubt, he would be safer."

Our audacious *magister utriusque militiae* had defeated the Huns in the battle of Maurica and suppressed the Visigoths' expansionist greed that, frightened by the presence of Attila, would not break the *foedus* by raising their hosts against Rome. Interestingly, the Hun king was more beneficial to the Empire alive than dead.

"Rome is collapsing and Aetius is running out of time," Optila continued. His eyes revealed deep sorrow and despondency, as if after trying to swim across an angry river he was sinking into the dark depths just when his hand was about to reach the shore. "Our general has won hundreds of battles, he has made deals with the barbarians, he has protected *the limes* of the Empire, but he can do little more. Rome lacks *milites* like you," he said, looking into my eyes. "We are just a handful of legionaries, dear friend, and we need the best of our men to emerge to forge the heroes of the future."

37

"Are there no longer soldiers willing to fight and die for the Empire?" I replied ignorantly.

Optila looked at me with a mixture of pity and tenderness.

"Aetius's legion is made up of veterans," he continued, looking at Traustila, the hardened Sarmatians, and the *semissalis*. "And novices." he added, looking at Calerus, Arcadius, Ajax, and the rest of the *milites* that made up the delegation. "There are no more young people in our ranks. And do you know why?" He asked rhetorically, since he didn't take long to answer: "Because they're dead or confined to monasteries and churches. The barbarians have innumerable troops and for every soldier they lose another comes from distant steppes or frozen lands and takes their place: but we don't. We are unable to rebuild our *numeri* as well as immensely weaker after each battle."

I shook my head without adding fuel to what I was hearing. That Rome's survival depended on Attila was utterly alarming, since when he healed his wounds at the Pannonia barracks, he would return more furious than ever. An aggrieved king is as dangerous as a boar wounded by a hunter's spear; both rage, venting their inordinate anger on those whom they hold responsible for their affront.

"If only a good emperor ruled in Ravenna," Optila muttered through his teeth. His clenched jaws revealed that he had to hold back to keep from breaking into a disloyal comment. For a few moments we were silent, watching the fire lick the logs turning them into incandescent ashes. I looked into his glassy, sad eyes, pained after so many years of sterile struggle, but showing the incombustible glow that grants a remote hope. The Gaul was exhausted, his heart ragged by disappointment and failure, but he was far from feeling defeated.

He looked away and looked at me, holding my shoulder as if he were guessing what he was thinking, and he told me:

"Go with your friends and rest, a very long journey awaits us."

I got up and greeted him with my fist on my chest.

"Hail, Optila."

The Gaul looked at me and nodded with a smile.

"Hail, Salvio Adriano."

It was a dark night, but I would swear that his face shone with tears. Meditating, I led my steps to the fire where my companions were. There, Calerus demanded all the attention, as he was declaiming a poem by Claudius that dealt with the exploits of general Flavius Estilicus and his innumerable victories over the barbarians. Several Sarmatian *milites* and auxiliaries watched him silently. Hearing ancient stories from the once glorious Rome comforted both veterans and novices, giving us the illusion, even if it was ephemeral, that another world was possible.

We passed the walls of Tolosa shortly before sunset, when the sun was setting behind the tall pines, lengthening the shadows and dying the sky with a reddish hue similar to the color of blood. It was a formidable city, with sturdy stone walls, tall watchtowers, and well-manned with soldiers. The streets were crowded with people who watched us with curiosity, contempt and fear. The Visigoths were our allies, but in those confused times alliances were as fickle as the attentions of the ungrateful harlot, who always end up giving their careful care to those who paid the most to enjoy them. And the common people who inhabited that city knew it well.

We entered the castle and several *spatharii* escorted us to the stables. We left our mounts there, under the care of diligent barbarian grooms. Later, while Mansueto and the Gauls were presenting themselves to the *domesticorum comes,* we went to the military barracks where the Visigoths offered us a succulent dinner made of roast pork, wheat bread and Gallic wine. For now, our hosts were entertaining us with all kinds of considerations.

I was enjoying my meal sitting with Calerus, Ajax and Arcadius on a bench, when, just behind me, I heard someone belching excitedly.

"Yes, my friends," Demetrius Tancinus grumbled to the group of four *semissalis* who accompanied him. "Now Rome rewards children with handsome features... we don't know why..." he muttered maliciously, making obscene gestures, arousing the laughter of his friends. "instead of rewarding those who really deserve it. This is disgusting," he concluded, spitting on the ground.

"An army of damsels and barbarian," one of his friends intervened.

"There is no future for true soldiers, for the brave ones who have sown the battlefields with the dead," Demetrius Tancinus insisted and, deliberately raising his voice, he added: "Have you seen the new *centenarii?* He could be my son; in fact, I think I met his mother in a brothel in Lugdunum. Ha, ha, ha, ha!"

The laughter of the veteran and his friends echoed in the barracks, drawing the attention of the Visigoths and the Romans who were there.

Tancinus was clearly testing me in front of the rest of the soldiers who made up the delegation. After Mansueto and the Gauls, I was the highest ranking officer, and I couldn't allow anyone to disrespect me. If I tolerated such an affront, he would not hesitate to humiliate me when the opportunity arose. I had to halt any outbreak of insubordination as soon as possible or I would be caught in the tangled branches of discredit and disobedience.

"You are very audacious with your tongue," I said, without getting up from the bench. "And cocky for daring to offend a superior..."

"I don't see any superior here, just a little boy who wears a wrong uniform," he interrupted, and took a long swallow from his jug of wine.

The barrack was plunged into a sea of silence. Both Visigoths and Romans watched us carefully. A murmur and the subsequent shuffling of bags revealed that they were making bets, although I didn't know what kind. I gulped, not really knowing how to respond to the insult. But I had to do something, and I did it.

"Demetrius Tancinus, you have offended a *centenarius* and you must be punished." I sat up and took the small whip that hung from my *cingulum militare*. "Now it will be up to you whether you receive a few lashes or a greater punishment."

The legionary stood up followed by his friends. Arcadius, Calerus and Ajax did the same.

"Really, boy? You lack the courage to punish a veteran," he muttered angrily.

Visigoths and Romans got up from their benches so as not to lose any detail of the challenge. Demetrius Tancinus approached me, our faces being a foot apart. His gaze was defiant and trusting; as if he expected me to make the slightest mistake to pour out on me the alleged suffered injustices. But I gave him no opportunity. A sharp blow to the throat was enough to take his breath away. Then a knee in the face and a kick in the genitals as he flailed painfully on the pavement left him completely at my mercy. His friends reached for their hilt, but the sharp *spatha* of Arcadius, Calerus and Ajax threatening their throats deterred them. Moreover, to my aid came the Sarmatian soldiers, who had no great regard for the veteran legionary.

"Take him by the arms and undress him," I ordered the Sarmatians, who complied with pleasure.

"You won't be able to," one of Demetrius Tancinus' friends replied.

"Shut up or you'll be next," I warned him.

The *semissalis*, who was still sore from the blows, stirred furiously calling out any number of expletives and resisting to be undressed by the Sarmatians. But, finally, and not without effort, they managed to remove the coat of mail and the military tunic, leaving him only dressed in the *subligar* and the *campagi,* a complete humiliation for the brave soldier.

"Damn bastards!" he screamed. "I will kill you all!"

The Visigoths laughed with amusement while Romans exchanged complicity glances, surprised by the way events were unfolding.

"Lay him down," I ordered, and Demetrius Tancinus was launched on the cold pavement of the barracks. "You have seriously offended me, legionary," I began to say. "And you'll receive your punishment."

"Bastard, I'll kill you!" he was roaring beside himself.

I was about to lash him with my whip when a shout stopped me.

"What the hell is going on here?" Mansueto asked, accompanied by the Gauls.

He approached us and observed how Demetrius Tancinus remained immobilized on the ground dressed in the *subligar* and the *campagi.* Then he looked away at me and noticed my riding crop.

"What has this man done?" he asked me.

"He has seriously offended me, *domine,*" I replied. My words were reinforced by the nods and murmurs of various Romans and some Visigoths.

"He's a *semissalis*…" Optila observed, not hiding his amazement.

"And he has him at his mercy," Traustila intervened, outlining a smile.

The *Hispaniarum comes* knelt down, and bringing his face close to that of Demetrius Tancinus, asked him:

"Have you offended the *centenarii*?" The legionary didn't respond and Mansueto insisted in a shouting voice: "Have you offended the *centenarii*?"

"I have told the truth, *domine,*" Demetrius Tancinus muttered between his teeth, imprisoned by the arms of the Sarmatians. "I met her mother in a brothel in Lugdunum."

Mansueto squeezed his jaws making an angry gesture and stood up.

"Punish him as he deserves and let his bloody back serve as a lesson to all those who dare to insult an officer," he told me, and then he left the barracks accompanied by the Gauls.

41

I didn't enjoy whipping the *semissalis*, but I had no choice. On my back I felt the lacerating looks of hatred of his comrades, enraged at the humiliating scene. Their friend, half naked, was receiving hurtful lashes as punishment for his insubordination. Now they would rethink it before questioning my authority. With my act I didn't get his esteem, but I truly got his respect.

Two days after the unfortunate incident we went towards Bracara Augusta accompanied by Euric and his escort: about fifty *spatharii*. The prince was young, his face was shaved, and his brown hair and deep black eyes radiated a cold determination. It was a quiet trip, without excessive setbacks, which allowed us to know the situation of the cities in Tarraconense after the Suevian incursions and the predation to which they were subjected by Basilio's *Bagaudae*. Thus, we visited Barcino in Ilerda, which was still shocked by the assault of the Suevian and the *Bagaudae*, Caesaraugusta where its inhabitants looked at us with anger and contempt wondering where we were during the attack of the barbarians, Clunia, Pallantia, Brigecium and Asturica Augusta, the last city of importance before reaching Bracara Augusta. We camped on an esplanade near the city, we had been tirelessly marching for several days and Euric and Mansueto agreed to rest for a couple of days before resuming the march. It was dusk and under the shelter of a bonfire we met several legionaries, among which were the Gauls Optila and Traustila. We were immersed in a deep silence, reflecting on what we had seen and heard during the journey. We were concerned and not only about the decaying state of many of our cities, but also about the gazes and hostile attitude with which we were received in many places.

"A woman spat the floor we stepped on in Caesaraugusta," Calerus said. "She was holding a three year's old little one… In her eyes I noticed a visceral hatred and resentment."

"Perhaps that child is the unwanted fruit of the barbarian assault," I said regretfully. "Possibly her husband was murdered and she was forced, it is not surprising that she blames us for her misfortunes."

Arcadius nodded and said:

"An old man took my arm and asked me where we were when the barbarians devastated the city, where were the legions that they support with their taxes."

"In Ilerda," Ajax intervened. "I heard someone shouting that it would be better for them with the barbarians, at least their armies are close and can protect them. They feel on their nape the breath of the *curatores* demanding the payment of the *annona militaris*, while our *spatha* are in Gaul, hundreds of miles far from their homes."

"The Suevian incursions and the looting of the *Bagaudae* are devastating the farmlands in Tarraconense," Optila pointed out. "Which without hands to work them will become barren wastelands."

"Which implies more hunger and fewer taxes for Rome," Traustila said. "Which won't be able to collect the *iugatio capitalino* corresponding to those crops."

"And the *adiectio sterilium*, the forced allocation of the peasants to these lands, will not exactly help to win the sympathy of the Hispano-Romans," Optila observed.

"Honestly," Traustila said, "I doubt very much the fidelity of the provincials and the Hispano-Romans *dignitates* if there is a foreign invasion, since they are suffering in their flesh the abandonment and oblivion by the Empire."

"They just want to live in peace and feed their families," I replied. "If Rome is not able to guarantee its safety, they will give in to another people who do it. We must not censure them for this; it is the Empire's obligation to protect them."

"I hope Requiario accepts the peace treaty," Calerus put in. "and the spirits of the Hispano-Romans subside. Rome needs Hispania as much as Hispania needs Rome."

We nodded at his words, but the silence, a somber silence, enveloped us with a cloak as black as the night that loomed inexorably over the lands of the Suevian.

At dawn we headed towards a village near Asturica in Augusta to stock up on provisions. As a sign of good will and to express our intention to pay for the merchandise, Mansueto and Euric led the detachment, both accompanied by fifty *milites,* mostly Visigoths. We entered the village before the frightened gaze of the peasants, not used to seeing Roman and Visigoth soldiers in those lands. Dogs barked at us restlessly and men fiercely clutched their farm implements, ready to make use of them if the lives of their families were threatened.

"Greetings, my name is Mansueto, *Hispaniarum comes.* And he is Euric, prince of the Visigoths. We are peaceful and we are heading to Bracara Augusta to meet with Requiario, your king. We need provisions to continue our journey and for this reason we have landed in your village."

The men wrinkled their faces and advanced threateningly towards us, considering that our intention was to steal their food.

"You have nothing to fear," the *Hispaniarum comes* hastened to say. "We are a peaceful delegation, we don't wish to cause you any harm. We will buy the goods we need and pay you back in good gold coins."

Mansueto's words reassured the peasants, who exhaled a long sigh, persuaded of the unequal combat that fighting against us would entail.

"Who is your boss?" Euric asked.

"It's me," said an old man, emerging from a stone and straw hut. "My name is Pervinco, and you will be well received in my village if your intentions are peaceful and honest."

"That's right, old man," Mansueto said with a nod.

"Come into my hut," said the village chief, pulling the mat that covered the door. "We can talk more calmly here. I will listen with interest to your requests. I'm confident that we can reach a good agreement that satisfies both parties. Woman," he ordered a young woman. "Bring beer to entertain our guests."

The girl nodded and went to a hut monopolizing the glances of the soldiers. She was very beautiful, her eyes were dark and her hair was black, long and slightly wavy. She wore an ocher robe fitted to a slender figure. Mansueto and Euric entered the hut escorted by a pair of *spatharii*. We remained vigilant on our horses. The peasants, now calmer, continued with their chores, but without ceasing to give us suspicious glances. The girl entered the hut with an amphora and left shortly after, getting lost inside one of the houses. One of Euric's *spatharius* dismounted and entered the house. Anticipating his intentions, I directed my mount there. Presently, a cry was heard and the girl came out of the hut with her clothes torn. She clung to my horse and begged me for help. I looked into his black, wet and terrified eyes. They exuded a mystical beauty. Behind her emerged the imposing figure of a giant barbarian with blond hair and long mustaches. He had his pants down and his penis upright.

"Come on, bitch, this time you won't escape," the barbarian yelled, pulling up his pants.

"Stay there," I ordered, threatening him with my *spatha*.

"This is mine, Roman, find yourself another one and leave me alone," he replied in a rough, ragged accent, trying to grasp the woman from behind.

The Visigoth horsemen came to the aid of his companion and soon surrounded me. The peasants, alerted by the shouts and movement of the horsemen, came carrying sticks, hoes and sickles, but they kept a safe distance, without venturing to intervene.

"We are on a mission of peace!"

Arcadius, Ajax and Calerus, followed by the rest of the *milites,* drew their swords and faced the Visigoths.

"Roman, I don't want any problems with you. I'll take this bitch and when we're done with her," he said looking at his friends, who burst out laughing while making obscene gestures. "She'll be all yours."

"I guess that you have not understood me. I won't tolerate any barbarian ruining this mission by damaging the interests of the Empire. This woman is under my protection, and unless you want to try the edge of my sword, you'd better go and vent with one of your friends. I'm sure you won't find any difference."

The barbarian growled furiously and lunged at me with his bare sword. From my horse, I managed to avoid a couple of attacks, but fearing that the barbarian, in his madness, would attack my chestnut, I decided to dismount. ¡Big mistake! In a few minutes I was surrounded by a crowd of Visigoths. But the legionaries also approached and challenged the barbarians with their *spatha.* The girl took advantage of the confusion to move away from the giant's claws and take shelter. The Suevian peasants looked at us confusedly, not understanding what was happening, but hoping that we would kill each other or get out of their village as soon as possible, since we had burst into their placid lives like a stormy gale.

"In Bracara Augusta you can vent to the whores you want," I suggested soothingly. He was a formidable warrior and I had no interest in fighting him.

"¡Bastard!" he snapped, throwing himself furious at me.

He was strong as a bull and he threw accurate lunges at me. Despite his size, he moved with agility and I had a hard time withstanding his thrusts. Then, another Visigoth came to his aid: fighting against two veteran warriors, my hopes of getting out of that fight alive were limited. But a legionary came to my aid: it was Ajax. The fight was even. The angry shouts of both sides thundered through the air like a raging storm. The confused bustle caught the attention of Mansueto and Euric, who came over to see what was happening. Ajax's rival prudently abandoned the fight, leaving the giant and I alone, surrounded by Visigoths,

Romans, and the odd Suevian. I felt like an ancient gladiator, fighting for his life before a crowd eager to see mutilated limbs and bloody swords.

"What the hell is going on here?" Mansueto asked.

"Let them be distracted," Euric grumbled, placing his hand on his shoulder. "It will be interesting to see a combat between a Roman officer and a king's *spatharius*."

"¡I can't allow it!" the *comes* replied.

"But it is not up to you to prevent this fight," the prince replied, and several Visigoths stood in his way with their swords drawn.

Mansueto took his *spatha* but a barbarian grabbed his arm tightly.

"This is treason," he muttered under his breath.

Euric smiled and said:

"Call it whatever you want. You can go on," he added with a wave of his hand.

"I'm going to skin you alive," the barbarian growled with a terrible smile, realizing that he had the consent of his lord.

I didn't have time to reply. With lightning speed, he lunged at me waving his sword from side to side. I barely held his thrusts, and the virulence of his beatings prevented me from counterattacking. I tried to get out of his siege, but it was impossible, it seemed that he sensed my movements: each of my attacks was responded with skill and forcefulness.

So, we were for several minutes: the barbarian throwing lunges at me and I limiting myself to blocking them with my sword, being unable to counteract him. I was exhausted and didn't know how long I could take his onslaught. The barbarian was fresh, and in one set of combat I could glimpse a wicked smile on the corner of his lips. He considered himself infinitely superior and, what was worse, so do I. Tiredness took its toll on me, forcing me to lower my guard. The Visigoth launched a thrust wounding my left arm, which began to bleed profusely. The Visigoths cheered loudly for their companion while the *milites* looked at me with concern. Emboldened, he launched a furious attack again, forcing me back.

"I'm going to strip your skin off and, once I'm done with you, I'll skin the bitch that you have uselessly protected," the Visigoth snapped with a malicious smile, approaching with a slow step.

"You'll have to kill me first and you still haven't succeeded."

"It's a matter of time. Rest assured that I will enjoy killing you, dirty Roman."

I took advantage of those moments of truce to breathe some air, before throwing myself into a desperate attack. I knew I had only one chance to beat him and I must take it or it would be my end. I threw a thrust at him that he stopped with ease, then another, and another, and another… but the Visigoth stopped them with insulting dexterity and a smile on his lips. Then he made a feint and the tables turned, now it was he who was attacking me. I was exhausted and my arm kept bleeding. He gave a loud cry and lunged at me in order to finish me off once and for all: he had already had enough fun. He sent me one thrust that I managed to block with my *spatha*, and another that I managed to avoid with a feint, but with the last one I stumbled and fell unarmed to the ground.

"Your time has come, pig roman," snapped the Visigoth, and pointed his sword at the sky ready to take my life.

I looked into his yellow eyes and realized that they were not human, but belonged to a hungry animal, thirsty for blood and eager to devour his prey. His sword was dyed red from the dried blood of his victims.

"Stop it, Walder!" a voice yelled and the giant stopped his sword a foot from my neck.

The Visigoth looked at Euric confused, refusing to obey the command of his *domine*.

"All right, Walder, sheathe your sword," the prince ordered paving his way with horse. "The Roman has already learned his lesson."

Reluctantly, and not without first spitting a look of contempt at me, the Visigoth holstered his weapon and lost himself among the barbarians that surrounded us. I stood up conscious of my luck and my eyes met Euric's, who was looking at me with pride and offensive arrogance.

"Are you fine?" Mansueto asked me.

I nodded among gasps. I was exhausted and my heart was beating with force and anguish on my chest, persuaded that the Grim Reaper had grazed me with his grim robe.

"If these are your allies…" Pervinco intervened. "I don't want to think how fierce your enemies will attack you."

Euric laughed behind us and said:

"I don't know if you are extremely brave or foolish. Walder is the *spathariorum comes,* the captain of the king's spacers. He is a German, a great warrior, without a doubt the best of our army. I've seen him fight countless times and it took just a couple of slaps to exterminate his rival. On the other hand." He continued approaching me. "You have given him a lot of work. It hasn't been easy for him to beat you."

"I'll take it as a compliment," I replied.

"Don't tempt your luck, legionary; you are alive today thanks to me. Maybe next time I won't be so condescending to you," he replied and left followed by his barbarians.

The prince's words were thrown into the air with the scent of threat. It was obvious, and that is how Mansueto and I understood it, that Euric hated the Romans.

"I hope this man is never anointed *Gothorum rex*," said the *comes*, watching him walk away. "In him, Rome will only find a formidable enemy."

I nodded at the truth of his words, but for now we had nothing to worry about. Turismund had three brothers and Euric was the youngest, therefore, he was very far away in the succession line to the throne and his chances of being crowned king were quite remote.

"Heal that wound," he added, pointing to the cut that the barbarian had inflicted on my arm. "I need my men to be in good shape for anything that might happen."

And patting me on my shoulder, he walked over to Pervinco. We loaded the wagons with the food bought from the Suevians and prepared to leave the village under the urgent gaze of Pervinco and the peasants, impatient for us to leave as soon as possible. But Walder was unwilling to give up his reward for beating me in combat and, with Euric's approval; he sent a pair of stick-wielding *spatharii* to capture the young woman. The Visigoths entered a hut leaving shortly after with the girl kicking and screaming, while their companions formed a wall with their horses to avoid the angry response of the Suevians.

"What does this outrage mean?" Pervinco asked angrily.

"Thank us, old man," Euric answered from his mount. "We will only take that woman, and we will respect your village."

"If we take the girl, we will jeopardize the peace treaty with Requiario," Mansueto replied.

"Requiario is a coward, as soon as he is informed that you have our support, he will agree to all your demands."

"But we promised them that our mission was one of peace, that only..."

"It was you who promised that," the prince interrupted. "Come on, get the woman and let's get out of this filthy village!"

The woman was sobbing trying to get away from the barbarians. She averted her gaze to the Suevians, Visigoths, and Romans, imploring their help. Her eyes were shining with terror. Then she looked at me, and in her eyes, I read a request, a plea impossible to ignore. I dismounted and headed towards the Visigoths. My friend Arcadius did the same.

"Let her go," I ordered them.

Euric, flanked by Walder and his *spatharii,* was watching us closely. The Visigoths looked at him bewilderedly without knowing what to do, but the prince shook his head and made them a disdainful gesture with his hand. We got trapped in a tense silence, similar to the one that precedes a violent storm.

"Let us pass, Roman," said the barbarian, pushing me contemptuously.

I took him by the arm, which he regarded as a threat. In response, he threw me a stick which I managed to dodge and then I replied with a blow to his jaw that sent him to the ground.

"It's two against two, let's have some fun."

"Haven't you had enough?" Mansueto said angrily, fed up from the prince's whims.

"Don't fear," replied the prince. "I suspected that one of your men would protest and that is why they are armed with sticks. If your Romans win, the woman will remain with her relatives, but if my *spatharii* do, we will take her."

Mansueto swallowed hard and nodded convinced that it was the only chance that the girl was not kidnapped by the Visigoths, a gesture that would irritate the Requiario king and make peace negotiations difficult.

Arcadius and I engaged in a fierce combat against the two barbarians. Their sticks flapped in the air, cracking with a menacing hum. I dodged my opponent's stick, but he moved with agility avoiding my blows. I drew my sword but a strong blow to my arm disarmed me, causing me to drop my *spatha* on the ground.
Arcadius managed to disarm his opponent who fell lifeless to the ground after receiving a succession of forceful blows. But suddenly another *spatharius* appeared and struck him with a stick on the head, knocking him senseless.

"No!" I screamed, as I watched my friend faint like a rag doll.

I threw myself over the barbarian like a rabid wolf fearing for Arcadius's life. I dodged a couple of attacks and with a fury born from revenge, I drew the *pugio* that hung from my *military cingulum* and stuck it in his neck. The barbarian put his hand on his throat, and, choking on his own blood, made foul guttural sounds. I was so absorbed in combat that I hadn't noticed the gaze of the *milites* around me. I saw a deep concern in their eyes: I had killed a *spatharius,* a very serious crime from which I would hardly escape unscathed. But in those moments what mattered least to me was my integrity.

"You will be executed, Roman!" Euric exclaimed, pointing an accusing finger at me.

"He only defended himself against your *spatharius*!" Mansueto replied.

The prince gave him a look full of hatred and said:

"But my soldiers were armed with sticks, and he used his dagger. It is a cowardly act that deserves a just punishment."

Visigoths and Romans drew their swords and looked at each other threateningly ready to use them.

"Seize him!" Euric ordered, staring at the *comes* waiting for a pretext to launch his *spatharii* at us.

"This won't stay so," Mansueto snapped. "You have tried to kidnap a Suevian in order to provoke Requiario' wrath and now you intend to arrest a *centenarius* for defending her life. Your task was to facilitate the signing of a lasting peace, but all you seek is to ruin the mission and spoil the relationship of the Empire with the Suevian. I will turn to Aetius and Turismund himself if necessary, but this act of treason will not go unpunished, prince."

"We'll see..." Euric challenged. "For the moment, we will arrest the *centenarius* and take him to Tolosa, where he will be tried according to our laws for the cowardly murder of a *spatharius*."

Four Visigoths dismounted and headed towards me with bare swords, but suddenly several whistles broke the silence and a Roman and two barbarians fell down from their mounts.

"They are attacking us!" shouted a Visigoth, and a shower of arrows, coming from a nearby forest fell on us.

"Protect yourselves!" Mansueto ordered, drawing his *spatha.*

From among the grove and shouting atrocious war cries, several warriors appeared armed with sticks and axes: they were *Bagaudae*. The

50

Suevian took advantage of the confusion to try to free the young woman, but the Visigoths prevented it by killing two of them. Pervinco tried to appease the anger of his people, but failed. The Suevian, enraged by the death of the two men and emboldened by the irruption of their *Bagaudae* allies, rushed against us.

"Kill them all!" Euric ordered from his restless horse, immersed in the bloody melee.

The *Bagaudae* were numerous, but most lacked a chain mail to protect them from our sharp irons. Still, they launched into combat with the courage that emanates from deep hatred. The Suevians persuaded of their fate if victory smiled upon us, fought with the ferocity of a she-wolf that protects her litter. Dozens of corpses from both sides carpeted the ground, staining it the red color of blood. The Suevian village was engulfed in a mob of angry war cries and howls of pain. I was fighting alongside Mansueto when he, after getting rid of a Suevian grabbed me by the shoulders and said:

"Run away, Adriano! Return to Lugdunum as soon as possible avoiding the Visigoths!"

At that moment, a *Bagaudae* attacked us with a huge ax, but I managed to get rid of him by sticking my *spatha* in his unprotected belly.

"If Euric takes you to Tolosa, you will be executed!" He went on.

"But…"

"You saved my life," he interrupted. "Now I intend to protect yours. Flee, it's an order!"

The battle was getting worse turning into a cruel butchery, so I hated even more having to leave my friends and comrades in arms abandoned there. But he was right. For the prince, my head was a precious trophy to show off to the rest of the barbarian nobles. And perhaps it even represented a future warning: Euric would bow to no one, not even to the armies of Rome.

"Go away," Mansueto urged me with a push.

Taking a last look behind me, I mounted a horse and, pushing my sword through the surrounding barbarians, fled that village, leaving behind the piercing screams of fury and fear, and the crack of swords and sticks. I went into the forest with a shrunken soul and glassy eyes. Although I had received orders, and prudence indicated that I remained as far away from Euric as possible, I couldn't help feeling like a coward who had abandoned his companions to their fate during the battle. I wished with great force that they would emerge from that fray, and that

I could meet them in Lugdunum where I was heading my mount. I was crossing the forest at a gallop wounding my face and arms with the branches of ash trees and oaks, when my horse stumbled and fell to the ground dragging me after him. Suddenly my vision blurred until I got involved in a black night.

I woke up startled grabbing my hilt. I was lying in the forest with my back against an ash tree. My heart was pounding in my chest; I was puzzled and confused after the fall. It was getting dark and the light of the last sun was leaking between the trees, dying the forest with the languid light of the twilight.

"Are you fine?"

I turned around and my eyes met the young Suevian's.

"You have suffered a serious fall," she added.

"My... my horse." I stammered.

"He tripped over a root and fell, but you don't have to worry about him, he hasn't suffered any damage," she said, pointing at me with her eyes at my sorrel which was grazing carelessly tied to a log.

A little more recovered I got up, although I was still stunned and bruised. My forehead was stained with blood from the blow.

"Here, drink, this will be good for you," the Suevian said, handing me my helmet with water.

I drank gratefully without taking my eyes off his bewitching black eyes.

"What is your name?" I asked her, once I had quenched my thirst.

"Alana, and you?"

"Salvio Adriano."

For a moment, an awkward silence enveloped us. She turned her gaze to the ground and I gazed at her rapt, as if I were in the incarnate presence of a goddess.

"What are you doing here?" I asked puzzled, evoking the terrible battle that had taken place a few hours ago.

The girl's eyes got veiled and she sat down by an ash tree. Her body shocked convulsively as if she had witnessed a heinous and abominable act. Suddenly she burst into tears and her cheeks got pierced with tears. I approached to Alana and comforted her in my arms.

"They've all been killed..." she whispered through tears.

"What Happened?"

Alana shook her head and replied:

"It was horrible... horrible... The Romans and Visigoths defeated the *Bagaudae*, who fled to the forest, abandoning the wounded men, leaving them at your mercy. But many of your companions died and the Visigoths' prince was furious. Our men surrendered and threw their weapons to the ground, but the Visigoth had no mercy on them. Pervinco was brutally murdered, and with him all the men of the village. The women cried pleadingly with their children in their arms, but the soldiers snatched their babies and killed them. Then they fell on the women like vermin on carrion. I managed to escape on my horse while the village was sacked and the women outraged." And with watery eyes she added: "The wailing and piercing screams of women still ring in my ears when they were forced by those soulless beasts."

The young woman paused briefly and continued:

"Then, while I was fleeing through the forest, I saw you on the ground, unconscious. I approached you and healed your wounds."

"Why did you do it?" I asked for. "We have exterminated your people, we are enemies. Why did you save me?"

She looked at me with her arcane black eyes and replied:

"I'm not a soldier, nor do I wish death or suffering to my fellow men, even if they are my enemies. Besides, you saved me from the Visigoths, it would not have been right to leave you abandoned in the forest; I would not have felt right."

"Thank you, I owe you my life."

Her lips drew a warm smile.

"Do you have relatives or somewhere to go?" I asked.

"No," she answered with moist eyes. "They're all dead. I have no one now."

I hugged her and felt the warmth of her body, her scent, her sweetness... I caressed her beautiful face, wiping her tears with my hand.

"If... if you want you can come with me to Lugdunum," I suggested uncertainly, fearing that I would be rejected.

"As a slave?" she asked me frightened.

"¡Never!" I answered. "You will always be free to go and do what you want. For your safety, you will remain under my protection until we arrive, but then you will be free to go wherever you wish if you see fit..."

In her eyes I could see doubt and concern for the uncertain future that awaited her.

"Lugdunum is a great city," I insisted. "You will easily find work there and maybe you can forget the horror that has devastated your people, rebuild your life far from wars and destruction. You can trust me," I added, taking her by the hands.

"You defended me from the Visigoths," she began to say. "And I heard how Euric ordered your arrest for killing that soldier. You risked yourself for me, for a stranger. You asked me why I helped you, now I ask you why you helped me, why you saved me from the clutches of that atrocious Visigoth."

I gazed with fascination into her deep, mysterious black eyes, her brown hair and her beautiful lips. My heart pounded and for a few moments, I didn't know what to say. A confusion of feelings fluttered in my gut in a rush. I sat up and simply said:

"I couldn't allow that savage to outrage you."

"But why?" she insisted.

"Because, although I'm a soldier, I don't wish death and suffering to my fellow men," I replied, repeating her words. But my motives were quite different.

Alana narrowed her eyes as if scrutinizing my thoughts and smiled.

"I'll go with you," she finally agreed with a slight nod.

My heart leapt in my chest and I clenched my jaws trying to suppress the joy that coursed through every inch of my body. And letting out a snort I said:

"We must leave; it is possible that Euric has sent his soldiers in my search.

"Or in mine..." replied Alana with her eyes veiled by anguish, possibly her mind evoked the Germanic's sinister image. A terrifying shiver ran through her body.

We headed eastward, avoiding the main roads and spending the night in crags, caves, or shepherds' huts. We had to hurry, since I was convinced that the barbarian troops had set out to capture us. We crossed the lands of Hispania. Years of plunder and depredation had turned Rome's most beautiful orchard into a desolate wasteland. Hispania, the most beautiful jewel of the Empire, was now nothing but a heap of abandoned villages, shattered causeways and burned pastures. The hand of the Empire had long since disappeared from those ruined lands. Along the way, we passed hundreds of peasants wandering aimlessly, accompanied by their hungry children. They looked at us with empty and pleading eyes, hunger and misfortune had taken their toll.

Misery carves its imprint in the souls of the most disadvantaged with the execrable chisel of injustice and unreason.

We were in a deep oak grove furrowed by countless streams that split through the drivel like crystalline veins, drowning the air with their soft, gentle gurgling. It was dusk, and the grove was so dense that the last rays of the sun hardly touched the ground. I have never believed in monsters, or witches, or spirits that dwell in the forest, stalking naive travelers or reckless pilgrims behind the shadows, but if they existed, I'm sure they would have chosen that forest as their home.

I was scrutinizing the oaks and beeches, watching for any threat, when the sudden caw of a crow surprised me, and I pulled the reins of my horse.

"Wait" Alana suddenly exclaimed.

"What's the matter?" I asked in alarm, drawing my *spatha*.

"I guess I was here when I was still a child," she said, looking around restlessly. "Yes, I remember."

"What do you remember?"

She didn't answer, dismounted and started walking.

"Alana!" I exclaimed, but she didn't hear me. She kept walking as if she knew the way, as if some strange magic was guiding her steps, as if she was sure of where she was going. Concerned, I dismounted and followed her. I shouted her name again, but she did not hear me. I approached her and saw that her eyes were lost in infinity, as if she were possessed by something or someone. Frightened, I grabbed her by the shoulders and shook her to wake her from her trance.

"Let me go!" she said in an imperative tone.

I obeyed her in bewilderment, surprised at the strength she radiated. She walked for a few minutes, until she reached the trunk of a huge yew tree. There she stopped.

"Are you all right?" I asked her worriedly.

For a few moments she looked at me in confusion, as if she didn't recognize me.

"What... what happened?" she asked.

A crow gave a high pitched squawk and from behind the yew tree emerged the figure of a man in a white robe. He was an old man with a weathered face and a long white beard. His eyes were gray and crystalline, and his hair was thin and gray. A white ribbon girded his forehead and he walked with the help of a staff.

"Many years have passed, but the omens have been fulfilled," said the old man with a smile. "Easy, little one, I'm also very happy to see you."

"Lughdyr!" Alana exclaimed, throwing herself on the old man, who almost fell because of his impetus.

I remained silent watching the scene, I was afraid to break the spell that surrounded Alana and the old man. They held each other for several minutes without noticing my presence. I was beginning to think that I had become invisible... The squawk of a crow seemed to wake them up, and then the old man looked at me.

"Greetings, Salvio Adriano."

"How do you know my name?" I asked puzzled.

"Lughdyr is a druid, a great wizard and a fortune teller. He knows everything," Alana said.

I had heard of the Druids, wise elders from distant lands, but I had never seen one, and until now, I doubted their existence.

"Are you a fortune teller?" I asked skeptically.

"I can read the future in the behavior of animals, the movement of the wind or the flames of fire," he replied.

"And can you see my future?" I challenged him.

The old man closed his eyes, pondered for a moment, and then said:

"You must be careful."

"With..."

The horrible squawk of a bird flying near my head thundered in my ears, forcing me to duck and protect myself with my hands. When I sat up, I saw the old man looking at me amused with a black crow perched on his shoulder.

"Our future is written in the unfathomable arcana of the stars, animals, fire, the water we drink or the earth we walk on... but it is necessary that the Mother grants you the prerogative of being able to decipher it. Now let's go home, it's getting dark," said the old man, who began to walk, ending the divination session.

It became dark as we arrived at the druid's house: a small round hut, built in stone and with a heather roof. We entered and I noticed that he had a fire ready and over it hung a cauldron. He gave us a wooden bowl and then served us a leek soup with onions and bread. During dinner, Alana told Lughdyr about the destruction of her village by Roman and Visigoth troops. The druid's eyes conveyed a deep

56

sorrow, and he shook his head in lamentation for the fate that had befallen the wretched Suevians.

From time to time, the old man and Alana gave each other knowing glances and nodded silently. I felt a little uncomfortable, as if I were at a banquet to which I hadn't been invited. When I finished my broth, I decided to inquire about the peculiar relationship between the two of them.

"Well, how do you two know each other?" I asked interested.

They both smiled. So much connivance was beginning to exasperate me.

"Lughdyr was a friend of my father," answered Alana.

"Was your father a druid?" I asked.

"I barely knew him; I was very little when he died."

"Her father was a great man," the old man interjected, looking at me with his enigmatic gray eyes. "When he died I took care of Alana, who was just a child, and I took care of her in these woods until I entrusted her to her aunt and uncle."

I looked at them without understanding anything of what they were talking about.

"Can someone start from the beginning?" I asked.

The old man smiled.

"Alana was the daughter of a respected physicist who, for years, was my student…"

"So you indoctrinated him as a druid?" I asked.

"Divination, magic, the ability to talk to the spirits is not learned in the scrolls, it is necessary to be born with very special qualities," Alana answered offended.

"I understand," I lied.

"Mother Nature blesses you with her grace before birth," explained the old man.

"And Alana's father lacked the gifts that Nature bestows, but he wanted to have the medical knowledge to help his people, didn't he?"

"That's right," the old man confirmed.

"And what about your mother?" I asked.

"She died during the childbirth," Alana replied regretfully.

I looked at her confused, until that moment I had assumed that her parents, like the rest of her family, had died in her village. I hadn't asked her about them so as not to further deepen her grief. I understood that

57

Alana was a stranger to me, despite the days we had been traveling together.

"Her father tried his best to save her, but he didn't succeed. Even so, and thanks to his great skill as a doctor, he managed to save the girl's life," said the druid.

"What happened after?"

"He had a long trip to take and I was left in charge of looking after Alana, who was barely four years old."

"He never came back," Alana said.

"He was addressing to Lucus Augusti when he was attacked by a group of bandits. Despite the fact that he was known and respected by all, the robbers showed no mercy, and they killed him," the druid continued. His eyes were veiled with sadness. "He was a great man; he alleviated many ills thanks to his healing gifts."

"At ten years old, Lughdyr handed me over to the care of my father's brother. Since then, I hadn't heard from him again," Alana said, taking the old man's hand. "My uncle died along with my aunt and my three cousins during the attack."

I had no choice but to look at the ground in shame, my troops or those of our federated Visigoths had murdered her family. Embarrassed, I asked her for forgiveness again. She smiled at me and stroked my cheek. I couldn't help but kiss her. The old man looked at us tenderly.

"When you saw us in the forest, you said that the omens had come true. What did you mean?" I asked the druid, remembering his words.

The old man, who was sitting on a footstool, heated his hands in the fire and closed his eyes. So, he remained a few moments ignoring my question. Then he looked at me and smiled.

"When I left her in charge of her uncle and returned to the forest, I had a premonition. In it I saw a young woman accompanied by a Roman, they were fleeing from some danger and hid in an oak grove: my oak grove. The young woman was Alana and the Roman... was you." the old man suddenly fell silent, as if he were afraid to continue with the story.

"Is that all? "I asked for.

The druid ignored my question and looked away at the fire.

"Is that all, Lughdyr?" I insisted.

"Do you really want to know the rest of the omen?"

He gave me a look that I couldn't interpret, the truth is that a disturbing chill ran down my spine. I tried to compose myself and nodded, staring into his eyes. The old man got up, took a small cauldron, poured in some water and put it to heat. When the water began to bubble, he introduced greenish roots along with dark purple berries. He stirred it up and the scent of rainforest embalmed the cabin. He took a ladle, poured some into a bowl, and handed it to me.

"Drink," he ordered.

I looked at the greenish liquid and breathed in the smell of slime and wet earth it emanated.

"You asked me recently if I could read your future," the druid said, turning to me. You will do it yourself," he added, waving his hand and encouraging me to drink the potion.

I looked at Alana, and I could see in her eyes that her mind was somewhere else, far away.

"Are you afraid to know your future?" the old man challenged me.

The crow uttered an unpleasant screech and flew around the hut, brushing me with its black wings. Then it landed on a rickety cupboard, looked at me and opened its beak as if trying to burst into laughter, as if the bird was mocking at me.

I looked at Alana, trying to scrutinize her hieratic face, but her gaze was still lost in infinity. The warlock's gray eyes stared at me, and a new squawk of the hateful bird resounded in the hut. I would be lying if I said that the situation didn't frighten me: Alana was completely absorbed with her mind wandering God only knew where, and the crow was staring at me defiantly, as if it wanted to tear my eyes out of their sockets. The druid spoke in a strange language, radiating a magical, evil, supernatural halo. Immersed in that disconcerting scene, I brought the bowl to my lips and drank…

We left the druid's hut shortly before dawn, wrapped in a sea of mist that prevented us from seeing a few steps beyond our horses. We didn't speak for hours, the effect the drink had had on my mind was still fresh. Alana remained somewhat dazed, and it was not until well into the morning, when the sun had dispelled the fog with its warm rays, that she spoke.

"What did you think?"

Her question startled me; I had become accustomed to the silence of the forest.

"They are just conjectures, absurd visions provoked by the effects of some drug," I answered with pursed lips.

"Can't you accept what your eyes have seen?" 0020yhe asked me irritated, stopping her mount.

"They were nothing more than shadows caused by the effects of the drink the old man offered me."

"I didn't take the potion and I had the same visions as you."

"Are you a druid woman?" I asked with a harsh smile.

She looked away angrily and said:

"Remember the words of the druid."

"Those were simple nonsense words."

"And what about the vision?"

"It was caused by the herbs that he gave me to drink," I replied.

Alana's face conveyed great pain and regret. I walked over to her horse and took her hand.

"You have great faith in that man and I don't blame you, since you were little you have been raised between superstitions and false beliefs."

"They aren't false beliefs! Lughdyr is a great druid, a wise and clairvoyant man!" she protested vigorously.

"It is fine," I said. "He's a wise man…"

"You don't know him," she insisted. "Travelers from distant lands come to his cabin to ask him for advice. He can see the future and he has seen ours."

I stopped my horse and staring into her eyes I said:

"In the forest, when you healed my wounds, you asked me why I saved you from the atrocious intentions of the German, why I risked my life to free you from the slavery to which the Visigoths wanted to subdue you." she looked at me carefully with her glassy black eyes. "Well, I did it… I did it…" A lump in my throat, caused by an absurd childish blush and the fear of feeling rejected, prevented me from expressing my true motives and feelings.

"Why did you do it?" she asked.

I brought my horse closer to hers and replied:

"Because I love you and if you… and if you feel something for me, nothing will separate us, much less a blurred vision and the prophecy of a…" I was going to say crazy, but I preferred to be more prudent, "…old druid."

My words sounded in the air like an unanswered prayer, since Alana looked down at the ground without saying anything.

"Of course, if you don't..."

"While fleeing from the German I tripped over your mount," she interrupted. "I looked up and fell in love with that Roman soldier with pure black eyes. Then I found you in the forest badly injured and my heart suffered. When you asked me to accompany you to Lugdunum, I asked you why you saved me. You answered me with empty words, but in your eyes I read the real reason. Since then, I believe that my heart is linked to yours."

My lips broke into a wide smile, and a pleasant tingling similar to the fluttering of butterflies ran through my body. But that moment, as magical as it was marvelous, disappeared as if struck by a furious gale when she continued:

"But our paths must part, remember his words."

I pulled furiously my horse's reins and stopped him. I dismounted and helped her dismount. I looked into her deep eyes, her full lips and kissed her. I remember how my heart was beating and how a mysterious energy flowed between us, enveloping us with an invisible, magical halo.

"This is love," I said with glazed eyes. "And it is stronger and more powerful than any bad omen, portent or prophecy. Forget the druid and his false words; forget the vision and its false message. Believe in me, believe in us... and believe in our love."

She smiled and kissed me, freeing my heart from the tyrannical chains of doubt and distrust.

We didn't speak about the druid again for days. The old man had been erased from our minds along with his prophecies and visions, or so I thought.

Despite our arduous situation, the days I enjoyed with Alana were, without a doubt, the happiest of my life. At her side I felt immensely happy and fortunate, and in peace with myself and the world.

We were riding through Spanish lands. Towns that were once rich and flourishing had turned into heaps of stone and ruins. Their walls, which were destroyed, had been plundered to build crude buildings or the walls of inhospitable caves. As we went deeper into the Tarraconensis, the greater the number of disinherited people we met on our way.

"We must hide in the forest, there are too many people wandering around here," I said.

We were crossing an old stone bridge and came across several villagers dressed in torn rags. Many of them looked at us in distress and despair. They approached our horses begging us to give them some coins or food, but others, united in small groups and hiding hoes and sticks, watched us with resentment and greed. They were farmers who, overwhelmed by the impossibility of providing food to their families, had become low life thugs and highway robbers greedy for a few coins.

"Why? They don't seem dangerous," she asked in surprise.

"They are hungry and desperate. At any moment they can attack us to steal our saddlebags or our horses."

"And is the forest a safe place?" she asked skeptically.

"No place is safe," I replied, looking behind me, afraid to see a Visigoth patrol arrive. "but the forest will allow us to hide from prying eyes."

"Are the *Bagaudae* hiding there?" she asked me.

"They are the ones that worry me the least," I replied, watching a group of raggedy men looking at us with malicious intentions. "We'd better hurry," I added, spurring my horse on.

We left the road as night fell on us, lengthening the shadows of the pines. We had to find a place to shelter soon or we would end up sleeping in the open, however, it would not be the first time either. We found a small cave carved into a hillock. It was protected by a small stone wall, which revealed that it was a rickety shepherds' shelter. The cave was no more than six paces high and as many long: it was like a palace for us when compared to other places where we had slept. A little more than a stadium away a stream ran and we took water. It had been many days since our last hot meal and we took advantage of the protection of the cave to build a fire. Alana prepared a tasty soup of leeks, garlic and onions, which warmed our cold bodies in the cold night.

The memory of the druid and the potion he gave me to drink came to my mind. We hadn't talked about him and his fateful prophecies for the past few days, and that was comforting.

"Lughdyr only thinks of our good," Alana said suddenly, as if she were guessing my thoughts.

"In the end, I'm going to conclude that you really are a druid woman. I was thinking precisely of the old man," I growled.

"We must separate and each of us must continue with his path, we are two very different people who belong to different worlds... the prophecy..."

The damn prophecy again. I cursed the day the wizard crossed our path. Not wanting to talk about it again, I lay down on the litter that I had prepared for me with dry leaves and covered myself with the blanket.

"We will get back together and never part, that's how it is written," Alana insisted.

"I don't want to talk about this, nothing will separate us: our love is stronger than any magic," I replied, turning my back on her. "Or is it that you don't love me?" I asked, dreading the answer.

But she didn't respond, she remained silent and wrapped in her blanket. I turned around and walked over to her. Despite the darkness, the sparkle in her eyes revealed that she had cried. I caressed her soft cheeks and kissed her. She kissed me back, I lay down next to her and we covered ourselves under the warmth of the blanket.

A few barks woke me up; I quickly got up and grabbed my *pugio*. I looked at Alana and motioned for her to remain silent. I cautiously made my way out of the cave. The dogs' barking became more and more insistent and were accompanied by unintelligible shouts.

"Quick Alana, we must flee!" I shouted, but it was too late.

A huge dog rushed at me, growling as if possessed by thousand demons. I felt its weight on my chest and fell to the ground dropping my *pugio*. He tried to tear at my neck and his drool fell on my face showering me with slimy, foul smelling froth. But Alana grabbed my dagger and plunged it into his back. The dog let out a piercing howl before falling dead in a pool of blood. I sat up and thanked her with a smile. Suddenly, half a dozen dogs emerged from the grove and came snarling toward us, threatening us with their huge jaws.

"Stop!" commanded a voice, and the dogs obediently ran towards their master.

Through the mist that veiled the forest, the sinister silhouettes of several horsemen mounted on spirited war horses emerged. One of them was followed meekly by the six dogs. His malicious smile and yellow eyes were unmistakable.

"Well, well, what a surprise, you are together," he said wickedly. "Did you think you would get away from me?" Walder asked. His voice was similar to the growl of dogs. "Now the prince is not here to save your Roman ass, and no one will be able to prevent your death."

He dismounted and headed to the small wall that protected the cave. Several of his men followed him, while others, from their horses, pointed his bows at us.

"But before I kill you, I want you to witness how I enjoy your little bitch."

I protected Alana by threatening the barbarian with my *pugio,* who had already jumped the wall accompanied by his men. I regretted that my *spatha* was stored in the *balteus,* hanging uselessly from the saddle. ¡Big mistake!

"I have to cut off your head," the German continued. "That's what Euric ordered me to do." he paused briefly, basking in his triumph in the same way a beast enjoys contemplating its cornered prey. "The prince wants to offer it to King Turismund, as an evidence of your cowardice and treachery. You don't mind right?" he asked with a wide smile, showing a string of yellow teeth.

"You'll have to come and get it," I told him.

"Ha, ha, ha!" he laughed out loud. "I already beat you once, what makes you suppose I can't do it twice?"

"Then come here, this is between you and me."

"No, no, no," he replied, wagging his finger "¡Between you, the bitch and me! don't leave her aside! I have my friend eager to finish what you prevented me in the Suevian village," he grumbled, clutching his genitals.

He drew his sword and raised it to the sky. I noticed how his archers sharpened his weapons. The German had no intention of killing me, his men would. A hiss was heard through the air, and I hugged Alana with my back to the Visigoths. I thought it was all over. A dry noise caught my attention; I turned and saw how an archer lay inert on the ground with an arrow stuck in his chest. There was a new hiss and another barbarian archer fell to the ground before Walder's confused gaze.

"Drop your weapons and we won't cause any more casualties," a familiar voice commanded from the undergrowth.

The Visigoths were reluctant to part with their swords and bows, and several darts converged on a Visigoth horseman who fell dead to the ground.

"You won't be able to escape, drop your weapons or all of you will die."

Walder reluctantly threw his sword to the ground and ordered his men to do the same. He looked around, searching among the pines and junipers for those who were decimating them, but he didn't manage to see them. Enraged, he mounted his horse.

"We will see each other again," he snapped me.

"I'm sure of that," I muttered convinced.

He turned his mount and got lost in the grove followed by his men and the dogs. Alana and I hugged each other in relief. The neighing of a horse startled us, we looked into the forest expecting to see the shadowy figure of the German appear again, but it was not the barbarian, but four Roman *milites* mounted on their warhorses. I smiled and headed towards them.

"Friends!" I exclaimed, and greeted them with a hug. They were Arcadius, Calerus, Ajax, and Arius Sidonius, Ajax's legionary training partner. "What the hell are you doing here?"

"Don't blaspheme," Calerus replied with a smile.

"Mansueto ordered us to protect you from the Visigoths," Arcadius intervened.

"But…"

"Mount on your horses; we are under the risk of Walder's return as soon as he notices the deceit. We'll have time to talk," said Calerus.

Four legionaries had driven away more than a dozen barbarians, but Walder wouldn't be so easily fooled. We galloped quickly, glancing several times behind us, expecting to see the German's blond mustaches and yellow eyes. But, luckily, the barbarian didn't appear.

After a long and tiring day, we rested our mounts near a stream and settled down to eat. The sun was setting behind the mountains, staining the highest peaks a reddish color similar to blood. The night was closing in on us hiding us under a dark and protective cloak and, from among the tall pines; the sickle of the moon emerged powerful.

After unsaddling our saddles, we prepared for a well-deserved rest. We sat in a circle around a blanket on which our meager dinner was laid out: bread, olives and some cheese.

"Tell me; what do I owe your miraculous appearance? If it hadn't been for you, I would be dead and Alana enslaved," I said.

"We put the *Bagaudae* to flight, and the Suevian were exterminated…" explained Arcadius, turning a guilt ridden glance on

Alana. "Euric was furious and poured all his anger on the defenseless population. Mansueto tried to stop him, but the Visigoths were more numerous and we could only watch helplessly as they treat brutally the women and children. It was an atrocity," he added, shaking his head with compunction.

"Many of our people died both Romans and Visigoths," Calerus interjected. "The prince, in retaliation, ordered that the village be razed to the ground. We didn't participate in the massacre," he said, looking at Alana, as a way of apology. "The Visigoths were mad. They captured Pervinco and executed him after torturing him. The men were killed and the women…"

"Don't go on," I interrupted, noticing Alana's glazed eyes.

"I fled when the village was being devastated," said Alana with her voice contracted with strong emotion. "Do you know if anyone survived?" she asked, with a plea in her eyes, a last hope that soon vanished like mist on a cold winter's night.

"I'm sorry," Calerus replied, shaking his head. "All the men, women and children were killed, and their bodies thrown into the flames that devoured the village."

An indescribable pain disfigured her beautiful face. I approached her and comforted her in my arms.

"But Euric wanted more… he wanted you," Calerus continued.

"He looked for your corpse among the dead and, not finding you," continued Ajax, "he sent the Germanic in your search."

"Mansueto, fearing for your life, urged us to protect you from the claws of the barbarians," said Arius Sidonius. "We had to find you before Walder and accompany you to Lugdunum."

Once again, the *Hispaniarum comes* cared for my integrity, I could never be grateful enough.

"It wasn't difficult to follow the trail of the Germanic and his horde of Visigoths," said Arcadius. "And here we are, saving your ass," he added with a laugh.

"But…" interjected Ajax, pointing his finger at Alana and me, wondering what we were doing together.

I told them our story and my intention to take her with me to Lugdunum, omitting the meeting with the druid. It was no time for mysterious prophecies.

"We had better rest," suggested Arius Sidonius. "We must be on our way as soon as possible or Walder will reach us. I'll take the first watch."

"I'll take the second one," volunteered Ajax.

"Then I'll take the third one, with a couple of hours' sleep I have more than enough," said Arcadius.

The slit moon was rising in a diaphanous firmament, dotted with sparkling stars. It was cool and we wrapped ourselves in our blankets, scrutinizing the sounds of the night, trying to glimpse any danger.

I looked at those legionaries and felt a deep sense of pride in being able to call them friends. They were young, brave, and impulsive; the fire that glowed in their eyes could burn the city of Tolosa with all the Visigoths inside. We found ourselves in a lost forest, stalked by the barbarians and facing an adverse and bleak future. But they didn't lament their fate; on the contrary, they were concerned for mine and, above all, for that of Rome.

During the night I was assailed by horrible nightmares. In them, I beheld how a Roman city was set on fire. Dark rivers of blood flowed through its streets, impregnated with the pungent smell of death. Dozens of young women ran in panic pursued by the barbarians, while children were executed in front of their mothers. A group of *milites* defended themselves bravely against the enemy onslaught but were defeated by the savages. One of the barbarians severed the head of a Roman and raised it to the sky in victory, shouting heartrending screams. I awoke in spasms and cold sweats. I cursed the druid. That dream, that nightmare, was the vision that assaulted me in his hut after drinking the potion. A condemnation that would martyr me for years, perhaps revealing to me a terrible horizon filled with blood and death. Perhaps it embodied the unfortunate future that awaited the glorious Rome.

After several weeks of marching we arrived in the city of Calagurris, where a *clarissimus*, after being informed of our presence by one of his servants, invited us to his home: a beautiful villa a few miles from the *municipium*. Petronius Quintus was a senator in Rome, but, disgusted by the corruption and meanness that plagued the *Urbs,* returned to Calagurris, his native city. The villa retained the opulence and luxury of ancient Roman villas: marble sculptures, stone fountains, ponds and beautiful gardens adorned the home of the former curial. We arrived shortly before dusk, and were dutifully greeted by his servants, who took charge of our mounts. Two of them accompanied us inside the village. We entered the house through the *vestibulum,* a small corridor flanked by stone benches, and arrived at the *atrium,* a beautiful inner courtyard with a pond, (or *impluvium,*) in the center from which a small stream of water gushed through a stone fountain. The gentle gurgling of the water of the impluvium and the scent of the surrounding chrysanthemums and lilies comforted our weary spirits and gave us an almost forgotten peace.

Admired by the sumptuousness of the villa, we entered the *triclinium* where several *triclinia* and a large table with trays of food had already been placed. We took a seat and our host appeared. He was a middle-aged man with scarce white hair. Of slender build, he had watery gray eyes that conveyed great dignity. He wore a *praetexta* toga and *soleae.* He greeted us with a big smile.

"I greet you, brave soldiers of Rome," he said looking at us, the men. "And I greet you, beautiful girl," he added, looking at Alana.

"I greet you, *clarissimus* Petronius Quintus; we thank you for having received us in your villa," I said. "My name is Salvio Adriano and these are my companions Sextilius Arcadius, Lucius Calerus, Arius Sidonius, and this is Vedio Quirico Nabor, but we call him Ajax. This is Alana."

"It is a pleasure for me to have the visit of the true defenders of the *Caput Mundi*, please take a seat."

We stretched out on the *triclinia* and the servants offered us trays of pecorino cheese, hard-boiled eggs, and olives. My body was more used to sleeping on a litter in the open air and eating sitting on a rock than lying on a triclinium, and I decided to take a seat. My companions and Alana imitated me before the smile of Petronius Quintus, who did the same. The *clarissimus* clapped his hands twice and several servants entered the *triclinium* carrying trays of roast lamb, fish garnished with herbs and lemon, and chicken with coriander, all accompanied by several jars of wine and a bowl of *garum.*

"What has brought you to these lands? It is not very usual to meet a group of legionaries accompanied by a Suevian." Petronius Quintus said, squinting distrustfully.

We looked at each other without knowing what to say, but we would run an unnecessary risk if the *clarissimus* considered us deserters and we decided to tell him the truth.

"It was very noble of you to come to the aid of a defenseless young girl," he said, once he had heard our story. "and I'm very sorry that your village was destroyed," he added, looking at Alana. "The voracity of the Visigoths is immeasurable."

"Has it been a long time since the *milites* appeared in these lands?" I asked, taking a piece of cheese.

"The legion, as we know it, has practically disappeared. Our armies are made up of foreigners and mercenaries, since hardly any Romans fight in their ranks. We pay barbarians to protect us from other barbarians. This has been the unfortunate end that our legions have suffered. Now, they are nothing more than the remnants of the invincible hosts that once dominated the world," replied the *clarissimus* with regret.

For many years the legion had been supplied with auxiliary troops from the conquered provinces. The Roman army was made up of legionaries and *foederati,* barbarian allies settled within the *limes* of the Empire. In turn, the legions were divided into *comitatenses and limitanei.* The *comitatenses* were the interior troops and moved wherever they were required with great speed. The *limitanei* were regular units of trained troops whose mission was to patrol the frontiers and delay an enemy invasion, giving this way time to the *comitatenses* to prepare the counterattack.

"But the spirit of the ancient Roman legions remains alive in Aetius' army," said Arius Sidonius.

"Aetius..." Petronius Quintus whispered thoughtfully. "*Solus romanae gentis,* the last of the Romans. I knew him in Rome many years ago, a brave and noble soldier, faithful defender of the Roman tradition. It is a pity there are not more men like him. Unfortunately, he is no more than a legionary surrounded by enemies, and I don't just mean the barbarians."

The words of the Roman nobleman confused us. Petronius Quintus took a sip of wine and, fixing his eyes on the red liquid, said:

"Sometimes I think Rome deserves to be destroyed. Corruption, excesses, nepotism and greed have debased leaders and citizens. The emperors, governors and other dignitaries don't pursue the prosperity of the Empire but their own benefit. They only wish to enrich

69

themselves and to satiate their most abominable perversions. Sometimes, I believe what they say," he paused for a moment, his eyes were moist. "That Attila has been sent by the Lord to devastate Rome from its foundations, so that it could rise from its ashes purer and more righteous than it has ever been."

"If Attila destroys Rome, nothing assures us that it will be reborn," Arcadius replied.

We nodded in silence.

"Our hopes are placed in Aetius and in his ability to forge fruitful alliances with the barbarians," Arius Sidonius intervened.

"Only God can prevent Rome from falling into the hands of the king of the Huns," Petronius Quintus, a devout Christian, replied at Calerus's assent.

That the survival of Rome depended on the grace of God didn't offer me too many guarantees, but our host was a pious man, and no one wanted to enter into theological discussions. It would have been discourteous.

"What a predicament the scheming Honoria has got us into," said Petronius Quintus suddenly.

"What do you mean?" I asked puzzled.

"Don't you know"?

We all shook our heads. The *clarissimus* settled down as if he were about to tell a long story.

"Attila has returned," he said.

"Attila?" we asked in unison as we sat up in the *triclinium,* not giving any response to his words.

"And more furious than ever," he added. The light of the oil lamps reflected in the glassy eyes of the *dignitate,* betraying that they were tired, dejected, and hopeless.

"What happened"? Calerus asked.

"The Hun's hosts have crossed the borders of Pannonia and have destroyed all the cities in their path, including Aquileia," he answered.

"Aquileia?" Ajax asked in horror.

"It has been burned and destroyed to the ground. Most of the population has been brutally slaughtered, only a few have managed to escape by hiding in the nearby marshes and swamps."

Aquileia, located on the Postumian Way, connected Italy with Dalmatia and with the east of the Empire. It was one of the most important and prosperous Roman cities. It had never been conquered, its strong walls and high towers made it impregnable. So it was, during the siege of the Quadi and the Marcomans. And now it was nothing but a mountain of rubble and ruins.

"*Flagellum Dei*... God's scourge. Attila has been sent by the Almighty to punish the Romans for our sins. The Huns aren't men, they are bloodthirsty demons," muttered Petronius Quintus to Calerus's convinced assent. "They leave a trail of desolation in their wake, not a blade of grass sprouts where the hoofs of their horses hole. They are like the plague."

"Where is he heading?" I asked.

"To Rome, and the most worrying thing is that there is no legion that can stop him, his march is unstoppable. Only God can save us."

It was grave and unfortunate news. Attila, humiliated and enraged by the defeat in Maurica, had raised a powerful army with the sole purpose of destroying Rome. He would unleash his choleric vengeance by turning the Empire into a desert, a barren wasteland where not even the most miserable shrub would ever grow again.

"Can't any legion stand up to him?" I asked. "What about Aetius? He will stop Attila!" I exclaimed in search of a last hope, but the *dignitate* looked down, shaking his head.

"Aetius remains in Transalpine Gaul with a handful of legionaries. To attack the Huns would be suicide. He must wait..." he said.

"Wait for what?" I asked without finding an answer.

For a few moments no one said anything. Sometimes silences are more eloquent than endless speeches full of useless words and empty promises. We remained contemplating the pavement, avoiding meeting the furtive glance of a colleague that would betray the voracious anguish that was devouring our entrails.

"Aetius will make deals with other barbarians," I began to say. "If Attila destroys Rome, the next to succumb will be the Visigoths of Turismund or the Franks of Meroveo. We are all interested in signing a great alliance against the Huns, it happened that way in Maurica and we managed to defeat him. Aetius can do it again!" I exclaimed, searching the *clarissimus*'s gaze for support I couldn't find.

Petronius Quintus got up and began to walk.

"Valentinian has ordered him to stop the invasion, but Aetius is keeping his troops billeted in Lugdunum," he said. "He doesn't have enough *milites* and he doesn't want to sacrifice a single legionary to save the emperor's neck. He knows that defeat is inevitable."

71

He drank some wine and continued:

"The emperor, who was in Ravenna, fled to Rome due to the advance of the Huns."

"But if Valentinian has ordered him to intervene, Aetius must. It's an order from the emperor!" I exclaimed.

"The Augustus is not concerned about the future of the Empire, he simply wants to save his egregious ass," growled the *clarissimus*. "Indeed, as soon as he heard the echoes of the barbarian advance, he ran for refuge in Rome, leaving the court of Ravenna helpless, Aetius does the right thing."

I meditated for a moment on the disobedience of the *magister utriusque militiae*, and on the unforeseeable consequences of it. If Rome survived the Hun and he returned to his inhospitable lands of Pannonia, Aetius would be in serious trouble; ¿or would Valentinian the one who would be in such circumstances? Not in vain, Aetius had the support of the army and the Augustus only with that of a Senate made up of tricksters and entertainers whose sole interest was to maintain their prerogatives and privileges.

"You said before that Honoria got you in trouble," Alana interjected. "¿Does she have something to do with Attila's invasion?"

Petronius Quintus sat down, ate a piece of meat, and took a long swallow of wine.

"Honoria is the sister of Emperor Valentinian," he began. "She is a beautiful and intelligent woman, which was named Augusta by Emperor Flavius Constantius."

"So she is an empress..." interrupted Arius Sidonius.

"Flavius Constantius must have noticed the limitations of his son Valentinian and named both sons Augustus," continued Petronius Quintus, ignoring the interruption. "And he was right: Valentinian is a real inept man. He is a weak and pusillanimous man who for years has hidden under the robe of his energetic mother, Gala Placidia. But her death exposed his son's incompetence. He is overcome by circumstances and feels jealous of his sister, much more intelligent, skilled and therefore more valid to lead the Empire than he is. And, blinded by jealousy, he locked her in a room in the palace, being assisted only by a servant girl."

He took a sip of wine and continued.

"Thus she remained for several years, but, tired of her confinement, she made a decision which, according to recent events, is having dramatic consequences for the Empire: she got her maid to send a letter to Attila offering herself in marriage. As a gift, she would give him half of the Empire."

"By being named Augusta, half of the Empire is hers, right?" Calerus asked. "What she did is completely legal."

"Indeed, she offered Attila the half of the Empire that is hers as Augusta of Rome," continued the *clarissimus.* "When Attila received the letter, he accepted the marriage willingly and asked Valentinian for his sister's hand. The emperor evidently refused."

"And now Attila wants to take in blood and fire what he considers to be his, and the emperor has denied him," Arcadius observed.

"Honoria only wanted to be free, to escape from her confinement, but her imprudence has awakened the monster that can destroy our civilization," Petronius Quintus said.

"But Valentinian would have the same problem if Honoria married another man, Roman or not, I mean, whoever Honoria's husband is, he is entitled to half of the Empire," I concluded.

Petronius Quintus nodded and said:

"That eventuality had already been considered by the emperor, who arranged the marriage of his sister to a mature man of illustrious family, but who felt more attraction for young ephebes than for power. He was a docile man, without ambition, easy to please with a good batch of young men and several jars of wine. I suppose that Honoria, when she was informed of her future engagement, went into a rage and then made the decision to send the letter to Attila. She is empress, through her veins flows the blood of several generations of *nobilissimi* Romans. Her marriage to a depraved man was an affront that she was in no way willing to tolerate."

Valentinian had left no loose end except Attila. At no time did the emperor conceive the possibility that his sister, locked up in the palace, could send a letter to the Hun, offering him half of the Empire as a wedding dowry.

"Valentinian is in a difficult situation: if he agrees to Attila's request, he will lose half of the Empire, but if he refuses, he may lose everything. Will he finally grant him his sister's hand?" Arius Sidonius asked rhetorically.

"I don't think that matters anymore. I doubt very much that Attila, now that he has noticed our manifest weakness, will accept half of the Empire when he can have it all," Petronius Quintus replied

We nodded with concern. The situation was dramatic: nothing and no one could stop the Hun; his hosts were an overflowing river that swept everything in its path leaving a trail of death and desolation. The Visigoths were withdrawing their armies to await events, Aetius remained in Lugdunum watching helplessly as, one by one, the cities of the Empire were destroyed, and the Frank Meroveo was too busy resolving internal revolts and setting up his reign. Faced with this prospect, and much to my regret, we could only entrust the salvation of the Empire to Holy Providence.

"But let's not be sad, we'll have time to upset over worries and misfortunes! It's time to enjoy this beautiful night!" Petronius Quintus exclaimed, rising from the *triclinium* with his glass raised. "Let's drink!"

"Let's drink!" we exclaimed with a bitter smile drawing on our faces.

We ate and drank without moderation, just as ancient gladiators enjoyed one last feast before jumping into the arena. We had pigeon with pine nuts, meat and vegetable soups, lamb with honey, cheese and olives, along with a magnificent Hispanic wine that the slaves served us as soon as they heard the clapping of their master. The music of the lute and the pleasant gurgling of the fountain relaxed our souls and dispelled our restlessness.

We talked for hours. Petronius Quintus told us anecdotes about Rome, provoking more than one laugh, Calerus narrated fables by Gaius Julius Phaedrus, and Alana distracted us with stories and Suevian legends. It was a beautiful evening where we all laughed, danced and even sang. After several hours, the sad end of dinner came and each one of us headed, some more wobbly than the other, to their respective cubicles.

The good Petronius Quintus provided us with provisions for the long journey we still had to make. We said goodbye with emotion, but not before thanking him for the excellent treatment he had given us. Leaving behind the beautiful village and the pleasant memories of our brief stay, we continued our journey towards Lugdunum.

We crossed the Iber river and arrived in the city of Caesaraugusta. We crossed the wall through the gate of Toletum and walked along the *decumanus* via. Despite the multitude of half-ruined houses and buildings, it still maintained part of its former splendor. We headed to the public baths since we had many days of travel behind us and our bodies urgently demanded a bath. We spent the night at an inn and resumed our journey shortly before dawn.

Alana was very quiet; she had hardly opened her mouth since we left the villa of the *clarissimus*. Something was bothering her, but she was afraid to say it. More than once I asked her if she was well, if she needed anything, if she was tired, but she always answered with a smile and an "I'm fine, don't worry," but it did worry me. I had only known her for a few weeks, so she was practically a stranger to me. Although I quickly understood that she was the woman of my life and seeing her sad and saddened broke my heart.

It was getting dark, and we looked for a suitable place to camp. Providence blessed us with an abandoned barn whose rickety roof threatened to collapse at any moment, but, lacking other options, we decided to spend the night there. After inspecting it we lit a fire to prepare dinner. Calerus, helped by Alana, prepared a tasty onion soup and we roasted some of the pork that Petronius Quintus had given us. During dinner no one spoke, we were tired and restless. After dinner, I went for a walk and asked Alana to accompany me. I needed to talk to her.

It was a cool night with no moon or stars; the sky was overcast and it threatened to rain. I covered Alan's shoulders with my *sagum,* and we walked without getting too far from the barn.

"You seem very worried lately, as if you were absent, is anything wrong?" I asked her.

She didn't say anything; she kept walking, clinging to her cloak.

"I can't help you if you don't tell me what's wrong."

"You've helped me enough; I owe you my life, what more can I ask from you?" she finally spoke.

"I owe it to you too, and you can ask me for anything you want, I'm all yours," I said, clutching her by the shoulders. "Haven't you realized how much I love you yet?"

She looked away, refusing to look me in the eyes.

"But I have the impression that I'm unrequited. Am I?" I asked, with my heart pounding.

"What are we going to do when we get to Lugdunum?" she asked, changing the subject.

I sighed and my breath exhaled pieces of my broken soul: Alana didn't love me anymore.

"That will depend on you," I replied.

"We can't be together..." she said distantly, coldly.

"Why?" I asked confused.

"Remember the prophecy, the words of Lughdyr."

"I don't believe in druids, or gods, or anything but you! If you don't love me, tell me, but don't hide behind the stupid prophecies of an old lunatic!"

She burst into tears dismayed and ran to the barn. I was left alone, watching the love of my life flee from me perhaps forever. I knelt on the ground with my hands hiding my contracted face. A flash of lightning warned that a storm was coming, and the clouds soon emptied all their contents onto my weary shoulders. I stood outside the barn for a few moments, hoping that the rain would wash away the pain that was oppressing me with its drops. When I entered, Alana was curled up in a blanket.

We barely spoke to each other the rest of the way. Alana knew how I felt about her, and I knew how she felt about me: nothing. I thought she loved me that she wanted to be with me, that she enjoyed every moment we spent together, but I was wrong. I had saved her from the Germanic, and I mistook gratitude with love. She didn't love me; she simply appreciated and esteemed me as the man who had freed her from the clutches of the barbarians.

My desolate sadness didn't go unnoticed by my companions, who asked me what evil was enslaving my spirit. But they soon found answers to their questions in Alana's eloquent silences. The scars that afflict the soul are as deep as the abysses that lead to hell, and their healing is longer and more uncertain than those caused by the poisoned swords of the barbarians.

It was dusk and we decided to camp in an old hermitage almost in ruins. We lit a fire and warmed our chilled bones, since a cold north wind not only carried menacing black clouds, but also caressed us with its icy breath. An intense silence filled with concern and concern enveloped us. We were a day from the *castrum* of Lugdunum, and if the destiny didn't prevent it, from my separation from Alana. I tried to get close to her a couple of times but she avoided me. I couldn't understand the change in her attitude and I wondered why, if she despised me so much, she had agreed to accompany me to Lugdunum. Finally I gave up and there, in the dark night, I huddled in my litter watching distractedly as the fire licked the last embers, waiting for a comforting dream to grant me an ephemeral truce that came well into the morning, when fatigue brought down wall of disappointment and uncertainty that my destiny had erected.

We crossed the sturdy walls that protected Lugdunum and headed to the *praetorium* of the *castrum* to meet Aetius. In the meantime, Alana would wait for us at an inn since it was not wise for a Suevian to enter into a military camp. The castrum was surrounded by a wall built with granite ashlars and topped with wood. The stables, the armory and the barracks were in poor condition, badly deteriorated by the time and lack of maintenance. If the enemies of Rome knew the conditions of one its most unique fortresses, they would not have taken long to pounce on it like hyenas on a wounded animal.

We identified ourselves to the *circitor* and he sent a *miles* to announce our arrival to the *magister utriusque militiae*. Soon the soldier returned and whispered a few words to the non-commissioned officer on duty who, looking at us with narrowed eyes said:

"The general will only meet with the *centenarius* Salvio Adriano, the rest of you go to your *numeri* and present yourselves to your officers."

We exchanged confused and uneasy glances: something was not right. My friends went to the regiment wrapped in a deep silence full of concern and discouragement, while I, escorted by a couple of soldiers, entered the *praetorium*. A few minutes passed before Aetius made his appearance.

"Well, at last we have news of you," he said as soon as he entered the room.

"I greet you, *domine*," I said, bowing my head.

"You are in deep trouble, *centenarius*," he growled angrily.

It had been several months since we last saw each other, but time had not been kind to him. He still had the eminent, haughty bearing of illustrious men, but his hair was lightening and gaunt bags hung from his eyes. His forehead was chiseled by an infinity of wrinkles and his gaze conveyed, above all, fatigue and regret.

"*Domine?*" I asked without understanding.

"Shut up!" he snapped at me furiously. "I received a message from Turismund informing me of your crime. He has demanded that I look for you and deliver you without further delay." he stroked his short beard. "Obviously, I have not sent anyone to capture you, but now that you are here..." he mused for a few moments, "...I really don't know what to do with you."

"*Domine*, I killed that *spatharius* in self-defense, Mansueto himself can attest to that. It was he who urged me to return to Lugdunum as soon as possible to avoid being captured by the barbarians," I replied.

"You nailed the *pugio* in his neck!" Aetius replied angrily.

"Mansueto..."

"The *Hispaniarum comes* has sent a message telling what happened and interceding for you, but you killed an allied soldier and you deserve to be punished."

I could never imagine that I would be in more danger in Lugdunum than surrounded by Visigoths in Gallaecia. I was completely confused, not understanding what was happening, why Aetius was treating me so harshly. I had only defended my life and also prevented a woman from being outraged. And so I told the general.

"*Domine*, I tried to stop the Visigoths from enslaving a Suevian. If they had succeeded, the peace treaty with Requiario would have been seriously threatened."

"To kill an ally to save a Suevian?" he screamed. "Is that behavior worthy of a legionary, of a *centenarius*?

"It wasn't just to save the woman, but to prevent the Visigoths from spoiling the peace treaty with the Suevian," I insisted.

Aetius walked thoughtfully through the room with his hands clasped behind his back, possibly his mind was wondering what punishment to inflict on me, although I did not regard that I deserved any sanction.

"*Domine*, do you know Walder?" I asked.

"Of course, I know him, why is that question?"

I looked into his eyes, confident and finally resigned to my fate: who has nothing to lose, dominates any situation, no matter how complicated it may be.

"Walder tried to force her, but I avoided him. As we were about to leave the village, Euric ordered his men to take her away. I couldn't allow it."

"Don't our soldiers commit heinous crimes or capture female slaves? As I have been informed, the *Bagaudae* and the Suevians attacked you and Euric destroyed the village. This action, rather than harming us, will benefit us, since Requiario will understand on which side the Visigoths will fight if his troops cross our *limes* again. The futile attempt to save a Suevian doesn't justify your conduct. Don't claim that you committed a crime to facilitate the treaty with the Suevians; I know that the Suevian fled with you. Other interests impelled you to help her and not precisely those of Rome. Don't try to deceive me!"

The general's eyes burned like flaming torches, but I remained serene, persuaded that I had done the right thing. And, without intimidating me or avoiding his furious gaze, I replied:

"The pillars of ancient Rome stood on the solid foundation of honor and justice. But now, those pillars have been corrupted by the actions of petty and ambitious leaders. Years ago, we allowed barbarians to cross the borders of our Empire. Have they infected us with their savage ways? What has become of honor? What has become of justice? The judges pass sentences that benefit only the highest bidder, the senators will second the emperor who will best agree with their interests and shower them with favors and privileges, the barbarian kings intercede in the proclamation of the Augustans of Rome, as if their opinion should be valued, and if in addition the *magister utriusque militiae* allows an innocent girl to be raped by a group of barbarians before the indifferent presence of his legionaries, perhaps and only perhaps, the Empire is suffering what it well deserves, and its destruction is the just punishment for allowing such infamous outrages."

My words made a great impression on Aetius, who looked at me sternly, but also with confusion. His pursed lips and his clenched fists revealed that my speech had awakened in him feelings that had lain dormant for a long time… perhaps too long.

"Where is the girl?" he asked me with a disgruntled expression.

"In a safe place."

"Turismund has claimed her; he says she belongs to Walder as spoils of war."

"I'd rather die than give her to you."

"Damn you bastard!" he exclaimed, striding across the room.

His mind swarmed like a swarm of insatiable flies. He was torn between the loyalty owed to the Visigoths and his own convictions as a Roman soldier. He could have killed me right there and sent my head to the barbarians, he could have tortured me to death in the hope that I would reveal Alana's whereabouts; he could have executed me in the *castrum* as an example to the rest of the legionaries and recruits. But he did not. Aetius went to a large window and surveyed the camp. A chilly breeze blew in through the window, but he was unmoved, he continued to gaze at the fortress as if he were pondering the future that awaited those brave legionaries. He finally he turned around and said to me:

"You have killed a *spatharius,* and I must punish you. Turismund has claimed it from me."

"I believe that an injustice will be committed," I replied, "But I will obediently accept the punishment inflicted on me if it quenches the Visigoths´ thirst for revenge and strengthens the foedus signed with them."

Aetius looked at me and there was a gleam of admiration in his eyes. He took a deep breath as if the sentence he was about to pass caused him deep pain. Turismund had demanded my head and, perhaps, the *magister utriusque militiae* had no choice but to offer it to him, even though my sacrifice would be a new affront to the Empire, which bowed its knees submissively to the insatiable impositions of the barbarians.

CHAPTER III

The extermination of the *Bagaudae*.

Quae apud alios iracundia dicitur, in bagaudis crudelitas appellatur.[3]

The darkness embraced me with its dark mantle and I didn't know whether it was day or night. I didn't even know how long I had been there. I heard a distant cough, someone begged to let him go out and another sobbed. Perhaps some poor wretch had received a visit from a jailer impatient to unleash his most unspeakable perversions. It was cold. Covered only with a dirty and threadbare *subligar*, I tried to warm myself by rubbing my arms and legs. There was a dripping sound... a drop fell, then another, then another... The sound of water hitting the pavement was my only company since I was locked up in that dirty dungeon. How long had I been there? Weeks? Months, perhaps? Or was it years? Time passed slowly in the utter darkness.

I was seated, I tried to sit up but I couldn't, my muscles didn't respond. I stroked my frizzy beard and my flabby bones. Next to me there was an empty plate, since I had already eaten the crumb of hard bread that a jailer had given me. Aetius acceded to Turismund's demands, and I suffered the consequences.

The *magister utriusque militiae* understood that I killed the *spatharius* in self-defense and exempted me from the death penalty, but my sentence was no less merciless and cruel: twenty lashes and imprisonment until death in the dungeons of the *castrum*.

I never heard from Alana again. During all that time he only allowed me to receive a visit from one of my companions: Calerus. He told me that Alana had gone west towards Gallaecia. Perhaps she had gone in search of the druid: her only family. There were no words of

---

[3] *What in others is called anger, in the Bagaudae is called cruelty (phrase extracted and adapted from the book Latin Grammar by Santiago Segura Munguía).*

love or comfort, she simply asked him to remind me not to forget the words of the druid... the words of the druid... How could I forget the cursed prophecy of the sorcerer? But what was the point in a gloomy and dank cell? I had no strength even to cry... There were no words of love or consolation... *De profundis clamavit cor meum, sed cor tuum non respondavit et anima mea non requievit.* [Out of the depths my heart cried out, yet your heart did not answer, and my soul did not rest.]

A sound of footsteps was heard; the jailers were preparing to release or imprison someone. The door of my cell opened and the bright light of the torches wounded my eyes as if they had been stuck with sharp needles. I protected myself from the brightness with my hands and felt two soldiers grabbing me.

"Come on, you bastard, cheer up, today is your lucky day!" one of the jailers exclaimed, pulling me out of the cell.

His loud voice pierced my eardrums and I covered my ears with my hands. I closed my eyes; the light of the torches burned my pupils. I heard the cries of the prisoners begging for food and water, but the jailers banged on the cell doors, ordering silence, and insulting the wretches locked up there. I squinted and noticed that I was being led down a corridor; we went up a stair and got outside. It was night and I appreciated it. I breathed in a breath of fresh air and a clean, pure, almost forgotten smell entered my lungs comforting my languid spirit.

"Take him to the baths, he can't be presented to Aetius this way," said a familiar voice, which I couldn't identify.

I was weak and I let them do it; the slaves rubbed the dirt accumulated on my body with esparto grass, staining the water of the bathtub black. They not only shaved my face and cut my hair, but also perfumed and dressed me in a white linen tunic and leather sandals. One slave offered me an apple, which I ate greedily, and another helped me walk. I could barely stand on my feet.

"That's better, I will carry you in the presence of the *magister utriusque militiae*," said the same voice that had ordered to clean-me up.

There was a Roman officer stood in front of me. It took me a while to recognize him... time had taken its toll on my memory... and on him.

"Optila?" I asked with a whisper.

"I greet you, Salvio Adriano," he answered with a smile.

I nodded without being able to utter a word; I was exhausted and terribly weak. The Gaul didn't want to tire me with vain questions and, in silence, we crossed an eternal corridor and arrived at the *praetorium*, where we took our seats in our respective footstools. It was not long before a slave appeared with a tray of food. He left on the table a bowl of chicken soup, a piece of bread and a pitcher. I drank some hot wine with honey and felt its warmth run through my body, giving me renewed energy.

"You look better," said the Gaul with a smile, watching how the color of life tinged my haggard cheeks.

"Why did they take me out of the cell?" I asked, with my voice cracking from lack of use.

"Aetius will have to reveal that to you. How are you feeling?"

"Better than a few hours ago," I smiled. "Will I go back to prison?"

Optila noticed the terror reverberating in my eyes but kept silent. Just in case, I poured myself another glass of hot wine and drank it in small sips.

"When is Aetius coming?" I asked, impatient to know my future."

"Soon."

"What day is today? How long have I been locked up?"

"A little over a year," answered the Gaul, looking me in the eyes.

"It's horrible," I muttered. "Aetius has inflicted a harsh punishment on me, almost worse than death," I added regretfully.

Optila patted me on the shoulder.

"Sometimes our general is forced to make hard decisions. But I can assure you that he has suffered a lot because of your imprisonment. He has seen in you the honor and courage that characterized the ancient Roman legionaries. But we live in difficult times where diplomacy and politics play a more important role than *spatha* and *scuta,"* he said, rising from his seat.

"He imprisoned me to satisfy the Visigoths," the Gaul looked down at the floor, confirming my words. "I only hope that my sacrifice was not in vain," I said with regret.

At that moment a door opened and Aetius appeared, accompanied by Traustila. He had a serious countenance and a deep sense of guilt marked with fire on his forehead. He was very old. I tried to get up but I couldn't Aetius made a gesture with his hand indicating that it was not necessary. He sat at the table in front of me, with Traustila protecting his back. Optila remained at my side.

"I greet you, Salvio Adriano. You are strong; few have managed to survive so long in one of my cells," the general said.

"I salute you, *magister utriusque militiae*. I heartily desire not to be returned to the dungeons and that my sentence has already been served," I implored.

He smiled, and, shaking his head, replied:

"No, you are free."

I sighed in relief at his words and looked up, thanking the God of the Christians, or the ancient Roman gods for such pleasant news.

"Thank you," I mumbled with glazed eyes.

"Do you want to go back to the army?" Traustila asked me.

"I'm eager to do so," I replied. "Where are my comrades?"

"If you mean the *milites* who accompanied Mansueto's delegation, they are here in the *castrum*."

To my mind came the *Hispaniarum comes* and the peace embassy.

"Did the Suevians sign the treaty?" I asked.

"So, they did," replied Traustila. "Requiario withdrew from Tarraconensis and Carthaginiense, and up to now he hasn't crossed our *limes* again. Mansueto and Euric were very... persuasive."

"But unfortunately, the *comes* died a few months ago due to a serious illness," intervened Optila.

I was sorry about the death of the *perfectissimus* brave. I was convinced that he would have done all what he could to avoid my imprisonment, but giving in to the demands of the Visigoths was more convenient for the interests of Rome than dispensing justice.

"The Empire has lost a great man," I said regretfully, looking at the pavement.

"That's right," Aetius acknowledged.

I looked up and added:

"I want to be with them, with my companions."

The three men smiled.

"And that's what will happen, but you will remain in the *praetorium* until you are fully recovered," said Aetius, getting up from the table.

"Why have you released me?" I asked him.

The *magister utriusque militiae* began to walk around the room with a thoughtful look and answered:

"The Visigoth King Turismund has been assassinated by his brother Theodoric or, rather, by one of his *spatharii*," the terrible image of the Germanic Walder sprouted in my mind. "And has proclaimed himself king. Rome doesn't owe loyalty to Theodoric because he has not yet renewed the *foedus* that his father once agreed upon and that his brother ratified after his death." He stopped his walk and looking me in the eyes, added: "Your crime died with Turismund."

Optila and Traustila smiled, and the appearance of Aetius revealed that he felt great satisfaction for my release.

"Now rest, I'll tell my servants to accompany you to your room, you'll be my guest until you have enough strength to lead your century," Aetius said with a smile.

Accompanied by Optila and Traustila I went to the room that Aetius had made available for me in the *praetorium*. I was tired but happy, my captivity was over and I would join my companions soon. But the memory of Alana came suddenly to my mind and my heart got saddened. Where was she? Why didn't she leave a single word of encouragement? My legs faltered and helped by the two Gauls, I entered my bedroom.

It was a cold and stormy night. Since I had lain down on the mattress, it hadn't stopped raining or thundering for a single moment. Although I was exhausted, I was unable to fall asleep, since my mind was deeply restless. Finally, fatigue overcame my discomfort and I surrendered to a pleasant and restful rest.

The sun was rising over the horizon when a servant offered me bread with olive oil and milk. Once I finished my food I was visited by Aetius' physicist who, after auscultating me, confirmed that I was suffering from malnutrition, but that in general my state of health wasn't excessively precarious. Shortly after, Traustila and Optila entered the room. I implored them to see my companions, but they refused.

"Adriano," began Optila, who had sat next to me on an old footstool, "your friends have been informed of your release and they know that you are under Aetius' care..."

"I can assure you that they went crazy with joy when they heard the news," Traustila interrupted him with a smile. "And even more so when they knew that you would return with them to the army."

I smiled pleased.

"Be patient, in a few days you will be ready for combat," said Optila. "Until then, you will have to rest."

Since I was released from my confinement, a question had entered my mind and I decided it was time to ask it.

"Why am I staying in the *praetorium?* Why doesn't Aetius send me to the barracks to be cared for by the troop physicists?"

Optila looked at me sympathetically.

"The *magister utriusque militiae* appreciates you," Optila replied.

"He saw you fight against the Huns, and you risked your life to protect a Suevian," Traustila intervened. "You accepted your sentence with commendable dignity, and you did it for the good of Rome, despite being terribly unfair."

"You are loved and respected by your companions," Optila continued.

"Not for everyone," I interrupted, thinking of Demetrius Tancinus.

The Gauls smiled.

"It's impossible to be esteemed by every person," said Traustila with a laugh.

"Aetius told us about the conversation he had with you before locking you up," said Optila. "Honor and justice are meaningless values in these times, but soldiers like you, like the general, like us," he said looking at Traustila who nodded with a smile. "We will be able to build a new Rome, stronger and more fearsome, whose shining radiance will blind the eyes of the barbarians who stalk it from their filthy dens like hungry vermin."

"For this we must extirpate the corruption, the injustice, the vileness existing in the heart of the Empire, in the court of Ravenna," said Traustila.

"Do you mean Valentinian?"

The Gauls looked behind them, fearing to be heard. For years, the emperors had spies hidden in the most unsuspected corners.

"It's not just Valentinian, it's all of them," whispered Optila.

"The emperors have forgotten the people, worrying only about amassing colossal fortunes and maintaining their perks," explained Traustila, with the assent of his companions. "They have perpetrated the most abominable and infamous crimes, remaining unpunished for all of them."

"They have ignored the Roman laws and despised the ancient gods," said Optila.

"Wait; do you expect us to worship Mars, Apollo or Mithras again?" I asked skeptically.

The Gaul shook his head in denial.

"It is not so simple. That the irruption of Christianity has weakened the Empire is undeniable, but worshipping Mars, Jupiter or Mithras is not the solution."

"I don't understand why you say that Christianity has weakened the Empire."

"The Church wastes immeasurable amounts of gold in adorning its temples and maintaining an army of monks and bishops," Traustila interjected. "Those are valuable solids that could be used to hire and equip soldiers."

"The defense of the Empire is no longer a priority. The Romans are more interested in attaining eternal life than in wielding a *spatha* to protect the frontiers or their own families. The priests long to lead a flock of condescending sheep who don't protest, who don't bother the powerful under threat of suffering the most horrendous torments in the deepest of hells," Optila lamented vehemently.

"Young people are inclined to tonsure themselves and wear the habit, rather than arm themselves with a sword and fight for their homeland," Traustila grumbled.

I'd have liked to hear the opinion of my friends Lucius Calerus or the one of the Petronius Quintus *clarissimus* on the matter. Surely such pious men would have a very different perception about, according to the Gauls, the detrimental effects of Christianity on the future of the Empire.

"I'm sorry, but I still don't know what I have to do with all this," I replied somewhat wearily, ecclesiastical discussions didn't interest me at all.

Optila let out a sigh and said:

"Turismund wanted your head for having murdered one of his own, but Aetius persuaded him to accept that you would only be imprisoned in a dungeon for life, hoping that the *Gothorum rex* would one day take pity on you and cancel the punishment."

"The Visigoths have spies everywhere and Aetius was forced to treat you like another prisoner. I can assure you that his soul ached to see you locked up there," Traustila said. "So, as soon as he was informed of the king's death, he ordered your release."

"I think you remind him of himself, but of course, when he was young," Optila interjected. "He has noticed the honesty and generosity that shines in your eyes," and, taking me by the shoulder, he added: "He has high hopes set on you."

"What a responsibility... I'd almost prefer to be sent back to my cell!" I exclaimed, to the laughter of the Gauls.

I got up from the footstool and went to the window. An almost pristine blue sky greeted the new day, leaving behind the raging storm that battered Lugdunum. I looked out the window and observed the *castrum*. Some soldiers practiced with the *spatha* or *spiculum* while others paraded or honed their weapons. Suddenly I remembered that Attila had crossed the *limes* again and was heading unstoppably towards Rome.

"I've been locked up for a long time and without news from outside, except for a brief chat with a jailer. The last thing they told me was that Attila had returned destroying all the cities that he found in his path, including Aquileia. What has happened since then?"

"Many things, my dear friend," Traustila replied.

"After destroying Aquileia, Attila headed to Rome: his true objective. He devastated all the cities he found on his way except Mediolanum, which he only looted until there was nothing of value left inside its walls," said Optila.

"But he spared the lives of its inhabitants, something he hadn't done with the rest of the cities he had attacked," interrupted Traustila, continuing with the story. "After sacking the city, he continued on his way to Mantua, where he had a meeting with Pope Leo."

"There has been much speculation about the meeting between the Hun king and the Bishop of Rome on the banks of the Mincius," Optila said. "But the truth is that Attila turned around and returned to his cold Pannonian lands."

Attila's resignation to his long-awaited dream of conquering Rome thanks to a conversation with the Pope was hard to believe. Leo must be a saint or a ruthless negotiator.

"Did he just go like this?" I asked confused.

"As I told you, much has been speculated since then. Some say that Leo offered him a real fortune in exchange of returning to Pannonia with his hosts, leaving the city unscathed. Others say that the soldiers of the Hun king were exhausted after the long campaign and that, not being very used to the strong heat of the south they fell ill and many died. In short, the Hun's hosts weren't t in ideal conditions to withstand a long siege."

"Some say that Attila, superstitious as he is, saw in the Pope a holy man and feared that, by attacking Rome, his powerful God would punish him, as many believe happened to the Visigoth King Alaric, who died shortly after sacking the city," said Traustila.

"There are even those who claim that it was the appearance of an angel which prevented the disaster. What is certain is that he turned back and Rome was once again saved," concluded Optila.

Attila's weakness for omens, predictions and other superstitions was well known. Nevertheless, he always consulted obscure necromancers and sorcerers before making important decisions. Perhaps the Hun saw in the Pope an emissary of the Almighty, a sort of divinity, or simply a bold wizard or sorcerer... who knows. But, if I had to opt for a more plausible and earthly motive, I would choose the fact that the Hun king returned to Pannonia with mules and chariots full of gold and jewels: supposed payment from Leo for not destroying Rome. But romans wanted and needed to believe that their city was protected by the aegis of Jesus Christ himself and would never succumb no matter how strong and powerful their enemies were. Pope Leo's meeting with Attila, and the latter's subsequent departure gave them arguments to strengthen this claim.

"But he will return..." I whispered, pushing the confused or miraculous conjectures about the salvation of Rome out of my mind, and convinced that there was no gold in the world or angels in heaven capable of satiating the voracious greed of the Hun.

But to my surprise the Gauls laughed uproariously and Optila said: "I don't think so... he's dead!"

"How?" I asked with my eyebrows arched in astonishment.

"Yes, my friend," replied Traustila. "And he is quite dead."

"But..."

"It was shortly after he returned to Pannonia," Optila began to explain. "During his wedding night with the Gothic Ildico. As they say, he ate and drank excessively during the festivities and fell asleep on the mattress completely drunk, dying shortly after drowning in his own vomit..."

"Others say he was killed by his deputies, who didn't willingly accept the order to retreat to Pannonia and not to storm the walls of Rome," Traustila Interrupted. "One way, or another, the Empire has been rid of its greatest enemy."

"His men," Optila continued. "when they found his corpse, they cut their hair and wounded themselves with swords, since the greatest of kings couldn't be wept with tears but with the blood of his soldiers. That at least is what is said."

The Hun's death was the best news I could have heard. I imagined the citizens of Rome dancing and drinking happily, rejoicing over the death of their most ruthless enemy.

"Drowned in his own vomit... an unworthy death for such a brave warrior," I observed.

"He drowned in the pestilence he himself had spread. It was the final ending for a bloodthirsty savage," Traustila replied.

I didn't agree with his words, but neither had I enough energy to engage in sterile debates. Attila possessed all the virtues that shone in great warriors: he was brave, skillful with the sword, fair with his men, and implacable with his enemies. If the Hun king had fought on behalf of Rome, perhaps our limes would not be so threatened. But that, of course, is something we will never know.

Suddenly, Turismund's death, another barbarian king who was an enemy of Rome and who died at the same time as Attila, came to my mind, and I asked:

"How did Turismund die?"

"Oof!" Traustila exclaimed. "There isn't much information about that either. What is certain is that the Visigoth king appeared one morning in his bed over a pool of blood. His throat had been slit."

"It is said that it was his brother Theodoric, since he is the most benefited from his death..." Optila interjected, spilling the last words as a revealing insinuation.

"As Seneca declared: «*Cui prodest scelus, is fecit*» [to whom the crime benefits, that is the author]," Traustila said.

Optila let out a great laugh and added:

"Crystalline as an icy mountain stream…"

"But there are more than a few who claim that one of his *spatharii* slit his throat," Traustila continued. The image of Walder, the *spathariorum comes* of Turismund, came to my mind. "The truth is that he was assassinated and the new king did not bother too much to look for the guilty ones."

"Do you think that Rome had something to do with the death of the *Gothorum rex?*"

The Gauls exchanged a complicity glance and shrugged their shoulders indifferently.

"Well, I have certainly missed some important events during my confinement!" I exclaimed, before the laughter of the Gauls.

A month after my release, I was ready to return to the army. Equipped with my helmet, coat of mail and *spatha*, I went to the camp where my comrades were. Aetius, accompanied by his Gallic officers, watched me with satisfaction from the *praetorium*. I took a deep breath and a broad smile spread across my face. My heart was beating, I was impatient to meet my friends, but fate saw fit that, on my way, I should first cross paths with other elements.

"Well, it seems that the traitor has returned," a *semissalis* said to a legionary standing next to him.

"There is no doubt that some people are lucky; someone else's head would have been cut off for much less," grumbled the *miles* sharpening his sword with a stone.

"There is no doubt that Rome has changed a lot," the *semissalis* continued with a snort. "Now murder, instead of being punished, is rewarded. since I haven't been told that Aetius' slaves have treated him as if he were the emperor himself!"

"Killing an ally for a bitch," said another, spitting on the ground.

"I would have known what to do with her!" the *semissalis* exclaimed getting up and clutching his genitals with both hands, before the laughter of his friends. "What do you say friends?" he asked aloud, seeking the complicity of the soldiers.

They spoke to each other without looking at me, but their poisoned words filled with contempt reached my ears. Several soldiers abandoned their chores to see how I responded to their insults. There were not few who knew the sympathy I had for the good Demetrius Tancinus.

"Now that you ask, dear Tancinus, I could tell you that what you are grasping with your hands, only serves to shove it in the ass of the *miles* that you have by your side," I began to say, approaching him. "I could tell you that your mother eats seven or eight like those in the brothel where she works or, if you hurry me, much fatter. I could tell you that the last time you fornicated with a female, you did it with a goat and it was because you confused her with your sister."

91

Tancinus' face got a fiery vermilion hue, like that of a volcano about to explode. And the laughter that thundered through the camp helped to precipitate the eruption.

"I could tell you many things, soldier, but I'll tell you only one: I'm a *centenarius* and, as the marks on your back attest, I won't tolerate the slightest hint of insubordination. This afternoon I will summon you and you will appear before me together with those two," I ordered him, pointing contemptuously at the two *milites* that followed his joke. "So that I may inform you of the punishment I intend to inflict on you. Do you understand?"

Tancinus looked at me with very tight lips and a frown on his face. The anger that consumed his interior was as voracious as the larvae that devour the remains of a dead rat.

"Did you understand soldier?" I asked again, bringing my face close to his.

"Yes, *centenarius,*" he answered between his teeth.

"Better this way, you can go on with your talk," I said, looking him in the eyes.

Tancinus, reluctantly, turned and lost himself in his contumely followed by his two friends.

"Well, now I understand why Aetius didn't allow you to return to the camp until you were fully recovered!" exclaimed a few feet away a smiling Arcadius with his arms rose, accompanied by Calerus.

"You'll need all your energy to face shits like that!" bellowed a no less smiling Calerus.

We gave each other a big hug. I looked them up and down and noticed that they had hardly changed. Maybe Arcadius was stronger and Calerus a little thinner, but they both looked good. We chatted for several minutes as we walked to the pavilions. I was told that Arius Sidonius and Ajax were in our same unit and that they had been quartered for a year waiting for reinforcements that didn't arrive and probably wouldn't arrive.

"You have recovered just in the best moment," said Arcadius, giving me a strong pat on the shoulder.

"What do you mean?" I asked him.

"We'll get going soon Several bands of *Bagaudae* have risen up in Tarraconensis, and they are devastating the province," said Calerus.

"When they attack a village, they kill the masters, and the servants and slaves are ordered to follow them or they are executed on the spot. The choice is simple," said Arcadius.

"They ravage the villages, murdering their inhabitants in a cruel and merciless manner. The men are tortured to reveal where they hide the money, but the women suffer worse: they are raped and then killed in front of their children," explained Calerus, shaking his head in dismay.

"Only the youngest are given the option to follow them or die."

"They have already ravaged several towns and villages, leaving a trail of fire and destruction in their wake," Calerus said.

"Who are they?" I asked for.

Arcadius spat on the ground.

"Pariah, runaway slaves, ruined peasants, servants who have murdered their masters and found shelter among them… who knows, any unfortunate who has been left by fate can become one of them."

"They are also supported by the Suevians. Not many years ago Requiario, in collaboration with the *Bagaudae* Basilio, sacked Ilerda and Turiasso, killing Bishop Leo."

"For this reason, Valentinian sent the peace embassy headed by Mansueto to Gallaecia," I said.

"Remember the *Bagaudae* attack we suffered in that Suevian village..." Arcadius intervened.

"How to forget it!" I exclaimed, remembering an experience that guided my destiny along an unsuspected path.

The *Bagaudae* were outlaws who looted villages and farms. They consisted mainly of peasants unable to cope with taxes, slaves, deserters and all sorts of bandits. Besides, they also integrated their ranks a large number of discontents, who, feeling abandoned by the Empire, and asphyxiated by the disproportionate fiscal charges imposed by the curators, had rebelled by allying themselves on many occasions with the Suevians. They devastated the Tarraconense region, and due to the economic and social crisis that Hispania was suffering, their number rose alarmingly.

"They are as bloodthirsty as a hungry pack of wolves," Calerus observed.

I liked the prospect of participating in a military campaign again, I was eager to exercise my *spatha*. Besides, returning to Hispania would perhaps allow me to see again....

"Have you heard from Alana again?" I asked.

"We have no more information than what I told you when I visited you in the dungeons. She went to Gallaecia and we haven't heard from her again," Calerus answered sadly.

"Are you sure there is nothing else?" I insisted longingly, taking him by the arms.

"She only told me to remember the druid's words. I'm sorry."

I sighed regretfully, exhaling puffs of sadness and pain. Suddenly I felt tired and we took a seat on some nearby benches.

"By the way, what's that of «the druid's words»?" Arcadius asked.

And I told them the whole story, prophecy included. My friends gave me looks of surprise and disbelief, but finally they believed my fabulous story.

"He is a sorcerer, an evil being from hell," Calerus grumbled. "Christ has already warned us to get rid of false prophets and seers. Perhaps you should forget her, dear friend, I'm very afraid that she is also a pagan witch."

"But I still love her and won't be able to forget her."

"She's gone, and you may never see her again. You'll find other women, with so many dead men on the battlefield, there are plenty of them," Arcadius said with a half-smile.

I said nothing. Perhaps my friend Arcadius was right and it would be best to forget her. She had made her decision and so I must accept it. With my heart shrunk because of sadness I arrived at our camp, where I was greeted with great enthusiasm by Arius Sidonius, Ajax, and several of my former companions, Sarmatian auxiliaries included.

"Have they told you that we are part of the *palatina legio*?" a smiling Ajax asked. "We are with the best and you will have under your command a hundred brave legionaries!"

Ajax's words worried me. The most courageous and experienced soldiers served in the *palatina legio*. If we, young *milites*, were included in it, it meant that the Roman army was going through a difficult situation.

"Tribune Libius Asinius wants to meet you. Come on, he's in the officers' barracks," Arius Sidonius said.

And that's where we headed. On the way I observed the legionaries of Lugdunum, and I saw that indifference and exhaustion had taken their toll on them eroding their courage and esteem. In their looks I beheld the despair that dwells in the heart of the defeated. We arrived at the barracks and there I met the man who would be my direct superior. He was sitting at a table enjoying a jug of wine with several officers.

"So, you are the famous Salvio Adriano. The truth is that you don't look like much either." that was the kind greeting he gave me. His table companions looked up indifferently.

The tribune was about fifty years old and close to discharge, having served in the army for more than twenty years. He was a stout man, with bushy eyebrows and a clean-shaven face. He had fought for years with Aetius, which was a guarantee. Moreover, he was the commander of the *palatinae legion*, a position that could only be filled by demonstrating great courage and daring on the battlefield.

"I greet you, *domine,* it is a great honor to serve in the *palatina legio,*" I said, ignoring his cold reception.

Libius Asinius smiled.

"Let's go outside and take a walk."

I said goodbye to my companions and we began to wander around the *castrum.*

"Aetius has told me a lot about you, he thinks you are a great soldier and that you have a great future in the army, that's why he has assigned you to the *palatine* elite imperial guard. But I must warn you that, until now, I have chosen the officers of my regiment personally and I have based on their bravery, loyalty and honor. You are the first *centenarius* that has been imposed on me in all the years that I have served as tribune and, I hope for your sake, that you deserve it."

"I'm sure you'll never complain about me, *domine.* I'll fight for Rome and the legion until I shed the last drop of my blood."

Libius Asinius smiled and said:

"I hope it won't be necessary, *centenarius.* Now go and get ready, we'll soon be marching on campaign."

"Against the *Bagaudae*?" I asked.

"That's right. In Hispania we'll see what you are made of and if you are worthy to have a hundred soldiers under your command."

He tapped me on the shoulder and returned to the officers' quarters, ending the brief conversation. I swallowed saliva as I watched him lose himself among the *milites,* who squared their shoulders as he passed, raising their right fist to their chest. I exhaled a breath of air fed by trepidation and fear. Once again, much was expected of me: an inexperienced legionary that the capricious goddess fortune or the vicissitudes of fate had seen fit to erect as a *centenarius* before his time.

But little else can be done except to bend to the will of the one who pulls the strings of our destiny and, now, mine is to impose a just punishment to those who had insulted their superior.

Cleaning the latrines of the barracks is a job exclusively for slaves, a humiliating task for any legionary and much more so for three *semissalis* with several years of service behind them. After my conversation with the tribune, I sent for Demetrius Tancinus and his two friends. I informed them of the punishment without hiding the immeasurable satisfaction I felt at imagining them bathed in all kinds of filth and flooded with the putrid odor emanating from the sewers of the *castrum*. The eyes of the *semissalis* burned like terrible flames in protest, but they kept quiet and accepted the sanction with relative submission. They had no choice either. In the army, punishments had to be carried out, otherwise, the consequences could be dramatic and, most certainly, immensely more damaging to the integrity of the punished. Tancinus and his men had to resign themselves and swallow their pride, especially when Arcadius informed me that they were placed in the *palatina legio*. Thus they would fight under my orders until they were discharged or met their death on the battlefield. Whichever came first.

Except for a handful of soldiers belonging to the *limitanei* troops of Tarraco, the Roman legions had definitively abandoned Hispania years ago and, when some revolt or barbarian invasion broke out, the Empire responded by sending the troops stationed in Gaul. But Rome didn't have surplus of soldiers and to suffocate the *Bagaudae* insurgents, Valentinian required the help of the Visigothic *federates*. Thus «ex auctoritate romana,» in the name of Rome, the Visigoths under the command of prince Frederic, brother of Theodoric, crossed for the first time the Roman borders of Hispania. Our legion, about a thousand *milites*, accompanied them to prevent occasional outrages and looting by the Visigoths and, above all, to ensure their return to Tolosa once the enemy had been exterminated.

We crossed Gaul by the *Domitia via* and arrived in Iuncara. From there we marched to Barcino, Ilerda and Caesaraugusta, where we rested for a couple of days. On the way, we were informed that the *Bagaudae* had ravaged several villas and estates near Allabone, and there we set out in the hope of exterminating them before they caused more damage. But we were too late. Columns of black smoke dyed the sky, foretelling the ominous omen of the destruction of Allabone. The spectacle was desolate: the city had been reduced to rubble and its inhabitants stabbed to death. Rivers of dark blood flowed through the muddy streets and mutilated limbs and severed heads gave us a grim greeting. A few abandoned dogs joined the vermin from a nearby forest to feast on the remains of the townspeople. An archer, disgusted at the sight of a fox devouring the lifeless body of a child, fired his weapon accurately and the fox fell to the ground with an arrow in its side.

We buried the dead and Frederic ordered that we continue the march as soon as possible. The prince was impatient to leave that desolate place, touched by the dark and deadly hand of Lucifer. By their tracks, the bandits were heading to Calagurris. We had to catch up with them or the municipium would be in serious danger. I remembered Petronius Quintus, the *clarissimus* who lived in a village near the city, and I feared for him.

On the way we were accompanied by a deep silence: the horrifying scenes that we contemplated in Allabone were etched in our minds along with the acrid smell of burned meat. We only wanted to meet those savages and return them to the hell from which they had fled. We lightened our march and in a few days we were at the gates of Calagurris. Its mighty wall had deterred the bandits, who were inclined to assault the nearest towns and estates, much worse protected and easier to loot. Servilius Elerius, the *magistrate* of Calagurris, informed us that about three thousand *Bagaudae* were in the vicinity. I was even more alarmed by the fate of Petronius Quintus and so I said to Libius Asinius, who authorized me to inspect the area. Accompanied by Arcadius and Ajax, I left on my horse towards the *clarissimus* village.

The sun was setting behind the mountains, staining the twilight blood-red. I whipped my mount trying to ignore the black omens that hovered in my mind like hungry flies. I remembered the *clarissimus* and the good treatment he gave us when we arrived at his villa on the way back to Lugdunum. We were strangers, but he opened the doors of his house and his heart to us, entertaining us with exquisite delicacies and delicious wines. Like two old and cherished friends who meet casually after a long and painful separation rejoice and laugh remembering past times, with the *clarissimus* we enjoy an unforgettable evening, we laugh, eat, declaim poems and sing forgotten melodies as endearing and inseparable friends, although we were just strangers. Petronius Quintus was a great man who didn't deserve to die under the iron of those vermin. But a plume of black smoke that was confused with the darkness of the incipient night, and some distant lights that simulated dancing according to the whim of the wind, augured that the *Bagaudae* had already visited the hacienda, leaving their sadly famous trail of fire and death.

"Go!" I shouted, whipping my horse with my heart beating anguished in my chest, before the already illuminating and terrible image of the powerful flames that were relentlessly devouring the town.

On horseback and with our *spatha* drawn, we crossed the burning embers that had become the strong gate in the wall that surrounded the hacienda. The corpses of the slaves were found scattered throughout a ravaged village, abandoned to looting and destruction. The *Bagaudae* had been cruel to the women, whose naked bodies lay lifeless covered with stabs and blows. We direct our mounts toward the domus and dismount still with our swords drawn. We entered with caution, as it was very likely that some other bandit drunk with wine or blood still remained in the building, searching among the dead and the rooms for something interesting to loot. In silence, with heavy hearts, we walked through the vestibulum and arrived at the *atrium*. The sculptures had been smashed and their pieces were scattered on a pavement dirty with debris and blood. In the *impluvium* the corpses of two slaves floated meekly and others were found scattered around the courtyard. The fire devoured the villa fed by a gentle breeze, embalming the air with the smell of burning wood.

"Look," Ajax said, pointing to a crucified man.

We ran towards him with the certainty that it was the *clarissimus*, because the *Bagaudae* used to get angry with the owner of the property they raided. And, to our regret, it was so. Petronius Quintus had been tortured and crucified. His toga was soaked in blood and his face was swollen and disfigured from the blows he received. Under the cross they lit a fire that didn't burn with the virulence that the savages would have desired. We released him and found that he was still alive. I put him on my lap and gave him some water. His eyes reflected the horror he had witnessed.

"Fri... friend Adriano, I knew you would come, an inner voice assured me," the old man whispered.

"Calm down *clarissimus*, everything is over, you are safe now," I told him.

"Soon I will meet Jesus Christ, I hope that my sins will be forgiven and the Almighty will allow my soul to cross the gates of Paradise."

Petronius Quintus closed his eyes and died. As he would have wished, we buried his remains and crowned his tomb with a rough wooden cross. I mourned his death quietly and swore revenge. The *Bagaudae* were close and it was time to find them. Filled with hatred, we left the ruined village and rode on horseback until we found the dignitary's killers. Hidden behind some bushes, I noticed that they had camped in a clearing in the forest. Confident, they had built neither palisades nor moats. There they were, about three thousand *Bagaudae* and Suevians, since the barbarians, as we feared, had allied with them for the purpose of plundering the province of Tarraconensis with the promise of a large and easy booty. The *Bagaudae*, armed and trained by Suevian officers, had become a fearsome and implacable army, ravaging the cities and estates with the ferocity of a pack of hungry wolves.

Their perverse laughter could be heard several stadiums away echoing in the air, as if it were the screeching of insatiable crows struggling for the remains of a dead animal. They drank, played dice or copulated like animals before the indifferent gaze of the rest. It was the degeneration of the human being at its most vile and abominable degree. Avoiding making the slightest noise, we return to our camp. As soon as I informed Libius Asinius, and after requesting the mandatory authorization of prince Frederic, a detachment consisting of Romans and Visigothic federated people was organized. The tribune commanded it. To avoid making excessive noise, we cover the hulls of our horses with rags and march towards the enemy camp. We arrived unseen and unheard. Many of them were sleeping half-drunk while others were fornicating with both men and women. The poor wretches, persuaded of the terror they provoked, were confident that no one would dare to face them. Such was their arrogance that they had not even bothered to set-up lookouts Protected by the night, we approached the bandits in silence, and using our *pugio,* we slit their throats without making the slightest noise. Hidden among the trees, several dozens of archers made easy target on the motionless bodies of the sleeping ones.

"Wake up, we are under attack!" shouted a voice, before being silenced by the accurate arrow shot of an archer.

We take hold of our *spatha* killing and severing all that bulk that we found in our path, in an orgy of blood and death. The legionaries, with the still fresh image of the cruel extermination of the inhabitants of Allabone, murdered men, women and children without distinction.

"Kill him, the larvae turn into lice," a *semissalis* ordered a legionary, who doubted whether to skewer a boy of about five years old with his sword. Shortly afterwards the boy lay in a pool of blood and with the expression of death reflected on his face.

Few were those who managed to escape by hiding in the thick of the forest. The sun greeted a new day when Frederic arrived at the *Bagaudae* camp. Some of us finished off the wounded men, while others went into the forest in search of a fugitive. The spectacle that greeted the Visigothic prince was devastating. Hundreds of dead *Bagaudae* and Suevians were scattered on the ground, many of whom had been tortured and dismembered. The *milites* were viciously applied to the last bandits and had entertained themselves by cutting off their limbs, cutting off their ears and burning their eyes. Frederic ordered the dead to be piled up and cremated; we had to avoid any kind of pestilence or disease.

I watched how the soldiers set fire to the bandits when Libius Asinius, from his horse told me:

"You've done a good job; maybe it wasn't a bad idea for Aetius to recruit you for the *palatina.*"

"Thank you, *domine,* I told you that you wouldn't regret it."

"This is only the beginning; you still have twenty years to show what you are capable of. The ragged and trusting *Bagaudae* aren't worthy for the *spatha* of a *centenarius*. But they have undoubtedly been very useful for your training."

Wounded in my pride, I was about to reply that I had also fought in Maurica against the fearsome Hun hordes of Attila, but the tribune must have read my thoughts because he added:

"I know that this is not your first combat, since you fought against the Huns with Aetius, and with great valor I might add, at least so I have been informed, but your military career has only just begun. You know how the Huns fight, the *Bagaudae* and," he paused and looked around to prevent his words from being heard by inappropriate ears, "the Visigoths. Take a close look at our *foederati*, they are formidable warriors. You will learn much from them, and their teachings will be very useful to you in the future. Of that you have no doubt." the tribune spurred his mount and directed it towards Frederic, who was conversing with several of his officers.

My lips turned up in a bitter smile as I watched Libius Asinius give me a discreet glance and nod. His «suggestion» would not be disdained.

An army of *Bagaudae*, even more numerous and fearsome than the one we had exterminated around Calagurris, was ravaging unopposed the Hispanic lands bordering Gallaecia. Thus, we left behind the villages of Vareia, Virovesca and marched towards Segisamo, the last important city before reaching Pallantia: our objective.

The road ran through a deep and well-known forest. Without quite knowing why, I distanced myself from the column I was marching in and got lost among the ash and beech trees. Soon I found myself in an oak grove crisscrossed by countless streams. I rode slowly looking among the brambles and ferns for some trail that would lead me to the huge yew tree where the druid appeared to us. I had not forgotten Alana and I was sure that the old wizard had the answers to all my questions. In the thicket I recognized the path that led to the druid's house. My heart was pounding.

It was getting dusk and I had to meet the wizard before nightfall or risk getting lost. The squawk of a crow startled me, and soon after, a black bird flew over my head to perch on an old man's shoulder.

"You're as stubborn as a mule," Lughdyr mumbled, shaking his head.

"Where is Alana?" I asked from my horse.

"She doesn't belong in your world."

"What do you mean?"

I got down from my horse and went hostile towards the old man. The crow, frightened I think, flew up and perched on a nearby branch.

"His father was a great physician, but the goddess nature was not kind enough to enlighten him with the power of the druids, but Alana…"

"Is she a druid-woman?"

He touched my shoulder and looked at me tenderly.

"I know you love her. Your eyes give it away and your aura confirms it, but she has to follow her own way."

"Where is she?"

"On a faraway island called Hibernia, there she is receiving the necessary instruction to channel her power."

If what the magician was telling me was true, I could forget my beloved forever. I had never believed in omens, premonitions or auspices, but now I had to cling to the druid's prophecy if I wanted to have any hope of seeing her again. Lughdyr's words sprang from my mouth.

"I'll find a pure and beautiful love, a love blessed by the Mother, a love forced to abandon me to return at the moment I need it most, when my body lies wounded and exanimated, when my last breath is about to expire, and the Grim Reaper is about to tear out my soul to drag it to his world of suffering and desolation, then, my beloved will return to free me from his clutches and we will never part," I said with tears in my eyes.

The crow, now calmer, perched on Lughdyr's shoulder again.

"Does she love me?" I asked with my heart beating.

"She loves you and her soul is broken for being separated from you. But Nature has bestowed upon Alana her lofty grace, blessing her with the magic of the Druids. She cannot escape her destiny; she isn't in a position to choose. She is a druid woman and she must face her own reality."

"Relegated to a life of loneliness and mysticism? Will that be the future that awaits her?" I asked angrily.

Lughdyr looked at me regretfully, and shaking his head said:

"Your ignorance and prejudices prevent you from seeing beyond your own eyes. We, the druids, cure the sick, instruct the physicists and help the needy, is there anything more beautiful than saving a man's life, training a doctor, or helping those who need it most? Our home is the forest because our Mother lives here, and the spirits that guide our omens are manifested. Yes, our life is lonely and sacrificial. Being a druid is a heavy slab that, as you help those in need, lightens until you are finally grateful to have been blessed with the favor of Mother Nature."

The night covered us with her dark cloak, and I noticed that the path disappeared lost in the thicket of the oak grove. I couldn't go back to my companions.

"Come with me to the cabin, you'll be back with yours tomorrow," he said, as if he knew what I was thinking.

We walked for several minutes until we reached his home. There, he prepared me a very spicy soup of bread and onion. My eyes were veiled; I was convinced that I would never see Alana again.

"She was born to help others, think of the lives she will save when she returns. She will be venerated among her people as a goddess. Rest assured that you will see her again, it is written so," the old man assured with a smile.

"I believe she has made her decision. If God or the gods see fit for us to meet again, so be it, but in the meantime, I'll do my best to forget her. Her memory is bitter as gall to me."

I didn't even try to stifle my tears, and they flowed with virulence, a somewhat distressing image for a *centenarius*. Lughdyr felt sorry for me and tried to console me.

"Alana loves you and will always love you," he said with conviction, then walked over to a small cauldron, poured a greenish liquid into a basin and handed it to me. "Here, drink this, it will help you sleep."

I wiped away my tears and drank from the bowl without even asking what it was. Soon after, I felt how my body relaxed freeing me from the anguish that nestled in my soul. My eyelids began to weigh me down as if they were made of iron, forcing me to close my eyes.

And my mind flew. It crossed immense meadows and deep cliffs, leaving behind rugged mountains. I floated on a brave and frothy sea of endless waves until I was enveloped in a thick fog. I didn't know if I was heading north or south, east or west, but an invisible rope, a strange energy was driving my flight towards an uncertain destination. Suddenly the fog vanished, revealing several small islands defending a rugged cliff. A beautiful green land opened up before my eyes. In the distance, I could see a mound crowned by colossal dolmens forming several concentric circles. Several druids, dressed in long white robes, were praying around a large fire. It was about to dawn. I approached and found that Alana was among them. I stopped my flight in front of my beloved. She smiled at me and I touched her soft cheek with my hands. Without a word, she took off a leather cord with silver mistletoe on it and hung it around my neck.

"My love, this is my place, this is the village where I belong. When the time comes... we'll be together again at last," flustered she lowered her eyes to the ground, as if those last words had given her more pain than joy. "Now you must leave and go back to your people," and with her eyes submerged in tears, she added: "I love you...."

The rattling of the wagon woke me up. I looked around confused; I didn't know where I was. My heart was pounding in my chest; I tried to calm down and realized that I was in one of the wagons transporting the wounded. I peeked my head through a tarpaulin.

"Well, you've finally woken up," said the *miles* that was driving the cart.

I sat down next to him. Without knowing how, I found myself with my fellow legionaries. We had left the oak grove far behind and were marching through a wheat field.

"What happened to me?" I stammered, still confused.

"They brought you in this morning just before dawn; apparently you had fallen from your horse. You should be more careful, those falls can be fatal."

What had become of my conversation with Lughdyr? And of my journey to those inhospitable lands? Was it all the product of a hallucination provoked by the fall from the horse? Suddenly, I remembered that Alana had given me her pendant. Quickly, I put my hand on my chest and, fascinated, I gazed at the silvery figure of a mistletoe leaf.

The distant walls of Pallantia, outlined in an ocher and crenelated horizon, revealed to us the arrival at our destination. From there we would set out in search of the Bagaudae and their Suevian allies. We camped outside the walls of the city and remained there for two days, recovering from the tiring journey. Well rested, Visigoths and Romans marched southward in order to annihilate the plague that had spread throughout Hispania, infecting it with the miasma of death and desolation.

We headed towards the city of Septimanca. The federates were in the vanguard and, covering the rear-guard, we were the legionaries of Rome. According to the latest information, the *Bagaudae* had made their own along the region.

It was getting dark and we camped near the Pisoraka river, in a forest of holm oaks and shrub oaks. It was hot and accompanied by Calerus, I went to cool off in the river.

During the whole campaign I had forgotten him and his long hair and blond mustaches. The army was so numerous and there were so many bearded and long-haired Visigoths that it would have been impossible to find him. But to my misfortune, he did manage to do it.

"Well, well, Roman, it seems that we meet again!" Walder exclaimed, accompanied by several *spatharii*.

104

I was squatting down to cool off when the German's gruff voice echoed from behind me. I stood up, reaching for my hilt, and Calerus did the same.

"They told me that you got rid of Rodrik's death." That was probably the name of the German I killed in the Suevian village. "Well, he deserved it. One shouldn't underestimate the enemy, no matter how effeminate he may seem."

The *spathariorum comes* gave a huge laugh that was jovially accompanied by his entourage. I didn't fall for the provocation and remained observing how he circled around us as if looking for a loophole to attack us.

"Where is the little bitch?" he asked standing in front of me.

"Far away from your dirty paws."

The Germanic burst out laughing again.

"You and I have some unfinished business, and I think the time has finally come to settle them," he said, drawing his sword.

"Stop there," a voice commanded from a towering chestnut.

"My lord, this Roman and I have an account to settle," replied the interpellated.

"The Romans are our allies and I won't allow quarrels between us."

The German reluctantly obeyed and holstered his weapon, losing himself among the oaks, but not without first giving me a furious look. His amber eyes had the prerogative to terrify the bravest of soldiers.

"My officer is quite a temperamental man, but you have nothing to fear as long as he remains under my command."

It was prince Frederic who spoke. Handsome young man, with had black hair and a shaved face. If it weren't for the Visigoth garb, I would have thought that he was a Roman tribune or curial.

"We've known each other for a long time, and between us... let's say irreconcilable differences have arisen," I said.

The prince smiled.

"I'm more or less informed," he said from the horse.

I was surprised that Frederic knew of my existence and more that he was aware of my enmity with Walder.

The prince smiled.

"I'm more or less informed," he said from the horse.

I was surprised that Frederic knew of my existence and even more surprised that he was aware of my enmity with Walder.

"I must tell you that you have to be careful. The *spatharius* is a great warrior and stubborn as a mule, he won't give up trying to finish what my brother Euric prevented him from doing in the Suevian village."

"I thank you for your advice, *domine*," I said with a nod.

"Your act was very courteous and I would regret your death. Take care, *centenarius*," added the prince, setting his mount at a trot.

Calerus and I watched him until he got lost behind the oaks.

"I have been told that Theodoric has become like him," said Calerus.

"What do you mean?"

"That he has become Romanized. Now he cuts his hair, shaves, and even, reportedly, reads the Roman classics."

"They are once again faithful allies of Rome, that's the important thing."

Shortly after his coronation as king of the Visigoths, Theodoric ratified the *foedus* signed by his father with the Empire. The *Gothorum rex*, like Frederic, considered Rome as the center of culture and knowledge, and logically, they were not without reason. Turismund was persuaded of our weakness and would not have hesitated to fight us if he had the slightest opportunity. On the other hand, the new king adored Rome and longed to get acquainted and absorb the knowledge and wisdom that our immense cultural heritage treasured. But Euric was completely different and, like with Turismund, he saw in Rome only a vast territory to conquer or plunder. I prayed that Theodoric would enjoy a long and prosperous reign, for the fate of the Empire, in one way or another, was linked to that of the Visigothic king.

We met our enemy a few miles from the thick pine forests that surrounded the city of Cauca. This time it wasn't the ragged, smelly *Bagaudae* we slaughtered in Calagurris. These were led by a Suevian officer called Agilulf. The barbarian had deserted along with several hundred soldiers, in search of greater fortune in Spanish-Roman lands. He had settled in an old abandoned *castrum* near Cauca, and his army had been worryingly increased with disinherited, deserters, outlaws and with all those who came to the protection of the Suevian under the promise of a great booty, as the sweet flies rush to honey.

Agilulf's *Bagaudae* had grown strong in the old *castrum*. They reinforced their walls, erected palisades and built a deep moat. More than three thousand men protected themselves behind the walls of the old camp. Surely the Vandal knew what he was doing. We camped in a meadow far from the forest, a few miles from *Bagaudae* fort to avoid night ambushes. As a customary measure of protection, we built a palisade surrounded by a ten-foot moat.

It was not dawn yet and we were already forming on the esplanade. Frederic departed with the officers while the Visigoths on the right flank, and the Romans on the left flank, stood firm, expectant at the orders of our generals. That day would mark the end of the *Bagaudae* in Hispanic lands. It didn't take long to get going and, in a few hours, we were in front of the Bagaudae *castrum*. From the walkway, Agilulf gave orders left and right to some soldiers who moved with leadership and speed, knowing exactly what their mission was.

The first to advance were the Romans. We formed a wall of shields and, protecting the ram, we marched the *palatina legio* with the mission of distracting the defenders, while the federated, supported by the *sagitarii,* placed ladders on the walls of the *castrum*. We had not advanced very far when a shower of arrows fell on our shield. Well protected, we overcame enemy darts without taking any casualties, but the *Bagaudae* weren't going to stand idly waiting to be pierced by our swords. A thud startled us, then another was heard, and a final rumble confirmed our fears. A huge stone fell on our column causing a great number of deaths. The confusion in our ranks was taken advantage of by the archers who made an easy target on us.

"Run and protect yourself under the wall!" cried the tribune.

And so we did, but already on the walls we were greeted with boiling oil and tar. Our legion was being decimated. Fortunately, several Visigoths had reached the wall and set up the ladders. With no choice but to climb them, or die burned, we climb the walls in the hope of reaching the walkway. So we did, and supported by a handful of Visigoth infantrymen and archers, the *milites* of the *palatina legio* were the first to crown the walkway. Hundreds of Suevians and *Bagaudae* received us with their beats. I saw Arcadius fight bravely surrounded by various enemies. I went towards him, but several *Bagaudae* blocked my way. They were dressed in filthy rags and were armed with large clubs and sticks. There were three of them and they looked at me with evil intentions. I had no problem getting rid of one of the raggedy men by feinting and stabbing his right thigh. But without giving me the slightest rest, another attacked me with a huge wooden mace. I managed to dodge several of his blows, but the savage was also right-handed and he protected himself well from my attacks. I looked at Arcadius and noticed with horror how a Suevian stabbed him with a spear in the back, making him fall inert into the *castrum*. Impelled by worry, I managed to break free from my adversary and jumped onto the roof of the armory, tumbling to the ground, very close to where my friend lay. I approached Arcadius and saw that, although badly injured, he was still breathing. Suddenly I realized that he was completely surrounded by *Bagaudae*. One of them ran toward me, waving his pike, yelling heartrending howls. It was the last thing he did before being pierced by an arrow fired by one of the *sagitarii*.

"*Centenarius* here is the *palatina legio* to kick the asses of these lousies!" the soldier shouted, as he jumped onto the roof of the armory followed by several *milites*.

A loud crash confirmed that the battering ram had done its job, and the main door of the *castrum* gave way. Hundreds of Visigoths, riding on war steeds, burst into the camp sweeping away every Suevian and *Bagaudae* in their path. I ordered several legionaries to take Arcadius to the *valetudinarium*, while the rest of the *milites* were preparing to annihilate such a troublesome enemy. I was running towards the ragged ones when I felt a strong blow on my back that made me fall to the ground. When I sat up, I noticed that I had been hit by a horseman, but it was not a Suevian or a *Bagaudae*. His malicious grin exhibited a string of yellow teeth. He dismounted and approached me, brandishing his sword.

"The time has come!" Walder shouted, throwing a thrust at me.

Taking advantage of the confusion in the fight, the barbarian intended to finish me off once and for all. I was able to stop his first attack and, in addition, I threw a couple of blows that he blocked with difficulty. But the German returned to the charge with a strong thrust that I managed to deflect. He was as strong as a bull. Around us, Romans and Visigoths were fighting against *Bagaudae* and Suevian without paying attention to our particular combat. The fall of the *castrum* was a matter of time, but I had other worries and the strong blow he gave me in my side confirmed it. I was completely exhausted, almost out of breath, but I noticed in Walder's yellow eyes and in his gasps of air, that he was not feeling much better. For a few moments we stood facing each other, without attacking, studying each other, looking for a weak point or a low guard that would allow us to put an end to our eternal quarrel. Then I noticed a movement behind the German's back, I gripped my *pugio* tightly and threw it at the chest of a *Bagaudae* who was about to slit his throat. A terrible smile appeared on Walder's lips. The German was persuaded that he had missed the attack, but he felt on his back the inert body of the *Bagaudae* pierced by my dagger and he understood. He looked at me with a frown and clenched his fists in bewilderment. If it hadn't been for my accurate intervention, his body would be rigid on the ground with his tongue sticking grotesquely out of his neck. Finally, he pulled my bloody pugio from the *Bagaudae*'s chest and threw it at my feet.

"Don't consider roman that this will prevent me from killing you someday, but the gods would punish me if I killed the man who saved my life today. I'll have to wait for another time," he said, before taking all his anger out on an unfortunate Suevian.

Many decades have passed and I still don't know why I didn't allow the bandit to rid me of the stubborn German. I don't understand how the folly of throwing my dagger at that ragged man came to my mind, killing him instead of waiting for him to kill Walder. Many years have passed and I haven't stopped a single second to curse that wrong decision...

Panting and exhausted from the effort, I fell on my knees. All around was death and destruction. I managed to get up and, like a ghost; I walked among the corpses and the wounded. Once more, the smell of human misery permeated every inch of my skin with its miasma. Several Visigoths tortured a Suevian before cutting off his head, while others dragged several women out of a house and outraged them over and over again, before the jokes and laughter of their companions. I had the feeling that all this was unreal, as if the scenes that my eyes contemplated were a dream or, rather, a horrible nightmare. The cries of pain were confused with the pleas for mercy, the laughter of the victors with the laments of the vanquished and the moans of the rapists with the cries of the raped women. I approached a trough 8abrevadero ok) with the intention of cooling off, but the water was stained with blood. The Grim Reaper had covered every inch of that castrum with his gloomy cloak.

There were no prisoners, all the *Bagaudae* and the Suevians were executed. His leader, Agilulf, as a lesson to his foolish rebellion, was skinned alive and his remains thrown to the vermin.

I went to the *valetudinarium* concerned about Arcadius's condition. Behind me I left a *castrum* devoured by flames, hidden by a thick curtain of black smoke suffused with the acrid smell of burned meat.

A big smile greeted me as soon as I entered the store. There, Arius Sidonius, Ájax, Calerus and naturally, Arcadius were waiting for me.

"Well, I see you sport a beautiful war wound," I said as soon as I entered.

"It's bigger than yours."

"And I think more painful."

Arcadius exhibited a bulky bandage that covered his torso, his face reflected the traces of deep pain.

"One more fight and we can still tell about it," Arius Sidonius observed.

"Thank God we're still alive," Calerus intervened.

"To God and our swords," Ajax added, drumming the hilt of his steel.

A grimace of pain blurred from Arcadius's face, preventing him from sharing our joy. Soon we left, letting him rest. The important thing was that he was alive and that his injury would not leave any serious consequences, except for a shocking scar on his back.

CHAPTER IV

Aetius, the last Roman.

Omnia neglegunt, dummodo potentiam consequantur.[4]

Once exterminated the *Bagaudae* and consolidated the alliance with the Visigoths, we returned to our quarters in Lugdunum where we took refuge from the rigors of the summer. The primroses and snapdragons painted the green meadows with shades of crimson, the nightingales cheered the spirits with their trill, and the rivers Rhodanus and Araris flowed peaceful and serene, with their beds full of crabs and trout. A beautiful scene very different from the one we witnessed a few weeks ago in the vicinity of Cauca. But our brief moment of contemplation and rest vanished when Aetius received a letter from Emperor Valentinian requesting his presence in Rome.

It was a magnificent day, where the sun shone brightly in an unblemished blue sky and a gentle breeze carried the sweet scent of wildflowers. I was walking outside the *castrum* accompanied by Optila, who had informed me of the Augustus' message.

"He wants to thank him for the services rendered: his victory over Attila's host and the *Bagaudae* hordes, the renewal of the *foedus* by the Visigothic King Theodoric, his staunch defense of the Empire..." said Optila with a gesture as we walked. "For all this, he has granted the hand of his daughter Placidia to Gaudentius, the son of Aetius."

"That is good news."

"It is," confirmed the Gaul with a smile. "It is well known that Valentinian envies our general. However, while he is safe in Ravenna or Rome, Aetius arms himself with the *spatha* and commands the troops. This invitation may help to iron out certain disagreements."

"What do you mean?" I asked confused.

Optila paused for a moment, looked around and began to speak.

---

[4] *They despise everything, as long as they get the power (phrase extracted and adapted from the book Latin Grammar by Santiago Segura Munguía).*

"The *magister utriusque militiae* is still reproached for his impassivity when Attila returned, destroying Aquileia and devastating half of Italy."

"But he could do nothing, he barely had soldiers," I interrupted.

The Gaul nodded.

"Aetius is a great general; his countless victories have allowed the Empire to resist the constant barbarian attacks. It is very weakened, it is true, but it resists. But the successes of some bring with them the envy and suspicion of others."

The confusion that radiated from my gaze encouraged him to continue:

"Many in Rome accuse him, unjustifiably, of wanting to dethrone Valentinian to establish himself as the new emperor. The army is on his side, but there are many enemies that our general has made in the heart of the Empire."

I pondered his words. It is true that I was unaware of the importance of politics in Rome, how gullible I was, I considered that it was enough to be a good legionary, demonstrate courage in combat and loyalty to the Empire, to forge the admiration and appreciation of others. But Optila was right, the useless, the cowards, the incapable, can only survive at the cost of insulting, lying and conspiring against those who surpass them.

"But the emperor's letter," the Gaul continued, "it is certainly good news. Both Valentinian and Aetius must work together for the good of Rome."

"That's how the emperor would have understood it."

"Indeed, his support will silence many mouths and will force more than a few senators to hide in their burrows waiting for another moment."

"Traitors inside Rome?" I asked, unable to believe that assumption.

"They are the most terrible and dangerous," Optila replied. "Because they don't attack from the front as our enemies do, but from behind, like the cowards who murdered Julius Caesar."

"Can the *magister utriusque militiae* be in danger in Rome?"

The Gaul nodded slightly.

"Have you talked to him?"

"Yes, he is calm and confident. What is more, he is really exultant at the possibility that his son, in the future, may wear the purple. He is aware that the letter is surrender on Valentinian's part. Besides, the senators conniving behind his back don't worry him in the least.

Moreover, the senators who connive behind his back don't concern him in the least."

"When will he leave?" I asked.

"Next week."

"Will he be escorted?"

"With a *numerus* de *vexillatio*," replied the Gaul. "You've never been to Rome, have you?" I shook my head. "Well, start polishing your coat of mail."

The Gaul's words excited me, and a broad smile broke out on my lips. Ever since I was a child, I had longed to visit the capital of the Empire, and now I could see my longed-for dream come true.

"I hope that our fears are unfounded, and that this trip will serve to raise our general to the glory he well deserves," said Optila, trying to banish from his mind dark thoughts, but in his eyes, I saw a concern that was difficult to mask.

"We will protect him from conspirators and traitors. Protected by his men, he won't suffer any misfortune."

Optila smiled and said:

"May the God of the Christians or the ancestral gods of our ancestors hear you."

On the way to Rome a deep emotion seized me. Visiting the capital of the Empire was a dream for Hispanic *miles* like me. Besides, I was marching with my companions Arius Sidonius, Ajax, Calerus and Arcadius, the five of us would undoubtedly enjoy the trip.

We entered the city through the Flaminian gate and, there, I suffered my first disappointment. I was persuaded that our troops would be received by an exultant population, who would acclaim us with tremendous gratitude for saving their skins on countless occasions, but it was not so. All around us there was nothing but beggars and foreigners of very different kinds, not very different from the *Bagaudae* we find in Hispania. We crossed the Mausoleum of Augustus, which was very deteriorated due to lack of maintenance. Then we crossed the Campus of Agrippa, the Arch of Claudius and finally, we arrived at the Palatine Hill. Yes, Rome was a real disappointment. Its streets were dirty and neglected, given to abandonment and indifference of the authorities. Everywhere there were beggars, pariahs and ragged people of the most diverse origins and languages. Its once colossal buildings and monuments were very deteriorated and not a few of them had been plundered and their columns and marble ashlars were now part of some church or *domus* of some influential *dignitate*.

We stopped in an esplanade in front of the staircase leading to the emperor's palace. I watched as Optila spoke to Aetius and Aetius shook his head. Finally, the *magister utriusque militiae* ascended the steps without an escort. At the entrance to the imperial palace, the patrician Petronius Maximus was waiting for him.

The grooms of the *palatinae scholae* took over our exhausted mounts, and Libius Asinius ordered us to break ranks, giving us a few hours of rest. Arcadius insisted that we go to the Maximus Circus, where there were dozens of taverns and brothels. My friend was looking forward to a good party. I convinced them to wait for me there, as I had a business to discuss with Optila. And I went to where the Gaul was, who was frowning in conversation with Traustila. Despite the distance, I saw deep concern on the faces of the veteran officers.

"Is everything fine?" I asked them when I had reached their height.

"Aetius has entered the palace alone, he is easy prey if they attack him," he replied worriedly.

"What can we do?"

"We must try to get in," Traustila answered, ascending the stairs.

Optila and I followed him, but at the door, a large group of Imperial Guards prevented us from entering.

"Too many imperial guards are protecting the entrance to the palace," said Optila.

"I don't like this, something is being plotted here," interjected Traustila.

The soldiers of the *palatinae scholae* watched us defiantly, and I noticed that some of them had already reached for their hilt. It was evident that they had orders to prevent any unauthorized entry into the palace. Powerless, we descended the steps and told Libius Asinius of our fears.

"I'm worried too," said the tribune, stroking his chin. "Petronius Maximus has received him, and the patrician's hatred and envy for him is well known. But we can't storm the palace; we would be exterminated by the *scholae*."

"I will wait at the door until the general comes out," said Traustila.

"I will wait with you," said Optila.

I wanted to meet Arcadius, get drunk in some tavern and who knows if I could visit some brothel or other, but I decided to

114

accompany the Gauls waiting to see our *magister utriusque militiae* go down the staircase safe and sound.

"I'm staying too," I said before the smiles of both Gauls.

"Well, half a dozen *milites* will wait with you at the entrance, in the meantime, I will patrol with the *centenarii* and the *semissalis* around the Palatine Hill," Libius Asinius said.

We remained several hours waiting for our general. There was no movement in the palace and, during that time, only a harmless slave came out of it. The Imperials didn't take their eyes off us, they hardly spoke to each other and their stern faces revealed tension. Suddenly, I saw one of our *semissalis* running towards us. When he reached our height, he was panting exhausted from his exertion.

"We saw an *equites* riding at full speed through the ancient temple of Apollo, Libius Asinius ordered him to halt, but he practically ran over him," the veteran legionary said, one of those who patrolled with the tribune.

"Where do you think he was going?" Traustila asked.

"He was riding along the Patrician way; we fear he was going to the castrum of the *palatinae scholae.*"

It didn't take long for the *semissalis'* suspicions to be confirmed. Within minutes, hundreds of horsemen from the *palatinae scholae* surrounded the palace and faced us with their swords drawn. We were a little more than twenty legionaries and we could do little against the emperor's elite soldiers. We soon understood that the slave who left the palace was carrying some sort of message.

"Who is leading you?" the tribune of the *palatinae scholae* asked from his horse; a sturdy soldier in his early forties whose gaze radiated an unwavering loyalty to the emperor.

"The *magister utriusque militiae* Aetius!" replied a panting Libius Asinius in the distance.

The tribune wrinkled his lips in displeasure.

"Order your men to form up in front of the palace and throw their weapons to the ground."

"My men are on leave."

"Then find them and do as you are ordered!" the tribune exclaimed drawing his *spatha.*

With a gesture, Libius Asinius ordered the *centenarii* to search for the rest of the legionaries.

"What is going on?" Optila asked, stepping forward.

115

"You will be duly informed in due course. Drop your weapons!" The tribune ordered from his restless horse.

We exchanged confused looks; we didn't understand what was happening. The noise of hundreds of *campagi* echoing on the roadway of the Via Longus caught our attention. Hundreds of soldiers and auxiliary archers came to support the horsemen of the *palatinae scholae*. The tribune raised his hand and the archers aimed their bows at us.

"Drop your weapons," Libius Asinius ordered.

"What the hell is this all about?!" Optila asked beside himself, to the officer of the *palatinae scholae*, refusing to obey the order of the tribune.

The archers sharpened their weapons, determined to make use of them. They were soldiers and obeyed orders. They didn't choose the target of their arrows, nor the moment to shoot them. For that purpose were the officers. The *sagitarii,* as disciplined legionaries, limited themselves to obey. The horsemen of the *palatinae scholae* bared their swords and a metallic and disturbing sound flooded the steps of the imperial palace.

"By all the gods of our ancestors, throw down your damn weapons!" Libius Asinius exclaimed, looking determinedly at Optila. "I won't tolerate that the sword of a legionary finishes with the life of another legionary, throw down the damned weapons! I don't know what the hell this means," he added, looking decisively at the tribune of the *palatinae scholae*. "Nor why we must disarm before you, but I trust there is a good reason, since my sword has never been thrown at the feet of a barbarian and it turns my insides to have to do so at the feet of a Roman."

"We all obey orders," replied the tribune, "and mine are concise and firm. Obey, and you won't have to fear anything."

"Who ordered you to disarm a detachment of legionaries of Lugdunum, of legionaries of Aetius?" Traustila interjected, remarking the name of our general, verifying in truth whom those *milites* served.

The tribune approached his mount to the Gaul and with an angry gesture replied:

"We are imperial guards and only obey orders from our emperor," and turning his horse he exclaimed: "Now, damn it, throw down your weapons or I order my archers to skewer you with their arrows!"

The tribune's reply didn't satisfy us in the least, indeed, it worried us greatly. What motives could have led Valentinian to communicate

116

such a disconcerting order? The legionaries of Aetius looked at each other with an irritated and confused gesture and, gritting our teeth, we threw our spatha to the ground. The metallic sound of our weapons hitting the pavement echoed in the air with the echo of a strange defeat. We had not fought, nor soiled our *spatha* with the blood of our enemies, nor succumbed on the battlefield, but our spirits languished as if we had sold our services to Attila himself during the battle in Maurica. We felt invaded by the icy breath of disloyalty and treachery, as if we had abandoned our general to his vilest and most perfidious enemy. And, perhaps, we had.

Little by little the legionaries arrived and watched the scene with bewilderment. Hundreds of horsemen surrounded the palace, protected by auxiliary archers. In front of us, we Lugdunum milites stood totally unarmed with our swords on the pavement. I could see the joyful arrival of my companions Arius Sidonius, Ajax, Arcadius and Calerus, and how the smile was wiped from their lips as soon as they saw us in that manner.

The soldiers of the *palatina legio* were formed in a dense and worried silence, when the door of the palace opened. A sorrowful Petronius Maximus stepped outside accompanied by several curials. For a few moments, they watched us in silence, their faces contracted with unfathomable grief. Petronius Maximus descended a few steps, while the rest of the senators remained at the entrance of the palace. The *scholae* closed ranks, encircling us with their mounts, and the archers drew their weapons, with the purpose of preventing any outbreak of tumult or rebellion. The patrician stopped at a prudent distance from us and twelve imperial guards approached him to protect him from an eventual attack. Then he snorted, as if what he was about to announce would cause him unbearable suffering.

"Legionaries... legionaries of Lugdunum, glorious defenders of the Empire, I have the sad obligation to report a terrible event to you!" the patrician finally exclaimed, with his face streaming with tears. "Today is a painful, infamous, disastrous day!" he continued. "Comparable only to the despicable sack of Rome by the barbarian Alaric!"

A murmur of concern spread through our ranks. The legionaries exchanged nervous and uneasy glances. We were impatient to hear the news that the patrician was trying to convey. What could have happened; Petronius Maximus was on the steps and Aetius was still in the palace everything seemed to be fine.

"Our... our beloved Aetius," he continued, "*magister utriusque militiae* of the armies of the Empire... is dead!"

Looks of annoyance and desolation followed each other among the Lugdunum legionaries, incredulous at what we had just heard. It was not possible that Aetius had entered the emperor's palace and, there, in what was practically his house, he would have met death. No, it couldn't be. Our general, victorious in a hundred battles against the most implacable enemies of the Empire, could not die in the heart of the *Urbs*. The capital was protected from Visigoths, Ostrogoths, or Huns, and supposedly free of any hint of threat to the general. But, of course, it was not. Annoyance gave way to fury and the legionaries stirred uneasily before the attentive gaze of the *scholae*.

"How is it possible that he died?" a soldier asked. "He came in under his own power, and now you say he's dead? How the hell is that possible?!" he insisted. His fists were shaking with anger.

"What has happened?" asked another, no less wrathful.

"You killed him, you murderers!" Optila cried angrily.

The archers drew their bows and the guards of the *palatinae scholae* prepared to charge at us.

"Soldiers of the *palatina legio,* your grief is my grief! Today all Rome mourns the death of the best of its generals!" exclaimed Petronius Maximus. Tears were running down his cheeks and his lips were trembling with compunction. "It was an unfortunate accident."

"Traitors!" a legionary shouted at him.

"Now return to Lugdunum and wait quartered for the orders of our Augustus!" he exclaimed, ignoring the legionary's accusation.

The patrician, fearful that an angry revolt would end his life, quickly took cover inside the palace, followed by the twelve imperial guards.

"Take your weapons and leave right now as you have been cordially urged, or by the founding fathers of Rome that I won't have so many considerations and I'll order my men to slaughter you as if you were a flock of sheep!" exclaimed the tribune of the *palatinae scholae* doing a gesture to an imperial guard, who returned shortly accompanied by the grooms and our horses.

With clenched fists and teeth, we took our *spatha* and sheathed them. Libius Asinius mounted his horse and commanded the march. We were escorted by several hundred soldiers and auxiliary troops until we left Rome, but several horsemen followed us at some distance until we reached the castrum of Lugdunum.

Our faces reflected like a mirror the dejected spirit of our souls, since we were all convinced that Aetius had been murdered. Once again, the envy, spite, ambition, and meanness of the powerful had precipitated the death of a great man.

For days, a deep silence flooded the entire *castrum*. Without our general, we would feel like orphans, left to our own devices in a gloomy forest full of stalking beasts. The light that guided our path had been extinguished forever, leaving us in the darkness of perfidy and cowardice. I realized that the true enemies of Rome were not in distant steppes or snowy mountains. As Optila pointed out, the worst threat that loomed over the Empire had to be sought within its *limes*, and it corresponded to the name of treason.

"This won't remain this way," Optila said.

It was a beautiful night and the stars illuminated the celestial dome with their throbbing brilliance. Several of us legionaries were sitting around a large fire, watching the crackling of the embers and the capricious movement of the flames.

"What do you mean?" Traustila asked.

"I will find out what happened to Aetius in the emperor's palace even if I have to dig through the shit that runs through the sewers of Rome. I swear it by all the gods," Optila answered, throwing a branch into the fire.

We looked at him with concern. We all suffered with great pain the death of our general, but there was little else we could do... except take revenge.

"I asked the tribune for permission and he granted it," said Optila. Tomorrow I leave for Rome.

"If they recognize you as an officer of Aetius, they will kill you," I warned him.

"I will go dressed as a common peasant."

"It is very risky to go to Rome alone," Calerus interjected.

Optila nodded his head.

"I know, but this way I'll go unnoticed," he said, without taking his eyes off the embers.

"May God protect you," Calerus said.

"God will have to protect Aetius's assassins!" Optila replied, jumping up and disappearing shortly after among the tents of the *castrum*.

The same day that Optila left for Rome, we received a visit from the *praefectus praetorium Galliarum* Tonantius Ferreolus and from Vicentius, the *Hispaniarum dux*. The *praefectus* had a good relationship with Valentinian and Petronius Maximus. He was a mature man in his sixties. Distinguished by his lousy character and arrogant attitude, he was used to commanding and being obeyed. The *dux* was a young man, with black hair and an aquiline nose. His gaze reflected the contempt he felt for all those of us who didn't share his noble lineage. The first decision of Tonantius Ferreolus was to disperse the ancient legions of Aetius, with whom he was characterized by a bitter rivalry. He assigned us, the Hispanic soldiers, to our old *castrum* in Tarraco, under the orders of the *Hispaniarum dux,* who years ago, decided that *foederati* soldiers and foreign mercenaries would be the ones to swell the ranks of his armies. Thus, he surrounded himself with barbarians of Visigothic, Heruli, or German origin, who would serve him faithfully as long as he could pay their high stipends. The *dux* had put the fox in the henhouse, entrusting the defense of the province of Tarraconense to the enemies of Rome.

Menacing black clouds greeted our departure from the Lugdunum *castrum*. Arius Sidonius, Calerus, Arcadius and I said goodbye to our good friend Ajax, making strenuous efforts so that the tears didn't flow from our eyes. We, the Hispanic legionaries were lined up in front of the *dux,* when the rain began to wet our saddened bodies. Tonantius Ferreolus looked at us with arrogance and pride, impatient to get rid of all those legionaries related to Aetius. The emperor had ordered it so. Reviled, annoyed and humiliated, we left Transalpine Gaul and returned to Hispania.

CHAPTER V

Treason and death in Rome.

Vim vi reppelere licet.[5]

They were a few quiet months, dedicated to patrolling the cities near our *castrum* in Tarraco, such as Barcino, Ilerda or Dertosa. Rome survived despite the death of Aetius, and the limes of the Empire were respected by our enemies. I often practiced the use of the *spatha* with my friend Arcadius, whom I had finally managed to beat on more than one occasion. I knew that sooner or later I would have to deal with Walder, and I needed to be as well prepared as possible. Several months of inactivity allow a lot of time to think and the memory of Alana flowed hopelessly in my head. I wondered where she was and what would become of her. There weren't few times that I evoked the Druid's prophecy, and I wished that the moment would come when the Grim Reaper would prepare to steal my last breath, so that my beloved would come and snatch me from its clutches.

It was an excruciatingly boring year, only punctuated by the occasional skirmish against bandits and outlaws. I longed for Transalpine Gaul, I missed the great Aetius, my Gallic friends and, of course, the giant Ajax.

I was walking through the castrum absorbed in my thoughts and consumed by nostalgia, when, in the distance, I saw Calerus calling me making gestures with his hand.

"We return to Gaul!" he exclaimed smiling.

"What?" I asked, not understanding what he meant.

Calerus was out of breath; he bent down and took a breath.

---

[5] *It is lawful to repel force with force (phrase attributed to Senator Cassius by the jurist Domicius Ulpianus).*

"Valentinian wishes to commemorate the victory over the Huns and has summoned all the legions that participated in the battle," he said, breathing heavily. "The tribune has just informed us, we leave tomorrow for Lugdunum and from there we will march to Rome."

The words of my friend cheered my saddened spirit; we were returning to Lugdunum and we would meet again with our friend Ajax, with the tribune Libius Asinius, with the Gallic officers Optila and Traustila, and with the other companions of fights and fatigues. Optila... What would have become of him? The last time I saw him he was about to travel to Rome. I wished with all my strengths that he had succeeded in his mission, and had discovered who was behind Aetius' death. But, above all, I hoped the Gaul to be safe and sound.

"That's great news; I can't wait to meet up with old friends," I said happily.

"Aetius's soldiers together again!" Calerus exclaimed grabbing me by the shoulders.

"Is the reason known?" I asked.

"The emperor has organized several festivities and celebrations, which will culminate with the re-enactment of the battle against the Huns."

At that time, I didn't know if Valentinian had anything to do with the death of the *magister utriusque militiae*, however, the *milites* of Aetius remembered that our general entered the palace alone and we never heard from him again. His legionaries of Lugdunum, we were separated, undermined and destined to different and very distant places. Some were sent to Ravenna, others to Placentia, Ancona, Narbo Martius, we returned to Tarraco, and not a few legionaries were scattered throughout the borders of the Empire.

"I don't know if Valentinian intends to gather us all together to verify our loyalty, or to show that he no longer fears us," I said thoughtfully.

"Soon we'll now."

We arrived in Lugdunum on a beautiful day at the beginning of March. We entered the *castrum* overwhelmed by the exultant joy of our fellow Gauls, who approached us greeting and embracing us with sincere joy. I felt very happy, that camp had been my home, my shelter and my life. With those damned soldiers I was united by the unbreakable bond of those who have shed their blood on the same battlefield, of those who have fought for the same objective, for the same mission, of those who have seen their comrades, their friends and their brothers die and then avenged their deaths by snatching the enemy's soul. Men whose only desire was to defend the Empire, offering their lives if so required.

We stopped in front of the *praetorium*, where a serious and ill-faced Vicentius was waiting for us, accompanied by the *praefectus praetorium Galliarum*, Tonantius Ferreolus. The *praefectus* raised his hand and ordered silence. Little by little, the shouting of joy ceased. With my eyes, I looked for my companions and I could only recognize Libius Asinius and some other legionary. I began to worry about Ajax and, above all, about Optila. Suddenly, the figure of a giant waving to me emerged among several hundred helmets and I could make out Ajax. I smiled calmer.

"Soldiers of Rome," began Tonantius Ferreolus, erected from a dais. "You have been summoned to celebrate the glorious triumph of our army over the barbarian Huns and their allies. Our beloved Emperor Valentinian has invited all of you to participate in the festivities that are going to be organized in the capital of the Empire."

The *praefectus* spoke before our distracted gazes. We were entertained looking for a familiar face in the crowd.

"As many of you already know," he continued, "the festivities will end with a performance of the combat against the Huns. The *Hispaniarum dux* Vicentius will lead the rehearsals with the help of tribune Libius Asinius," he said, doing a gesture to the official to take the dais, "along with senators Traustila and Optila."

The Gauls took the stage and greeted us. I was more comforted to know that my friends were alive, although I was impatient to see if Optila had succeeded in his risky undertaking.

"I hope you take this representation very seriously," the *dux* said sullenly, "and make the name of the legion stand out. We'll leave for Rome in a couple of days," he added, before descending from the dais, followed by the Gauls, the tribune Libius Asinius, and the *praefectus praetorium Galliarum*.

"We are fine if the name of the legion depends on a sham," one legionary said quietly.

"What audacity the *Hispaniarum dux* has. Well, isn't he going to direct the show when he wasn't even there?" another said.

"Hush, soldiers," I was forced to order, suppressing a smile.

We broke ranks and I went in search of Ajax, whom Calerus, Arcadius and Arius Sidonius were already greeting. My giant friend maintained the splendid form that characterized him. We were all excited to get back together.

"Long time without seeing you *centenarius*, I see that life is treating you well."

Said a voice behind me, I turned and saw that Optila was walking towards me with a big smile.

"I salute you, *senator*. It's a joy to see you again," I said, and we clasped each other's forearms.

"How are things going in Hispania?"

"Everything is excessively quiet since we exterminated the *Bagaudae*."

"Well, well, we haven't seen each other for a long time and we sure have a lot to talk about. Come by the officers' barracks this afternoon and we'll talk long and hard."

"I will."

Optila smiled and walked over to Traustila, who was conversing with the *praefectus* and Libius Asinius.

"I hope he succeeded in his endeavor to discover who Aetius' murderers are," Arcadius said, looking at the Gaul.

"At least he was able to return safely," Calerus intervened.

"Maybe this afternoon I'll tell you something about it," Arcadius said, and everyone looked at me.

"We'll see..."

I amused myself during the morning by greeting my former companions, among them being Traustila and Libius Asinius, and how could I forget Demetrius Tancinus and his cronies! It was the cold and distant greeting of those who do not even care about appearances. I also had the opportunity to be introduced to the *praefectus praetorium Galliarum,* Tonantius Ferreolus, who greeted me with indifference as one who contemplates with indifference the fall of the ocher leaves in autumn. With him was Vicentius. The *dux* looked at me in annoyance, as if I were an unpleasant fly that had disturbed his dinner. Those men lacked my liking and sympathy. Their cloudy looks and arrogant gestures only made me suspicious and distrustful.

124

The afternoon arrived and with it my meeting with Optila, I was impatient to meet my friend. I was on my way to the officers' barracks when the Gaul came to meet me.

"Let's go for a walk," he said as soon as he saw me.

We crossed the gates of the *castrum* and headed for a nearby stream. On the way we hardly opened our mouths, Optila wanted to be sure that his words would not be heard. The wrinkles on his forehead betrayed unfathomable worry. He walked slightly hunched over, as if he had to carry all the weight of the world on his back. It seemed that the death of Aetius had affected him more than the rest of us. We took a seat on a rock located on an esplanade. From there, we could observe the walls of the castrum and speak without fear of being overheard. On the horizon some black clouds were approaching and a cool breeze rocked our *saga*. They were the last throes of a winter that was reluctant to surrender Transalpine Gaul to the incipient spring.

"I'm glad you're back from Rome, I feared for you," I said.

"I still know how to move with some skill in the muddiest and foul-smelling environments of the Empire. But I won't deny that it was a difficult undertaking. The foundations of the Senate of Rome are rotten as the entrails of a dead rat, since Aetius has died before the indifferent gaze of several curials. I had to be slippery as a lamprey if I intended to achieve my objective without being discovered. Possibly, the *agents in rebus* at the service of the *magister officium* were on the alert, attentive to anyone who asked more than the opportune questions about the death of the general. But the desire to know the truth urged me not to falter, to keep on investigating until, at last, I found the person who revealed to me what I wanted to know."

"Did you find out who killed Aetius?" I asked, between admiration and surprise.

His eyes clouded over and his face contracted, wounded by an unfathomable pain. I felt a great bitterness for him.

"Rome respects nothing, not even the men who have shed their blood to protect it. Now more than ever I'm persuaded that it must be destroyed, it is not worth the death of one more legionary so that the patricians, senators and emperors may continue to maintain their privileges and remain unpunished for all their crimes."

The Gaul began to speak without taking his eyes off the *castrum*. His heart harbored a deep sorrow.

"I'm tired, dear friend," he continued. "I have years of hard fighting behind me and I don't think I can take much more. But I don't feel sorry for myself, I have already lived long years and there is little more left for me to do. I feel sorry for you." he looked me straight in the eyes and took me by the shoulder, "and for the noble and brave young men like you and your friends."

"I don't understand what you mean."

The Gaul shook his head.

"You are great legionaries in a decadent and corrupt army, led by inept men whose only interest lies in amassing great fortunes and maintaining their privileges. If you were led by worthy and upright generals, more concerned with the glory of Rome than with themselves, you would drive all those damned barbarians out of our *limes* and the Empire would rise again. Of that I'm absolutely certain. But Aetius is dead and in the whole Empire there is no one like him. It is only a matter of time before our frontiers crumble and our walls collapse."

"The legions will fight to the last to prevent that from happening," I replied.

The Gaul began to speak without taking his eyes off the *castrum*. His heart harbored a deep regret.

"The defense of Rome is not in the hands of the legions. Haven't you seen who Vicentius surrounds himself with?" I remembered the barbarian soldiers the *dux* had recruited. "The Roman *milites* are part of a triumphant and glorious past. Thanks to our *spatha* we have dominated and subdued powerful tribes and nations. Yes, we were heroes in distant and forgotten times, but now we are nothing more than a nuisance, a stumbling block to get rid of. We are treated with contempt, despised and relieved by barbarians of strange languages and dubious loyalty. Legionaries are ghosts of a victorious past that will never return. The legion languishes, dear friend, like the withered flowers scorched by the summer, like the condemned man who remains postponed in a cold dungeon, waiting for the executioner's ax to free him from his agony." He stopped for a moment and remained with his gaze fixed on the horizon, as if searching for memories cornered in memory. "Unfortunately, the defense of the Empire is not in the hands of the ancient legions, but of inept, corrupt and... murderous people," he added, clenching his fists.

The gentle breeze that greeted us turned into a chilly wind. A shudder ran down my spine. I tried to attribute it to the change in temperature rather than the Gaul's words, but I couldn't.

"When I arrived in Rome," he continued. "It was enough to enter the right brothel and ask the pertinent questions to find out who was in the imperial palace when Aetius died. That was simple the hard part came later; avoid being discovered by the *agents in rebus*, avoid the patrols of the *palatinae scholae* and, above all, be received by Lucretius Crassus."

"Lucretius Crassus?" I asked, even though I knew who he was.

The Gaul nodded and continued:

"He is one of the most sympathetic senators to the emperor. He comes from an illustrious and traditional Roman family, connected with that of several illustrious patricians, and even, I believe, with that of some Augustus. A *clarissimus* of noble ancestry and noble lineage, but more inclined to amuse with a beardless slave than to work for the defense and prosperity of the Empire. Well, everyone is quite free to choose his distractions and pursuits," he added with a bitter smile. "One night, hiding behind a hooded robe," he continued. "I managed to avoid the patrols and arrived at the door of his domus. Two guards impeded my way with their hilt, but I introduced myself as senator in the service of the *praefectus* Tonantius Ferreolus, and I ordered them to announce my arrival to the senator at once, since I was the bearer of an important missive. The guards looked at me suspiciously, but they must have realized that I wasn't lying and dutifully obeyed."

"Why did you introduce yourself as *praefectus* of Tonantius?" I asked him confused.

The Gaul smiled indulgently, aware of my unfamiliarity with the world of politics and the tangled web of friendships, patronage and influence that, like the twisted roots of a century-old oak tree, binds the high dignitaries with the brittle bond of shared interests. And, just as the roots nourish and sustain the tree, the Roman senators, with their intrigues, confabulations, pacts and compromises, nourish their excessive ambition and sustain their privileges and influences.

"Lucretius Crassus and Tonantius were bitter enemies of Aetius," he replied. "Whom they accused of setting himself up as emperor in the shadows. They are so petty that regarded the triumphs of our general with hostility and antipathy, since they increased his power and prestige. But with the *magister utriusque militiae* dead, the Senate and the Augustus now stand as the new guarantors of the Empire. It is to them whom the people must be grateful for their protection and welfare, and not to an impertinent and awkward general, distinguished by an inordinate pride and arrogance. And, Tonantius, freed from the obstacle that Aetius posed to his ambitions, and supported by some of the most influential curials of Rome, sets himself up as the new general in chief of all the legions."

"Please continue," I insisted, realizing how lost I was in that intricate, putrid, and despicable world of politics.

"The curial greeted me with a warm welcome," Optila continued. "He attended to me in the atrium, but I whispered to him that I was the bearer of an important message and that we should be protected from prying ears. I dared to caress his worn face and smile at him with some impudence. The senator licked his lips and looked at me with desire, since his sexual inclinations are well known. Then he led me to some private baths attached to the *triclinium*. I told him that I wanted to enjoy a nice hot bath after the long journey, and that it would be very nice to do it with someone. Excited, the pig began to undress me, but I urged him to get into the bathtub while I undressed, and he proceeded. I still remember his look of surprise when I pounced on him and plunged his head into the tub. It didn't take long for him to tell me everything I wanted to know while taking his last bath."

Some drops began to fall, auguring a storm, and we returned to the *castrum*.

"Lucretius Crassus revealed to me that Aetius was received by Valentinian, who showered him with flattery and adulation," Optila continued. "Petronius Maximus, Heraclius, the eunuch *primicerius sacri cubiculi* of the emperor, and some senators of the highest confidence of the Augustus were in the room. The general took a seat and several slaves served trays of food and wine. For several minutes they chatted in a relaxed manner and agreed on the marriage of the two sons. All was going well, until Petronius asked iniquitously who, if Gaudentius married Placidia, would inherit the purple after the emperor's death."

"Valentinian has no male children, only Placidia."

"Indeed, upon his death, his successor should be the son of Aetius, but Valentinian showed no enthusiasm."

"But it would be the most logical thing to do."

"The Augustus hates Aetius; he would in no way tolerate his son being proclaimed emperor. He agreed to the marriage of his daughter Placidia to Gaudentius because he had been advised to do so by several senators. It would be nothing more than a political wedding that would calm the tempers of the legions and the curials linked to the general. Valentinian, in conspiracy with several patricians, already had another candidate in mind."

Once again, the envy and anger of the powerful surfaced, always concerned with their own interest more than with the safeguarding of the Empire.

"Besides, Valentinian accused him furiously, of appropriating part of the loot captured in recent campaigns," he continued. "Huge amounts of gold and silver that corresponded by right to the emperor and the people of Rome, and that were illegally in the hands of the general. Then a terrible discussion ensued. Aetius seriously insulted Valentinian, calling him a liar and incapable, and the latter branded him a thief and traitor, ignoring his order to defend the Empire from Attila's advance."

"What happened next?"

"Not pleased with slandering him, Valentinian exclaimed that Aetius wanted Gaudentius to be appointed emperor, so that he could handle him at will, as if he were a puppet, our general being the true master of the Empire."

"I suppose Aetius had to restrain himself from hitting him."

"The general rose from the *triclinium* and faced him. He called him powerless and exclaimed to the curials that while the emperor sodomizes eunuchs, he risks his life to protect the Empire. Then…"

Optila fell silent; we were near the entrance of the *castrum*, and the soldiers outside were running for shelter from the persistent rain. We stopped for a few moments, until we were completely alone again.

"When Aetius was about to leave the room, Valentinian, in a fit of rage, drew the spatha and rushed at him, thrusting it into his back."

I couldn't believe his words. The emperor himself had stained his own hands with the blood of the first of the Romans. What person so dastardly, cowardly and petty would be capable of such an affront? To kill in the back the man who had given everything for the Empire. I held my hands to my head in shock at such a revelation.

"He fell to the ground badly wounded," he continued. "Despite the severity of the wound, perhaps he would have had a chance to leave the palace alive if Heraclius, aggrieved by the words of the *magister utriusque militiae*, had not discovered a dagger hidden in his tunic to stab him. From his neck began to gush a stream of blood before the

129

perplexed and helpless gazes of the senators, who in no way would have imagined that the encounter could have had such a dramatic outcome."

"Did the damned eunuch stab him?" I exclaimed, in a louder voice than prudence advised at the time.

Optila waved his hand for me to lower my voice.

"This can't go on like this," I continued with my fists clenched, oblivious to the deluge that was falling on us.

"Let's go back; two soldiers talking outside the *castrum* under this rain can cause suspicions."

Aetius' death couldn't go unpunished. Our general had been vilely assassinated and it was time to claim justice. The furious anger that burned within me demanded that I kill both, the coward emperor and the eunuch Heraclius. Rome, Rome, Rome, a great Empire ruled by the incapable, conspirators and traitors obstinate to achieve a glory that they in no way deserved. That was possibly the only time Valentinian wielded a sword, and he did it to treacherously kill the great Aetius. Let history judge him as he deserves.

If our *magister utriusque militiae* had had more ambition, if he had wanted to be appointed emperor, he would surely have achieved it. He had the support of the legions and several senators, among them Boethius, who noticed in him a more prepared and capable candidate than the indolent Valentinian. But Aetius didn't yearn to get dressed in purple; he only loved Rome and spared no effort to defend it from her many enemies. Aetius was a great soldier who lived for the Empire and died a victim of the misery of an unworthy emperor. The pettiness of men is only matched by their inordinate ambition.

We arrived at the *Caput Mundi* praised by crowds, being greeted by a multicolored shower of rose petals, by the low rumble of drums and by the high-pitched blast of *litui*. Valentinian had spared no expense, and the streets had been cleansed and beautified for the occasion. The pariah, ragged, and tattered that I had encountered on my first trip had been hidden or eliminated, who knew, but what is certain is that this Rome had nothing to do with the one I had known only a year before. We entered through the Flaminia Gate and marched along the road of the same name, arriving at the Via Triunphalis. We left the Parthenon, the Baths of Nero and the Domitian Stadium to our left, and camped near the Aelius Bridge, in the so-called *Campus Martius*, a large esplanade in front of the Capitoline Hill. The monuments I came across had been restored, giving them some of their ancient splendor. The emperor insisted that Rome evoke what it had ceased to be many years ago, and he lavished a real fortune in offering the Romans several days of festivities and celebrations with the purpose of making them forget their worries.

"It's like Nero and his gladiator show. *Panem et circenses[6]*, offer the people bread and circuses and you will have it at your feet..." Calerus observed.

We had just reached the esplanade and we were still forming. The cheers of the crowd and the persistent music had not ceased for a single moment. The Romans seemed happy.

"Let them enjoy, God only knows when they will smile again," Arcadius replied.

Calerus shook his head.

"The ancient emperors squandered vast resources in order to entertain the people with fights of gladiators and beasts. Now, Valentinian wants to do the same; entertain the people instead of feeding them. Bad business."

"Does anyone know where the beggars are?" Arius Sidonius intervened. "Since we have crossed the walls I haven't seen any."

"I suppose they will play the role of Christians in the Coliseum," Arcadius replied with a smile.

"It's not funny," Calerus protested, looking at him with wrinkled eyebrows.

"The truth is that they are gone," Arius Sidonius said.

"The same, they are underground, in the catacombs built by the ancient Christians," Arcadius insisted, determined to annoy Calerus.

Calerus was about to answer him when the sound of the *cornua* and the *litui* announced Valentinian's arrival. They had built a large platform for the occasion, covering it with tapestries and fabrics. The emperor approached the *pulpitum* accompanied by a whole retinue of senators, patricians and illustrious *dignitates*. A young man with mannered movements caught my eye; I looked for Optila and noticed that he was nodding at me from a distance. The sound of the trumpets ceased, and the emperor addressed the audience and the legions.

---

[6] *Bread and circus (Decimus June Juvenal).*

"People of Rome, in these troubled times, we must remember more than ever the glorious deeds of our legions, and not relegate them to ostracism and oblivion! Therefore, I have decided to organize a great feast in honor of the great Aetius in commemoration of his immortal victory over the Huns of Attila!"

A shout of approval spread through the vulgar until a pleased Valentinian silenced them waving his hand.

"Three days of festivities that will culminate with the representation of our victory over the invincible Huns." More exclamations burst out from the crowd. "People of Rome; behold our valiant soldiers, all of them true heroes, defenders of the ideals of justice and civilization that our Empire represents. Bold milites who keep the barbarians away from our borders, and who will not hesitate to shed their blood and risk their lives for each one of you. Roman citizens!"

The crowd broke into thunderous shouts and «Long live the invincible army of Rome!» alternated with «Hail Rome, Hail Rome!» «God save the emperor!» and «Long live the Empire.» We stood firm in front of the *pulpitum*, oblivious to the hustle and bustle that enveloped us. I could perfectly distinguish the legionaries Valentinian was referring to. We were around six thousand *milites* in total, of which the Roman soldiers would not even reach a thousand. The rest of the troops were made up by the federated Scythians, Heruli and Germans that so pleased the *Hispaniarum dux* Vicentius, in addition to a handful of Franks, Visigothic and Burgundian mercenaries. This was the real army that supported the defense of the Empire. An army of Romans, but without Romans.

A week to recreate a battle in which thousands of soldiers died is not a long time, and even more so if we add that the chief of ceremonies was a real incompetent more interested in monopolizing all the prominence, than in sticking to the events that occurred. It was common to see the Gaul officers and Libius Asinius discuss the details of the performance with the *dux*. Finally, and after hundreds of trials, any resemblance of this "comedy" to reality was only due to chance. Naturally, Vicentius played the role of Aetius and, in his judgment; it was practically our late general along with a handful of legionaries who achieved the victory. But such a pantomime was completely indifferent to me, and there were not a few of us legionaries and federation tired of marching, fighting and dying under a blazing sun. Thank God, the day of the performance, or rather, of the farce arrived. It was the sixteenth day before the kalends of April.

Thousands of people were clustered around *Campus Martius*. The senators, patricians, *praefecti*, *praefectus urbi* and other *dignitates* of Rome had the privilege of doing so in the emperor's rostrum. Barbarians and Romans were lined up and ready for combat, the dux stepped forward, standing right in front of Valentinian, and raised his spatha to salute him.

"*Nobilissimo* Valentinian, Emperor of Rome, witness the events that took place in our glorious victory over the barbarian Huns! Attila himself had to bite the dust before our formidable troops!" Vicentius exclaimed before thousands of cheers.

Valentinian enjoyed the show from the *pulpitum*. In Calerus's words, he simulated ancient emperors watching gladiators sacrifice their life in his divine honor. I could see that Heraclius, the eunuch, was sitting to his right. Petronius Maximus had taken his seat in a place away from the emperor, a fact that caught my attention, since it was common for the emperor to surround himself with flatterers, sycophant, and other fawnings. It was just sunny and sweat was gushing down my forehead. At least, in that it did resemble that farce with the actual combat against the Huns.

"Let the battle begin!" shouted the emperor.

The *Hispaniarum dux* galloped into formation at the sound of the *litui* and drums. The people shouted in fever, harangued and insulted the barbarians as if it were a real fight. Perhaps the Emperor Honorius wasn't very clever in banning gladiatorial fighting. They are barbaric, cruel and bloody, but isn't that what the common people want? Admittedly, he kept the public entertained and distracted from his petty existence. The fact is, when our mock charge against the false Huns began, the public roared with enthusiasm. However, any resemblance of this with the battle that took place in Maurica, was pure coincidence and more, when the only one who had taken it seriously was Vicentius.

The slow and exaggerated movements, the feigned cries of pain, soldiers who are mortally wounded and soon get up amidst loud laughter to continue the battle... it was a real disaster. Nothing of what was rehearsed. Each one did whatever he wanted and attacked whoever he considered appropriate, without following any guidelines. A real comedy. While I was arguing with a Hun who refused to die, I noticed how around me the soldiers were chatting, laughing and even playing dice. The *dux*, who was in the front line of the battle mounted on his horse, was trying to attack the fake Huns, but they were moving away making contemptuous hand gestures at him. His face was a reflection of anger and helplessness. His glorious performance in honor of Aetius, though we all knew he had staged it to gain the emperor's favor, was nothing more than a pantomime. We looked like five-year old boys playing battles. The crowd soon showed their anger and began to throw fruit, pieces of bread, and any throwable item of little value they could lay on their hands at us. Despite the distance, I noticed that the emperor was sitting restlessly in the *pulpitum*, astonished and bewildered. The cries of "out, out!" followed one after the other; the public was becoming more and more annoyed. The emperor had promised him three days of feasting and celebration and his words had come to nothing. The wine ran out on the first day; we *milites* were already there to give a good account of it, the plays were boring and the chariot races in the *Circus Maximus* were rigged. The only hope the emperor had of getting off lightly from the sad festivities he had organized was the reenactment of the battle against the Huns, and so far it was proving to be a real disaster. But I must admit that I enjoyed seeing Valentinian's confused face and, above all, the dux discomposed gesture. All around me was confusion and idleness. I looked again at the pulpitum and saw that the emperor was giving orders to an officer of the *palatinae scholae*. He didn't give him time to do more. An arrow, arising from the uproar caused by Romans and federated, pierced his chest, turning his spotless purple robe into crimson. The *palatinae scholae* rushed to assist him, while the dignitaries abandoned the rostrum fearing for their lives. That should have done the eunuch Heraclius, but he didn't. Scared, covering his face with his hands, he stood still and motionless, he didn't flee or attend the dying emperor. Fear gripped him, making him an easy target. And the Grim Reaper surprised him, since the dart dug into his forehead, piercing his skull and plunging into his devious brain. Heraclius rolled down the rostrum until he hit his bones on the ground. The arrows came from *Campus Martius*, but who had thrown them? I looked around, but it was all confusion. The common people fled in terror, stepping on each other, the nobles were terrified, some ran, while others hid like rats under the seats of the rostrum. I was puzzled; chaos and madness had taken over that esplanade.

134

"Come on, let's go back to camp! There's little more we have to do here!" a voice ordered me as he grabbed my arm tightly.

It was Optila, accompanied by Traustila, who was carrying me back to the camp.

"What else do we have to do?" I asked, but I got no answer.

CHAPTER VI

The Vandals go up the Tiberis.

Ignavi coram morte quidem animam trahunt,
audaces autem illam non saltem advertunt.[7]

The emperor died and for days no one could enter or leave Rome. Our *numerus* remained quartered in the *castrum* near the Aelius Bridge. Hundreds of soldiers belonging to the *palatinae scholae* patrolled the streets night or day and interrogated the soldiers, torturing the suspects if necessary, to extract from them the most meager information. Senator Petronius Maximus took charge of the investigation and had no doubt that the arrows that killed the emperor and Heraclius came from Roman ranks. All of us legionaries who at one time or another had served under Aetius command were interrogated. But they were unable to extract any confession from us, since we didn't know who had made the attack on the Augustus. We were then decimated. But in this case not every tenth legionary was executed, as was customary when a legion mutinied disobeyed an order or fled in combat, but every tenth soldier was imprisoned. Rome couldn't afford such a waste. The dice was cast and the goddess fortune saw fit to make me one of the condemned. We would remain locked up until the culprits of the murders were caught, which probably meant that we would never see the sunlight again.

I was locked in the dungeons of the subway prison excavated under the *castrum* of the *palatinae scholae*, in the camp of the ancient *praetorians*. Located outside the city walls, it was accessed through a trap door and a narrow, slippery staircase. A hundred other companions accompanied me. Fortunately, none of my friends were among them. It was a confinement a thousand times more cruel and infamous than the one I suffered in Lugdunum. The unfathomable darkness, the sticky dampness, the lack of air, the smell of detritus and putrefaction, the bugs... The cells were infested with insects; there were winged and

---

[7] *Cowards agonize in the face of death, the brave are not even aware of it (Gaius Julius Caesar).*

wingless ones, with six and eight legs, that bit or sting, flew or crawled, bugs and more bugs. I didn't know where they came from or what they fed on, but the truth is that many of us got sick, and I'm completely convinced that those damned and disgusting insects had a lot to do with it.

Each cell was occupied by ten men and I have to admit that I didn't get along with the fellow prisoners I was assigned to. I was the highest ranking prisoner in the cell, but in those conditions that detail was unimportant. But if we wanted to survive, we had to organize ourselves: ration the little food and water that the jailers gave us, assist those who got sick and do the minimum cleaning work to at least get rid of the bugs. I tried but did not succeed. We fought like wild beasts for every crust of bread or jug of water that was offered to us, and we abandoned the sick in a corner, stealing their meager ration. It was a struggle for survival, where only the strongest could survive.

It didn't take long for the first one to die. A few weeks later a second one fell and then a third. My relationship with the other six soldiers did not improve with time, and even less so when they tried, blinded by hunger, to eat the third one. Or rather, they ate him. What's more, they didn't even wait for the disease to precipitate his death. No, they didn't wait. Hunger made them impatient and one of them shortened his agony by breaking his neck. They cut him into small pieces with the help of a sharp stone and ate him in silence, avoiding being discovered by the light of the jailers' torches. I still remember with horror how they surrounded the corpse, bent down to tear off pieces of flesh and looked at me with the shining eyes of wild beasts and faces red with blood. They were no longer men, they had become beasts.

The great difference between my captivity in Lugdunum and the confinement I suffered in Rome was that, in the Gallic prison, I was alone in the cell. I could sleep more or less peacefully at night without fear of being attacked and I didn't have to fight every day for my ration of food and water. In Rome, I was afraid, very afraid. It was like being locked up in a cell with wolves, monsters or demons from the deepest hell. During my captivity, I could hardly sleep. I was always alert, restless, waiting to be attacked at any moment by those beasts eager to kill me in order to cut me into little pieces and thus satisfy their hunger.

But a surveillance round noticed the remains of the prisoner. I don't know if it was day or night, since the cell was completely devoid of natural light, and only the torches in the corridor dimly illuminated the gloomy dungeon. It was a regular round, but this time the jailer was concerned about the condition of who, according to what he had been told, was very ill. He had been curled up in a corner of the cell for several days and the jailer became suspicious, especially when he saw the good appearance of some of those imprisoned there. He approached the supposedly ill man, took off the blanket, and his eyes gazed in horror at the corpse of a man that had been partially eaten. He brought the torch close to the face of the deceased, unable to believe the macabre scene. Then I checked to what extent the barbarism of my cellmates had reached. They had eaten the face, the arms and part of one leg. They had cut the man in half and devoured his heart and part of a lung.

"Wild assassins!!" the jailer exclaimed in terror, between convulsions and nausea. "What have you done?"

It was a mistake: he should never have entered our cell alone. Like a pack of wolves, they pounced on him and killed him. One took off his military tunic and sword, and they left the cell. For a few moments I didn't know what to do. I looked around in confusion, and after weighing my few options, I decided to join them. I didn't get it.

"You'll remain here," one said scornfully, closing the dungeon door as he passed.

They didn't get very far. The soldiers of the *palatinae scholae* didn't ask questions, they were the emperor's elite guard for a reason. As they climbed the stairs, they were already waiting for them. They were killed on the spot. As I later knew, two guards were making the rounds. While one was inspecting our cell, the other was delayed since he had got attached to a young prisoner. When he heard the screams of his companion, he ran to the guardhouse and alerted the soldiers.

I was interrogated to elucidate if I took part in the massacre of the torn prisoner, but it was enough to look at my dismal appearance in comparison with that of my cannibal companions to understand that my diet lacked the same sustenance. As for the murder of the guard, the tribune of the *palatinae scholae* wisely understood that I had nothing to do with it.

Fortunately, I was locked up in a cell alone. At last, after long months, I could sleep peacefully without being startled by the terrifying possibility that someone might slit my throat during the night.

Eventually, I became a friend of a jailer who gave me information from the outside. From him, I learned that Petronius Maximus had been invested with the purple, and that he had married Licinia Eudoxia, the wife of the late Valentinian. He also informed me that the investigations about the murder of the emperor had concluded, even though the culprits had not been arrested. My luck was cast: I would rot forever in that miserable cell.

"Something must need to hide Petronius Maximus when he has stopped the investigations," the jailer told me one day.

As Traustila said, recalling the illustrious Seneca after the murder of Turismund: *«cui prodest scelus is fecit»* [whoever benefits from the crime that is its author].

"Do you think he's behind Valentinian's death?" I asked for.

"Aetius's soldiers are blamed, who in turn accuse Valentinian of having murdered the *magister utriusque militiae*," he replied, spitting on the ground. But Petronius Maximus is a rich and powerful man. Furthermore, he is not lacking in ambition and there are many who claim that he instigated the murder of the Augustus."

I remembered Optila's words at *Campus Martius* shortly after Valentinian's murder: «We have little else to do here.» Until that moment I had believed that the Gallic officers had something to do with the death of the emperor, but after the words of the jailer, many doubts flourished in my mind.

"There are those who say that he even encouraged Valentinian to kill Aetius, accusing him of wanting to seize the throne from him," the jailer continued. "I don't know, I think the new emperor is an untrustworthy conspirator. Have a good day."

He always said goodbye with the same phrase before locking the door. I smiled bitterly «Have a nice day…».

The jailer's words took their toll on my idle mind. I understood how petty and dastardly politics was in Rome: a man had been executed simply because someone had unjustly accused him of treason, an emperor had been assassinated and the authorities had not bothered to discover the culprits, and a hundred innocent legionaries had been locked up on the whim of a senator eager to wear the purple. Rambling on about human folly and tightly clutching the silver mandrake hung from my neck, I fell asleep.

My rest was short-lived, since the sound of a loud commotion awakened me. The jailers were opening the cell doors, urging the prisoners to come out of the cells. I heard the door of the next cell being opened, and I prayed to all the gods that the next one would be mine.

And so it was. My friend the jailer quickly opened the door, accompanied by a slave carrying a large basket full of swords.

"Come on Adriano, get out of the cell, you are free," he told me as soon as he opened the door.

I didn't think about it, any other option was better than staying in that filthy prison.

"What's going on?" I asked confused, watching as other jailers opened the rest of the cells.

"The Vandals have landed in Italy and are heading for Rome. Take a sword and wait upstairs," he replied nervously.

I obeyed and went up the stairs, run over by the rest of the prisoners, who ran quickly towards freedom, fearing that, at any moment, the jailers would change their minds. It was night and a sky full of pulsating stars greeted me. Outside, chaos reigned in the castrum of the *palatinae scholae*. The imperial guards, whip in hand, prevented the prisoners from escaping, making them line up in front of the prison. Several hundred *equites* horse man and *milites* of the emperor's personal guard were forming up in the camp.

"Move!" exclaimed a guard hitting me with a cane.

The pain woke me up and I followed some prisoners who were forming up in front of the soldiers.

"Line up in threes!"

Exclaimed a *circitor* and so we did. Despite the dim light, I noticed that most of the prisoners were the legionaries condemned for the assassination of the emperor. Dirty, malnourished and dressed in rags, we looked like a real army of outcasts. Even the *Bagaudae* looked better than we did. In a short time, all the prisoners were forming up under the watchful eye of the guards. Then the tribune of the *palatinae scholae*, mounted on a powerful warhorse, addressed us.

"Legionaries of Rome!" he exclaimed before our surprise. Weren't we prisoners anymore? "The Vandals of Genseric have landed in Italy and are on their way to *Urbs*."

I was beginning to understand.

"Emperor Petronius Maximus has granted you your freedom on the promise to defend Rome from the barbarians. You will all be reinstated in your former positions, you will be provided with uniforms and weapons, and you will be fed so that you will be in the best condition for the imminent arrival of the enemy," said the tribune from his restless horse.

Rome didn't exactly have an abundance of *milites*, especially when the threat of the Vandals loomed over her. A hundred legionaries, or rather several dozen ragged soldiers, since many had died in the unhealthy dungeons, were better than nothing, and the promise of freedom was a more than reasonable payment for risking their lives with Genseric's barbarians.

"Who among you is willing to lay down his life for Rome!" shouted the tribune.

"We always have been!" exclaimed a prisoner.

"We will put an end to these barbarians!" cried another.

"Hail Rome!" was heard from the front row.

The cries of «Hail Rome!» spread throughout the prisoner formation like fire on tar. Soon the soldiers of the *palatinae scholae* imitated us and a thunderous shouting flooded the castrum infusing new vigor into our exhausted spirits.

The tribune looked at us with satisfaction, raised his hand and from the camp kitchens came out several slaves carrying steaming pots, baskets of white bread and jars of wine.

"Now eat and rests, tomorrow at dawn go to the storehouse where the *biarchi* will deliver your equipment."

The mutton stew was wonderful for all of us. I enjoyed my dinner alone, sitting on the parapet leading to the warehouse. After my experience with my cannibalistic companions, I had become wary and suspicious. I ate and drank with delight, a guard handed me a blanket and I slept curled up against a wall.

A strange nightmare assailed me during the night. In it I saw a village attacked by *Bagaudae* among whom I was. It was a massacre. The men tried to defend themselves, but we were more numerous and soon the land was strewn with corpses. We burned the stone and heather huts, while the women and children fled in terror. A barbarian horseman emerged through the smoke, raising his sword, ready to cut down the life of a little boy, about four or five years old, who was crying disconsolately in the middle of a mud and blood quagmire. The horseman gripped his sword tightly as a woman appeared out of the mist and ran to the little boy, protecting him in her arms. I recognized her at once. I ran quickly to the horseman, but I was too late. The barbarian pierced the woman's back with his weapon and she fell limp to the ground. I still remember the child's tearful eyes and her look of

141

terror before the barbarian severed her head. I woke up uttering a piercing scream, but luckily no one heard me, or so I thought.

"It is up to you that that does not happen."

I was confused and wondered if I was still dreaming.

"Dreams have the prerogative to warn us of future events, but sometimes, it is in our hands that such events do not come to fruition," said a familiar voice, and the figure of an old man dressed in a white robe loomed out of the darkness. "Even the humblest of peasants, if his heart is brave and determined, can reverse the course of history."

"It was Alana and a child, I watched them die," I said, more startled by the dream than by the sudden presence of the druid.

"Our destiny is written in the stars," Lughdyr said, raising his hands to the sky, "but Nature or mere chance rewrites it, allowing us to modify it."

"Alana cannot die. You said it!" I exclaimed angrily.

Lughdyr sat next to me and looked at me compassionately, just as he would with a child who doesn't understand why hunger or diseases exist.

"You can stop it," he assured.

"How? What can I do? I don't even know where the village is," I protested helplessly.

"I'll guide your way, trust me."

Those were his last words. The druid as he had appeared vanished, leaving my soul constricted and a deep sorrow in my heart. I had to find that village and avoid the death of my beloved and the little one... Suddenly, I wondered who that child was and why Alana sacrificed her life for him. Was he her son? Would she have married? I rejected this possibility, since she was a druid-woman, but... what if he was her son? Who would be the father? A chill ran down my spine and I was forced to dismiss the absurd suspicions that sprouted in my confused mind. I decided to consider that that experience had been nothing more than a dream, a horrible nightmare fruit of long months of confinement...

Rome was in a deep chaos. Alarmed by the arrival of the Vandals, the crowd fled in panic, crowding the city gates. The servants, with blows of whip and cane, made way for their masters, powerless before the quagmire created by wagons and goods. A part of the desperate common people got into a tumultuous fight, while a group of skillful petty thieves took advantage of the confusion trying to snatch their belongings. The women cried, cursing their luck, the children looked around terrified and without understanding what was happening and the men, anguished and trapped between the wagons that blocked the exit and the exasperated people who tried to escape, hit each other in a vain attempt to escape from a panic-stricken city. Shouting, kicking, pushing, shoving and hitting were all to no avail. The wheel of a chariot had broken due to the enormous weight it was carrying, blocking the Ostiensis gate, which was to the south of the city, near the Tiberis river. Every effort was futile and many tried to turn around in search of another way out. But between those who wanted to leave and those who wanted to return, they formed a chaos preventing any kind of movement. Overcome by anxiety and anguish, many began to faint, and fell to the ground, being trampled mercilessly by the crowd.

"Repent, people of Rome!" cried an old monk in the distance, waving a long wand menacingly. "God has forsaken us because of our sins!"

"My God, save us!" cried a woman carrying a child in her arms.

"Help me, my wife has fainted!" cried a man helplessly, who was dragged by the crowd while his wife remained inert on the ground.

Several columns of smoke emerged on the horizon revealing that the city was being given over to pillage, and not precisely by the Vandals. For the unscrupulous and evildoers, any occasion is a good one to get their hands on a good booty, and a city in deep chaos was an unbeatable opportunity.

"Bastards, let me pass!" shouted a burly merchant, swinging a riding crop at anyone who got in his way.

That was the last thing he said. Before long, he suffered the wrath of an irrational mob that fell upon him, tearing him to pieces and stealing his belongings. His wife, who was right behind him, was fortunate enough to flee with her children and return the way she had come escorted by her slaves.

"Repent for your sins, people of Rome or you will suffer eternal damnation, and your souls will rot in hell!" the monk shouted again in exasperation, as if he had lost his mind.

"God, I want to get out of here!" a man claimed crushed by the crowd.

"My son, my son!" cried a woman, looking through the crowd for her lost little boy.

Dressed in my *centenarius* uniform and supported by five legionaries, I was trying to organize the evacuation of Rome through the Ostiensis gate, the route chosen by the majority of the Romans, which caused its collapse. More so, when a chariot got stuck in the arcade. We tried to push it aside but it was impossible, so we decided to unload it to facilitate its removal but its owner, a rich merchant, tried to oppose. He had to be unceremoniously submitted. It took us several minutes to free the door, but the crowd was crushing against the cart, making our maneuvers difficult. Finally, and not without effort, we managed to free the door and the people overflowed the exit as if it were a furious torrent, leaving behind several inert bodies on the ground.

"Make way for the emperor!"

In the distance the unmistakable voice of the tribune of the imperial guard was heard. The family of Petronius Maximus was preparing to leave the city escorted by a not excessively large group of equites from the *palatinae scholae*, who made way for the procession banging hard with their sticks and using their mounts. They had decided to flee through the gate of Ostiensis to take the road of the same name that communicated Rome with the port city of Ostia Antica. Once there, the emperor would embark on a ship putting his egregious ass safe from the invader. They were still some distance away, but it was evident that the common people didn't like to see how their emperor, who established himself as the maximum protector of Rome and the Empire, fled in a hurry, using his personal guard to clear the way from the common people that crowded the streets.

"There you have the one who caused the ruin of Rome!" cried the monk again, his eyes bloodshot and foaming from his mouth. "Because of him the Vandals are going to kill us all!"

"Let's finish him off!" cried a giant with a bull's neck and hands like shovels, before a murmur of approval. "Rome will be condemned due to his abominable sins!" cried the indefatigable monk again.

"Death to Petronius Maximus!" exclaimed another.

The threatening shouts went on and on under the alert gaze of the tribune, who ordered his soldiers to draw their *spatha*. Two men, exited by the shouts of the crowd, shook the gestatorial chair in which the emperor was riding, and the tribune was forced to use his sword. The crowd went into a rage when the tribune of the *palatinae scholae* killed the

144

two assailants, and from threats, they passed to the action. Several men pounced on the men carrying the gestatorial chair, knocking them to the ground with blows and slashes. The imperial guards fared no better. The bull-necked giant pounced on the tribune, hooked him by the arm and, with little difficulty, threw him to the ground. He never got up again. The rest of the imperial escort, feeling lost, prudently fled to the barracks, abandoning the Augustus to his fate and taking the empress Licinia Eudoxia and her daughters Placidia and Eudoxia to safety.

The emperor, still recovering from the fall of the gestational chair, was easy prey to the mad mob, who massacred him with kicks, bites and punches until they left him inert on the ground. My legionaries tried to intervene, but I urged them not to do so. The crowd was enraged and had completely lost their minds. Any attempt to save the life of the Augustus would have been futile and our lives would have been in unnecessary danger. Besides, if the jailer's words were true and the emperor had had anything to do with the murders of Aetius and Valentinian, his cruel death would have been well deserved.

"He is the son of the devil and must not have a Christian grave!" exclaimed the monk, continuing with his harangue. "His remains must feed the fish in the Tiberis!"

The bull-necked giant didn't hesitate and taking the sword of a dead imperial guard, he severed the limbs of the unfortunate Augustus. The fiery mob burst into fierce howls as the improvised butcher threw the bloody remains at them. More out of curiosity than to maintain order, something impossible in that city immersed in madness. I followed the crowd who, forgetting their haste to leave Rome, headed for Tiberis, lifting the emperor's bloody pieces with satisfaction. Leaving the Testaceus Mount spillway on the left, we crossed the Galbae warehouse where a group of looters was devouring several jars of oil from Hispania, grain from Egypt and wine from Gaul and we arrived at Aemilia Porticus, a complex arcaded warehouse located next to the Tiberis. Those who carried some of the emperor's spoils stood on the bank of the river. They all awaited the arrival of the monk, who, panting after the enormous effort arrived after a few minutes. My legionaries were terrified. They had never seen such a cruel and merciless spectacle. All around us, the crowd laughed with bloodshot eyes. Shouts of acclamation preceded the arrival of the monk. I noticed that he was a man of about fifty years of age, short stature, scarce hair, with a lost look and a trembling mouth. He wore a threadbare and dirty brown woolen robe. I wondered when reason decided to leave his troubled mind.

"Brothers, throw the corrupt remains of Petronius Maximus into the Tiberis and may his soul never enjoy rest!" cried the monk with his arms raised. "May his sacrifice satisfy Our Lord, and with His infinite goodness, free us from the relentless plague of the Vandals that descends upon us like a swarm of hungry locusts! Impious Rome must walk towards the Light; abandon the excesses and depravity to which she has been dragged by a lascivious and greedy people! Brothers, remove from my sight those bloody remains, corrupted by an immensity of unutterable sins! Tiberis will devour the material body of Petronius Maximus and Hell will consume in burning flames his immortal soul!"

The mutilated limbs of the emperor were thrown into the dark waters of the river, before the acclamations and the jubilation shouts of the maddened people. There, gawking, gazing at the Tiberis with their eyes averted and lost, they remained there for several minutes until, not knowing what to do, they returned the way they had come and walked, in a guilt-laden silence, in the direction of the Ostiensis gate.

Many were the inhabitants of Rome who abandoned the city, others, on the other hand, dedicated to looting in the face of the imminent arrival of the Vandals.

"It is preferable that Rome be sacked by the Romans themselves than by the barbarians," said a *miles*, as we patrolled the deserted streets.

All around was nothing but ruins and debris. The fires followed one another in a city abandoned to looting. The *Urbs* was being devoured by its own children. Slaves were picking up the corpses scattered in the streets and loading them onto wagons. No, I didn't quite agree with the soldier's observation.

Two days after the assassination of the Augustus, in the kalends of June, the air resounded with the menacing snort of hundreds of war tubas. The Vandals were about to arrive in the city. From the northern wall, one could watch as an endless line of soldiers moved inexorably toward their goal: Rome. It was a cool late spring morning and the sky was completely limpid, unblemished, showing a beautiful and almost unreal celestial color. I was a beautiful day that invited to enjoy life, if it were not for the terrifying presence of the barbarians and the piercing sound of their tubas. From the walls inward all was silence and restlessness. The Vandals positioned themselves about twenty stadia

146

from the city to get protected from the range of our ballistae and projectiles. It was a well-trained and disciplined army; they knew what they were doing. Celsus Galenus, the *praefectus urbi* and highest authority in Rome after the emperor's death, observed the enemy movements with attention. He had been *praefectus praetorium Galliarum* for many years and through his veins ran the blood of censors and praetors. He was a nobleman of noble ancestry. He was about sixty years old and still had an abundant tuft of white hair. Thanks to his long military life, he had a stout constitution and his powerful arms were capable of splitting in two anyone who dared to stand in his way. He had expressionless gray eyes and his features showed no hint of concern. Undoubtedly, he was a great general of well-tempered nerves, the *praefectus urbi* that the city needed in those terrible moments. Now, surrounded by soldiers, he was looking attentively at the army that threatened to destroy the *Caput Mundi*. Next to him was Pope Leo. He wore a long white tunic with purple bangs that reached his ankles. He had a dark complexion and, in spite of his advanced age, he still had some golden tones in his beard and hair. His gaze was serene and calm. I wondered if, as had happened with the arrival of Attila and his host of Huns, he would be responsible for negotiating with the Vandal king for the salvation of the city. I looked around me to calculate how many troops we had, and I think that we were no more than six thousand soldiers ready to defend Rome, while the Vandal hordes numbered around thirty thousand. The situation was really desperate.

The movement from the barbarian ranks of a group of horsemen caught my attention. I identified the *Vandalorum rex* Genseric by his sturdy and warlike bearing, very different from that of the Augustans of Rome. A man of advanced age, possibly close to seventy, he sported a full head of brown hair brushed with silver strands at the temples and his face was hidden behind a frizzy beard. He was accompanied by ten horsemen from his personal guard. The two most powerful men in Rome looked at each other and exchanged a few words that I didn't manage to hear. Genseric stopped halfway and sent one of his guards. When he reached the walls he reported, loudly, that the Vandal king was willing to negotiate the surrender of the city on his word that not a drop of Roman blood would be shed. The two men looked at each other and descended the walls to meet the invader, escorted by the imperial guard.

"Pope Leo is a great negotiator, he has already prevented Attila from destroying Rome and I'm sure he will repeat such a feat," said a legionary.

"The Hun king had little interest in traveling further south; his troops were sick and exhausted. The agreement he signed with the Pope was most advantageous to his own interests," said another.

"It is true, the tribute that Valentinian had to pay him to return to Pannonia left the coffers empty," interjected one more.

"Gold is only gold, but a human life is irreplaceable. Thanks to the Pope, Rome is still alive, don't forget that," insisted the first one who spoke.

"Until today..." replied another, whom we looked at with apprehension.

Celsus Galenus, accompanied by Leo and several *equites,* went to meet the Vandal king. The future of Rome, and therefore of the Empire, was being negotiated on that esplanade. Behind me, some women wept quietly for fear of breaking the thick silence that enveloped us. The hurried beating of hundreds, thousands of hearts could be heard in that sea of tension and anguish, while their owners wondered if they would be witnesses of a new dawn.

"This waiting is going to kill me," a man said without taking his eyes off the negotiators.

"I have a wife and three children, I fear for them," said another, to the assent of several men who were next to him.

"And you have good reasons for doing so. The *praefectus urbi* will have to bow to his demands if we want to get out of this alive," another explained, shaking his head.

As time passed, the number of women who burst into tears increased, plunging the city into an incessant lullaby of whimpers and sobs. I didn't blame them, if Rome fell, they would be the first to suffer the consequences. During the assault on a city, men died pierced by swords, spears or darts, that is, they suffered a more or less rapid death, even dignified, but with women the most ruthless cruelty was unleashed. First they endured the loss of their husbands, fathers or brothers, then they witnessed how their sons or daughters were killed, but not before being brutally forced. Later, and if the horror of seeing their loved ones murdered, mutilated and outraged were not enough, they would be the ones who would suffer the derision of rape. In the end, fate had only two possibilities for them; slavery or death. For this

148

reason, it didn't surprise me to observe how many husbands gave daggers to their wives, convincing them to kill their children before falling into barbarian hands. It was only necessary to wait for the good Lord to grant them temperance to conclude such sacrifices before it was too late.

The minutes were hours and the negotiation seemed to have no end. We observed those men scrutinizing in their gestures or expression, some indication that revealed the slightest information about the course of Parliament, but it was not like that. Both Genseric and Celsus Galenus, and naturally the Pope, were intelligent and skilled men in the use of the word and avoided giving any opportunity to their adversaries through a bad gesture, a snort or the slightest smile.

For whatever might happen, the *magister officiorum*, the commander of the *palatinae scholae* and the *agents in rebus*, had ordered to place large cauldrons of boiling water, tar, and burning sand along the entire length of the wall. Catapults, ballistas and onagers would keep the barbarians at a certain distance, while the *sagitarii* would try to halt those who dodge our first defensive line. Already on the walls, soldiers of the *palatinae scholae*, legionnaires and civilians armed with knives, clubs and axes formed the last defensive line. If the wall fell, we would retreat our position and fight house to house. They fought for loot, we fought for our lives, very different motivations that could lead to victory or defeat if the battle was even.

"They're coming back," said a soldier.

The Pope and the *praefectus urbi* were returning to the city accompanied by the imperial guard. Their faces were serious, but also serene. Impatient, the imperial guard opened the Flaminia gate, and the great men crossed the walls.

The high *dignitates* of Rome were required by *the praefectus urbi*. They would be the first to know the result of the negotiation. Few senators and illustrious people attended the meeting called by Celsus Galenus, as most had fled in panic, abandoning their people, the Romans for whom they should pour out their concerns and concerns, to their fateful fate. While the nobles gathered, the defenders of the city remained vigilant for any enemy movement.

The position of the sun marked the sixth hour when an official of the *palatinae scholae* informed us of the conditions of the agreement between the *praefectus* of Rome and the Vandal king: the city would be sacked by foreigners without using violence. All Romans, rich or poor, free or slave, would remain at the doors of their *domus or insulae* with all their furniture, jewelry, money and any other valuables. Not a single drop of blood would be shed, the city would not be destroyed or burned, and the churches would be respected. Only those who tried to deceive the Vandals and hide their wealth would be executed.

Rome would be sacked, but it would survive. For those of us who only possessed a sword, the agreement was most advantageous, but the rich and the powerful raised their voices, refusing to accept the humiliating terms of the Vandal. But they had no choice, because the decision had already been made. The next day, the fourth day before the fifth day of June, when the sun rose over the horizon, the city would open its doors to the invaders and would be sacked in a consensual and supposedly peaceful way.

We lined up and flanked the Vandals, who passed through the Flaminia gate and entered the subjugated Rome with sheathed swords, but displaying insulting smiles and sultry looks of contempt. At the doors of their homes, parents hugged their wives and children in the vain attempt to protect them from the barbarians. Genseric supervised the pillage under the watchful eye of Leo and Celsus Galenus. They quickly loaded the valuable furniture and pieces of jewelry into carts, before the sobs of the women and the panicked looks of their children. Legionaries were given the task of protecting the churches and houses of the notables in order to avoid probable excesses. A Vandal took a leather bag of coins from an old censor. Distrustful, he entered his house accompanied by several men, leaving a few minutes later carrying several sculptures and bronze busts. Without hesitation, the Vandal drew his sword and impaled it on the chest of the unfortunate old man, who hadn't had the common sense to consider the sculptures and busts valuable. A family of *clarissimi* nervously awaited the arrival of the Vandals. They stood at the door of their *domus* accompanied by half a dozen slaves, along with all their belongings and valuables. The Vandal officer claimed the slaves and the *clarissimus* refused.

"According to the agreement made with the *praefectus* of Rome," said the curial, not hiding his displeasure at such a pact. "You can only steal our valuables, not our slaves."

"You buy and sell slaves like furniture or cattle. They are valuable and we take them with us," the Vandal objected, grabbing tightly a slave, a girl who was no more than twelve years old.

One of the soldiers protecting the family drew his gun and threatened the Vandal.

"Let go of the girl," the impulsive young legionary ordered, without removing the *spatha* from the barbarian's neck.

The Vandal stopped confused. They had been plundering the city for hours and until now no one had dared to resist. He released the girl and turned to his men. The little slave ran towards a woman and took shelter in her lap. The legionary smiled and sheathed his *spatha*. Then the Vandal officer drew his sword and with an extraordinarily agile movement, turned and severed the legionary's head, which fell to the ground and rolled to stop at the feet of the young slave.

"Is anyone else against us taking the slaves?" the Vandal yelled, raising his bloody sword.

There were no protests, and the barbarian officer grabbed the young slave, snatching her from the fragile arms of the woman, who fell to the ground between pleas and cries. The Vandal approached the *clarissimus*, clutching the girl violently.

"Tell me Roman, are you going to prevent me from enjoying the charms of your slave?" he asked contemptuously.

The *clarissimus* looked down in humiliation.

"You Romans are cowards, you have surrendered your city without even fighting," snapped the Vandal, spitting at the curial's feet. "You have no courage to defend what is yours."

Without being blocked by anyone, he entered the *domus* dragging the unhappy and sobbing girl.

Genseric, accompanied by Celsus Galenus and the Pope, reached the Palatine Hill. A large group of soldiers of the *palatinae scholae* guarded the rich *domus* and buildings that surrounded the emperor's palace. He stopped his horse in front of the palace and climbed the steps. From the doorway, Empress Licinia Eudoxia, along with her daughters, her servants, and the imperial guard, watched expectantly at the arrival of the barbarian king.

"Is everything in the palace valuable?" the Vandal asked, looking down a hallway filled with furniture, sculptures, chandeliers, and hundreds of gold and silver objects.

"Yes," the empress replied coldly.

Genseric smiled satisfied by the loot; even so, he ordered several of his men to search the rooms.

"You promised to respect the life of the Romans," Pope Leo reminded him, fearing for the life of the empress.

"As long as they didn't try to deceive me," the king replied, without looking at his face.

Celsus Galenus ordered a senator from the *palatinae scholae* to order all available legionaries to strengthen the protection of the imperial family. There was no way he was going to tolerate Genseric hurting Licinia Eudoxia. His dignity was already being unbearably tainted by allowing the barbarians to ride the streets of Rome with impunity, plundering, burgling and raping female slaves, as if to indulge further excesses by foreign hordes.

And there I was, lining up on the palace steps, protecting the empress and her daughters from the vile intentions of the *Vandalorum rex*. For the first time I seemed to notice a trace of concern on Leo's face. He whispered in Celsus Galenus's ear as Genseric chatted with some of his officers. Licinia Eudoxia hugged her daughters tightly, protecting them from the pack of wolves that watched them with hungry gazes. She was a beautiful woman in her early thirties, exhibiting a haughty and noble bearing. Over the linen *subucula,* she wore a gray silk *stola* girded with a purple *patagium* embroidered with gold thread. Her dark eyes revealed an iron determination; she would not be intimidated by a bunch of barbarians no matter how wild they were. She is too much of a woman for the cowardly Petronius Maximus and, of course, for the inept Valentinian.

"My lord, we have found this."

One of the Vandals, who had entered the palace to search it, rushed out and handed a small silver chest to Genseric. Pope Leo and Celsus Galenus exchanged worried glances. The empress remained embracing her daughters with a haughty and imperturbable gesture. The Vandal king looked at her, and she responded by giving him a look full of hatred and contempt that Genseric did not take long to understand. With a frown, she opened the chest to find a large quantity of gold solids inside. She took out a coin, and observed that one of the sides was embossed with the profile of Valentinian. He smiled in satisfaction at the finding: Licinia Eudoxia had tried to deceive him and now she would suffer his punishment. With a calm step he approached the empress, who maintained the regal and haughty face of the Roman *nobilissimae.*

"You have tried to deceive me," Genseric said. "If we stick to the agreement with the *praefectus* of Rome, I could kill you right now."

152

The girls burst into tears as soon as they heard the Vandal's words. Without even looking at him, they clung tighter to her mother's breast.

"That chest is not mine," said the empress, staring into his eyes.

The Vandal burst out laughing and said:

"You disappoint me. I guess lying is not typical of a Roman *nobilissima*."

"If the empress says it is not hers, it is not hers," the *praefectus urbi* interjected, grabbing his hilt.

"Everything in Rome belongs to you, King Genseric," the Pope said, trying to calm things down. "What else do you want?"

The Vandal handed the chest to one of his officers. He felt strong and almighty. Yet the glorious capital of the Roman Empire was at his mercy.

Genseric was the king of a lesser people, but he had achieved what other kings much more powerful than him had not even dreamed or aspired: to conquer Rome by surrendering it to his barbarian feet, stripping it of its infinite riches, leaving it to ruin and desolation. And all this happened without spilling a single drop of Vandal blood. There is no doubt that this is an immeasurable and colossal feat, which will elevate him as one of the most audacious kings in history. He relished in such a sweet instant, getting drunk on the honeys of conquest as a disgusting fly licks the remains of a dead rat. He watched the concerned faces of the *praefectus,* the Pope, and the empress's daughters, who continued without taking their gaze from the tunic of their mother. The Imperial Guard took hold of his hilts and the Vandal smiled. After all, we were just a handful of men against an entire army. He approached the empress and stroked the hair of one of her daughters.

"I don't want more deaths, I only intend to return to Africa full of riches," said the *Vandalorum rex,* addressing the *praefectus* in Rome. "But the empress has insulted me, and I deserve compensation."

"What kind of compensation?" Celsus Galenus asked uneasily.

"I'll take the empress and her daughters to Carthago as part of the booty."

"Do not!" the *praefectus* exclaimed, drawing his *spatha.*

"Stop Celsus!" exclaimed the Pope.

The imperial guard and legionaries drew our swords and set out to protect the empress. Celsus Galenus stopped a few steps from Genseric with his sword drawn. The Vandal watched the scene with amusement.

"Are you going to stop me, *praefectus urbi?*" he asked contemptuously. "You, who will be censured throughout the Empire for delivering Rome to foreign barbarians without defending it?" the Vandal spat on the ground, drawing his sword and exclaiming. "I will take the empress and her daughters to Carthago whether you like it or not! What you will have to decide is how many Romans will die before this happens!"

"Enough!" the empress cried.

She withdrew from her daughters and entrusted them to one of her servants.

"That chest is not mine and therefore has never been found in my room," Licinia Eudoxia continued, pointing to the chest. "We both know it well. Unjustly accusing me of being its owner is nothing more than a ruse, a deception. The lie of a deceitful and unworthy king for, God only knows what dark purpose. But anyway, I won't have any more Roman blood spilled. Perhaps that is precisely what you want," she added, looking at the Vandal with frozen eyes full of hatred. "Yes, that's right... your cruel look gives you away." A sly smile appeared on Genseric's lips. "You cling to a pretext to; now that your armies have crossed our solid walls, throw Rome into a devastating fire and bloody destruction. It would be too easy. No, *Vandalorum rex*, I will meekly fall into the trap you have cleverly contrived. I fear for my people, I fear for my daughters and if you assure me that by surrendering us you will leave Rome and leave Italy without drawing your sword anymore, I will agree to be led to Carthago."

"Your guesses are wrong, *nobilissima* Licinia Eudoxia," replied the Vandal. "That chest isn't mine and my intention is far from ravaging Rome and razing it to the ground. No, noble Licinia Eudoxia, it is not. If that had been the case, I wouldn't have agreed with the egregious great men who now seek to protect you," he said, looking over at Pope Leo and Celsus Galenus. "But who had no qualms about flanking my entrance to Rome and opening the doors of your palace to me. They would even have opened the ones in your bedroom if I had required it."

The *praefectus urbi* was about to intervene but Pope Leo prudently took him by the arm.

"Soon my wagons will be loaded with your snatched riches and I'll return to Carthago," Genseric continued. "I have no interest in staying any longer in lands that have little else to offer me. So, *nobilissima*, once my purpose is achieved, I'll leave with all my armies," he added, holding out his hand to the empress. "I assure you."

Licinia Eudoxia nodded gravely.

"So be it. I'm your prisoner," she finally agreed, approaching the barbarian and offering her hands to be tied.

"Do not!" Celsus Galenus exclaimed, taking hold of her hilt, but the empress restrained him with a gesture and said:

"You have done the right thing, illustrious *praefectus urbi*. Rome will survive the Vandals. Now don't make a terrible mistake that will water the streets of our immortal city with Roman blood. No, don't do it. We will accompany Genseric to Carthago, because it is our duty, our firm obligation as patricians, as protectors of Rome. It is a despicable sacrifice if with it we achieve that no one, absolutely no one, dies as a result of the barbarian swords."

Celsus Galenus clenched his fists in anger, but persuaded by the empress' prudent words, he had no choice but to give in and accept his decision. Beside him, Pope Leo was drinking his tears, overwhelmed by deep regret. Meanwhile, Genseric, the great winner, smiled with satisfaction.

"You will live in a beautiful palace according to your noble condition," the Vandal assured her, pleased.

"But it won't stop being a prison for that," Licinia Eudoxia replied.

For two weeks the city was sacked by foreigners. Marble and bronze sculptures, beautiful gold and silver jewelry, huge amounts of coins, jewels and precious stones, thousands of horses and slaves... the loot obtained by the Vandals was formidable... But the city was saved. Few were the men killed and women forced, the churches were respected and the buildings were not burned. Truth be told, Genseric kept much of his word.

Mules and oxen pulled the heavy wagons with force. They could be counted by thousands. The barbarians shouted at the beasts, whipping them with their whips. The wheels got stuck in the potholes in the pavement making the effort of the pack animals useless, so the slaves had to divide the weight between different wagons or carry the heavy loads themselves. When the barbarians had already stripped

Rome of its riches, they departed, dragging with them the empress and her daughters.

In a long line they departed along the Via Portuense, which led to the sea. There the Vandals had anchored their numerous ships. The wagons, due to the enormous weight they carried, left deep furrows in the earth. Laughing, and drunk with wine and victory, the invaders marched off, leaving the *Urbs* at the mercy of hunger and disease. Thousands of slaves, horses, sheep and other livestock, closed the procession of shame. The *praefectus urbi* watched the march of the victors in silence, with his eyes moist and humiliated. Pope Leo was at his side, he tried to console him by placing his hand on his shoulder, but the praefectus slapped it away. No doubt he questioned whether he had done the right thing. The Vandals were returning contentedly to their North African lands with a huge mutiny, and without having suffered a single casualty in their ranks. The Romans, on the other hand, were humiliated and disheartened. The dishonor of shame was hanging over Rome, which continued to live but at the cost of being stripped of its dignity and glory.

"You have done the right thing, your act has saved many deaths and suffering," Pope Leo said to Celsus Galenus with tears running down his cheeks.

"I have surrendered Rome and allowed the imperial family to be taken to Africa. I'm nothing but a damned traitor," the *praefectus* whispered dejectedly.

"You couldn't fight the Vandals; they were superior to us. Rome was already doomed; they would have sacked it in the same way, but sowing the streets with corpses. Any kind of resistance would have been sterile."

The consolation words were lost in the air and had no effect on the sunken *praefectus,* who remained hidden behind the shield of ignominy and humiliation. His face was contracted, disfigured by an immeasurable pain.

"Rome has been plundered, the emperor is dead and Licinia Eudoxia has been abducted by Genseric. Our world is sinking, swept away by the raging and insatiable waves of barbarism," said an officer of the imperial guard.

Those of us who heard him nodded silently.

"I hope God forgives me," the *praefectus* mumbled, heading for his *domus.*

Pope Leo followed him with his eyes until he was lost in the crowd. His eyes watered and in a whisper, he said a prayer for the tormented soul of the *praefectus urbi*.

Celsus Galenus, after the death of the Augustus, was the highest protector of the city of Rome, and had not only failed to defend it from its enemies, but had offered it to him on a silver platter. And such an affront wounded his spirit with the sharp spear of treason, dragging him into an abyss from which it is impossible to escape. Since men of honor, soldiers who have shed their blood in defense of their homeland cannot tolerate the scorn that comes with the infamous surrender that springs from the absence of battle.

As I knew shortly thereafter, the *praefectus urbi* went to his *domus*, drew his *spatha* and knelt. He rested the hilt on the ground and, letting himself fall on its cold edge, ended his suffering, his shame and his life.

The once proud Romans were now specters wandering aimlessly through their streets. The silos were empty, as were the warehouses, corrals, henhouses and stables. There was no food and no possibility of getting it. The first to suffer the consequences of the lack of food were the dogs, then the cats and finally the rats. Every living thing became part of the diet of the starving Romans. It didn't take long for the city to fall into the hands of disease.

Abandoned to its misfortune, prophets and false messiahs emerged like weeds announcing the end of the world. Many were those who took their own lives by throwing themselves into the Tiberis or throwing themselves into the void from the *insulae* or the walls.

The fear for the plague forced more than one to wrap their few belongings in a cloth, tie them to a stick and leave that hell of desolation and bitterness.

Almost a month after the sack of Rome, the troops of the *magistri militum* Ricimero and Julius Valerius Majorian arrived in the city. I suppose they were not impressed by what their eyes saw as they marched past with their mighty warhorses. The streets were dirty and smelly, corpses crowded around the corners and no one had bothered to remove them, Imperial soldiers and legionaries lounged playing dice or lying in the shelter of any tree that offered some shade. Nobody kept order. Pope Leo had locked himself in his palace fearing for his life and the *magister officiorum* spent his time in brothels completely drunk, wrapped in the arms of the women who exercised their ungrateful work there.

For my part, there was little else I could do but let myself be dragged down by carelessness and indifference. When civilization is devastated and ruined, when God covers his children with the veil of indifference, when the guts protest because of hunger and the mind threatens to detach itself from reason, it is difficult to do nothing but try to stay alive in the hope that Providence will grant you a truce or send you a message of hope and salvation, and the troops of the *magistri militum* were that message. They carried with them several hundred wagons with grain, wine and oil that delighted the hungry population.

At once both generals took command of the city. Their officers took charge of the indolent soldiers, and in a few days, we looked like a real army. The streets were cleared of corpses and the population didn't lack a crust of bread or a glass of wine to pour down their gullets. With a full stomach, reality takes on a different perspective and is seen with hopeful eyes. Once again, Rome was being reborn from its own ruin.

The *magistri militum* made a pleasant impression on me. Ricimero was the son of barbarian notables, had been brought up at the court of Rome and during his youth had fought under Aetius' command. His black hair was streaked with gray, and his eyes were as dark as a raven's wing.

Although he was already fifty years old, he had the sturdy and martial bearing of one who had spilled his blood on the battlefield. Majorian was much younger; he would have been in his early thirties. His hair was intensely blond; his face was drawn with graceful and noble features, and his eyes revealed intelligence and cunning. These were two of the most powerful men in the Empire.

The heat augured a particularly hot summer, and we hurried to bury the dead we found in the streets. There came a time when they were so numerous that we were obliged to load them on wagons and transport them outside the city walls. There we piled up wood and set fire to them. Little by little, those who had left the city returned, carrying with them their belongings and families. They burst into tears and lamentations after seeing their houses plundered or burned, but it didn't take them long to understand how fortunate they had been when they heard of the fate of some of their friends, relatives or neighbors.

CHAPTER VII

Requiario invades Hispania.

Tempestas minitatur antequam surgat.[8]

The city was resuming its usual pace, obstinate to overcome the humiliation and deaths that had occurred a few weeks ago, when I was informed that my days in Rome were coming to an end. Avitus, the *magister militum* of Gaul, had been proclaimed new emperor with the acquiescence of the Gallo-Roman senators and, above all, of the Visigothic hosts, who fostered his appointment in Arelate, the capital of the region. About a thousand legionaries were entrusted with the mission of going to meet the new Augustus.

As soon as I arrived in Arelate, the reasons that led Ricimero and Majorian to accept his appointment became clear. Behind its walls, in a sea of tents, thousands of federated Visigoths were camped. Theodoric had taken the appointment of his friend Avitus very seriously, and Rome was already in too much trouble to face her only allies.

We crossed the city walls before the suspicious gaze of the Visigoths, who doubted our intentions towards the new emperor. Our commander, tribune Constantius Trebius, had to assure the captain of the Visigoths that our mission was to escort Avitus to Rome, where he would be ratified by the Senate.

We went to the *castrum* of the Roman garrison and the grooms took charge of our horses. I was exhausted after the long journey. I refreshed myself with fresh water from a bucket and ate some bread and cheese that I carried in my saddlebag while sitting under a barrel in the parade ground.

"He has protected himself by barbarian troops, Avitus has sold us."

"What have you said?"

The legionary took a seat next to me, he was a young recruit with a serious look and a disgruntled gesture. By his accent I identified his Gallic origin. He kicked a stone reluctantly and replied:

---

[8] *The storm threatens before breaking out (Lucius Anneo Seneca).*

"He has put all his trust in his Visigoth guard, disdaining the soldiers of Rome. It is a shame."

"Perhaps he has his reasons," I replied, remembering the murders of Aetius, Valentinian, and Petronius Maximus, all caused by Romans.

The recruit looked at me suspiciously, starting to regret the conversation he had started. I looked at him and noticed that he had blushed.

"What is your name?" I asked to reassure him.

"My name is Clodio Larcio, *domine*, and I'm a Gaul."

"I imagined it. My name is Salvio Adriano and I'm Hispanic."

"I imagined it," he answered with a smile that bordered on insolence. "You have come to escort the Augustus, haven't you?"

"So is."

"He will reject you; he will surely order you another mission. He will go to Rome accompanied only by the federated Visigoths and by the legion quartered in Arelate. They are the only Romans he trusts."

"It would be an absurd risk for him."

I observed the *castrum* of Arelate. It was a solid stone construction and was in very good condition. The soldiers were well equipped and seemed well fed. But, as was the case in the *castrum* of Lugdunum, they were very few. They numbered no more than two thousand. In case of an enemy attack, the defense of the city would depend on the Visigoth *foederati*.

"I hate those barbarians; the only thing they want is to take over the Empire," Larcio growled.

I smiled, the memory of my friend Arcadius came to my mind, he thought exactly the same of the barbarians as the young Gaul. What would become of him? Where would the good Arcadius and the rest of my friends be? I prayed that they were okay and that we could meet in the future. Larcio was looking at me as if his words had affected me.

"Now they are our allies and it is thanks to them that we still keep our *limes*," I replied.

"They will end up betraying us; it is only a matter of time."

I saw our tribune leave the *praetorium* of Avitus, he walked with long steps and stroked with force. Despite the distance, I saw that he was very angry.

"I think I should go, it has been a pleasure Larcio, I hope to see you again," I said.

"Hail, *centenarius,* and good luck," said the recruit with a martial gesture.

The Gaul was a sensible young man who knew the new emperor very well. Just as he had predicted, Avitus refused our escort and ordered us to quarter in Arelate until further orders. Our tribune was in a rage, he had undertaken a tiring journey for nothing, or so he thought.

I don't know what it is that drives us men to kill each other, what wild and primal instinct leads us to dismember, stab or cut our throats. The truth is that inactivity inflames us when the weeks go by idle. It must be that the fiery impetus that develops from being accustomed to living on the edge calls for some reckless occupation where to spill part of the accumulated violence.

Requiario, the king of the Suevians didn't recognize the new emperor of Rome and had the audacity to plunder Carthaginiense, subjecting the province to depredation. The Emperor Avitus sent ambassadors to establish peace with the Suevian king, but the latter, presumptuous and persuaded of the weakness of the Empire, ordered that they were beaten and sent to Rome half dead. But the Augustus was reluctant to engage in hostilities with the Suevian, and persisted in the attempt to agree on a peace by sending to Bracara Augusta, a new legation. But the ambassadors were again beaten and ill-treated, evidencing the contempt which the Suevian professed for the Empire.

Insatiable, and in the absence of any response from Rome, Requiario invaded Tarraconensis, capturing a large number of Hispano-Romans and dragging them as slaves to Gallaecia. Due to the constant outrages committed by the Suevian, the Augustus had no choice but to resort to the help of the Visigothic federates, and sent King Theodoric and his hosts *«cum voluntate et ordinatione Aviti imperatoris»* with the will and order of Emperor Avitus, to neutralize the persistent Suevian invasion. The Visigoth stood, once again, as the great champion and maximum protector of the Empire. And we, a handful of *milites,* as already happened in Frederic's campaign against the *Bagaudae,* would accompany him to avoid possible outrages and excesses while they were in Hispanic lands. Thus, we left for Tolosa, where we would join the troops of King Theodoric, who in addition to contributing thousands of men, had also agreed to the participation in the campaign of the Burgundians and the Franks. It was clear that Avitus didn't intend only to punish Requiario for his insolent invasion, his goal was to exterminate him and with him all the Suevian of Gallaecia.

A fine rain hit our helmets while the east wind waved a sea of Visigoth banners and flags. The ten *centenarii* who made up the *palatina legio* proudly formed in front of our *milites*. The tribune inspected us mounted on his handsome war chestnut and nodded pleased. Our legion was well equipped and educated; I can vouch for that, thanks to the maneuvers and training I witnessed. It was made up mainly of Italians, some Hispanics and especially Gauls who were supporters of Avitus who had fought by his side on countless occasions. The tribune Constantius Trebius led us. A brave man, his face was cut by a deep scar that would have delighted the good Arcadius. He had the haughty and noble countenance of former officers. We all respected and appreciated him, because he was severe but fair, he knew how to give the appropriate punishment according to the fault or infraction committed. Not many years ago, he had shared the battlefield with Aetius, and with the Emperor Avitus, defending the limes of Gaul from the barbarians from the North. He looked suspiciously at the Visigoths, whom he considered no more than self-serving and petty barbarians. Whether or not he was successful in his impressions of our federated, the truth is that they were there, a few hundred steps from our legion, forming alongside us to defend Tarraconense from his Suevian cousins.

Twelve thousand soldiers, including Visigoths, Burgundians, Franks and Romans, made up the army that was preparing to give the troublesome Suevian a scolding. King Theodoric himself led the troops. He was a strong and capable man, with a powerful look and an authoritative voice. A true Visigoth. Theodoric's participation in the campaign made me uncomfortable. Undoubtedly, Walder, as *spathariorum comes*, would accompany him. He would try to avoid the barbarian hosts at all times. If there was a way to elude the Germanic, it was to stay as far away from our allies as possible.

The unremitting rain poured down on us, soaking helmets, breastplates, military tunics and bones. Constantius Trebius was stood in front of us. The tribune looked at the *Gothorum rex* sideways, without any intention of concealing a frown and displeased gesture. Fighting subordinate to the orders of a barbarian must have been a lacerating humiliation for such a battle-hardened Roman. But that was the way the Empire worked and the tribune had no choice but to obey. The new times required us to swallow our pride and dignity, even if it tasted bitter and repulsive as gall.

The rain raged and lightning crossed the dark sky of Tolosa, making our helmets and shields reverberate in blue. A last clap of thunder frightened the horses and unsettled the most novice soldiers. Theodoric looked at the sky and spat cursing his luck. A long march under a heavy rain and on a wet road was not the best of beginnings. Unable to delay the march any longer, the Visigoth ordered our advance.

We crossed the Pyrenees and Requiario fled, like a fox discovered in a henhouse, from Tarraconense. The very uncouth hadn't counted on the invaluable help of our Visigoth allies. For several days we chased him, but the Suevian moved with agility and speed, always leaving us behind just at the moment that it seemed we could catch up with him.

We reached the once glorious city of Clunia, now half demolished by the looting and fires caused for years by the barbarians, on a leaden and tremendously rainy day. The clouds had parted, throwing cascades of water from the sky with the sole intention of drowning us all, as if a new flood was closing in on us in order to punish us for our infinite sins.

I was sheltered from inclement weather under a portico of the old theater in Clunia when the tribune approached me and said:

"I greet you, *centenarius*."

"I greet you, tribune," I said, sitting up in surprise.

"Easy." Constantius Trebius smiled, sitting next to me. "Did you know that this theater was carved out of the rock and that it had a capacity for about ten thousand people?"

I shook my head.

"This city, in its maximum splendor, once housed more than thirty thousand souls and now you see," he said, pointing to the ruins. "There are no more than five hundred who live among its rubble."

"It is only the reflection of many Roman cities."

The tribune nodded regretfully. In his eyes I noticed the exhaustion of one who struggles to cling to an unrealizable dream. Heroes from another magnificent and glorious age who refuse to acknowledge reality, no matter how obvious it may be.

"I will defend Rome from all his enemies, as long as a single drop of blood runs through my veins," he said with fierce determination.

"And you are not alone."

"I know."

Constantius Trebius looked at me with affection. He was aware that I had fought under Aetius command against the Huns in Maurica, and this fact had helped me gain his appreciation and sympathy.

"I have spoken to King Theodoric; he has told me that after the hills to the north of the city, there is a small village."

I looked at him carefully.

"He asserts that a Spanish-Roman traitor that has collaborated with the Suevian hides there."

"Who is he?"

"I don't know, some bastard who has sold his honor to the Suevian for a handful of coins. You must capture him alive, it is necessary for him to reveal who else has helped the barbarians during the invasion."

I nodded regretfully, because there were more and more rumors that assured that in Hispania there were not a few who were more inclined towards a stable government, even if it was barbarian, than for the disinterest and abandonment that provided them a Rome only worried about collecting the disproportionate taxes corresponding to the *iugatio capitalino*, and the *annona militaris*, the annual tax that contributed to the maintenance of the army. The Hispano-Romans paid their tributes, but Rome didn't protect them from their enemies, abandoning them to their fate. They wondered why they should maintain an army that didn't help them when they needed their help. It was reasonable that the disaffection that Hispanics felt for the Empire was on the rise after each barbarian invasion.

"You will be a group of twenty men, ten Romans and ten Visigoths dressed as *Bagaudae*."

"A surprise attack."

The tribune nodded.

"He must not escape and you must kill all the inhabitants of the village as an example to all those who dare to betray the emperor."

"When?"

"You will leave at dawn and attack before dawn."

"As you command, *domine*."

The tribune nodded and left under a blanket of water.

It was a dark night and it was cold. The stubborn rain had granted us a little respite, and gradually the exhausted clouds melted into languid swirls that faded away, swallowed up by a black sky dotted with palpitating, timid stars. Dressed in rags, covered with coarse goatskins or threadbare blankets, and with our faces smeared with blight and mud, we formed the chosen Romans and Visigoths to capture the traitor.

"Remember, there must be no witnesses; old men, women and children must die."

We rubbed our chilled bodies while the Visigoth officer who commanded us drew a rough map of a village in a mud.

"According to our scouts, the traitor is here," he said, pointing with a stick at a hut drawn in the mud. "The Romans will surround the town making sure there are no lookouts." He looked up and looked at us to make sure we understood him. We nodded with a shrug and he was satisfied. "We will catch him and bring him to camp," he continued. "When we have captured him, you will kill the villagers."

"How many?" one of the Romans asked.

In his eyes I read that he wasn't enthusiastic about the idea of killing Hispano-Romans, no matter how treacherous they were. After all, all they wanted was to protect their family from him. The imperial troops were too far from their lands and the Suevian army too close.

"What difference does it make?" the Visigoth replied with contempt. "You kill everyone you see."

"I ask because there are only ten of us," the legionary insisted.

"Are you Romans not even capable of killing a group of unarmed women?"

The Visigoths laughed maliciously.

"Anyway, some of us will give you a hand if the traitor doesn't cause us too much trouble," the barbarian graciously conceded.

"Thank you for your generosity," agreed the *miles*, before the pleased look of the Visigoth, who must not have understood the sarcasm.

I smiled at the legionary's audacity.

"If there are no more questions… go ahead," the Visigoth ordered.

The night hid us with its black cloak and we walked almost without seeing where we were stepped on. Small torches guided our uncertain steps. The silence was almost total, being only interrupted by the sound of some owl or the wet dead leaves that crunched under our footsteps. So we walked for an hour until we came to a hill.

"Look," said the Visigoth officer, pointing to some huts looming further down in a small valley.

"There is little left until dawn, we must hurry," observed another barbarian, before the agreement of the one who commanded us.

As ordered by the Visigoth officer, we set out to surround the village to make sure there were no lookouts. The sun was about to break behind the mountains, there was no time to lose. With extreme stealth, we crossed the town, which was made up of just eight stone and straw huts. A dog barked at us and a voice came from a cabin that silenced him. We looked at each other nervously with our hearts pounding. The mud reached up to our ankles and made it difficult for us to step. Suddenly, a door opened and an old woman came out. We hide behind a hut without being seen. The old woman walked around the hut, lifted her skirt, and began to urinate. We looked at each other and smiled. When she finished she went back into the house.

"I think there are no lookouts," said a legionary.

"I agree. Now this is the plan," I started to say. "We will divide into groups of two. Each couple will stand behind a hut, when the Visigoths capture the traitor, we will enter them and kill everyone inside. The three houses in the center will be attacked by those who finish first."

The legionaries looked at the ground, they hadn't been trained to kill women and children while they slept, and the very idea disgusted them exceedingly. But we were obeying orders. Once again, we had to swallow our principles, even if it burned our guts and we ran the risk of becoming one of those barbarians we so loathed.

"Come on guys; remember it's for the good of Rome," I tried to encourage, without much conviction.

"I'll go warn the barbarians that there are no lookouts," said a legionary.

"Well, the rest of us will go to the huts. When you report to the Visigoths, go to the hut that is further west. Your partner will wait for you there."

The *miles* nodded and left, lost in the thick of the forest.

We split into pairs and, in silence, we headed towards the huts. There we remained hidden, waiting several minutes until a slight noise from the forest warned us of the arrival of the Visigoths. The officer greeted me and nodded when he passed me, then, accompanied by the barbarians, he headed towards the hut where the traitor was. It was beginning to dawn.

The door of another hut opened. This time a young man came out, it seemed that he was about to urinate. He walked around his house, but something behind him caught his attention and he headed towards a neighboring shack.

"They attack us!" he yelled in horror, opening the cabin door. He had seen the group of Visigoths.

A legionary ran towards him to silence him. The boy ran like a soul that the devil carries, crying out loud. Men armed with canes, hoes, and sticks began to emerge from the huts. The Visigoths, not knowing what to do, entered the house where the traitor was hiding.

"They're bandits, let's go get them!" a burly peasant yelled, brandishing a menacing stick.

Several men followed him. For a moment, we didn't know what to do. It seemed that the mission was doomed. The Visigoths came out of a house dragging the inert body of a man. The sun was lighting up a new day and more men and women came out of the huts carrying any object that could be brandished as a weapon. They fell on the Visigoths who defended themselves as best they could from the crowd. There would be about twenty who prevented the kidnapping of the traitor. The Romans remained quiet, hidden behind the huts avoiding making the slightest noise, attentive to how events were unfolding.

"They are Visigoths disguised as *Bagaudae!*" a man shouted who had just finished off one of the barbarians.

"Let's search the surroundings, there are sure to be more!"

His words alerted us. One of the legionaries unable to stand the tension any longer, fled, giving away his position. Several peasants ran after him, catching up with him a few steps away. A brutal blow to the head ended his life.

Suddenly the earth shook under our feet. The peasants looked at each other for an explanation, but it didn't take long to find the cause. Along a muddy road, several hundred horsemen burst into the village, swords at the ready, to the surprise of the villagers who did not expect the sudden attack. Now they were the ones running for safety. Taking advantage of the arrival of the Visigoths, we came out of our hiding place and gave a good account of the fleeing population. For much of the fray we were hidden and did not show any sign of presence until the arrival of the barbarian horsemen. And now we were about to cut down the lives of some Hispano-Romans who were fleeing in terror. It was not a brave or heroic act, but in those confused times bravery and honor were nothing more than a masked fraud, a grotesque lie dressed with beautiful gestures and sweet words. The noblest virtues were as questionable as the supposed purity of a girl after being abandoned to a horde of barbarians. The only important thing was to stay alive. Everything else was of no consideration. Scruples were a luxury we could do without.

The piercing howls of pain and distress were confused with the galloping of horses and the crunching of bones and broken skulls. The huts were set on fire and a thick white smoke enveloped the village. The sun's rays illuminated a red mire of spilled blood. I rushed upon a man that was running into the forest, and without a second thought I slit his throat. Then I went for another, and another and another... The corpses piled up and were trampled by the horses' hooves. In the confusion, I watched as a horseman grabbed a man by the legs and clutched him to his horse.

A boy came out of a hut and stood still in the middle of the mud. He was crying inconsolably.

"The time has come," said a familiar voice.

Through the smoke, the figure of a Visigoth horseman emerged. His sword was unsheathed and he was riding at full speed towards the little boy.

"No!" shouted a woman running towards the child.

I looked at her and a cold shiver like the breath of death ran through my body. The woman reached the child, hiding him under the protective cover of her arms. I ran towards them. The barbarian was close behind. He spurred his horse fiercely and raised his sword. I immediately recognized his blond whiskers and amber eyes. Unable to reach the woman and the little boy, I rushed toward the barbarian's horse. I had only one chance and I had to take it. I swung my sword and with a single slash I severed one of the sorrel's hind legs. The horse uttered a wild whinny full of pain and rolled shockingly on the ground, dragging the Germanic in his fall, and leaving him badly wounded, inanimate on the mud. I approached him and found that, although he had lost consciousness, he was still alive. His pagan gods had protected him from certain death. The German had his helmet crushed and a trickle of blood ran down his dirty with mud and sweat forehead. The horse, in its terrible fall, had broken its neck, thus putting an end to what would have been a slow agony. I looked at the woman, who had not stopped protecting the child for an instant. I ran to them and put them in a safe place, hiding them behind some ferns. We were silent until the Visigoths left. Walder, the one I could see, was lying limp on the ground.

"Hello, Alana," I said with my voice cracking with emotion.

An endless number of emotions bubbled in my heart, and my hands trembled like those of a young boy ready to savor his first kiss of love. I had hundreds, thousands of questions to ask him, but above all there was one that particularly tormented my spirit: why he abandoned me when we arrived in Lugdunum, without granting me even a few brief words of love, or at least of affection or encouragement. But his presence and that of the little boy dispelled my doubts and insecurities, and I chose to live that magical moment with intensity and joy.

"Hello, Adriano."

"Mom, is it dad?" the boy asked, pointing a finger at me.

Alana didn't need to reply. The little boy had his mother's eyes, but his ears and nose were undoubtedly his father's. I picked him up in my arms and hugged him. His little arms wrapped around my neck and I felt the pleasant candor of his face on my face. I felt an indescribable emotion. My eyes moistened and I kissed him. Alana watched us excitedly and tears streamed down her beautiful face. I was happy, exultant, I had recovered Alana, and, in addition, I had found the wonderful gift of a son.

"What's your name, little one?"

"Adriano."

I couldn't contain the tears, which flowed from my eyes like a mighty torrent filled with water after the storm. I hugged Alana and so, wrapped in a sea of tears, we stayed for several minutes. We didn't want to break such a wonderful and unexpected moment.

"We're finally together and we'll never be apart again," I finally said.

"But the druid..."

"He misinterpreted the omens, forget it," I interrupted. "You are my family and I won't allow anyone to separate us."

My son smiled and hugged me tightly when he heard my words.

"Have you noticed how much he loves me? And he hardly knows me!" I exclaimed proudly.

Alana smiled.

"It's true, the boy adores you."

"How could he don't? I'm his father!" I said, full of happiness. "We will flee from these lands and go to some distant place, away from wars and misfortunes."

Alana hesitated, the druid's omen surfacing in her mind. She looked at the little boy who was still clinging to my neck. She was confused and indecisive: she didn't want to break the child's heart by separating him from her father, but she in turn, as a druid woman, had great confidence in premonitions, auspices and divinations.

"Lughdyr misinterpreted the omen; remember that he said that we would meet when I was at death's door and that you would free me from its clutches. He was wrong," I said vehemently.

"Your beloved will come back to free you from her clutches... that's exactly what he said..." Alana whispered. "... What if... what if your loved one wasn't I?"

Her face was contorted and her forehead was wrinkled. The doubts and the inner struggle she suffered were intense, devastating, and cruel. I must intercede for her, for our love. Illuminate the tortuous path of uncertainty through which she traveled, guiding her towards the path of truth... of my truth...

"It is you, my love, only you. We both know it," I started to say. "My love, tell me, tell me how it is possible that we would have found each other in this lost village if it weren't for the *fatum's* willingness to do so. Let us not seek an explanation for what doesn't t have it. The important thing... the really important thing is that we get back together. Listen to your heart as I listen to mine. They do not lie; feelings are the only certainty, the last refuge in this damned world flooded with the miasma of hatred and death." I pointed to the village engulfed by flames and the lifeless bodies of the peasants, scattered in a blood-red quagmire. "Believe in me, in us and nothing and no one will be able to separate us."

A bitter smile appeared on her lips and she averted her eyes to the floor.

"My heart loves you more than my life, but..."

"Think of the child, think of me..., together we will be happy," I insisted.

"Where will we go?"

"The place is the least important, as long as it is far from the war. Our home will be wherever we are together." I was euphoric, it seemed that after all my efforts, I had convinced her. "Whether it is the highest peak, the deepest abyss, the most inhospitable island, a wasteland or an orchard, what does it matter? We will be together and that is the most important thing!"

Still hugging the child, I approached Alana and kissed her. Her warm tears wet my face. I caressed her cheek. Her face was veiled in doubt, but her gaze betrayed that she loved me and had always loved me. My heart was pounding in my chest with an immense joy.

"We'd better go," I said, trying to shake off the indecision and uncertainty that had settled in her mind like a firm and unshakable foundation.

The cawing of a crow startled us. Suddenly, a black bird flew over our heads.

"I won't allow it!" I growled, leaving the little one on the ground and drawing my *spatha*.

Adriano looked at us without understanding what was happening.

"No one will separate me from my family!" I shouted to the crow.

The bird landed on a nearby branch, I drew my *pugio* with the intention of silencing, once and for all, its infernal squawks. The crow stared at me defiantly. Its pupils, as black as blight, reflected a human figure and it was not precisely mine. I gripped the dagger tightly but a strange energy prevented me from throwing it at my target. I was captivated its gaze. Then Alana exclaimed some words in a strange language and the bird took flight and lost itself in the thicket.

"What did you say to it?" I asked confused.

"I ordered it to go back to its master, we don't need it here."

I kissed her again. The morning was well advanced and the sun was shining on a beautiful day.

"What was that bird?" the little boy asked.

"Nothing, son, it was just a devil's envoy."

My answer didn't please Alana who professed a blind devotion for the druid. She reproved me with her eyes and I had to apologize.

"I'm sorry... it's just a little bird looking for a friend," I told the little one, who smiled at my inventiveness. "Now we'd better go."

"Where?" Alana asked.

"We'll go to Saguntum, where my family lives. Then we'll board a ship that will take us to Greece or Egypt."

"It's a long trip."

"I know, but the reward is well worth it."

Alana nodded.

A noise from the thick forest caught our attention. Startled, I reached for my sword and shielded my son and Alana, putting them behind my back. A flock of black birds emerged from the beech and oak trees. They uttered deafening squawks that hurt our eardrums. In pain, we covered our ears. In the meantime, hundreds of birds surrounded us and perched on the branches of the trees.

"What's wrong, mom?" my terrified son asked, clinging tightly to his mother's arms.

"We're lost," Alana muttered, aware of what was happening.

"What do you mean?" I asked alertly.

She didn't answer me and with her right arm she pointed to the thicket. The birds perched on the branches of the nearest trees. The crows stopped cawing and a deep silence enveloped the forest. Alana was still absorbed, pointing at some bushes with her gaze lost. I watched the birds around us. In their black eyes I saw the image of sinister figures. A black cloud, arising from some enchanted spell, hid the sun, and a thick, dense fog rose from the ground and, in a short time, hid us with its cold mantle. I could hardly see more than a few paces. I hugged Alana and the little boy tightly. My sword was tightly clutched, ready to prevent anyone from separating me from my family, whether they were hundreds or thousands of wizards, soothsayers, sorcerers, witches or druids. No one could take my family from me. No one.

"She doesn't belong to you," a voice from out of the darkness boomed.

"Go away, you cursed sons of Lucifer!" I shouted defiantly.

"She is Nature's child, and must return to her service," said another voice.

"I won't allow you to part me from Alana and my son. I love them more than my life, and I will kill anyone who dares to come near us."

Out of the darkness, several figures began to appear and surrounded us, preventing us from fleeing. They wore white robes, carried long staffs and hid their heads with hoods.

"She is a druid-woman, born to serve Mother Nature in love, kindness and charity," said one of the sorcerers.

"You don't know what love is, what kindness is or what charity is!" I exclaimed furiously. "You speak of Mother Nature, but you don't know what her essence is, you are nothing more than wolves dressed in sheepskins, hypocrites who don't hesitate to enslave a woman and separate a child from her father to achieve your dark purposes. You're just a bunch of old lunatics!"

One of the witcher approached us, I immediately identified Lughdyr. He walked towards us with outstretched arm.

"Come with me, my daughter," the witcher said in a hollow voice from another world.

I felt how Alana separated from me and enchanted by the words of the witcher headed towards him. I took her by the shoulders and shook her back so that she came around. She looked at me and I saw in horror how her eyes were completely white.

"A... Alana," I stammered.

"Let me go, I must go back with them," she whispered.

"Don't! I exclaimed, grabbing her tightly. You are haunted!"

"Your efforts are useless, she belongs to us."

The witcher's words inflamed me, my heart was filled with anger and I wanted, with all my might, to drive my sword into his chest and stain his immaculate tunic with the red color of his blood.

"Dad, let us go."

A chill ran through my body when I heard my son's words. Like Alana, his eyes had lost their color and turned completely white. They had both been bewitched.

"No, my son, I won't allow these sorcerers to separate us. I won't allow it!" I exclaimed, hugging him tightly.

"You can do nothing," Lughdyr replied, raising his arms to the sky.

"Our love is more powerful than your black magic!"

I hugged Alana, who was trying to get away from me and march towards the witcher. The darkness was dissipating, and timid rays of sunlight illuminated the forest. It seemed that we had defeated the wizards.

"She is not from your world. Fate..." said Lughdyr.

"Fate is written, but we have a chance to change it!" I interrupted, remembering his own words.

"That's why you're here today, and you've saved Alana's life and your son's. It is possible that in the future you'll see them again, but your meeting will be fleeting, as each of you must continue on your own path."

"I love them and I will never part with them," I replied.

"That is not in your hand."

The fog lifted and the figures of dozens of warlocks became visible. They were all old men with long beards and white robes. Alana and my son were still spellbound with their eyes rolling. I held them tightly, preventing them from escaping to Lughdyr, but suddenly I was seized by an unfathomable weakness, and my strength left me. Exhausted, I fell to my knees. The last thing I remember was how Alana and my son got lost in the thick of the forest followed by the witches. Then a deep darkness enveloped me. Before losing consciousness, I felt the soft caress of a sad tear run down my cheek.

I woke up and they had disappeared. I looked for them in the forest but could not find them. Submerged in a sea of despair, I sat on a rock and wept bitterly. When I had no more tears to shed, I got up and walked towards the remains of the village. I felt like my body and my soul underwent a terrible transformation. I clenched my fists and jaw, and a deep hatred was born in my heart. My muscles were tense, contracted with arousal. There was only space in my mind for one purpose: to find my family, and if this meant killing every Druid in my path, then so be it. God would gladly bless me for exterminating that string of heathens and sorcerers. I hated them with all my might: they had separated me from my family, and made the happiest day of my life the most sad and painful. He would kill them all, and they would pay with their blood for all the damage they had caused me.

The German was lying on a quagmire of blood and mud. I walked over to him and found that he was still breathing. Still not knowing why, I got him on a horse that was wandering disoriented and we started our way back to the camp. We arrived just as they were preparing to leave. My companions greeted me with shouts of joy and claps of thanks. Both Visigoths and Romans thought we were dead. I had a lost look, I was not aware of what was happening around me. My heart cried, moaned, howled invaded by immeasurable pain. My eyes burned with terrible tears of fire. I stopped being a man to become a monster, a soulless being driven by an insatiable desire for revenge.

"Good work, Adriano."

The one who spoke was Constantius Trebius, who received me with a big smile.

"Get off your horse and rest, you look terrible."

The good man of the tribune didn't know it very well. I dismounted without saying a word. The German was in charge of the Visigoths.

"Are you okay?" a worried Constantius Trebius asked me.

"Perfectly, I just need to rest."

"What happened in the village?"

I looked at him not providing an answer and walked towards my tent. I was grateful that it had not yet been disassembled.

"You can rest for a couple of hours, we'll delay our departure!" The tribune yelled, but I didn't bother to turn my back to thank him for the gesture.

Like a ghost I wandered towards my store. At first the *milites* greeted me and congratulated me on my return. However, I was the only legionary who had made it back safely. But my serious and contracted countenance alarmed them. They stopped greeting me and limited themselves to flanking the path. There were few who considered that that fateful day I made a pact with the devil himself or that I was possessed by some demon or spell. Some claimed that I had died and returned from hell in exchange for selling my soul to Lucifer himself. Fantastic stories that the passage of time would take care of, erasing from the memory of the most credulous and ignorant.

A Visigoth woke me up, freeing me from a recurring nightmare that would haunt me for years. Theodoric required my presence. I washed myself in a bucket and dressed in the military tunic and a coat of mail. I was led into his presence escorted by his *spatharii*. Theodoric received me seated on a wooden throne covered with sheets of gold and precious stones. He had undergone a major change from the barbarian whom I fought with a few years ago in Maurica. His gestures were more refined and his bearing, as good old Calerus would say, more Romanized. He had a shaved face, short hair, and wore a military robe similar to that of Roman magistrates. To his right was Sisemundo, the commander of the Visigoths, a powerful warrior with a tight, sullen face. To his left, scowling was tribune Constantius Trebius.

"So it was you who saved the life of the captain of my *spatharii*," said the Visigoth king, just bowing to him. "Who would have guessed that the person Walder wanted to take his life would be his savior."

"The designs of the good Lord are inscrutable," I said, concluding that my relationship with the German was known by all Visigoths.

"It's true, sometimes fate shows us its most... ironic side," observed the king.

I clenched my jaws; I couldn't bear hearing about fate.

"I have summoned you to personally thank you for saving the life of the best of my soldiers. I'm sure he'll do the same when he recovers from his condition."

"How is he?" I asked out of courtesy, in truth the life of the German was completely indifferent to me.

"He has suffered a severe blow on his head, but physicists believe that he will recover."

"I'm glad," I lied.

The Visigoth king smiled, not very convinced of my happiness.

"I consider your heroic act worthy of recognition," said the king, rising from his throne. "I have consulted with Constantius Trebius." he looked at him and he nodded, "and he has agreed to my wish to appoint you *ducenarius* of the *palatina legio.*"

At any other time, that promotion would have filled me with joy, but when you are separated from the woman you love and your child, any news, good or bad, was of relative importance. Still, I forced a grateful smile and nodded accepting the position.

"I'm sure you will serve Rome with honor in your new position," said Constantius Trebius.

"Defending it from all its enemies," I added, looking at the Visigoth king.

"That's fine; loyalty is an increasingly rare commodity in these difficult times," Theodoric said with a harsh smile. Surely in his mind sprang the tragic death of his brother Turismund, killed by himself or by one of his henchmen.

"Now go and get ready for the march Salvio Adriano, we will leave in a short time," said the tribune.

I said goodbye to the *Gothorum rex* with a nod of my head, and returned to my tent. There a *biarchus* was waiting for me with my new uniform. I think I was the last to know of my promotion.

We continued our march through Gallaecia in pursuit of the coward Requiario. We ravaged several villages on our way, and in all of them I asked about wizards, sorcerers and druids, but I always got the same answer: the false deities had been expelled from those lands thanks to the priceless work of the Christian monks. If I wanted to find the druids, I had to head further west. According to what I was assured, their villages were full of legends of witches, goblins, sorcerers and other heretics. There, possibly, my family was to be found. And we were heading west when, on the third day before October noon, we came across the *Suevorum rex*.

He had no time to escape and prepared his troops a few miles from the city of Asturica Augusta. The battlefield was a large esplanade bathed by a river named Urbicus and dotted with small hills. A perfect place for the maneuvers of our infantry and for the charges of the Visigoth cavalry. Either the Suevian king had prepared some stratagem, or his end would be very near.

We met the Suevians on a cool autumn day, where the sun remained hidden behind leaden and threatening clouds. I inspected my *milites*. During the short time I had been their superior, I knew how to gain their trust and respect. Something very complicated when it comes to war veterans. I was a man of few words, quick decisions and accurate thrusts, everything an officer needs to be respected and obeyed. In the sky I saw an eagle fly over the Suevian troops, and I smiled. If I were superstitious or trusted in deceitful omens, I would have considered it a good auspiciousness.

We legionaries occupied the rear of the allied army, so the brunt of the campaign would be borne by the Visigothic, Burgundian and Franks *foederati*. Although the objective was to definitively expel the Suevians from our borders, we were little more than mere observers. A battle for Rome but without Roman soldiers.

Theodoric led the center of the formation, while Franks and Burgundians flanked him. The sound of the tubas and the *litui* of war, on both sides, burst with a thunderous roar on the battlefield, scaring away all kinds of birds that flew through the sky in search of a safer place to shelter.

Constantius Trebius, mounted on his sturdy warhorse, led the way. On his restless sorrel, he checked that each of the units that made up our legion was well equipped and prepared for combat. Once he was sure that everything was correct, he looked at the Visigoth king and nodded. Theodoric gave an order to his aide-de-camp and he obeyed immediately.

"Roman allies!" shouted the aide-de-camp. "Forward"

Surprisingly, the federates outflanked us, allowing our advance to the vanguard of the army. Theodoric must have considered that it was our war and that the more Romans perished in it the better for his interests. Once we were in the front line of combat, the tribune raised his hand and directed it towards the enemy; then we marched against them. Shoulder to shoulder, shield to shield, legionary to legionary, each of the ten units was a compact, impassable structure, a machine created to kill and destroy. So, it had been for hundreds of years and thousands of battles. And now the Suevian king would witness the devastating power of the fearsome Roman legions.

We were a few hundred paces from the Suevians when a rain of arrows and javelins fell upon us, the *ducenarii* ordered the formation of a wall of shields and we felt how the darts and spears stuck in our shield. We stopped our advance for a few moments, a moment that our enemies took advantage of to send in their horsemen. From the small opening between my shield and that of my companion, I saw how hundreds of Swabian horsemen were heading towards us, brandishing swords and pikes, raising an immense column of dust. My detachment was the most advanced and therefore the first to receive the enemy attack.

"Prepare your javelins!" I ordered.

The legionaries armed their javelins behind their shields. The ground groaned under the enemy gallop. The Suevians horsemen were heading inexorably towards us, like a colossal and furious flood, threatening to crush us with the hooves of their horses, sweeping us away in their path.

"Wait for my order!" I shouted, gripping my javelin tightly.

My heart was pounding in my chest, and I seemed to feel the heartbeat of the two hundred men who made up my unit. They were veterans, seasoned soldiers, protagonists in dozens of battles. The legionaries of each numerus had to think as one, act as one and fight as one. There was no place for individualism, the life of each legionary depended on the companion next to him. Protecting him meant protecting oneself. This was the difference between victory and defeat, between life and death.

The Suevians spurred their horses more virulently and pointed their weapons at our formation. A gentle wind brought with it the smell of their horses and their own sweat. The time had come.

"Legionaries!" I exclaimed. "Now!"

In a single, precise, thousand-times-trained movement, two hundred soldiers pushed aside our shield, stood up, and threw our javelin at the enemy, who was at close range. Then, with lightning speed, we returned to take cover behind our shield. Not a few horses and horsemen were wounded with our javelins. Due to the inertia of the ride, many Suevians fell before our feet being finished off with our *spatha*. Through the slit of my shield I noticed that the Suevian horsemen, terrified by such ferocious carnage, stopped their charge. The one who commanded them looked around confused, not knowing what decision to make. A crass mistake. If a captain orders a cavalry charge, the cavalry must advance towards the enemy to the last consequences. On the battlefield there is no place for indecision. If a captain hesitates, his men die. It is as simple as that.

So it was. Theodoric, attentive to the indecision of the Suevian commander, ordered his archers to pour out their quivers on the enemy horsemen. We, protected behind our shield, received the odd Suevian bolt, but they collided ineffectively against our protections. But hundreds of Suevians fell dejected, skewered by thousands of Visigoth arrows. Defeated, few were those who managed to flee, protecting themselves behind the rear.

"Forward!" I ordered. "¡Roma invicta est! ¡Roma invicta est! [Rome is invincible!]" I shouted, and my voice evoked the memory of Publius Cornelius Scipio, of Aetius, of Julius Caesar, of Hadrian, of Trajan, of Aurelian and of so many emperors and generals whose immortal exploits glorified the Empire. My cry was seconded by the voices of hundreds of legionaries and echoed through the air with the cry of victory and glory. We were not legionaries, but proud heroes of a long-forgotten time, as were Achilles and Hector, Priamo and Agamemnon, Aeneas and Ajax. Zeus, stormy, would watch us blissfully from the heavens, as he beheld the Priamid Hector fight against the Peleid Achilles.

Two hundred soldiers, followed by the rest of the *palatina legio*, and surrounded by the barbarian foederati, we advanced trampling the dead and finishing off the wounded. Requiario, disconcerted, ordered the advance of his infantry. Thousands of Suevian soldiers advanced toward us, striking the shields with their swords in a terrifying roar.

"Hold formation!" I ordered, as we marched towards the barbarians.

The Suevian, inflamed at the sight of the red ground littered with their dead comrades, charged at us with an atrocious force, and clashed with a roar against our shields. A melee ensued. Chaos took over the battlefield. We held formation long enough for the Visigoth horsemen to enter the scene. Sisemundo on the left and Theodoric on the right surrounded the Suevian who soon found themselves trapped and with no way out. Requiario, unable to recognize defeat, sent his last troops and his own personal guard to the aid of his cornered infantrymen. The Suevian king did not lack courage, for he himself commanded them.

Unable to maintain our defensive formation any longer, we broke through the shield wall and charged the Suevian, who, feeling trapped, fought fiercely. On the battlefield, in the heat of battle, there is no fear, there is no terror, and sometimes there is not even prudence. The excitement of battle turns us into irrational, bloodthirsty animals. Cutting down lives, severing limbs, feeling the warm blood of the defeated enemy splashing on your face, more than a duty, it was a pleasure. And my *milites* were prone to be swept away by such delight.

Several Suevians fell pierced by the edge of my *spatha*. As if possessed by Mars, I punished every one with my sword at will, snatching lives and widowing Suevian. The ground became slippery with blood and it was difficult not to step on a dead or severed limbs. A Suevian attacked me with a large double-edged ax. I managed to stop his attack by protecting myself with my shield, but I stumbled and fell to the ground. Defeated, the Suevian pounced on me, impatient to deliver a fatal blow to a Roman officer. And so it would have happened if it hadn't been for the sudden appearance of a Germanic giant who, mounted on a mighty war horse, pierced him through with his sword, the sharp and bloody point protruding from his sternum.

"I'm no longer indebted to you. Roman!" Walder shouted from his horse with a terrible smile, showing a string of yellow teeth. I thanked him for his help with a nod.

The din of an enemy charge caught our attention. The Suevian king, persuaded that the battle was lost, launched one last attack with the few horsemen that still protected him. The German and I exchanged a knowing look. Walder spurred his horse and headed for the *Suevorum rex*. I looked around for a mount. I was lucky, a few steps away there was a Suevian rider fighting with a Burgundian. I ran towards him and managed to dismount him. After slaughtering him, I mounted his horse and rode swiftly toward Requiario. But Walder arrived earlier. Protected by his personal guard, the Suevian king defended himself bravely, but we were far superior and the German one forcefully got rid of every Suevian that stood in his way. I spurred my horse, but it was very slow. While I, helplessly, spurred on the horse that had been my lot, Walder easily got rid of two royal guards and was already fighting Requiario. He had won me the game. Cornered, dejected, and without any hope of victory, the Suevian king turned his mount and began to retreat. But Walder cleverly managed to hit him on the back. A wounded Requiario managed to flee to the rear, while several of his personal guards protected his retreat. Walder didn't give up and continued the chase, but the Suevian were very numerous, and he was forced to give up. We had defeated the Suevian, but his king had managed to escape from our clutches.

The victory was overwhelming and the dead on the enemy side could be counted by thousands. But the objective of the campaign hadn't been completed: Requiario had managed to flee. After the battle, Theodoric summoned the staff and I, by order of the tribune, was authorized to participate in it. We were summoned to the *praetorium*. There were the best and most illustrious warriors who were part of the army. All of them headed by King Theodoric himself. Few hours had elapsed since the battle, but we were as fresh as if we had enjoyed a day of hunting or played an entertaining game of dice. Victories infuse renewed vigor into the exhausted bodies of the victors. We took seats on wooden benches and some servants brought us some cold food and watered wine to satisfy our hunger. The *Gothorum rex* was happy, and he was enjoying a chicken thigh.

"Gentlemen, I congratulate you on this great victory," he said when he had finished swallowing a generous piece of chicken.

Those present, including Walder, nodded gratefully.

"What is more," added the king, rising from his footstool, "Requiario's flight will justify our incursion into Suevian lands." He began walking around the room. "We are talking about a criminal who has assaulted the Roman regions of Carthaginiense and Tarraconense and mistreated the ambassadors sent by Rome to negotiate peace. I understand that Emperor Avitus would have no objection," he added, looking at the tribune.

Constantius Trebius didn't lack much time to understand the true intentions of the Visigoth. Even so, he had no choice but to give in.

"The Suevian king is a danger to Rome... and also to our Visigoth allies," he said, looking at Theodoric. "His extermination will be beneficial for both nations."

"Indeed, we will go to the very heart of Gallaecia if necessary to find him," said the king, before the cheers of the federated officers.

The Visigoth's purpose pleased me. My objective was to find Alana and my son, and I could only achieve it if we remained in Gallaecia where, I was convinced, they were being held by the sorcerers.

After several more minutes of discussion, the decision was made to leave for the southwest. We agreed that Requiario had fled to the city of Portu Cale. From there he had direct access to the sea and if he managed to board a ship, we would probably have lost his trail forever.

Satisfied with the meeting, the Visigoths left the *praetorium*. The tribune and I, the only Roman representatives, left last. I was about to walk through the door when a hand gripped my shoulder tightly. I turned and could see the Germanic's yellow eyes. The tribune tried to intervene, but I made a gesture to reassure him and smiled.

"Calm down, *domine,* we are old friends."

"It is true, *domine.* Very, very good friends," the Germanic said sarcastically.

"I'll see you at the *castrum*, in a few minutes I'll join you," I said to Constantius Trebius, who went away unconvinced.

"We are at peace, Roman. You saved my life and I saved yours," said the German.

"I don't think so," I replied, remembering the attack on the *Bagaudae*.

The German spat on the ground.

"We were fighting and a bastard *Bagaudae* interrupted us, that was all."

"What do you want?" I asked, disgusted by his presence.

"We are allies and as long as this situation continues, I won't fight with you. But one day Visigoths and Romans will be enemies. Then I'll look for you and you can be sure that I'll find you."

"I'll wait impatiently for that moment." I turned my back on him and headed toward the Roman camp.

"Adriano!" he yelled.

He surprised me when he called me by my name. I stopped without turning around.

"But I have no agreement with your Suevian bitch and if I find her, I assure you that I'll recognize her and know very well what to do with her crotch! Ha, ha, ha!"

For a moment I was tempted to turn and skewer him with my sword, but I managed to restrain myself. I clenched my fists and continued on my way, leaving behind the German laughing out loud.

Walder's threat worried me I knew that the barbarian was capable of the most heinous atrocities. I had to find Alana and my son before he did, or their future would be quiet uncertain. But where could I look for them? I was in unknown lands full of myths and legends, where the supernatural was confused with the daily, without in many cases, discerning any difference. Stories of witches, goblins, powerful wizards and even dragons were told throughout the Suevian's heretical lands who had accepted Arianism, including Catholicism after the conversion of Requiario himself, but without completely denying their pagan beliefs and superstitions. I had been myself a witness of several-difficult-to-explain events and my skepticism towards everything supernatural had begun to unravel. The thick forests and their haunting sounds, the crystal clear whispering streams, the gentle howling of the wind, its scent… all of Gallaecia was mysterious and enigmatic.

"What did that barbarian tell you?"

Immersed in my musings, I arrived at the Roman camp where a worried Constantius Trebius, whom I hadn't noticed until I bumped into him, was waiting for me. I hesitated to tell him the truth, but I preferred to remain silent. It would be too embarrassing to explain to the tribune that my beloved Suevian and my son, whose existence I hadn't known until recently, had been kidnapped by a group of old druids in white robes.

"We have had a score to settle for years and we can't wait to settle it," I answered.

"He seems dangerous," observed the tribune.

"He is."

We broke camp and continued along the southern road towards Bracara Augusta. We arrived at a small village made up of several stone and straw huts scattered along the banks of a crystal clear stream. There we were greeted by more than terrified villagers, who, unable to escape, bought their lives in exchange of betraying the path their king had taken. As we concluded, Requiario was heading towards Portu Cale.

We camped five *stadiums* away from the village. It was cool in those lands and hundreds of fires warmed our terrified bodies and illuminated the dark night. Restless, I inspected the guard and then made my way to one of the huts. In it lived the man who had identified himself as the village chief. I knocked on the door and a woman with a tired face and fearful eyes opened it.

"My name is Salvio Adriano and I'm an officer in the Roman army. I'm here to see your husband," I said around the door.

"Open up, woman," a male voice ordered.

The Suevian obeyed and I entered the hut. Round in plan, it was built of stone with a braided heather roof. A fire, placed in the center provided some warmth to the room, and at the same time heated a soup of onions and garlic, which would serve to deceive the hunger of the whole family.

"Welcome to my house," said the man, trying to appear serene, which he lacked.

"Thank you," I said, sitting down on a pile of clean straw that the woman, very kindly, had diligently prepared for me.

Gomado had six children, since that was the name of the leader of the miserable village. The oldest was no more than ten years old, and the youngest was only a few months old. All of them were dirty and malnourished. They wore threadbare clothes and looked at me with a mixture of fascination and fear. Gomado was a young man, although he was aged as a result of the harsh conditions of the place. Barren and rocky, the Suevian lands demanded a high price for every grain of wheat or rye its inhabitants were able to extract from its greedy soil. His wife was extremely thin. She walked with a limp and half a stoop. Some disease or the malnutrition that also affected her children had taken its toll on her, leaving her half crippled for the rest of her life. The man handed me a bowl of soup which I refused, the poor wretch already had too many mouths to feed to take care of mine as well. I opened my saddlebag and handed him a loaf of wheat bread and a piece of cheese. Gomado looked at me gratefully, and divided it between his wife and children, who ate with appetite and delight.

"You may be wondering why I came," I said when I saw that he was partially satiated.

The man answered me with a nod of his head.

"Myths and legends abound in this land," I continued. "I have heard of certain wizards you call druids, who use their skills to heal the sick and alleviate some of the ills that overwhelm you."

"If myths fed us, my children would be as fat as the lords who command us," Gomado replied, not hiding certain resentment.

"Don't you believe in them?"

184

"Wizards, witches, sorcerers or druids are part of our customs," he acknowledged.

"So, they exist?"

"Yes."

"Have you seen any of them or witnessed their spells or wonders?"

Gomado looked at me with distrust, as if he were before a Christian monk eager to wrest him from the clutches of paganism.

"Don't be afraid, your beliefs and customs are indifferent to me," I assured him.

"She is a living example of their power," he said, pointing to his wife.

I looked at him in intrigue as the woman tried to hide behind her creatures.

"What do you mean?"

The peasant closed his eyes as if searching in his memory for distant, almost forgotten memories. His mind must have flown far away, since it took him several minutes to open his mouth.

"It was a cold winter night. My wife was writhing in pain from a complicated childbirth, but her screams were veiled by a strong storm. Outside, snow surrounded us and the blizzard prevented her from taking a single step to call for help. I could barely see beyond my nose. My wife was dying and I could do nothing to stop it. Then he appeared."

The woman shifted uneasily, uncomfortable at her husband's statement. I looked more closely at the hut and noticed that it was adorned with leaves and branches of mistletoe, yew, and oak. In addition, snake heads and animal skulls hung from the ceiling. Although the Suevian were Arian I didn't notice a single sign in the hut that would give away that belief. I was in the house of a fully pagan family.

"Who showed up?"

"The druid."

"Go on," I requested.

"Everyone in the shire knows him; it is common to see him gathering plants and berries in the forest. He only comes to town to cure or alleviate people's suffering. He is a loved and respected man."

"What is his name?"

"Thordor."

I was very disappointed to hear that name. I would have given my right arm to have listened to Lughdyr's one. But maybe this Thordor

185

guy was there the day the Druids took Alana and my son from me, and maybe he could lead me to them. I gestured for Gomado to continue.

"He touched Laira's head with his hand and her pain disappeared," he continued, looking at his wife. "Gently and without taking his eyes off her, he ordered me to put water to heat. I obeyed while he was busy covering her with a blanket, invoking with phrases of magical and unknown origin. I heated the water and brought it to her. Laira's eyes conveyed a pleasant peace and deep calm. The druid continued his intoxicating chants until Laira fell asleep. Then, Thordor, I'm not sure where from, he took out a blanket, hung it from the ceiling, and hid behind it with my wife. He was confused, I did not know what to do, I feared for my wife's life. Suddenly, a purr caught my attention. The purr turned into a loud cry and behind the blanket, the figure of the druid appeared carrying a little boy in his arms. With tears in my eyes, I could see that both my son and my wife were in good condition. Filled with happiness, I hugged them and thanked the druid for all that he had done for my family. Thordor looked at me, smiled, opened the hut door, and was engulfed in the blizzard."

"He is a holy man!" exclaimed the woman.

"Shut up!" the man commanded wrathfully, looking at me with fear.

"Calm down, I have already told you that I'm not here to convert pagans to Christianity," I said to calm him down.

"Then what are you looking for?" asked the woman from her corner.

The woman's question surprised me. Until that moment she had avoided me by hiding behind her children, and now she looked at me with certainty and firmness. I looked into her eyes, black, deep and mysterious. They didn't look like hers. A shudder ran down my back.

"Forget them. If you want them to live, you have to stay away from them," the woman burst out, in a deep, cavernous voice, before her husband's astonished gaze.

"Never!" I exclaimed, turning to her.

"Your presence puts them in danger! Don't you realize that?" The woman asked me in a voice that was not hers.

"Where are they?" I asked, shaking her.

"Let her go!" Gomado exclaimed, throwing himself at me.

I fell to the ground under the peasant's weight. With great effort I managed to free myself from him and approached the woman, but it was too late. In her eyes I saw confusion and fear. The druid had left and abandoned her body.

"Where can I find Thordor?" I asked.

The couple fell silent.

"Where can I find Thordor?!" I cried angrily, drawing my *spatha*.

The children burst into tears, flooding the hut with sobs and wails full of dread. Gomado looked frightened at his wife, and she shook her head. To betray a rich and powerful king but insensitive to the needs of his people was one thing, but to hand over the man who saved the lives of your wife and son was something quite different. In the man's eyes I could see the pain that his decision was going to cause him, but he was aware that he had no other choice if he wanted to stay alive. With his head bowed, he turned to me and told me everything I needed to know. His wife burst into tears, covering her face with her hands, more to avoid her husband's cowardly face than from the shame of her own crying.

I left the hut and headed for the camp. It was nightfall and to venture into the dark, unknown forest in search of Thordor would have been foolhardy.

I hardly slept that night; nightmares assailed me and prevented me from a pleasant sleep. The dawn had not yet broken when I put on my coat of mail and left my tent. Restless, I mounted my horse and got lost in the depths of a beech forest. Bad omens and dark thoughts swirled in my confused mind. What if Gomado had lied to me and was leading me into a trap? What if Thordor was just a simple healer of no importance? What if I got lost in the forest and never found my way back? Too many doubts, too many questions, and only one reality: I longed to find my family. I crossed crystalline streams, climbed steep hills, crossed lost paths, until I reached a thick oak grove. For the moment, the farmer's directions were correct. I had been walking for several hours and began to feel tired, so I decided to take a rest by a stream. I plunged my hands into the icy waters and refreshed my face. For a brief moment, my soul felt calm, as if I had forgotten the hardships that the inclement fate was bringing me. More comforted, I resumed my journey.

"Here I am. Your search is over, since you have found me."

The voice startled me and I almost fell off my horse, which was turning nervously on itself. When I managed to get hold of him, I approached the man who had said those words. It was undoubtedly

Thordor. He wasn't excessively old, being no more than fifty years old. His hair was thick, long, and in spite of his age, very black and devoid of any gray hair. His face, gentle and calm, was shaved and I must admit that his features were graceful. His eyes were very dark, almost black, and conveyed a great peace. He wore an old, threadbare brown tunic with a hood and was helped by a staff similar to that of Lughdyr.

"I understand you are Thordor," I said, getting off my horse. The druid nodded. "Then you know why I seek you."

"I can't help you; your wanderings in the lands of Gallaecia have been useless."

I drew my sword and walked towards him.

"I'm a desperate man capable of desperate things. I simply want you to tell me where my family is."

The druid didn't flinch, he continued to look at me calmly, I would almost say with tenderness, but at no time did I notice anything similar to fear or concern in his eyes. I lifted my *spatha* to a span from his throat.

"Put your sword away, your eyes tell me you're not going to use it," he said, without moving a muscle.

"I don't want to kill you, but have no doubt that I will. Tell me what I want to know and I'll go."

"Alana and your son are in a safe place, away from their greatest danger."

"Their greatest danger?" I asked confused.

The witcher nodded.

"What or who is their greatest danger?" I asked, dreading the answer.

"I think you already know," he simply replied.

"No, I don't know. You tell me," I lied.

A gust of cold wind brushed its icy cloak across the forest, taking the fallen leaves of the oaks with it. An overwhelming shudder ran through my mind. To tell the truth, the presence of these druids, sorcerers or witches, made me uneasy. Thordor stared at me and shook his head.

"You are their greatest danger," he said, not taking his eyes off my eyes.

"I don't believe you."

"You must trust Lughdyr's words and stay away from them. It will be the only way for you to meet again."

"Tell me why I'm their greatest danger and maybe, just maybe, I'll give up the idea of looking for them."

The squawk of a crow caught the druid's attention. Suddenly a black bird landed gently on his shoulder. His eyes, round and black, looked at me, or rather, scrutinized me. I stared at them and concluded that I was going mad when I seemed to see in them the sinister figure of the druid Lughdyr.

"It's Lughdyr's bird, isn't it?"

"So is."

"Can the old druid see through his eyes?"

"Lughdyr is very powerful."

I accepted the presence of the crow and, therefore, of the old druid. After all, there was little I could do.

"Tell me why I'm a danger to them," I insisted, sheathing my sword.

Thordor nodded and began to walk along a narrow path with the bird resting on his left shoulder. I walked next to him on his right side; I hated that bird and wanted to keep him as far away as possible.

"The lives of men are intertwined, just as roads intersect and distance themselves along the same route. In these paths the travelers meet, and separate to meet again later. Destiny is the builder of the road and we are the travelers. The point is, we don't travel alone," the druid said, stopping abruptly.

"What do you mean?"

"In our transit we carry heavy loads that can affect those travelers we meet on our hazardous path."

Thordor, using his staff, raised a stone, revealing a sleepy viper that lay dormant in order to keep warm. He gave her a little bump and woke her up. The serpent, confused, gave a pair of angry snorts, attacked the druid's staff without much success, and hid in some bushes.

"Our path has crossed that of this snake and, thanks to Nature, without major consequences. But unfortunately, this isn't always the case."

"I think I understand."

"Your path is linked not only to Alana's, but to someone else's. Let's say it's the heavy load you carry on your journey."

I looked at him carefully.

"And that load can hurt Alana, right?"

Thordor nodded.

189

"Who is he?"

The druid resumed his path.

"Think of Alana and the times you have met during the trip and you will find the answer."

For a few moments I thought about Alana and the moment I met her, our trip to Lugdunum, our separation and the reunion of a few days ago. I tried to find out what the druid was referring to, but couldn't find an answer. So, I considered that it was some ploy to avoid revealing where my family really was.

"Don't try to fool me, I'm not a kid. Tell me where they are! I snapped, grabbing his shoulder."

The scared bird flew to a nearby branch. Thordor looked at me pityingly.

"There is no worse blind than the one who doesn't want to see, but in your case, the sick stubbornness aggravates your blindness. Seeing them again puts them in serious danger. Don't you realize?"

"You lie!" I screamed furiously. "I don't consider you venerable saints as many think, I don't even consider that you are physical. You cannot fool me with your lies masked with wise words. You are nothing more than cruel sorcerers who feed the ignorance and superstitions of the villagers, for only God knows what dark purpose."

"The consequences will be dramatic if you persist in continuing on your way and Alana's and your roads converge before their time," he replied, ignoring my offenses.

His eyes were moist and showed deep regret. I unconsciously took a step back. The grief and pain the druid was transmitting were unbearable. Without knowing why, I burst into tears. I felt that my heart had broken into a thousand pieces. I fell to the ground on my knees in a sea of tears. Submerged in deep pain, and with my face hidden by my hands, I remained for minutes until a deep sleep soothed my tormented soul.

When I awoke, the druid had disappeared. I was tired but relieved, as if all my anguish had vanished with my tears. I mounted my horse and headed for the camp. Once again, those damned sorcerers had tricked me, mocking me.

I pondered Thordor's words on the way back to camp. The druid assured me that I was carrying a heavy burden on my journey, someone who could become dangerous to Alana, and for that reason, I must stay away from them. If I find my family, so will he... so will he... An image, a man, sinister amber eyes flashed in my mind and with them his name: Walder. If the druid was right, that heavy, harmful and dangerous burden, possibly answered to the name of the Germanic.

But what should I do?... Believe the druid and return to Gaul, staying away from my beloved and my son until our roads crossed again? Or forget his words and look for them, putting them in grave danger?

Distressed, bewildered and confused, I arrived at the camp, where a great movement in the Roman ranks attracted my attention. I was immediately summoned by the tribune, who had on several occasions demanded my presence. I entered the praetorium where Constantius Trebius was waiting for me with the *ducenarii* and *centenarii* of the *palatina legio*. He had a frown on his face and a worried look on his face.

"For God's sake, where have you been? We've been looking for you for hours," he said as soon as I entered the *praetorium.*

He didn't even let me open my mouth to justify my disappearance with some pretext as implausible as ridiculous.

"We have received a message from Gaul, we must return to Arelate urgently," he said, raising his hand so that I would not interrupt him. Ricimero and Majorian have revolted and are leading their legions north.

"But why?" I asked, not understanding what was going on.

"That's none of our business, the important thing is that we have to return to Arelate and protect our emperor."

"Romans against Romans... We are talking about a war, aren't we?"

My question dragged behind it an eloquent sea of silence, and several officers fixed their eyes on the ground.

"Let us hope not," answered a *ducenarius.*

"Don't we have enough Vandals, Germans, Suevian and other barbarians to kill each other?" I exclaimed indignantly.

Nobody said anything; after all, we were all thinking the same thing.

"We are soldiers and we obey orders, prepare your legionaries, we'll leave as soon as possible," said the tribune.

"Ricimero and Majorian are also soldiers and under their orders they have thousands of legionaries. What are the reasons that have led them to rebel? Don't they owe obedience to the emperor?"

"If they don't come to their senses, they will be fiercely punished for it," Constantius Trebius answered sternly.

"How many Visigoths will accompany us?" I asked naively.

We were barely a full legion, a little more than a thousand soldiers and five hundred *equites*. The emperor would have as many legionaries available in Arelate who, together with his personal Visigothic guard, made up his insufficient army. On the other hand, Ricimero and Majorian were the *magistri militum* of the Italian legions and had under their command more than ten thousand men.

"Only Avitus's personal guard," answered the tribune. "Theodoric claims that he needs his soldiers to exterminate the Suevian."

"But the Visigoth fights the Suevian in the name of Rome, «*ex auctoritate romana*,»* surely he has received orders from Avitus to return to Tolosa..." It didn't take me long to understand the true intentions of the Visigoth king. "He won't leave." I muttered and looking at the tribune I added: "If Theodoric defeats Requiario, he won't abandon Hispania; his troops won't return to Tolosa and will occupy Carthaginiense and Tarraconensis."

"He is a faithful ally of Rome, when he has exterminated the Suevian, he will return to his lands beyond the Pyrenees." replied Constantius Trebius vehemently, but his eyes were veiled with worry and doubt.

"May it be so," I wished without much hope.

Now, what worried me most was the certain possibility of having to fight against other *milites* in an internal war that would bleed even more the exanimate Empire. Whether or not Theodoric remained in Hispania was irrelevant: the Suevian and the Visigoths would fight each other like hungry wolves for the meager remains of skin and bones of a deer devoured by the larvae. A meager booty for so much spilled blood.

But no complaint or protest came out of my mouth, I was a soldier and I had to accept orders with obedient devotion. It was useless to complain. If the emperor did not reach an agreement with the *magistri militum*, we would fight an unequal battle, Romans against Romans. There would be no winners and only one loser: the Empire.

Moreover, leaving for Arelate meant separating me from Alana and my son, and a confused and ambiguous feeling martyred my heart. I feared that Thordor's words were true and that my mere presence would put them in danger, but also the possibility of never seeing them again broke my soul into a thousand pieces. Crestfallen, afflicted and deeply saddened, I ordered my *centenarii* to break camp. We were returning to Gaul.

192

CHAPTER VIII

The battle of shame.

De duobus malis minus est semper electdum.[9]

The negotiations failed and from Arelate we marched to Italy. We were just a handful of soldiers, mostly Gallo-Roman, who intended to put down the rebellion of the insurgents Ricimero and Julius Valerius Majorian. The bad omens of Constantius Trebius were confirmed: the Emperor Marcus Mecilius Avitus had implored Theodoric for help, far exceeding the limits established by the imperial dignity, but the Visigothic king refused to offer it. Thus, we met our enemies in a plain located in the north of the Apennines on the fourteenth day before the kalends of November, a few miles from Placentia, a city abandoned by its inhabitants when they noticed the arrival of such powerful armies. A very sensible decision, since a city near a battlefield is easy prey to pillage and plunder by both defeated and victors.

Both armies stood impassive under the inclement weather. The sky was black like the future of Rome, and on our helmets and coats of mail the icy rain pattered, wounding our faces and hands with sharp sleet drops, that numbed muscles and frightened bones. In our ranks no one spoke, we all looked expectantly at our comrades, turned into enemies. Avitus was leading us and, next to him, his personal guard: a few hundred Visigoths that king Theodoric had allowed to remain protecting his ally. Constantius Trebius watched the Romans of Ricimero and Majorian, no doubt, looking for some companion, some friend to avoid wounding and to avoid being wounded. An absurd battle that benefited no one, not even the ambitious Ricimero.

---

[9] *It is always better to choose the lesser of two evils (Marcus Tullius Cicero).*

Why had we got to this extreme? What were the reasons that had led two Roman armies to confront each other? I found the answers to these questions when the battle ended and abundant Roman *modius* watered the fields and dyed the rivers. But right now, I had a bigger issue to worry about: surviving.

Like the tribune, I looked among the Romans for a friend and my heart sank when I noticed, among the enemy ranks, the banner of the legion of Lugdunum, the ancient legion of Aetius. I prayed to the good Lord that Ajax, the Gauls Optila and Traustila, and dozens of other companions and friends, wouldn't be in front of me, in that green and prosperous field that would soon become a quagmire of mud, blood and death. I sharpened my eyes, but couldn't identify anyone. With their hooves pierced and hidden behind coats of mail and scuta, it was impossible to distinguish a familiar face. But unfortunately, I did recognize another banner. I was about to abandon, to run towards my enemies, throwing my spatha to the ground as a sign of surrender when I made out, veiled by the downpour, the banner of the *limitanei* of Tarraco. Without a doubt my friends Arcadius, Calerus and Arius Sidonius were in front of me, with their hands tightly gripping the hilt of their swords, waiting for the order of their superiors to advance towards us. Probably they didn't do it willingly, but we were soldiers, legionaries of a dying Rome, brave warriors ready to kill and die if we were ordered to do so. And it can be assured by God himself that the legionaries of Lugdunum and the *limitanei* of Tarraco were the most formidable warriors who have ever trod the earth.

A neigh caught my attention, Avitus, accompanied by several Visigoth officers, had advanced to the front line to inspect the troops. He was joined by Constantius Trebius, who repudiates that battle as much as the rest. I saw the tribune gesticulating vehemently while the emperor tried to moderate his manners with appeasing gestures, but he was unsuccessful. Meanwhile, the *foederati* Visigoths watched the enemy, scrutinizing the chances of victory. I noticed an officer shaking his head in denial, and then he walked over to a colleague and whispered in his ear. The behavior of the Visigoths worried me.

"Roman legionaries!" Avitus exclaimed suddenly. "In front of us are the traitors Ricimero and Majorian, who, eager for power, have raised their soldiers against the emperor and against Rome!"

The Augustus harangued us from his horse, which was moving nervously in front of the formation.

"It's a very painful circumstance for you, but believe me that it's also painful for me! Romans against Romans, brothers against brothers!" he roared, shaking his head. "Believe me when I tell you that I have done everything possible and impossible to avoid this confrontation, but the rebel *magistri militum* have not listened to reasons at all! Ambition and greed have clouded their minds, and they are willing to sacrifice the Empire for their vile purposes! We cannot allow it; we must destroy the enemies of Rome, be they barbarians... or Romans!"

A deep silence, broken only by the patter of the rain, accompanied the emperor's words.

"After this battle!" he continued, "a new era will loom over Rome, we'll be once again a great Empire, feared and respected, where a Roman will never raise his sword against another Roman! I swear to you by the most sacred!"

No one cheered his preaching, but we remained in eloquent silence. His harangue had not obtained the expected result, in truth; it had not served any purpose. Frustrated, he sought refuge among his Visigoths, before the indifferent gaze of the legionaries.

Constantius Trebius, with a disgruntled and uncomfortable gesture, prodded his horse, drew his spatha, and ordered the advance of my regiment. The battle had begun.

The field was muddy and there weren't a few legionaries who, despite their campagi slipped, breaking the formation and throwing the nearest soldier off balance.

Three *numeri* marched, three regiments in low spirit and with the certainty that, on that fateful gray day, we would die at the hands of our legionary brothers. In front, the enemy wasn't making any movement, but was waiting under cover behind the *scuta*.

"Stop legionaries!" the tribune ordered, and we obeyed. "Come closer *ducenarii*."

Without understanding the order very well and attentive to any enemy movement, we went to meet the tribune.

"This is a futile battle and lost beforehand," he told us, once we caught up with him.

"What can we do if we don't fight?" asked a *ducenarii*.

"We owe loyalty to the emperor and we must die for him if necessary," replied Cassius Belenus, a cold-eyed *ducenarii* with unrelenting fidelity.

"I don't fear death, but I don't wish to die pierced by a Roman *spatha*," the tribune said. "I have always been faithful to Rome and the Empire."

"What do you mean?" I asked.

Despite his rain-soaked face, his glassy eyes revealed that he was crying. He sheathed his sword and unsheathed the *pugio*. We looked at him in horror fearing his intentions. Cassius Belenus approached him, but the tribune stopped him with a wave of his hand.

"I'm a man of honor and owe loyalty to my emperor, but I would rather die than stain my sword with the blood of Roman miles. No, I won't be the one who participates in this barbarism." he shook his head, and looking at me with sorrowful eyes added: "Salvio Adriano, I name you *praepositus* of these troops, fight with courage and honor and may God keep you for many years to defend the Empire not from our brothers, but from the barbarians that stalk our borders."

"Domine..."

With a quick movement he brought the pugio to his neck and slit his throat, falling lifeless to the ground from his horse. We dismounted and came to his rescue as soon as we could, but it was too late. The tribune was dead. His blood was the first to stain the battlefield red. A blood given to the most unfathomable despair. Those lands, which soon would be sown with the corpses of thousands of Roman legionaries, were watered with the courage, honor and unwavering loyalty of a soldier, of an officer of Rome who chose to die rather than disobey an order of his emperor. But we had no time for regrets, since Ricimero didn't lose any detail of the scene and as soon as he saw the tribune fall from his horse, he ordered two detachments of *vexillationes* to charge against us. Avitus, confused and not knowing what to do ordered his Visigoths to carry out a counterattack that didn't take place. The barbarians observed the inert and lifeless body of the tribune and then the charge of Ricimero' cavalry and realizing that this was not their war and persuaded that defeat was certain, they marched to the rear-guard leaving the Augustus escorted by a handful of soldiers of the palatinae scholae.

"Traitors, you will be punished for your cowardice!" a wrathful and terrified Avitus shouted at them.

"The throne of Rome is not worth the life of a single one of my men, this war is not our business! Kill each other; we will come back for the remains!" the barbarian officer shouted, before the laughter of his companions.

Ricimero's *equites* rode at full speed towards us. We quickly mounted our horses and headed for our respective regiments.

"Salvio Adriano, as *praepositus* of the army, you are now our commander!" Cassius Belenus shouted to me.

He was right. The tribune had committed suicide, the emperor remained in the rear, tearing his clothes and cursing his fate, and I, as *praepositus* appointed by Constantius Trebius, now exercised command over an entire legion.

"Protect yourselves with the *scuta* and at my command throw the javelin at them!"

It was my first order and so they did.

The horsemen charged at us with force, but protected with shields and armors, we managed to withstand the first attack.

"Throw the javelins, now!" I exclaimed.

A hail of javelins fell on the unsuspecting horsemen, causing a great number of casualties among their ranks. Having done as much damage as possible, we returned to take cover behind the protection of our shields.

Through the slits in my *scutum* I noticed how a wrathful Ricimero ordered one of his legions to attack. With horror, I saw that it was the *limitanei* of Tarraco. The rain was pouring down and puddles and streams flooded the battlefield. The horses had difficulty riding and were relegated to the rear. The fight would be between legionaries: *scutum* against *scutum*, *spatha* against *spatha*. We were greatly outnumbered, but even so, I allowed the brunt of the battle to fall on only three numeri. My purpose was to cause as many casualties as possible among the enemy ranks, and then the rest of Avitus's meager army, more rested and fresh, would finish the job. A very optimistic vision considering that our enemy was four times our number.

It didn't take us long to feel the shock of the Hispanic legion on our shields. The hand-to-hand combat was brutal and the resounding of our scuta thundered in the mountains dragging an omen as ominous as useless. We defended ourselves with courage, but the Hispanics were great warriors, especially when Arcadius was among them, as I could well notice. I saw him throwing punches everywhere, as was usual for him, and I think he also saw me, because I watched as he moved away from my position to avoid a painful confrontation. So, defending ourselves, enduring one and another enemy onslaught, we remained for hours, until Majorian, fed up with our stubborn resistance, ordered the milites of Lugdunum to go into action.

"Legionaries of Avitus, attack!"

I ordered all available soldiers to enter into combat. *Alea iacta erat* [the die was cast] as Julius Caesar sentenced when he crossed the Rubicon with his legions, thus initiating the civil war that devastated the Empire. Only a dignified and honorable death awaited us. The Emperor Avitus, from his horse, led the rest of the *numeri*, who with less experience and much more youth, were easy prey for the brave Gauls and fierce Hispanics.

It was a slaughter. The ground was strewn with Roman corpses and the sludge and mud puddles were stained with the dark color of blood. Surrounded as we were by enemies, we fought bravely to defend our lives. I don't know how many men I killed that day, but with each thrust, with each thrust of the sword, with each Roman life that I cut down, my soul languished. I remember the confused eyes of a young legionary who gazed at me without understanding why we were fighting, as I skewered him with my sword.

Night was hovering over the battlefield and threatening to envelop us with the shadows of twilight. And the insurrectionist generals, eager to put an end to that aberration as soon as possible, ordered the Italian legions to enter the battle. We were lost.

"Salvio Adriano!" a voice exclaimed in the din of battle.

"Salvio Adriano!"

I heard my name again, but I didn't know where it came from. Suddenly, a *senator* came towards me with his sword drawn. I pushed a legionary out of the way and faced him with the desire to take the life of an enemy officer before I fell dead.

"Salvio Adriano, it is me, Optila!" he shouted at me, detaching himself from his helmet.

I looked at him confused, his eyes veiled by blood and mud.

"Get out of here or you'll die, Avitus has already surrendered!"

"What... what did you say?" I asked in bewilder.

"You have been defeated; there is no point in more Romans dying. Avitus has surrendered!"

I looked towards the enemy camp and saw that our emperor had abandoned his men and surrendered his weapons to Ricimero, before the pleased gaze of Majorian. So many dead legionaries, so much

Roman blood shed uselessly. No emperor was worthy of deserving that a single legionary should sacrifice his life for him, much less that such a legionary was I. Filled with rage, I tightened my grip on my hilt before throwing it to the ground.

Fed up, I looked around and contemplated my men. Panting, exhausted, sunken, they threw their spatha before our enemies who looked at them with admiration, nevertheless, they had sold their defeat. The rain, always capricious, ceased and a timid ray of sunshine tore through the gray clouds illuminating the thousands of corpses and mutilated limbs that were scattered across the battlefield. Defeated, sunk, I fell to the ground on my knees. Thus, I remained for a few moments: dejected under the weight of countless misfortunes.

"Don't fear for yourself, nor your men. You are Roman soldiers and you have fought bravely to defend your emperor. Your lives will be respected. I wish I had in my ranks men as brave and faithful as you."

"No emperor deserves my loyalty," I replied, without taking my eyes off the ground and without noticing who was addressing me.

"I hope you change your mind someday."

"I doubt it," I replied, raising my head.

Before me stood Julius Valerius Majorian, one of the rebel generals, dressed in the military uniform of *magister militum*. He looked at me with sympathy and I could see in his dark eyes that he was a noble and dignified man. He took off his plumed helmet revealing blond hair, and a serene and confident face.

"Perhaps the *magister militum* of Italy can make me understand why my sword is stained with Roman blood and why thousands of legionaries have died today at Placentia."

I looked him in the eye and he held my gaze. Around us, dozens of curious onlookers gathered, interested in the conversation between a victorious general and a defeated legionary. Majorian held out his hand and helped me to sit up.

"All of us here are heartbroken. It has never been my wish." He interrupted himself and looked at Ricimero who was talking with a dejected Avitus. "It has never been our wish." he corrected himself, "that two Roman armies fight each other, but I can assure you that the outcome of the battle has been the most beneficial for the future of the Empire. *Cum finis est licitus*... [When the purpose is licit]."

"The Empire?" I interrupted him. "What Empire? What purpose can be considered licit when it has caused such devastation?" I turned with outstretched arms, showing the desolation that surrounded us. "Rome doesn't exist, because all its emperors have exterminated it."

"Have confidence," he said, placing his hand on my shoulder, "Rome will rise again, and I hope I can count on you to make it so."

I smiled bitterly and turning my back on him, I returned to the remains of my army.

Majorian kept his word and the defeated milites were neither imprisoned nor punished. It is true that Rome had no legionaries to spare and to have dispensed of our services would have been foolish. Finally, I was able to converse with my old comrades: Arcadius, Calerus, Arius Sidonius, Ajax and, of course, with the Gauls Optila and Traustila.

After collecting the dead and burying them with Christian dignity, we were able to rest well into the night. It was curious to see how some soldiers, who a few hours ago were killing each other like hungry beasts, now gathered around a fire as if they had forgotten the devastating battle in which they had participated, and told jokes, sang, laughed or chatted about the most trivial topics.

After a desolate fire, among the blackened and smoky embers of the infinite wasteland, under the lean and charred branches, a tender stem always sprouts brimming with life and hope.

I counted the casualties and, with deep regret, counted over eight hundred legionaries killed. It was even worse for our enemies, who lost about twelve hundred. In all, nearly two thousand soldiers, slightly more than a legion, had perished sunk in the mud that flooded that plain north of the Apennines.

It was very cold and we legionaries warmed ourselves under a generous fire. As the hours passed, the mood subsided and the pain and sorrow for our dead comrades faded like our warm breath, swallowed up by the freezing night. In the love of a good fire, groups formed around a poem, a song or a legend. I approached one of these groups. It was the largest, and I wasn't surprised why.

"Every day the wild horse quenched his thirst in a shallow river," said Calerus, before an expectant audience. "A wild boar also went there, which by stirring the mud from the bottom with its snout and feet, muddied the water. The horse asked him to be more careful, but the boar took offense and called him crazy. They ended up looking at each other with hatred and distrust, like the worst enemies. Then the wild horse, full of anger, went to look for the man and asked for his help: "I will face that beast," said the man, "but you must allow me to ride on your back." The horse agreed and there they went, in search of the wild boar. They found him near the forest and before he could hide in the thicket, the man threw his javelin and killed him. Free from the wild boar, the horse headed towards the river to drink in its clear waters, sure as he was that he would not be disturbed again. But the man had no intention of dismounting: "I'm glad I helped you," he said. "Not only did I kill that beast, but I captured a splendid horse." And although the animal resisted, he forced it to do his will and put a rein and a saddle on it. He, who had always been free as the wind, for the first time in his life had to obey a master. His fate was cast, and from then on he lamented night and day: "Silly me, the annoyances caused by the wild boar were nothing compared to this! By magnifying an unimportant matter, I ended up being a slave!"

Everyone applauded and thanked Calerus's story, which distracted them, even briefly, from the barbarism they had suffered a few hours before.

"What conclusion can be obtained from this fable?" Calerus asked the devoted audience.

"We shouldn't trust a horse that talks!" shouted a *miles* before the laughter of the rest.

"That we ally ourselves with whom we shouldn't!" said another.

"You're not on the wrong track." Calerus smiled.

"As the great Gaius Julius Phaedrus would say, sometimes, in an effort to punish the harm they do us, we ally with those who only have an interest in dominating us," I replied.

Calerus smiled at me and made a place for me next to him.

"Of course, my good friend Adriano, we must be skillful when looking for the solution to a problem, lest we find another even worse problem."

"And not to trust our allies," intervened Cassius Belenus, whom I hadn't noticed, remembering how the perfidious Visigoths withdrew in the middle of the battle.

We nodded and a slight murmur of approval ran through the huddle.

"I know of another fable even more appropriate than that!" a young legionary of Gallic origin exclaimed with exultation.

"We are all ears," Calerus said with a smile.

"Do you know the fable of the two dogs?" the soldier asked excitedly, enjoying his fleeting moment of glory.

"Of course we know it!" Arcadius exclaimed bravado, sitting next to Calerus. But here is a string of ignoramuses, who will be delighted that you enlighten them with your immense wisdom, young soldier!

"You don't know it, do you?" I asked Arcadius.

"Well... no," he replied sheepishly, looking away at the fire.

We broke into a thunderous laugh and more than one had to dry their tears. Arius Sidonius, who was sitting next to Arcadius, slapped him on the back and he shrugged, acknowledging his ignorance.

"Well, this bunch of louts has one more member. Welcome to the group of the ignorant, dear Arcadius!" Ajax exclaimed from the other side of the fire.

"Not all of us have had the opportunity to read the classics," the one questioned tried to allege.

"Let's take advantage of the fact that we are surrounded by such good speakers, to cultivate our intelligence," I suggested, looking at the young legionary, who was impatient to tell his story. "Tell us the fable."

The young man got up and began to gesture, drawing the attention of those present who looked at him with sympathy.

"One dog asked another for permission to give birth to the litter that she was waiting for in her den, a favor that was gladly granted. Time was elapsing and the moment didn't arrive for the dog in labor to leave with her litter the den that had been so generously given to her, claiming, as a reason for this delay, that it was necessary to wait for the puppies to have the strength to walk on their own. The dog took pity on the young, inexperienced mother and allowed her to remain in her den for a few more months. After this time, she returned to claim what was truly hers and that she had only left to borrow, and these were the words that the young mother told her: «I will get out of here if you have the courage to fight with me and with my litter that, as you can see, they have grown up and are sturdy now.»

"And the dog, with her tail between her legs, had to leave her home and find another one far from her land," Calerus finished.

"Did you get the message?" the legionary asked, looking at us all uneasy to see if we had liked his fable.

"The barbarians crossed our *limes* fleeing from hunger and the Huns, they asked us for asylum, and Emperor Valens granted it. Now these ungrateful dogs want to take over our lands. This is the message, right?" Arcadius answered.

In the year 376 of Our Lord, more than two hundred thousand Goths, carrying their few belongings in carts drawn by oxen and mules, crossed the Danube fleeing from the pressure exerted by the Hungarian troops to the east. The Emperor Valens, impressed by such a huge number of refugees, gave them asylum and authorized them to settle in Thrace. The problems didn't take long to surface and, either due to the impossibility of providing food to the huge number of refugees, or to the abuse of certain Roman officials, who saw in the starving Goths a magnificent opportunity to get a huge fortune, the altercations and skirmishes followed one another until Rome, powerless and overcome by circumstances, had no choice but to accept foreigners into her limes.

"If you bring the enemy into your house, he will drive you out of it." the young legionary replied.

"Then I have understood it perfectly."

Arcadius got up, spat on the fire and was lost in the darkness of the night. An awkward silence enveloped us, and the young legionary sat hiding among other soldiers. The fable of Gaius Julius Phaedrus had reminded us of the precarious situation in which Rome found itself, surrounded by barbarians eager to pounce on it as the Suevian and Vandals had already done. All of them peoples who were allowed to settle in our lands, and who prospered and multiplied protected from hunger and the Huns within the *limes* of the Empire.

Little by little we each went to our tents. The night was late and the next day a long and bewildering day awaited us. However, victors and losers, we didn't know what our destiny would be and what steps Ricimero and Majorian would now take once Avitus had been defeated.

The morning greeted us with a light drizzle, which, thank God, lasted a short time, but black clouds like smut threatened to unload all its contents on our chilled bodies. I was numb from the cold and damp, and only when I warmed my body with a more than decent chicken broth did I begin to stretch. Around the camp, thousands of sleepy legionaries wandered wearily through the camp, not quite sure where to go. It was the *ducenarii* of each of the legions who, shouting, ordered their soldiers to line-up. It was then that I remembered that I had been appointed praepositus of my legion and as such, I had to behave. I was heading towards my men, when an old friend called my name in the distance.

"Adriano!" Optila exclaimed, showing a big smile. "How did you spend the night?"

"I'm soaked; I'm wet to the *subligar.*"

"Ha, ha, ha! You're not the only one," he said, taking me by the shoulder. "I have news."

"Tell me," I said, interested.

"Your legion, lacking a tribune, will remain under the command of Tonantius Ferreolus..."

"Does that mean we're going back to Lugdunum?" I asked hopefully.

"Yes, and not."

I looked at him confused.

"Today the camp will be dismantled, and we will go to Rome," he continued. "The Empire needs a new emperor, and it is vital that he be proclaimed as soon as possible. Ricimero and Majorian have ordered that all the troops leave for *Urbs*; they want to transmit a message of unity to reassure the people."

"What will become of Avitus?" I asked, more out of curiosity than any real interest in the future of the maligned Augustus.

"He has reached an agreement with the winners and his life will be respected, I suppose they will confine him in some distant village and assign him a generous pension for life."

"Not a bad ending for a defeated emperor."

We were heading towards the *praetorium* where, possibly, Ricimero and Majorian would meet.

"I don't think Avitus will have a long life," an enigmatic Optila countered. "A defeated emperor when dead is less of a problem than a living one."

"Will we go to the *praetorium*?" I asked when we were a few steps away from its entrance.

"You are more skillful every day! Julius Valerius Majorian wants to talk to you." The Gaul stopped. "Be prudent with your words Adriano, the *magister militum* will be possibly invested with the purple."

"Thank you for your advice, my friend."

We entered the *praetorium* and there Majorian was waiting for us, accompanied by his personal guard and several assistants busy dismantling the main tent of the camp. The *magister militum* was having a piece of bread for breakfast with a piece of cold meat. This austerity surprised and pleased me in equal measure. As soon as he saw me, he stood up to greet me. By his demeanor, gestures and behavior, he reminded me to a great extent of Aetius. I looked at Optila and he nodded as if the Gaul had read my mind. I was grateful that Ricimero was absent. That man made me uneasy.

"I greet you, *magister militum*," I greeted, beating my chest with my fist.

"I greet you, *ducenarius*. I think Optila has already informed you," he said, without further ado. "We return to Rome, where a new emperor will be proclaimed."

Majorian began to pace distractedly around the room, no doubt expecting some question from me. I said nothing, as the Gaul had advised me, I tried to be prudent.

"What qualities do you think a Roman emperor should have?" Majorian asked me, noticing that I didn't open my mouth.

"He must be worthy of deserving the charge," I answered with restraint.

"And how must be the man on whose shoulders the purple mantle rests and on whose shoulders the imperial scepter is raised in Rome? What merits must he treasure to be worthy to wear the imperial insignia?"

I looked at Optila, who remained totally silent. Who was I to suggest what qualities an Augustus should possess? I touched my chin and decided to be cautious in my answer.

"He should represent the values that have distinguished the Empire since its foundation: honor and justice. The new emperor must be a brave, noble and, above all, just man," I finally answered.

The *magister militum* looked at me and smiled with satisfaction.

"You asked me a question on the battlefield, do you remember it?"

"Yes, *domine*, I asked you why my sword was stained with Roman blood and why thousands of legionaries had died."

Majorian approached me and looked me straight in the eye he said:

"Avitus had placed numerous supporters in important positions in the administration; these officials have emptied the already meager coffers of Rome by appropriating a large part of the Treasury. Moreover, retired in Arelate and under the protection of his barbarian guard, he ignored messages warning of a Vandal sea blockade until it occurred. Now, due to his indolence, the people are starving because they can't pay the high food prices. The population hates him and even more so when he melted down several bronze statues of ancient emperors to pay his Visigoth mercenaries."

The *magister militum* stroked his beard and resumed his walk.

"It was terribly painful to face your legion, and I mourned at length the death of Constantius Trebius, whom I knew personally. But believe me, there was no other choice. If Avitus remained on the throne any longer, he would have ended up selling Rome to Theodoric himself. Now a new and hopeful future looms over the Empire," Majorian continued, with his gaze fixed on an indeterminate point, as if his mind already envisioned a flourishing, prosperous and, above all, invincible Rome. "And I hope I can count on your help," he finished, returning to the real world.

If I accepted Majorian's generous offer and joined him, a future of glory and prosperity awaited me. Who knew if I would eventually be designated senator or even tribune? I still wonder why I made such a wrong decision. Every day of my life I cursed myself for it. I forgot the words of the druid Thordor, or rather; I obviated the importance of them. For months, my mind had been thinking about the possibility of returning to Hispania in search of my family. I knew that, according to Thordor's words, if I set out on their quest, Alana and my son could be in serious danger. But as time passed, I wanted to deceive myself into believing that the druid said or meant something very different. The truth is that I needed to see them again, life without them was meaningless and I was suffering from not being able to kiss or hug them. At that moment, I was persuaded that the druid only wanted to keep me away from my family. When a man looks for a justification for something he intends to do, or has already done, you can say by God himself that he finds it, and I, unfortunately, found it.

"*Domine*, I thank you for your proposal, but I haven't seen my family in Saguntum for years and I would like with all my heart to take a few days off to be near them," I lied.

Optila looked at me with surprise on his face. Majorian scrutinized me looking for the real reason for my rejection of his proposal.

"I could order you to accompany me to Rome," the *magister militum* said with an imperturbable face. "But I won't do it; I want the people who are by my side to do it by conviction and not by coercion. Go then to Saguntum and rest, I think you deserve it. Come back when you are ready, the doors of my *praetorium* will always be open to you. You may leave."

"*Domine.*"

I said goodbye to Majorian and left the *praetorium* accompanied by a sullen Optila, who didn't understand the reason for my decision until the light reached his tired mind.

"It's because of the girl you saved in the Suevian village, isn't it?" he asked, as we went towards my numerus.

"That's right."

"Is there something else?" asked the Gaul.

"I have a son. I can't be separated from them; I must go and look for them."

"Where are they?"

"I don't know."

The Gaul stopped and looked at me in surprise. The *castrum* was bustling with the hustle and bustle of the auxiliaries, who were loading the wagons, dismantling the tents and taking care of the horses. Optila gestured and we sat down on a wooden box.

"I think you have a lot to tell me."

And I told him.

When I finished, Optila looked at me with concern. He didn't believe in saints, but neither did he believe in druids, sorcerers or witches. He was a pragmatic man with his feet on the ground. But my words caused him some shock and more so when I showed him the mandrake leaf pendant hanging from my neck. He stood up and began to pace thoughtfully with his arms behind his back. He stayed that way for several minutes.

"I'll go with you," he said at last.

"How?" I asked, jumping to my feet.

"It is a dangerous journey, and more so with that barbarian in your way."

"But I must do it alone," I replied. I appreciate your help, but I have to refuse it.

"If that druid... Thordor is right; your family will be in danger if you find them. I will go with you, but not to protect you, but to protect them."

I pondered his words and looked at him. In his eyes I read that he would not accept a negative answer. I smiled at him and he answered me with another smile.

"I'll go talk to Majorian," Optila said, returning to the praetorium.

"Wait!" I exclaimed.

He didn't hear me, or if he did, he ignored me. Be that as it may, shortly afterwards he returned with a safe-conduct from Julius Valerius Majorian, authorizing us to travel through Suevian and Visigothic lands as legates of the *magister militum*. He had granted us a year's leave on condition that we would return to Rome after this period of time had elapsed. If I didn't want to serve him, so be it, but my obligation was to serve Rome, these were the words that Majorian transmitted to the Gaul. Little did our general know how wrong he was.

CHAPTER IX

Return to Gallaecia.

I fall, qui haec ante non viderim.[10]

As it was mandatory in the case of two ambassadors from Rome, we went to Tolosa to offer our respect to king Theodoric. We showed our credentials to the guards, who after making us wait more than two hours, informed us that Frederic, the king's brother, would receive us, since the *Gothorum rex* was still on the campaign against the Suevian. Escorted by several *spatharii,* we entered the castle and reached the throne room. There, seated next to a long oak table, a smiling Frederic was waiting for us, accompanied by his brother Euric... and Walder.

"I greet you, Roman officers," prince Frederic said affably.

"I greet you, *domini,*" the Gaul and I said in unison.

"Allow me to introduce Euric to you, my little brother," he said, gesturing at a nobleman dressed in sumptuous robes... "and Walder, *spathariorum comes*. Although you already know both of them, right Salvio Adriano?"

"Yes, my lord," I replied with a slight nod. "I greet you, Euric; it is a great pleasure to see you after such a long time," I greeted politely, leaving old quarrels behind. The prince saluted with a listless wave. "I salute you, Walder, *spathariorum comes* of the mighty king of the Visigoths," I added with a smile. The German answered me with a nod.

"My lord," Optila said.

"Sit at our table and drink our wine, it comes from Betic," said Frederic.

We took a seat and an attendant served us two jugs of wine, which we drank with pleasure, savoring its sweet taste. Walder, standing between us and the princes to protect them from any possible attack, presided over the table while I sat on his right side, just in front of prince Euric. Optila sat next to me.

Euric watched us with a scrutinizing gaze, as if he were trying to find out through our appearance, the true power of Rome.

---

[10] *Blind am I, that I have not seen it before (Marcus Tullius Cicero).*

"I realize with distaste how Rome favors murderers, and not only does she not punish them harshly enough, but she also names them ambassadors. It is evident that something is changing in the Empire..." Euric mumbled with contempt, shaking his head.

It was obvious that the Visigoth prince hadn't forgotten me. He still remembered how I killed one of his *spatharii* to protect a young Suevian.

"Salvio Adriano suffered a severe punishment for his mistake. I can assure you, prince Euric, that the dungeons of Lugdunum are not at all welcoming," Optila asserted.

The Visigothic prince looked at us with an inquisitive look and made a disdainful gesture with his hand, as if we were flies that had annoyingly barged in during a well-deserved rest. An uncomfortable silence occurred, which Euric himself was ready to break:

"How is it that Rome, after its civil war, is capable of dispensing with such brave soldiers to entrust them with an administrative mission? I suppose that the casualties suffered in Placentia must have been numerous. Now the Empire must be weaker than ever and will need all its troops."

"On the contrary, *domine*," the Gaul intervened swiftly. "Rome is stronger than before, because we have overthrown an incapable emperor, who was only invested thanks to the conditional support of his barbarian friends."

Optila wasn't very diplomatic, since it was precisely thanks to the auspices of the Visigoths that Avitus was proclaimed emperor.

"Marcus Mecilius Avitus is a great man, only the treachery of a Suevian and the excessive ambition of a general, caused his overthrow. I don't foresee much future for the glorious Empire of Rome."

"Certainly more promising than the one that awaited us with Avitus," Optila replied, entering into the provocation.

"Gentlemen, gentlemen, we are among friends and allies, let us not forget it. Let us drink some wine in honor of the new Augustus, whoever he may be, since he will surely be a great friend of the Visigothic people," Frederic said, calling several servants to bring more wine and something to eat.

More than four years had elapsed since the embassy of Mansueto, last time I had been in the presence of prince Euric, and his appearance had changed considerably. He had a bushy, curly beard, and his aquiline nose gave him a certain aristocratic air. His face had the deadly look of

210

a bird of prey. He was a pernicious man, driven by an inordinate greed. He was the youngest of four brothers, so he was far from the Visigothic line of succession, but his steely determination could drive him to reverse the future that the fickle and always unjust *fatum* had written for him, since an irrepressible and insatiable lust for power beat frantically in his heart. And the prince was ready to satisfy his ambitions, regardless of the price he had to pay for it.

"He likes us Romans, less and less each time," Optila whispered to me, in a moment of Walder's distraction.

"It seems so," I answered, looking at Euric, who was drinking distractedly from his jug of wine.

Soon the servants entered the room bearing a succulent meal, consisting of roast pork and grilled lamb. Moreover, our jugs were well attended by diligent servants, who filled them without giving us time to empty them.

"King Theodoric is still in the Suevian lands, isn't he?" Optila asked, with the idea of obtaining some information about the king's campaign.

"Have you located Requiarius?" I asked.

"The cam..."

"Indeed," interjected Euric, interrupting his older brother, who gave him an irritated look. "Our brother Theodoric arrived in the Suevian city of Bracara Augusta, where he was received in the praise of crowds, more like a liberator than a conqueror. Its gates were opened and only the Suevian notables were seized and their possessions confiscated. There were no more executions, and the lives of the rest of the inhabitants of the city were respected. The people applauded such a decision, and as a token of gratitude, not a few fingers pointed to the hiding place where Requiarius was hiding. Our king had no difficulty in locating him and, naturally, shortly after falling into our hands, he was executed."

Euric lied. As I later knew, Bracara Augusta was sacked, and thousands of citizens were cruelly killed through unjustified violence. The city was devastated, and the few survivors condemned to slavery.

"It seems that the mission entrusted to Theodoric by Avitus has been a success," I said. "Therefore, shouldn't he return triumphantly to Tolosa instead of remaining in the ravaged lands of Gallaecia?"

"*Cum voluntate et ordinatione Aviti imperatoris,*" answered Euric with a cynical smile, "the emperor deposed, orders prescribed. Our king will remain in Gallaecia as long as he sees fit. Moreover," he continued, "he may have decided to invade Lusitania. Who knows if perhaps he attacks Emerita Augusta, your ancient diocese capital, which is now in Suevian hands."

The prince's look was defiant and haughty, since he was persuaded that Theodoric's disobedience, in not returning to Tolosa once he exterminated the Suevian, wouldn't be answered by Rome. As I feared, the Visigothic king, after plundering Gallaecia and perhaps Lusitania, would remain with his Burgundian and Franks allies in the lands of Hispania.

"Who rules the Suevian now?" Optila asked absently, as if the subject was irrelevant to him.

"A Theodoric henchman named Agiulf," Frederic put in quickly, anticipating his brother.

"He's a lieutenant of the king," Walder said. "I know him, I've fought with him. He is the perfect man to subdue those dogs."

I looked at Optila, who kept eating indifferently. He took a sip of wine, looked at Frederic and asked:

"Will the Suevian accept a king chosen by the Visigoths?"

"Do they have another option?" Euric anticipated the answer again.

Frederic glared at him, while Walder smiled at the prince's impudence. There was no question who the German served in the king's absence.

"And you, Walder, why aren't you in Suevian lands accompanying your lord?" I asked.

The German looked at me in surprise, because he didn't expect me to address him at any time. He bit into a piece of pork and with his mouth full, began to speak.

"I was wounded in a battle and the king authorized me to return to Tolosa," he said, while scraps of food spilled from his mouth.

"I'm really sorry about that... and is it serious?"

Optila, who was drinking a sip of wine at the time, nearly choked. Even Prince Frederic smiled at my sarcastic question.

"Not as much as you'd like, Roman," The German muttered reluctantly, but still chewing, dropping more pork scraps from his mouth.

I smiled.

"Thanks to our victory over the Suevian, we are now stronger and more powerful," Euric said, looking at us with quarrelsome eyes.

"The triumphs of our *foederati* are our triumphs," Optila said, not taking his eyes off the Visigoth. "The stronger and more powerful our allies are, the stronger and more powerful Rome will be."

"As long as we remain allies," Walder put in, to Euric's nod.

"Let's toast our victories, which are those of Rome!" Frederic exclaimed to calm an atmosphere rarefied by mistrust and suspicion. He stood up, lifted his mug, and drained it in one gulp. The rest of us did the same, but some were more convinced than others.

It was not good news. The Visigoths had conquered much of the Suevian territory and what was worse; they had crowned a puppet king who would be directed from Tolosa. Frederic, like king Theodoric, was loyal to the Empire, but Euric had other aspirations and would not allow Rome to get in his way.

"And you, where are you going?" Euric asked us, while we remained absorbed in our thoughts.

"Now that we have visited our Visigoth friends," he drawled his last words. "We will march towards the cities of Levantine: Tarraco, Dertosa, and Saguntum, as far as Carthago Nova," Optila lied.

"What is the reason for your trip?" the Visigoth insisted.

"Know the state of their defenses in the event of a Vandal attack."

"I can tell you that: they will fall as Rome itself fell," Walder burst out laughing. "You can save your trip now." His laughter increased in tone and was accompanied by Euric's laughter.

Frederic, more restrained than his table companions, looked at us in bewilderment. Optila's forehead throbbed furiously. I squeezed the knife with which I was cutting the meat, wanting to slaughter the two barbarians that I had in front of me. After a few moments and when Walder and Euric dried the tears that veiled their sight, Optila got up and very correctly and politely, how could it be otherwise in the case of an ambassador, asked for permission to leave the room. Frederic willingly granted it, and we both left the throne room, enraged and red with anger.

Two days we rested in Tolosa until we finally marched to Hispania. During the time we remained in the capital of the Visigoths, I sensed the disturbing presence of Walder on our napes. Euric, suspicious, must have sent him to spy on our movements. Not infrequently, a few days after our departure, I looked behind my back hoping to see the arrival of the German accompanied by several of his men. Fortunately, none of this happened.

Protected by our safe-conduct and, above all, by our *spatha*, we crossed the Visigothic fields and set foot on Suevian lands. We spoke little during the journey. I was absorbed in my fears and Optila, my good friend, didn't want to disturb me, allowing me to abandon myself to my thoughts. My mind was constantly wondering if I had done the right thing, if returning to Gallaecia had been a good idea. Something inside me assured me that I should give up, turn around and go back to Rome. But my heart longed to see Alana and little Adriano, and to know that they were well, safe and sound from harm.

"I just want to see them, and then I'll go," I said in a whisper, as I rode on. I was going crazy, martyred by contradictory and insane thoughts.

"Do what your heart or instinct tells you," Optila suggested to me, who must have heard my lament.

"My heart tells me to look for them, but also to go back the way I came. I feel confused, on the one hand I'm eager to see them again, but on the other..., terrified that this will happen."

"Let's rest, we have been traveling for many days and our minds are tired. Under that tree we will be protected," proposed Optila getting off the horse.

It was only a few hours before dusk and we were in a thick and beautiful beech forest. A few hours had passed since we crossed the last populated village we found on our way. Its inhabitants were sparing with words when we asked them about the druids. A hermetic silence envelops everything that has to do with them. Only a child, absent-minded and innocent, showed us the way to a hidden hut where, according to what his parents had told him, there lived a young druid-woman with a child and an old wizard. Since we didn't believe in coincidences and in the absence of other traces to follow, we continued along the path that the little boy had pointed out to us, hoping that his indications were correct and would lead us to our goal.

We lit a generous fire and roasted some beef that we had bought in the village. A good splash of wine warmed my body and spirit, and I began to feel in a better mood. I tightened my grip on the silver mistletoe hanging from my neck and prayed to see my family soon.

"Gallaecia is a land of druids, witches and sorcerers," said Optila. "I don't believe in such things: old men who levitate, sorceresses who turn into animals, people who appear and disappear... but when in regions as far away as Hibernia, Gallaecia or Gaul itself, there is talk of them and their descriptions are so similar, it makes one think that they really exist and have magical and supernatural powers."

"My pendant is an example of this," I confirmed as I showed it to him. "I have seen truly amazing prodigies, beyond all logic. I do believe in druids because I have seen them and witnessed their power. What worries me, what disturbs me, is to know what their intentions are with Alana and Adriano, and why they don't allow them to be with me."

"I think they already told you," Optila replied.

"It's true, according to Thordor, I'm a danger to Alana and my son, and that's why I must stay away from them."

"But you don't believe him."

"I don't want to believe him."

Optila stoked the fire to deter the nocturnal vermin. He looked around restlessly, trying to glimpse some hidden danger in the gloom of the forest.

"This forest gives me goose bumps," he mumbled as soon as he heard the hoot of an owl.

"I'm not surprised," I said, curling up in my blanket.

"I'll do the first custody," said Optila, still looking around for danger.

"All right, wake me up when you want me to relieve you."

I closed my eyes, but soon after I opened them, something had woken me up. I turned my head and saw that the fire had gone out, and that only the silver rays of the moon illuminated the dark forest. Optila, with his back leaning against a tree, was sleeping peacefully. I wondered how long I had been sleeping, because I had the impression that I had only closed my eyes for a brief moment, but the position of the moon and the extinguished fire revealed that I had been surrendered to the arms of Morpheus for more than a few hours. I sat up and understood what had awakened me: the silence. Nothing could be heard, neither the nocturnal birds that usually stalk their unsuspecting prey from their dark watchtower, nor the gentle wind brushing the ochre leaves with its cool breeze, nor the subtle footsteps of the little mice on the leaves as

215

they eat some fruit, attentive to any noise coming from the heights. Restless, I got up and picked up my spatha. I thanked the moon, whose blessed silver rays brought some light to the gloomy night. The cawing of a crow startled me. I looked at Optila; the Gaul continued sleeping oblivious to my fears. I saw the shadow of the bird perch on a nearby branch.

"Lughdyr!" I shouted, not caring to wake up my traveling companion. "Lughdyr!" I insisted, looking around. "You damned sorcerer, come out of your hiding place!"

In front of me, like a specter, appeared the sinister figure of the druid. He carried his inseparable staff and wore, as usual, an immaculate habit. He looked at me sternly as he approached me. His eyes were red with anger and he gripped his staff tightly, as if it were my neck. My presence in these lands wasn't to his liking.

"Where are they?" I asked him, not being intimidated by his unexpected appearance.

"You won't be quiet until one of them dies, will you?" was his reply.

"Where are they?" I said again.

The druid stopped a couple of steps from me. He was frowning with anger and his eyes were bloodshot.

"Do you really want to know it?" He snapped at me.

"Yes," I replied.

"Let your wish be granted then."

Lughdyr raised the staff to the sky and began to twist it until it formed a kind of small, pale blue fireball. The crow uttered a terrifying croak and got lost in the darkness of the forest. I watched in rapture as the ball grew larger and larger until it became the size of a man. Lughdyr, with his eyes rolled up, pointed his staff at an oak tree and the blue fireball crashed into it, spreading everywhere and greatly increasing its size. Before me, a kind of mirror appeared framed in a blue fire, where I saw myself reflected. I looked at Lughdyr, who was next to me but, curiously, the mirror only reflected my figure.

"I must be dreaming," I said.

"Always seeking justification for things you don't want to understand," the druid replied wearily. "Now you will witness what your distrust, stubbornness and arrogance have caused. Look at the mirror!"

I obeyed and observed that my figure vanished and in its place appeared those of several horsemen who stalked a small town hidden in the thick of the forest. I saw myself riding with Optila when we reached the last village and asked its inhabitants for a Druid-woman. Shortly afterwards, I saw myself talking to a little boy who was pointing to me with his little arm a path that was lost in the shady area of the thick beech forest. The sun went down and the horsemen continued to lurk, waiting for the moment to take action. My heart sank and a deep horror took over my whole being when I recognized one of the soldiers.

"Let's see what the hell the Romans asked them," Walder said to his men.

And, riding at full speed, they reached the Suevian village. Carrying thick torches, they entered house to house, throwing the terrified peasants outside, while women and children cried in fear at the presence of the Visigoths. One of them tried to defend himself with a stick, but was easy prey of a barbarian's sword, which pierced him mercilessly before the horrified gaze of his wife and his three children. Walder ordered that all the inhabitants be taken to an esplanade, and there they were interrogated.

"I just want to know what those Romans asked you!" the German yelled. "We don't want that any more people die," he said, looking at the poor wretch who lay inert on the ground, while his wife, on her knees, wept inconsolably, hugging her children. "But, if you don't respond and soon, you will die one by one like that bastard. The decision is yours."

My heart was beating so hard that it felt like it was going to escape from my chest. I looked at Lughdyr who, with a frown on his face, didn't take his eyes off the mirror and the scene it was showing.

"The Romans asked about a... a woman," one of them dared to answer, omitting that it was a druid-woman.

"What woman?" Walder asked, turning to him with his sword drawn.

"A... a Suevian woman with a child," replied the man, who was already regretting to have spoken.

Walder grabbed him by the neck and lifted him a few feet off the ground and then dropped him. The peasant fell down with a crash and began to cough, barely able to breathe.

"Who is that woman?!" the German shouted to the terrified villagers.

No one answered, no one wished to reveal who the woman really was and who she was with. She was a druid-woman and she was protected by a powerful wizard. To betray her would be to betray him,

217

and in addition to being esteemed, druids were also feared. Walder glared at them and spat on the ground. Then he fixed his gaze on a child and turned to him.

"The little boy knows nothing!" his father exclaimed, protecting him in his arms.

Walder struck him on the forehead with the hilt of his sword, causing him to fall back several feet. His mother came to his aid and the barbarian punched her hard, breaking her nose and knocking her senseless. Walder knelt down in front of the child and grabbed his shoulder. The peasants, terrified, embraced their wives and children, who sobbed quietly trying not to attract the attention of the Visigoths.

"Who is that woman?" asked Walder.

"She is..." the boy began to say with tears in his eyes, as he watched his father and mother lying unconscious on the ground, "she is a druid-woman; she lives deep in the forest with a boy and an old wizard. At least, that's what my parents told me."

The German man sat up confused at his answer. He wondered why we, two Roman legionaries, were so interested in finding the whereabouts of a druid-woman. Thoughtfully, he stroked his blond beard until his lips showed a smile full of yellow teeth.

"What a son of the bitch" he shouted his voice. "Will that druid-woman be the bitch he snatched to me in the Suevian village!?" and he broke into a thunderous laugh at the bewilderment of his men, who looked at each other and shrugged their shoulders without understanding what his boss was referring to.

Hearing Walder's words, a shudder ran through my body. I looked back at Lughdyr, but he was staring at the mirror, his eyes rolling. I wanted to ask him where Alana and the little boy were, what had happened to them, but I didn't dare to wake him up from his reverie for fear of losing the mirror images.

"Where does that bit... druid-woman live?" the barbarian asked the boy, getting down on his knees.

"Over there," the little boy replied, pointing to the path that he had indicated to us a few hours before.

Walder nodded in satisfaction and sheathed his sword at the relieved look of the villagers.

"Don't leave one alive," he ordered his men, and then he drew a small dagger and slaughtered the boy, who fell on her mother, wetting her blouse with the red color of her innocent blood.

Horrified, I watched as the Visigoths slaughtered and skewered all the peasants with their swords, whether they were old people, women or children. One of them tried to abuse a girl of no more than twelve years, but Walder stopped him, saying that they didn't have time. The barbarian protested, but he drew his sword and stabbed it into the young woman's chest. She barely moaned before falling inert into a pool of blood.

"Let's follow the path; we must reach the druid-woman's hut before the Romans!" Walder ordered, climbing onto his horse.

Lughdyr was in a trance, while nervousness and anxiety devoured my guts. I looked at the mirror and observed how a dense fog was drawing inside it, preventing vision. Believing that it was no longer going to reflect images, I approached the druid, but he stopped me with a gesture and urged me to look in the mirror again.

The fog dissipated, revealing a new image. It was a hidden cabin in the shade of a forest. Fire rose from the chimney and the movement of shadows behind its windows revealed that it was inhabited. Outside, protected in the gloom and stalking like wild beasts, were the Visigoths.

"There are people inside, we will surround the house and enter through the door; we are gentlemen, aren't we?" asked Walder, before the quiet laughter of his men. "Let´s go."

They dismounted, and avoiding making the slightest noise, surrounded the cabin. The people inside were oblivious to what was happening in the forest. Walder, escorted by four Visigoths, stood in front of the door. He checked that each Visigoth had taken his position and, with a strong kick, he knocked the door down.

"Do not!" I yelled, throwing myself towards the mirror when I saw Alana appear inside the hut.

"Wait!" Lughdyr ordered me, coming back from the trance.

I didn't listen to him, sword in hand, I went towards the mirror with the absurd purpose of crossing it to meet Alana and my son, but when I touched it, it vanished, reappearing the oak at which the druid had thrown the blue fireball.

"Where are they?" I asked, beside myself. "What has become of them?"

"You don't need to worry," he replied. "They are doing well… for now."

"What?!" I asked without understanding.

"Easy, for once believe in me, Alana and little Adriano are safe and sound."

"How did they manage to get saved?" I stammered.

"Walder hasn't found them."

I looked at the druid and he smiled at me. His face no longer reflected anger, or hatred, quite the opposite. In him I noticed serenity and peace, a lot of peace. I felt my heart and my muscles relax. Exhausted by the tension, I sat down on the floor.

"Can you explain to me what happened? What have I seen in that mirror?" I asked between gasps.

"The mirror reveals the consequences of our actions."

"Are Alana and Adriano well?" I asked with a heavy heart, still not believing his words.

"I already told you, you must believe me, they are fine."

"And... and the boy and the villagers?" I asked, dreading the answer.

"Safe and sound"

"Was it all a joke?" I snapped, jumping up.

"If you persevere in your decision and continue the path that you have taken, these misfortunes will happen and I won't be able to prevent it. On the other hand, if you go back the way you came, none of this will happen, and it will be nothing more than a horrible nightmare. The choice is yours."

"What a macabre game of yours, that you show me possible misfortunes by making me feel guilty about them."

The druid shook his head.

"We are solely responsible for our actions and these inevitably affect third parties. You have hidden behind the shield of mistrust, ignoring our messages, persisting in a harmful search. But there is little more I can or we can do. You are free to continue along the path of unreason by which you have insisted on directing your steps but, don't forget, the only person responsible for your actions is you, not us. Don't blame the «sorcerers» for your wrong decisions."

His voice was firm, determined, but it vibrated in the air wearily and exhausted, as if he had exhausted all his strength after consuming a titanic effort. he looked at me with the gloomy and sad eyes of one who has implored a last plea, a desperate plea that knows that it will not be attended. The resolute fearlessness of the ignorant is only comparable to his infinite foolishness.

"How can I know that I'm not a victim, once again, of your deception?"

"Listen to your heart, it will guide your way."

"My heart tells me to find my family and you insist on preventing it!" I yelled angrily at him.

"For the good of all, I have done so," he said in a jaded tone.

"It was a ghoulish joke to get away from Alana!" I snapped, remembering what I had just seen reflected in the mirror.

Lughdyr stared at me as I approached him threateningly.

"How many times have we warned you to stay away from Alana?" he asked me.

I stopped my step.

"And have you obeyed?" he asked me again. "Thordor warned you: your path and Alana's will come together in due course, but if you precipitate your encounter your beloved and your child will be in serious danger. Let destiny take its course and make your life apart from them."

He looked at me with wet eyes and took me by the shoulder.

"Stop mistrusting us. We druids want the best for Alana and for little Adriano."

Doubts crowded my mind again. What if it had all been a sham, a deception to permanently separate me from them? In spite of everything, I could not, I didn't want to trust the old wizard and suspicion and suspicion reappeared inside me, poisoning the little sanity I still treasured. Lughdyr looked at me with unfathomable pity. In the expression on my face he could read my feelings.

"Well, I see that, despite everything, you still don't believe me," he muttered disheartened. "Maybe and just maybe, fate will allow you to join your path to Alana's earlier than expected, but the price you will have to pay will be very high. Are you willing?"

"Yes, I'm. I want to see Alana and my son again," I replied, seized by a stubborn perseverance, by a tragic madness.

"You can also return to Rome without seeing them, and then your path will be more peaceful and pleasant..." I shook my head and continued. "Let it be then. Go back in your footsteps, later the road will fork, and you will have to make your decision."

"And I'll take it."

Lughdyr shook his head at my fatal stubbornness.

"I must tell you that not everything the mirror reflected was an illusion. The heavy load that you carry on your way, not only threatens your family, it is also a threat to you and those around you. But when you think that all is lost, your moment won't yet have come."

"What do you mean?" I asked, not quite understanding the meaning of his last words.

He didn't answer. As he appeared, he vanished. The moon was hidden behind the clouds and I was enveloped in a deep and thick darkness. I doubted again if the events I had just witnessed had been real or was it a dream. Almost groping, I reached our camp, and, in the shadows, I noticed that Optila was sleeping peacefully.

The sun was breaking through the mountains, turning the highest peaks a beautiful orange color, when Optila began to stretch. It was a bit chilly, and I was feeding a small fire, protecting myself from the cold, wrapped up in a blanket. I still doubted if the experience I had had the night before had been real or simply the result of a horrible dream. I was tired and slightly dazed. The doubts, always the tenacious doubts, tormented me and I didn't know what to do. I pondered the druid's last confused words, and as much as I tried to understand them, I couldn't. The truth is that every time I looked for Alana, her mysterious and sinister figure appeared preventing me from approaching her. I looked at the oak where Lughdyr had thrown the blue ball in the hope of finding some sign, some embers that would confirm that what had happened that night had been real. I searched the surrounding ferns, holly trees, and junipers, but found nothing.

"What are you doing?" Optila asked me, rising from his litter.

"Nothing, nothing, I heard a noise and I thought it might be our breakfast," I lied.

"God!" he exclaimed as the day dawned. "I slept like a child all night and I was on duty!"

"Don't worry, I've barely slept."

"I can't understand it, it never happened to me," the Gaul apologized.

"Let's eat a little, and then we'll start the journey... back." I told him.

Optila looked at me without understanding my words and approached me. He looked at my tired and worried face, and immediately understood that the night had not been as placid as he thought.

"You look awful," he said. "Let's sit by the fire and warm our frightened bodies, I think we have a lot to talk about."

We sat down and had some bread and cheese for breakfast. I hardly took a bite; a knot in my stomach prevented me from ingesting food. Optila asked me about my change of mind and my intention to return to Rome, and I told him about the experience I had had during the night. He stared thoughtfully into the fire for a few moments with his head working in search of the best solution.

"I don't know if your experience was real or just a dream, but that is not relevant. Be that as it may, I believe the druid is right," he finally concluded. "We must return to Rome, let the *fatum* guide you to your family, showing you the way."

"I only hope that the price demanded for meeting them is not too high," I told him.

"If we return, we do the right thing, the rest, as the druid would say, is in the hands of destiny."

The Gaul's words comforted me. I was thinking the same thing myself, but I needed the advice of a friend to reinforce my decision. With all the pain of my heart, I nodded and prepared my horse. I looked back to the oak tree in the hope of seeing one last sign, one last message from the druid, but I did not find it. I started my way back to Rome with the hope of seeing my family one last time, but with the uneasiness of not knowing what the price would be. Ambiguous feelings that saddened my spirit.

We retraced the path we had gone on, and arrived at the village that, according to the mirror images, had been razed to the ground by the Visigoths. My heart was glad to see the farmers carrying their tools, the women washing in the river, and our little guide waving to us in the distance as he herded a handful of goats. I returned the greeting with a big smile and my eyes grew excited.

"It looks like the German's sharp sword finally didn't make it this far," said Optila.

The villagers went on with their daily chores, oblivious to the fateful future that would have awaited them if he had persisted in his search for Alana and little Adrian... *felix ignorantia* [blissful ignorance].

"As long as Lughdyr's words had been true," I replied again skeptically.

"If your experience last night was only a dream, or as real as you and I are here, you will know before long."

"It's true. If I see you again, what happened last night will have been real and the images reflected in the mirror true. On the other hand, if we return to Rome and I have had no news of my family, everything will have been nothing more than a dream, or rather, a horrible nightmare, and the druid will have deceived me again."

"What will you do in that case?" the Gaul asked, sensing the answer.

"I will return, and this time I swear to you by the most sacred thing, that I won't cease in my efforts until I find them."

We rode for several hours until we found ourselves at a crossroads. We looked at each other in amazement; we could have sworn that this fork in the road didn't exist before. One of the paths led off to the right, was flat, wide and in good condition. On the other hand, the other was a little wider than an open path in the undergrowth and ascended the hill getting lost in the thick forest. We concluded that the first path was the safer and possibly the right one, but something inside me warned me to take the second, the steeper and more dangerous one. We stopped and assessed both possibilities, and after several minutes of discussion, I convinced him that we should continue on the steeper path for a few hours until nightfall. The next morning, if he was wrong, we would descend and continue on the supposedly correct path.

"I have a feeling," I said.

"Don't tell me you're going to have supernatural powers now, too!" he exclaimed sardonically.

"I have spent too much time in the company of the druids, and maybe they have passed some on to me..." I said with a chuckle.

We were about to begin our ascent when a strong wind startled us. Our horses became restless and we had difficulties to control them. It was not without effort that we managed to control our mounts. We looked at each other in amazement and hesitated to head for the trail.

"The time has come to make your decision!"

A voice shouted. I looked away from Optila. The Gaul was absorbed in staring at an indeterminate point in the forest. Concerned, I turned to him and, to my horror, noticed that his pupils were white.

"Optila!" I yelled at him, shaking him awake from the trance he was in."

"If you take the path to the right, you will arrive in Rome and your journey will be placid and calm, on the other hand, if you choose the path to the left, you will meet Alana and Adriano, but this decision will entail a huge sacrifice that will cause you unfathomable pain!"

The voice came from Optila, but it wasn't his. Lughdyr spoke to me through his lips.

"Optila awake!" I yelled.

"Take the decision!" the Gaul snapped, looking at me with his ghostly white eyes.

Instinctively I turned away from him. His voice shook me, freezing the blood that flowed through my veins. I was spellbound, unable to tear my gaze away from his terrifying white eyes.

"Go to Rome, I beg you, and you'll see your family again. I only ask you to be patient," the Gaul pleaded, but this time in his true voice. His eyes remained blank, since he was still in a trance.

For a moment I hesitated. What price would I have to pay to see my beloved and my son? Would it be wiser to return to Rome by the safest way? Optila was looking at me with vacant, searching eyes. Rider and horse had become rigid as if they had been turned into marble or bronze sculptures, and only Optila's neck moved following my movements. A crow flew over my head, landing on the Gaul's shoulder. I looked around, hoping to meet Lughdyr, but the old druid didn't appear. Scared, I decided to make the riskiest decision.

"I want to see my family!"

The crow flew off his shoulder, lost on the steep path.

"So be it!" cried Optila, in the voice of the druid and collapsed to the ground.

I dismounted swiftly and went towards the body of the Gaul who was lying inert on the ground. I laid his head gently on my lap uttering his name over and over again, patting his face gently. With a heavy heart, I could see a tear welling up from his closed eyes. After a few moments of bitter agony, Optila awoke.

"What... what happened?" he asked disoriented.

"Are you fine?"

"Yes, but... what am I doing on the ground?"

I sat him up carefully and verified that he was in good condition, although somewhat dazed. I gave him some water and related the experience he had just suffered.

"I'm not amused that a druid enters my body and… possesses me," said the Gaul, grasping his genitals with concern.

"Easy friend, he didn't give him time to enjoy your charms."

"Well, you never know, those druids spend long nights alone," he replied more cheerfully.

We broke into uproarious laughter and started up the path. Little by little, concern and a deep silence replaced our laughter. The path became more rugged and narrower with each step we took, imprisoned by the bushes and brambles that grew on its edges. In just a few hours, the sun began to set behind the tops of beech, yew and oak trees, and we had to find a place to spend the night. Restless by the gloom of the place, we reached a small clearing, and although there was still enough light to ride for another hour, we decided to prepare our litter and take shelter in that clearing. It was not that we did not find another more appropriate place to camp.

"I believe that tomorrow we will reach the top of this mountain," Optila pointed out, preparing a fire. "From there we will have a complete view of the entire valley and perhaps, we can better see where we are going."

"I don't know how to thank you for everything you're doing for me," I said, moving closer to the fire.

"We are legionaries, don't forget it," he said, taking me by the shoulder. "If we don't help each other, who will? barbarians like Walder or prince Euric?"

I nodded gratefully and a big smile broke from his lips. Suddenly, a sound in the bush startled us. We took hold of our *spatha*, as the noise was closing in on us.

"What was that?" I asked, looking around.

"They look like horses, and lots of them."

From the forest came the cries of several men, fiercely prodding their mounts. They had located us and had no intention of letting us escape. We still didn't see them, but their harsh booming voices were heard closer and closer and they would soon find us.

"Who could they be?" I asked for.

"I don't know, maybe they are Suevian, *Bagaudae* or simple bandits. The truth is that we are in serious danger if they find us," said Optila, looking for somewhere to hide.

But it was too late. An arrow, launched from the gloom of the thick forest, struck the Gaul's left shoulder, knocking him to the ground in pain. I was running to help him when I saw a dozen Visigoth horsemen come up to us.

"It hasn't been easy, but I've finally found you," Walder said, getting off the horse.

"You son of a bitch!" the Gaul blurted him out, rising in pain from the ground and brandishing his sword with his right hand.

"What are you trying to do?" I yelled at him, threatening him with my *spatha*.

The German gestured and half a dozen riders unmounted, unsheathed their swords and headed towards us. Their purposes weren't good.

"Euric has ordered me to follow you to know your intentions, but I have decided to kill you," he replied with insulting sufficiency.

"We are allies!" exclaimed the Gaul.

"Today, yes, tomorrow... Who knows?" the German drew his sword.

"You're a traitor!"

The sun was hiding behind the mountains and began to cool down. In a few minutes, a moonless night would cover us with his black cloak, and the German had no intention of granting us the possibility of escaping by covering us in the dark. He looked up at the sky and calculated how much time he had to take our lives.

"Roman, you and I have an account to settle, and today is the appointed day," Walder said, advancing towards me.

His amber eyes shone reflecting the last rays of light.

"You are protected by twelve Visigoths; there is no honor in this duel," I said, clinging to the meager opportunity granted by invoking the uncertain nobility of the barbarian officers.

The German busted into laugh and his men accompanied him.

"Honor? Nobility? Vain words that old women use to avoid being killed. The only thing that matters is who lives and who dies, and today you're going to die. And you won't be the only one. Kill the Gaul!" he ordered his soldiers.

Several Visigoths headed towards us. Optila had lost a lot of blood and was very weak, but even so, he managed to stop the onslaught of several enemies. I engaged two; Walder had no intention of staining his sword with my blood. Pressed by the need to help my friend, I threw off the Visigoths and rushed to his aid. Optila had been wounded in his right thigh and was struggling to stand up. Leaning his back against a yew tree, he was defending himself fiercely against two Visigoths who were playing with him as a cat plays with its prey before devouring it. They threw a lunge at him and laughed, they threatened him and the Gaul responded with desperation. Entertained as they were humiliating Optila, they didn't notice that I had gotten rid of two of their henchmen, and now I was behind their back. Walder, with a desperate cry, warned them, but it was too late, I skewered them with my *spatha* before they were aware of what was happening.

Optila, exhausted by the effort, fell defeated to the ground. He was very pale and his clothes were soaked in blood. Life was slipping away from the brave Gaul legionary.

"Hold on, my friend," I whispered, taking him by the shoulders.

"*Quasi non dolec, hic prope morn est.* [It almost doesn't hurt, my death is near]," he muttered, with glazed eyes.

The sound of trampling leaves warned me that someone was heading our way. I turned and met the German's yellow, angry eyes. The death of four of his men had not thrilled him.

"I'm going to skin you alive, you damned Roman!" he blurted me out before launching a terrible thrust.

Still on the ground, I managed to repel the angry attacks of the German, and even managed to throw two dangerous thrusts that he avoided with great agility, but that at least helped me to stand up. I moved away from Optila with the intention of taking the German with me so that he wouldn't notice the badly wounded Gaul. We stayed like that for several minutes, defending ourselves against each other, and trying to attack each other when we noticed the slightest crack. The night was closing in on us, and our relentless struggle continued without a clear winner.

We were both exhausted and gasping for breath. Then the German turned his gaze to Optila and then looked at me. Terrified, I understood his intentions. A terrible smile broke out between his blond whiskers.

"Kill the Gaul!" he ordered, and several Visigoths rushed towards Optila, who stood motionless with his coat of mail soaked in blood, resigned to his unfortunate fate.

"No," I cried, running to his aid.

Forgetting my own safety and with my mind absorbed in helping my friend, I neglected my right side and Walder skillfully thrust his sword between my ribs. A wrenching pain coursed through my body and I fell badly wounded to the ground. With tears in my eyes, I watched as the Visigoths raged against Optila, thrusting their swords into him again and again. Lying on the ground, face down and unable to get up, I stretched out my hand with the vain intention of being able to free him from such a horrible death.

"Now it's your turn," I heard Walder say behind me.

I entrusted my salvation to the Almighty just before I felt my back being pierced by the barbarian's steel. The pain was unbearable and I screamed with all the strengths that my growing weakness allowed me. But my body stopped responding and the last of my energy left me. A deep peace overcame me and the pain that dominated me faded away like the shadows of the night being caressed by the clarity of dawn. My eyes were veiled and I was engulfed by an icy black vapor.

I meekly offered my soul to the Grim Reaper, leaving it at the mercy of the dense darkness.

CHAPTER X

The Reencounter.

Fiet tamen illud quod futurum est.[11]

I have heard hundreds of stories about dying people who have been on the verge of death. Some have seen and even been able to touch or speak with the Almighty, whom they have defined as an old man with a long white beard, dressed in a robe of the same color. Others saw a bright, almost blinding light and, as if they were moths captivated by the light of a fire, they went towards it, waking up just as they brushed it with their fingers. Others affirmed to have woken up in a green and leafy paradise, where lions played with deer and its inhabitants wore radiant and happy smiles. There were those who swore they had been in a blue sky full of fluffy clouds, as soft as the plumage of birds and, from the heights, to have watched the rest of the mortals as if they were busy ants. I was on the verge of death and, I really didn't see any of that. Only a placid sleep accompanied me during the days I remained lying on a straw bunk.

As I later knew, I lay prostrate for ten days without being able to move, being fed and cleaned. And during all this time, I don't know if by luck or misfortune, I didn't see the Almighty, nor was I in the Paradise of the affable animals and smiling neighbors, nor did I climb to the heights of heaven to contemplate how my countrymen work, and the only light I saw was, in my awakening, that which illuminated the weak flame of an oil lamp. Due to the inactivity of the last few days, my eyesight remained veiled and I could barely distinguish blurred objects around me, but a faint light guided my eyes to a fire. Then I saw a shadow approaching me. I could not see it well, but I realized that it was a woman.

"Calm down," a voice whispered. "You are in a safe place, far from any danger."

---

[11] *In spite of everything, what must happen will happen (phrase taken from the Latin Grammar book by Santiago Segura Munguía).*

Her face was less than an elbow away from me, but I still couldn't recognize her. Even her voice was unfamiliar. I didn't know if I was still dreaming, or had come back to reality.

"Here, drink some broth; it will make your feel better."

She brought the bowl to my mouth and I was able to sip some of the hot soup, while I felt how, unfortunately, my body was loosening up and every one of my bones and muscles began to ache. My face contracted in pain and the woman gave me a drink of a concoction that tasted like a thousand devils.

"This will calm you down," she said shortly before leaving the house.

Little by little, the fog that veiled my vision dissipated and I could see that I was in a thatched hut. There was a small table to my left with an oil lamp and a wooden cup on it. I tried to move, but could not. I feared I had suffered some serious injury that would prevent me from moving my legs or arms, but I calmed down when I began to feel a gentle tingling in my fingers and could move them slightly. The sound of hinges disturbed me, and I turned my neck sharply, causing me a sharp pain.

"Be more careful, you haven't moved for several days and you could hurt yourself."

The slender figure of Lughdyr emerged before me. The druid left a small bag on the table, then touched my forehead and lifted my eyelids.

"The fever has subsided, I think he will survive," he said to the other person. "Bring me more water."

The door opened again and someone came out of the hut returning shortly after with a wineskin of water. The druid pounded some herbs in a mortar, weighed them on a tiny scale and poured them into a wooden cup. Then he poured some water and stirred it. Despite the concoction the woman offered me, my body, while waking up from such a long sleep, began to ache. The tingling I felt in my fingers flowed through the rest of my body until I was able to move my arms and legs a little. I sighed in relief.

"Drink this potion; it will ease the pains you will soon begin to suffer," the druid said handing me the wooden cup.

I drank the bitter concoction, but the pains were getting stronger and stronger. I tried to speak but could not, I was still very weak. Lughdyr waved me to rest and left.

231

I fell asleep again, but strong pains woke me up during the night. I opened my eyes; I was enveloped in a dense darkness. I looked to my left in the futile hope of seeing the light of the lamp. Terrified, concluding that I had finally died, I tried to sit up without success. I managed to move my right arm and tried to turn to my left, but a sharp pain almost took my breath away. The scream I uttered was so harrowing that it frightened even me. At least I had regained my voice. Someone lit a fire and then I saw her. Beautiful, fair and radiant as I had never seen her before, she approached me with concern written in her eyes and settled me on the pallet. Then the druid appeared carrying a lit fire.

"I think you're going to be a very troublesome patient," Lughdyr sputtered.

"I'm... sorry is that..." I stammered with difficulty.

"Easy, nothing's wrong," Alana said, stroking my forehead.

She smiled and my eyes got excited.

"Thank you," I managed to say.

"With your permission, we are going to sleep," the druid growled, who didn't like night frights.

"Good evening, my love," Alana said, kissing my lips.

Alana's words of love were the best balm, and her warm kiss gave me the strength to overcome the pain, not of that night, but of a thousand nights like that. Thankful to God for allowing me to be with my beloved, I fell into a peaceful and restful sleep.

I stayed in the druid's hut for several weeks, recovering from my serious injuries. Walder's sword had left deep and painful memories on my right side and back. I was lucky that he didn't injure any vital organ or muscle that would incapacitate me for life, and only indelible scars would remind me of the modest price I paid for my daring. Higher was the tribute paid by Optila, vilely murdered by the Visigoths because of my blind stubbornness. His unfortunate death fell on my mind like an unfortunate stone, from which I won't be able to redeem myself until the end of my days.

They were days where I found the longed-for peace and tranquility. Not only did Alana and Lughdyr, whom I began to know and appreciate, took care of my complaining wounds, but also, my little Adriano with his hugs and kisses, cheered my soul and helped me to bear the evils that lacerated my body and overwhelmed my spirit. I'll never forget the days I was hidden in the druid's hut, lost in the thicket of an oak grove and surrounded by my family. But everything comes to an end and unfortunately, that day came when I found myself fully restored. With no arguments to justify my longer stay in the cabin, I prepared to assume the painful but inevitable departure.

It was a cold winter day, Lughdyr asked me to accompany him to collect plants and mushrooms in the forest. We were warm, since the first snowflakes made their appearance accompanied by a fresh north wind. We had not been far from the hut when the old wizard sat on the fallen trunk of an old oak. I sat down next to him.

"There's something you want to ask me, but you don't dare," the wizard began to say. "And you'd better do it as soon as possible, because you'll soon be back with yours."

The druid was right, during all those days a strong feeling of guilt tormented my conscience. I hadn't asked the question for fear of knowing the answer, but my time was running out, and the time had come to know the truth. I took a deep breath and exhaled sharply. A cloud of mist emanated from my mouth that soon vanished into the frigid air.

"You don't miss any detail," I said with a tone of disgust.

"It's not enough to close your eyes to avoid danger, sooner or later you have to face it and the sooner you do it, the better," the druid said, looking at me with sympathy.

I smiled and got up. Then, looking out into the thicket of the forest, I asked him what he had long wanted and was afraid to know.
"Optila's life was the price I had to pay to meet Alana and Adriano again, right?"

I didn't turn around for fear of seeing his nod. I stood still, rigid, waiting to hear an answer that would fill me with guilt for the rest of my life. I heard Lughdyr take a deep breath and a slow exhale. No doubt he was doing that stomach breathing that he had taught me to temper the nerves and calm the spirit.

"Our actions affect third parties and only fate knows to what extent," he replied.

"But if I had followed the direct route to Rome, Optila would still be alive..."

"We all die, what changes is the when, where and how."

"Do you mean that Optila's days were already numbered?" I asked, whirling around.

The old man remained sitting clutching his staff. His gaze was lost in the depths of the forest, as if he were searching for the answer among the nymphs, the goblins or the spirits that inhabited it.

"Sometimes we druids see things," he began, without taking his eyes off the forest. "Confusing images that appear before our eyes and that we are forced to interpret. One night I fell into a trance and you appeared before my eyes making a difficult decision that, I soon realized would entail great suffering. At the time I warned you, but, unfortunately, I could not give you more information, because I didn't have it."

"Optila died, but it could have been me or even Alana or Adriano, right?"

"So is."

"But if I had followed the direct route to Rome, Optila would still be alive," I insisted.

Lughdyr got up and started pacing, I followed him. The cold was so intense that not a single animal was heard. The forest seemed to be in a cold, silent lethargy. We were only accompanied by the snort of the wind whipping the leafless branches and the crunch of our footsteps on the thin layer of snow.

"Don't beat yourself up; Optila was killed by the Visigoths. Who knows if he hadn't died before if he hadn't met you?"

The life of a legionary was exposed and hazardous, and there weren't few times that he bet his own life leaving it in the hands of the black Grim Reaper. Perhaps the druid was right, perhaps the fact of knowing me had extended his life more, perhaps Death granted him a truce before claiming his eternal presence. Maybe, maybe ... it was all conjecture and the only certain thing was that the Gaul was dead and I, at last, had met my family. Despite Lughdyr's words of comfort, I became more and more convinced that the price I had paid to meet Alana and my son had been his life. An excessively high and unfair price... But the decision had been mine, and I had to assume my responsibility.

"You didn't kill Optila," Lughdyr intervened, guessing my thoughts. "It was the Visigoths. Don't forget it."

"Thank you," I said with tears in my eyes. But his comforting words slammed against the wall of remorse and guilt. I will never forgive myself.

We continued walking in silence. Sometimes, the old man scanned the ground for a plant and then he scratched in the snow with his staff, showing a blade that he took delicately and put in a small bag.

"You must go soon," he said without looking at me, observing the long, thin stems of butterworts.

"I know."

"I understand that you won't look for them again."

"No, I've learned my lesson; I'll join them when the time comes," I said, clenching my jaws.

The old man nodded.

"I'll see them again, right?" I asked hopefully.

It started to snow and Lughdyr took me by the shoulder. It was very cold and it was time to go home.

"That's how I've seen it but..."

The old man stopped. I looked at him and begged to continue.

"Don't forget them Adriano, but live your life without thinking that you'll see them again."

"You told me…!" I exclaimed.

"And I keep it." Lughdyr interrupted. "When you are on the verge of death, your beloved will appear and she will free you from the clutches of the Grim Reaper... but it will take many years until that happens, and perhaps your true love won't be..."

Suddenly he fell silent, and his eyes narrowed in confusion, as if a blurry image or dark omen had arisen in his mind.

"Are you fine?" I asked worriedly.

Lughdyr looked at me, and his lips twisted into a forced smile.

"I was just trying to say that I don't want you to waste your life in a long wait."

"I must be the one who makes such a decision," I said decisively.

"It's true, *omnia vincit amor*[12] [love triumphs over all]," the wizard said with a smile, persuaded of the powerful and unwavering love I felt for Alana and my son. "Let's go home or this cold will freeze us to the bones."

We entered the hut and I felt the comforting warmth of a generous fire in my body. Adriano ran towards me and hugged me tightly; I picked him up and began to turn as I used to do every time I saw him. Alana looked at us amused. I put the boy down, begging for more fun,

---

[12] *"Virgil's Bucolics."*

and sat next to her. Due to my sullen behavior, she understood that I had to convey news to her that, as expected, was no less ominous. For a few moments we didn't say anything. We both watched as little Adriano amused himself with a wooden horse that Lughdyr had carved for him. Outside, the snow was thickening and a strong wind whistled the dry branches that covered the hut. The druid was heating up the food, the boy was fiddling with his toy, and I was sitting next to my beloved, a beautiful yet fleeting family scene. Unable to remain silent any longer, I decided to speak.

"My wounds are healed and I must go," I said with a lump in my throat, looking at the little boy.

Alana hugged me tightly without saying a word; I looked into her glassy eyes and kissed her. Her tears melted into mine and her warm, moist heat ran down my cheeks.

"When are you leaving?"

"I must get to Rome soon before the harsh winter makes the roads even more impractical."

"You should leave tomorrow," said Lughdyr, still stirring the pot he was heating on the fire.

I nodded silently.

"It will be that way," I agreed without protest.

"Adriano." the old man called the boy. "Take your coat and let's go outside, it's impossible to pick good herbs with your lazy father."

"But it's very cold!" Alana protested.

The druid smiled. He picked up the boy who had meekly put on his coat and opened the door. Our eyes arched in surprise as a timid ray of sunlight came through the doorway. I approached and saw that the storm had disappeared giving way to a limpid sky without blemish. Lughdyr left the hut accompanied by the little boy, but not before saying goodbye with a big smile. I closed the door and looked at Alana, who was watching me with sadness and tenderness at the same time. I walked over to her and sat next to her. We melted into a long, warm kiss, and our souls joined with the intention of never parting. It was beautiful and warm and fleeting like a bright sunset. I will never forget that happy moment. The tears flowed in our eyes in anticipation of the inevitable separation, but in our hearts we hoped that we would see each other again, that this passionate meeting wouldn't be the last and that the *fatum,* as a tribute to our painful separation, would grant us hundreds of moments as magical as that.

We got dressed and gave each other one last kiss just before the door opened and Adriano walked in, running happily with a frog in his hands.

"Look, dad is a frog!" he said happily, showing me the animal.

"I thought frogs were hibernating around this time."

"I picked up a stone and found it, it was curled up to keep warm." the little boy explained excitedly.

"Shouldn't you have left it there?" Alana asked a little annoyed.

"Don't scold the child, I told him to take it. Its skin has non-negligible medicinal properties…" Lughdyr intervened, stroking the boy's hair.

I walked over to my son and gave him a big hug. Unable to bear the tears any longer, I wept softly before Lughdyr's rueful gaze and Alana's silent sob.

Before dawn, in silence and with my heart broken into a thousand pieces, I gave the little boy a kiss, who, oblivious to my departure, was sleeping peacefully. I left the hut accompanied by Lughdyr and Alana. The stars predicted that a clear dawn would accompany my march, but it was cool and we protected ourselves with a thick woolen blanket. I noticed that the snow had disappeared, muddying the roads where I was about to walk.

"It will be a rough ride," I whispered, looking at the horizon.

"The omens are benign; your journey will be uneventful," Lughdyr assured, leaning on his inseparable staff.

I looked gratefully at the old druid. After many years, I had realized that Lughdyr loved Alana and little Adriano as much as I did. I was aware of how foolish and stupid I had been all this time. I had acted like an ignorant brute.

"Thank you Lughdyr, I will never forget that you have saved my life and, above all, how you have protected my family," I said, holding out my hand.

"May God guide your way."

We shook hands, the glint in his eyes revealed that the old druid had forgiven all my insults. Alana, who was watching us with wet eyes, ran to me. She hugged me tightly and started crying.

"Tell Adriano that I love him and that one day we'll get back together," I said, my voice cracking with emotion.

"I'll tell him."

Alana's face was flooded with tears.

"I love you."

"I love you so much."

We gave each other one last passionate kiss, and with my eyes veiled by tears, I began the path that separated me from them with my soul bitten by intense pain and unbearable uncertainty. I didn't stop looking back until I lost sight of them. I cried quietly for hours until my eyes went dry. I felt dejected, defeated, without the will to live. Nothing tied me to a ruthless and cruel life anymore. There weren't few times that I reached for my hilt intending to end my existence, since according to Lughdyr's words, my beloved would appear when the black Grim Reaper was about to snatch my soul. But I didn't have the courage to do it. I really didn't have it. During the weeks of my long journey, the memory of my family and, above all, the hope of seeing them again gave me the strength and courage not to lose heart, not to give in to bitter despair and to continue fighting, impelled by the burning desire to be reunited with them. Our paths had forked and now we were moving towards an inexorable future on parallel roads.

CHAPTER XI

A new life in Carthago Nova.

Bibamus, moriendum est. Et notile tempus perdere, cum vita brevis sit.[13]

I made a detour to Tarraco with the intention of gathering information on the situation in which Rome was immersed and I was informed that most of the legions were in the capital of the Empire, embracing who would be appointed as the new emperor, whose name still was unknown.

Exhausted after the tiring journey, I crossed the Flaminia gate and entered the *Caput Mundi*. The city was lavishly decked out and impeccably groomed for the festivities to be held after the coronation. The Romans seemed happier and more carefree than ever. Unaware of what was happening behind the walls of the capital of the Empire, they enjoyed and amused themselves hopefully with the new Augustus. I went to the hot springs with the intention of taking a good and comforting bath, cutting the hair that hung from my shoulders and shaving my curly beard. I couldn't present myself to the *magister militum* as a vulgar *Bagaudae*. After paying a more than reasonable price, a servant handed me a towel and pointed out where the dressing room was located. I undressed and gave my dirty clothes to a servant to clean it up in the best possible way; then I crossed the arena where some clients were doing physical exercises or lifting heavy bronze balls. I arrived at the *tepidarium* and enjoyed a bath of warm and crystalline water, which soon became cloudy due to the dirt that was impregnated on my skin. A servant horrified by the dirt that my body gave off, attended me diligently and rubbed me hard with an esparto glove. Sore but clean, I made my way to the *caldarium* and dove into a single tub. The hot water opened my pores and a pleasant sensation ran through my body. I was so relaxed immersed in the pleasant bath that I'd have

---

[13] *Let's drink, death is inevitable. And don't waste your time, since life is short (phrase extracted and adapted from the Latin Grammar book by Santiago Segura Munguía).*

fallen asleep had it not been for a servant indicating that it was time to immerse myself in the *frigidarium*. I left the hot spring and headed to an outdoor pool. It was cold outside, but nothing compared to the water in the pool. I submerged for just a minute and ran, frozen, towards the hot spring amidst the laughter of some servants and clients. Immediately I warmed up and headed to the *laconium* where I had a steam bath to dislodge the stubborn grime that had refused to separate from my skin. I entered the *laconium* and was enveloped by a thick mist. I greeted the five clients who were in the sauna, and sat down on a wooden bench. One of them was busy pouring water into a bucket full of hot stones, so that more and more steam would come out, as if the one already enveloping us was not enough.

"Well, I think that Ricimero is wrong favoring Julius Valerius Majorian as emperor," said one of my companions in the *laconium*; a chubby, half-bald man.

"Majorian is the best candidate, don't doubt that," replied a thin man with a long, thin nose.

"The best would be Ricimero, it's a shame that the barbarian blood runs through his veins and he professes the Arianism," intervened the client who was pouring water on the stones, a short and plump man.

"I keep saying that Majorian is the best emperor Rome could have. He is a great general, appreciated by his men and undoubtedly loved by the people," the long-nosed customer insisted.

"That's what worries me," grumbled the bald man.

His friends looked at him expectantly. He got up from the bench and took the wooden saucepan from his partner to prevent her from pouring water on the stones. He was scorching us with so much steam. I thanked him for his cautious gesture in silence.

"Majorian has an unhealthy fixation for the poor and the homeless." He began to explain. "I'm concerned that, at a certain point, he favors the populace rather than the dignitates."

"Ricimero wouldn't allow it," said the short man.

"Perhaps when Majorian is proclaimed emperor, it will be too late and the Suevian will be able to do little."

"Don't underestimate Ricimero' power, he already managed to get rid of Marco Mecilius Avitus, and I'm sure he could do it again," said another of the clients, who had not intervened until that moment.

"And what do you think?" the plump, bald man asked me directly, pointing at me with the saucepan.

They all watched me carefully. I was a stranger to them and naturally, they were also unknown to me. I had to be careful with my answer, since I didn't know who my interlocutors were.

"Majorian is a great general, fearless and brave on the battlefield. Ricimero is a cunning man and a skilled strategist. If he has supported his proclamation as Augustus, he must have good reasons for that," I replied.

A slight murmur of approval came to my ears.

"Do you consider he is the best of all the candidates to lead the Empire?" the fat man asked again. "Do you think he is better than Ricimero?"

I got up from my seat and addressed the plump character, which I beat by almost a head in terms of size. I took the dipper from him and poured more water on the stones. The rest of the customers looked at me attentively, and some even sat up to hear us better.

"Ricimero is of barbarian origin and will never be named emperor. To speculate on his worthiness to hold that position is an exercise in futility, since we will never be in a position to verify it. On the other hand, Majorian has proven to be a commander and to have extensive military knowledge. Virtues highly valued in an emperor, and if, in addition, we add that Ricimero supports him, what more proof of his worth do you need?"

"*Certum est* [it is true]," said one customer, with the assent of the others.

On the other hand, the plump, bald man said nothing, looked at me with disdain and sat down on a bench.

"What is your name and who are you?" he asked me as I was about to leave the *laconium*.

I turned around. I could barely make him out in the thick steam. He gestured to me to get my attention, and I turned to him.

"My name is Salvio Adriano, *ducenarii* of the *palatinae legio.*"

"A Hispanic and also a legionary. I understand," he growled, glaring disdainfully at his friends.

His companions in the *laconium* laughed at the joke.

"To whom do I have the honor of addressing?" I asked, undaunted.

"My name is Methylius Seronatus, *praefectus classis Ravennatium*, commander of the fleet of Ravenna," he answered pompously, rising from the bench.

241

"It has been a pleasure, *domine*," I said before leaving the *laconium*.

Uneasy, I went to the *frigidarium* where the fresh, clean water removed the sweat and the last crusts of dirt impregnated on my skin. I dressed in the apodyterium with my clothes already clean and dry, and I trimmed my beard and hair.

The conversation I had with those men in the *laconium* worried me. It was evident that Majorian was not to the liking of all the Roman generals, but that the commander of the Ravenna fleet spoke so blithely of his ability or inability in a public sauna and without knowing some of those present, was a sign that something was amiss in the Urbs. Discretion was conspicuous by its absence in these confusing times, where every senator, patrician, or miles fought to maintain their share of power, however ridiculous it might be.

Immersed in my thoughts, I walked along the Londus road towards the camp of the *scholae palatinae* where, as I had been informed, Majorian was installed. My heart pounded as I distinguished, in the distance, the walls of the *castrum* of the imperial guard. I will never forget, nor will I ever be able to, the days of captivity I suffered in the cellars of those barracks, confined in their dark and smelly dungeons. A deep emotion and fear seizes me when I evoke that confinement and the bloodshot eyes of my cannibal cellmates. I sighed deeply trying to get those terrifying memories out of my mind.

I was about to identify myself to the *circitor* when, in the distance, I heard someone shouting my name. I turned around and gave a big smile when I realized who it was.

"Adriano, my friend!" exclaimed Arcadius, raising his arm to get my attention.

"Arcadius!" I shouted, and ran to meet my dear friend.

We embraced each other tightly; then we separated for a few moments so that we could look at each other and contemplate the sharp traces that the passage of time had left on our suffering faces.

"You are like you always were! After the battle in Placentia, I was unable to congratulate you properly on your promotion to *ducenarii*. And of the first regiment; it's worth noting!" he added, taking a closer look at my uniform.

"You're not doing too bad yourself; I see you've been promoted to *centenarius*."

"Yes, well, we've been somewhat amused the last few months, and the *centenarii* are easy prey for the sharp and relentless barbarian archers."

"Don't be modest; I'm sure you've earned your promotion on your own merits," I said, pointing to a scar across the right side of his cheek.

"Do you like it?" He asked proudly. "I got it from an Alaman mercenary in the course of a hard battle." His eyes suddenly glazed over. "Unfortunately, many comrades died that fateful afternoon."

"It was a friend, wasn't it?" I asked, dreading the answer.

He nodded his head.

"Arius Sidonius."

"Arius Sidonius?"

"It was a horrible battle. The Alaman outnumbered and surrounded us. Our tribune, Marius Galvisius, didn't know what to do and began to issue orders at his will, without any sense. Then a *ducenarii* named Cassius Belenus…"

"Yes, I know him. A great *miles*," I interrupted him.

"He proved so on that fateful day," Arcadius continued. "Cassius Belenus took command of the army and we managed to put the barbarians to flight, but the price paid for the incompetence of the tribune was considerable."

"What about Calerus?" I asked him.

"He's fine, don't worry. He is here in Rome with Ajax, awaiting the appointment of Majorian."

"What happened to the tribune?" I asked.

Arcadius clenched his jaw and fists. The scar on his face took on a reddish hue.

"Although the victory was thanks to the intervention of Cassius Belenus, he managed to take the credit and the glory," he answered, spitting on the ground. He comes from a distinguished family and enjoys the support of the senators, who consider him the new savior of the Empire, a sort of Aetius," he added, laughing bitterly.

I shook my head in irritation, the rise in military or social rank thanks to lineage, rather than personal merit, was one of the reasons why the Empire was on the edge of the precipice.

"Genuine inepts of noble surname and rancid ancestry," I said with regret. "Is Traustila also here?" I asked, trying to change the subject.

"Yes, we are all here, together with the *limitanei* from Tarraco. Our camp is set up outside the walls, near the gate of Salaria, is something wrong?" he asked me, noticing my serious countenance.

"I also bring bad news, my friend: Optila is dead."

"Oh my God!" exclaimed Arcadius, throwing his hands on his head. "How did it happen?"

"He was murdered in cold blood by the Visigoths."

Arcadius looked at me without understanding my words, since he supposed, like the rest of the Romans, that the Visigoths were our allies.

"I think we have a lot to talk about, we'd better go to a tavern and unburden ourselves of our respective misfortunes," proposed Arcadius, pointing to a nearby building.

"Later, now I have to report to Majorian," I replied, rejecting the tempting invitation. "But as soon as I'm done, I'll come and look for you at the camp and then we'll go together to Circus Maximus to make up for our sorrows with wine and women, is that all right with you?"

"You've changed a lot if you agree to accompany us to the brothel," he grinned. "All right, I'll wait for you at the camp."

I said goodbye to my friend and entered the *castrum* of the *scholae palatinae*, where I was received by Majorian accompanied by Ricimero. The room was well lit and on a long wooden table they had arranged several trays with food and a couple of jugs of wine. An officer announced my arrival and the future emperor impatiently authorized my entrance.

"I greet you, *magister militum*," I said as soon as I entered the room, bowing my head as a sign of respect.

"Welcome Salvio Adriano, after so many months, it's a pleasure to see you again," said Majorian affectionately, turning to me.

"I greet you, *ducenarii*," said Ricimero sullenly.

"Drink something dear friend, I suppose you are exhausted after such a long journey."

I thanked Majorian for his invitation, and served myself some cold chicken and a jug of wine.

"I have been informed of your journey; I hope you have received the hospitality that an ambassador of Rome deserves and that our Visigoth *foederati* have treated you well," said Ricimero grabbing a jug of wine.

I almost choked on a piece of chicken meat.

"The Visigoths killed a *senator* of the Empire and left me badly wounded. Is this the hospitality our allies have extended to us?"

"Is Optila dead?" Majorian asked me, disgruntled.

"Yes, *domine,* killed by the Visigoths."

"It can't be, they are our allies. Theodoric renewed the *foedus* with Avitus."

"But Avitus no longer governs the designs of Rome," Interrupted Ricimero. "Those Visigoths are as faithful as the whores that infest the Circus Maximus. A Roman officer cannot be assassinated and his crime go unpunished. The new Augustus must punish such an affront with force if he intends to be respected."

The Suevian turned a stern look to Majorian, as if his comment was not a suggestion, but an order.

"The new emperor will know what to do," Majorian replied decisively. "We will act with determination but also with prudence. Maintaining the *foedus* with the Visigoths is indispensable to strengthen peace. I have ambitious projects for the Empire and a war against the Visigoths would be disastrous. Theodoric is a powerful and respected king, a word from him would be enough to make Franks and Burgundians join his cause and cross our *limes.* We must keep the agreement with him at all costs. When he is proclaimed Augustus, I'll send an embassy urging an explanation for this act of treason and I'll demand the immediate surrender of the criminal."

"I hope that in your prudent words Theodoric doesn't perceive any hint of weakness," Ricimero replied, walking around the room with a haughty and arrogant gesture. "For the moment, once he exterminated the Suevian..." the *magister militum* clenched his jaws with a clear gesture of pain "He penetrated into Gallaecia and Lusitania, engaging in depredation and devastating the cities of Emerita Asturica and Pallantia with unusual violence. Only the inhabitants of Coviacum resisted the attack of the Visigothic hordes and their Burgundian and Franks allies. However, the savage cruelty poured out on the Hispano-Romans of those lands will take years to be forgotten."

"Hispanic-Romans who agreed to kiss Requiario' ring, don't forget it." replied Majorian.

"Yes," Ricimero agreed. "But, where were our legions when the Suevian crossed the Tarraconense? Armed militiamen, a handful of *bucelarii*, and peasants carrying sickles and hoes, can hardly bear a charge from the Suevian cavalry. What could they do but accept the invader?

If Rome doesn't protect her own, they will seek refuge in the one who shelters them under his aegis, be he called Requiario, Theodoric... or Majorian."

Ricimero's words were true. Legio VII Gemina, and the five *limitanei* cohorts settled in Hispania, had been dissolved for years. Only in Tarraco did a *castrum* persist with several regiments of *milites* and a detachment of *foederati* auxiliaries. Lacking legionaries to defend them, the Hispanics organized themselves into armed militias or demanded the services of private armies, the *bucelarii*. Rome only came to the aid of her citizens when the barbarian invasion threatened not only to sack the cities, but also to conquer them, taking them from the Empire. Otherwise, Hispanics were left to their own devices and had to protect themselves with their own resources.

"That situation will change," Majorian agreed. "We must appease the Hispanic-Roman provincials so that they understand that Rome has not forgotten them. Only in this way will we ensure that they remain loyal to the Empire."

"Senator Magnus has a great influence over Hispanics," Ricimero intervened. "He could be the ideal person to travel to Hispania and involve *committees* and dignitaries in your ambitious project."

The last words were thrown into the air loaded with irony, but Majorian understood that, once again, the Suevian was right and he just nodded silently.

"By the way," Ricimero continued, looking at me with narrowed eyes, "I understand that you collaborated with the Visigoths in their campaign against the Suevian."

I remembered his Suevian origins, and his animosity towards the Visigoths. It was worth remembering that they had almost fleeced his people.

"I just obeyed orders, *domine*," I said, looking into his eyes.

"As is your duty," he replied, with a slight bow.

The *magister militum* proudly raised his chin and scrutinized me, trying to probe to what extent I was loyal to the Empire or the Visigoths. I don't blame him; traitors infested Rome and roamed its streets with impunity. Furthermore, I fought in Placentia on the side of the defeated legions of Avitus, emperor invested with the purple *paludamentum* thanks to the support of the Visigoths, which didn't exactly earn me his sympathy."

"*Domine*, I want to congratulate you on your imminent proclamation as emperor, I wish God bless you with a long and prosperous government," I said, changing the subject.

"Thank you, legionary, these are difficult times and I hope to have the favor of Our Lord," said Majorian.

Ricimero took a sip of wine and mumbled sarcastically:

"You have him for the moment."

Majorian looked at him suspiciously. We both understood perfectly what he meant by his offensive words. The future Augustus had Ricimero' support, who called himself the lord of Rome. Majorian would wear the imperial insignia, as long as the mighty Ricimero saw fit to do so.

"Ricimero, leave me alone with Adriano, he has much to tell me about his tiring journey," Majorian ordered, in an obvious gesture of authority and staring the Suevian in the eye, without hiding the displeasure that his comment had caused him.

The *magister militum* held him his gaze for a moment, as if he were preparing to unsheathe his *spatha* and fight right there, noting the deep hatred they both professed for each other. Perhaps the common goal of overthrowing Avitus, whom they had confined in a golden prison by appointing him bishop of Placentia, had united them, but once he was overthrown, misgivings and hatred resurfaced and nothing, not even working together for the good of Rome, united them. Finally, and not without first giving him a look full of anger, the Suevian left the room. I didn't know if Ricimero was as powerful as he claimed, but the truth is that Majorian would have to be careful and protect his back if he wanted to enjoy a long life as emperor.

"That bastard says I'll be anointed because of him, and the worst part is that much of Rome thinks the same."

Majorian's face was chiseled by a sneer of contempt but also of rebellion, since he refused to be a puppet, a doll that ruled Rome at the whim of the Suevian.

"Rest assured that it is not, *domine*," I lied.

"I have shed my blood and my men for the defense of the Empire. I owe nothing to him or to his German mercenaries," he whispered. "I'm the one who has used him, and not he to me!" He exclaimed, slamming the table. "He's still an Arian barbarian even though he dresses in a woolen robe and *calcei senatorii* (red boots for senators)," he whispered, sipping his wine.

His gaze reflected the hatred and contempt he felt for the Suevian. He sat down at the table and poured himself some more wine. For a few moments he said nothing, absentmindedly drumming his fingers on the glass with a lost look and a gesture of displeasure marked in fire on his face. His mind was restless thinking of Ricimero.

"The whole army supports you, *domine*. You must not fear."

"I know," he looked up at me and added. "But Ricimero has more than a few clients among the high dignitates, and even in the legion, I fear."

"Rome cannot tolerate another civil war…"

The words vibrated in the air, leaving a bitter taste on my lips, and my gesture contracted with pain, as if I had been lacerated by the swords of a thousand Visigoths.

"And there won't be, I'd rather abdicate for whom… Ricimero would consider opportune" said Majorian, recognizing the omnipotence of the Suevian. And rising from the table he continued:

"But let's forget the bastard Arian and tell me what happened to Optila."

"He was killed by Walder, captain of the *spatharii,* and I believe that behind it all is the hand of Euric."

"Euric, Theodoric's younger brother?" Majorian interrupted.

"That's right, he hates us and I think he'll wait crouching until the time comes to rush upon us."

Majorian smiled.

"He would have to get rid of his brothers Theodoric and Frederic first. We must not worry about him."

"*Domine,* you must not underestimate him. Theodoric killed his brother Turismund to seize power from him, and we have no assurance that it won't happen again. I know Euric, he is an extremely ambitious man, if his goal is to conquer Hispania, he will do everything in his power to achieve it, even if he has to kill his two brothers with his own sword."

The sun was setting behind the hills and the coolness of the evening came through the large windows. Majorian stroked his chin thoughtfully and looked at me with determination.

"To that purpose he feeds that German dog, to do the dirty work. Perhaps you are right. We should strengthen our alliance with the Visigoths and warn Theodoric of his brother's evil intentions," Majorian agreed.

"I think it would be the wisest thing to do."

"Now that Attila is gone, and the Huns have returned to their cold, dark lands in the east, the Visigoths stand as our most formidable enemy. It will be in Hispania that the fate of Rome will be sealed. When the festivities of my proclamation are over, part of the *palatina legio* of Lugdunum will join the *limitanei* of Tarraco, and protect Hispania from the Visigoths. Now we are allies, but no one knows how long this situation will last."

"From Tarraco we can respond to any Visigothic attack in both Hispania and Gaul. It seems to me a good choice, *domine.*"

Majorian sat down with a worried look on his face, picked up a glass again and looked at it meditatively. Many were the worries that were taking root in the tired mind of the future emperor and there was little I could do to help him. I asked for permission to leave and left the *castrum* of the imperial guard to go to the Salaria gate to meet my friends.

The night was covering Rome with its veiled cloak, and the cold of a winter that refused to give way to spring was responsible for the streets remaining almost deserted. The distant barking of a stray dog, the footsteps of vigilante patrols and the plaintive chant of a drunken beggar accompanied me to the gate of Salaria. Once outside the city walls, I came upon a sea of bonfires that rivaled the stars in the firmament. Thousands were the legionaries encamped awaiting the proclamation of the new emperor. Not without difficulty, and after asking half a dozen *milites,* I arrived at Traustila's tent. My heart was in my fist. No one likes to be the bearer of bad news and even less so when it affects him directly. The sorrowful feelings caused by the misfortune come back every time it is spoken of, and the remade heart breaks over and over again…

I opened the tent, and found the Gaul reading a paper under the dim light of a lighted fire.

"By all the gods!" he exclaimed, jumping up and down. "I can't believe it!"

"I salute you, my friend Traustila."

We embraced each other tightly. The Gaul was smiling at me and his eyes were shining with emotion. I sat on his bed without finding the appropriate words of mourning. Optila and Traustila had known each other since they were conscripts. A lifetime of fighting, war, destruction and death behind them, but also of friendship, courage and honor. The relationship between the Gauls reminded me of the one I shared with my friends Calerus and Arcadius. In an instant I felt my heart compress at the thought that one day I might be the one to receive the news of the death of one of them. Traustila sat down next to me and his face darkened with my silence.

"What's wrong, my friend?" he asked, tapping me on the shoulder. "It's Optila, isn't it?"

I nodded without having the courage to look at his face. My eyes were veiled by tears that rushed to flow uncontrollably. Traustila got up and clenched his fists.

"What happened?" he asked, laying his hand on my pained shoulder.

"It was the Visigoths. We were ambushed and Optila was killed. I miraculously managed to save my life," I replied, jumping upright, showing him my scars as a tormented apology for being alive while the Gaul was dead; pretending to allege that I could do nothing to prevent his death.

"What sons of bitches." he exclaimed furiously. Who was he?"

"Walder."

"The German…" he muttered, etching that damn name on his mind.

He sat down dejectedly on the cot and hid his face with his hands. He shook his head in shock, refusing to accept the tragedy of hiss loss. Rejecting the evidence that a *foederati*, a supposed ally, had taken the life of his friend, our friend.

"Son of the great whore!" he exploded with anger.

His furious scream must have been heard throughout the *castrum,* and unable to bear the pain any longer, he burst into tears. I tried to console him, but the Gaul was defeated, lifeless. Together we mourned Optila's death. I don't know where Traustila brought out a jar of wine and two glasses that he generously filled. The sorrows with wine subside and we didn't stop drinking and telling stories about our friend throughout the night. «*Vinum laetificat cor homini*» [wine makes the heart of man happy]. Laughter alternated with tears, and Traustila demanded more wine from the waiter which soon brought us two jars. It was going to be a very long night and what better way than to enliven it with the sacred elixir of the pagan god Bacchus. We drank, laughed, and cried until just before dawn, we fell into the arms of another pagan god, Morpheus.

The morning greeted us with a beautiful, fresh day. We were tired, but in better spirits, especially Traustila. We washed ourselves in a basin and prepared for breakfast. On the way to the barracks I met Arcadius and Calerus. They looked bad. Suddenly I remembered that I had agreed with Arcadius to accompany them to the brothels of the Circus Maximus. However, it seemed that the fact of my absence didn't prevent my friends from enjoying the infinite charms treasured by the women who practiced their self-sacrificing profession there.

"Well, the missing Adriano is here," Arcadius said, feigning anger. Well, you missed it" He added, nudging Calerus with his shoulder.

"Friend Adriano!" Calerus greeted more effusively. It's a shame you didn't participate in yesterday's party. It was epic!"

"Ha, ha, ha! Coming from you, surely your bacchanal will go down in history," I said, giving him a big hug.

"You must excuse him; we were drinking to Optila's health and memories all night," Traustila intervened.

There was an eloquent silence in memory of the Gaul officer. We all deeply felt his loss.

"Let's have breakfast; I'm hungry like a wolf," Arcadius suggested, breaking the silence.

And so, we did. Along the way I met Ajax and later *ducenarii* Cassius Belenus. That same morning I ran into my friend Demetrius Tancinus, who had finally been promoted to *centenarius*. Luckily, he was stationed in another detachment and would not serve under my command. Meeting my old friends comforted me and my mind was blown six years ago, when we were just inexperienced recruits facing the formidable army of the invincible Attila.

I fondly remember the weeks I stayed in Rome. There weren't a few nights that I accompanied Arcadius to the brothels of the Circus Maximus, where my friend had become fond of a young Ethiopian woman, black as ebony and an expert in the arts of lovemaking. I limited myself to getting drunk on the stale wine they served me in the sordid taverns, chasing away the whores that came by showing me their charms, whispering in my ear what they would allow themselves to be done, and what they would do to me for just a few coins. More than once I was on the verge of falling into temptation and, perhaps it was nonsense, but the love I felt for Alana prevented me from lying with any other woman, if only to vent all the energy that men, like beasts that we are, keep in our guts. There was no night that Arcadius didn't reproach me for not lying with one of the prostitutes, he even offered me his beloved Ethiopian. He assured me that abstinence wasn't good for health and that if I wanted to be celibate, I should wear a monastic habit. I laughed and changed the subject. I was aware that it would take many years before I could see her again, if this happened, but my love was more powerful than my animal impulses and in Rome I didn't find any woman who could fill, even in part, the enormous void that the druid-woman had left in my heart. But, as I found out later, time and distance heal everything, and love needs to be nurtured every day if we want it to keep its flame at its best.

We remained in Rome until the proclamation of Majorian as new emperor, shortly after, part of the palatinae legion of Lugdunum, or as I liked to call it, the legion of Aetius, we left for Tarraco commanded by the magister militum Nepotianus.

News reached the Hispanic city of the good government of the emperor, who in just two years had abolished taxes, punished corrupt officials and eliminated some of the most unpopular prerogatives of dignitaries. Meanwhile, and thanks to the indefatigable work of senator Magnus, he had secured the adhesion to Rome of the Hispanic provincials, and his authority was accepted both by the *magister militum Galliarum* Egidius, and by Galo-Roman senators. The renovation of the *foedus* by Burgundians and Visigoths was celebrated with rejoicing by the Romans, who looked hopefully as a horizon of peace and prosperity loomed over the turbulent sky of the Empire. They were years in which we all believed, we trusted that another Rome, another world, was possible. The Augustus became like the executor arm of the long-awaited dream of the famous Aetius.

We were training with our swords in the *castrum* of Tarraco when Nepotianus received a disturbing message from the *civitatis comes* of Carthago Nova. He had been informed that Genseric was planning an invasion of the city. With no time to lose, we immediately set off to the south of Hispania following the Via Augusta. But first I said goodbye to Traustila, since the Gaul would remain in Tarraco directing the training of the new recruits. We said goodbye with a big hug and excited eyes. The memory of our friend Optila quickly came to mind and we feared that this farewell would be the last. But this was not a time of bad omens, but of wishing us luck and hoping with hope that, as the druid Thordor would say, our roads would cross again. In Tarraco I left a friend, but luckily, the rest accompanied me to Carthago Nova.

We passed the city of Dertosa and reached Saguntum. It was years since I had left my family to enlist in the army and ambiguous feelings ran through my heart. I asked the tribune for permission and went to the docks accompanied by Calerus. The *castrum* of Saguntum was strategically located on a large cliff facing the sea and provided a complete view of the entire environment. We went down a poorly paved road that was neglected due to the lack of maintenance. Little had changed the city since I left; what's more, I think it was even more poor and depressing. Barefoot and malnourished children constantly assaulted us begging for coins. From the windows, fearful women with eyes sunken by hunger watched us uneasily. Many houses were abandoned or struggled strenuously to stay upright, rats crossed the streets with impunity, and dogs more famished than their owners were idly guarding the doors of the houses. I came to my old home. Before calling, I observed the flakes of lime that had exposed the adobe blocks with which it was built. I looked at Calerus, my heart was pounding. I knocked on the door hoping that no one would open it. Nothing united me neither my parents nor my brothers, but a feeling of deep roots, or let's call it arcane ties of blood, forced me to abandon the protection of the castrum and enter a decaying and ruinous city. I knocked on the door again and a hollow voice from inside warned me that it would soon be opened.

"Who are you?" a man asked, or rather, a lean, worn face, peering around the door.

"Father, I'm Adriano, your son."

My father looked at me suspiciously, brought his face closer to look at me more closely.

"Who is it?" asked a shrill, high-pitched voice from inside the house, unknown to me.

"Shut!" my father yelled, turning his head. "You seem to be doing well, son," he added, narrowing his eyes and looking closely at my uniform. "You aren't a simple legionary, are you?"

I saw the greed in his eyes and felt a deep pity. Calerus watched the scene in silence.

"Today we are leaving for Carthago Nova and I wanted to greet you before I leave," I said, changing the subject. "Where are my mother and my brothers?"

My father rubbed his hands, observing, with the greatest impudence, the bag that hung from my belt.

"Come in," he said reluctantly.

I hadn't seen my father for ten years and to say the truth, I think I still regret that visit. The long years he had worked as a stevedore had taken their toll on his lean body. He was extremely thin, stooped, and the bones of his hands were stiff, as if he had claws instead of fingers. Life hadn't been excessively generous to him, and it wouldn't have been correct to blame him for the sorry state he was in. But it was his greedy and mean look that pressed my heart. We went into the house and took a seat on some old, splintered footstools.

"Who the hell are these?" yelled an old woman, her face lined with a thousand wrinkles and dressed in tattered clothes.

"Shut up, old witch. It's Salvio Adriano, my son!"

The woman fell silent and looked at me more closely. Her gaze, just as it had happened to my father, drifted over my leather bag.

"I'd offer you some wine, son, but as you can see, I'm even poorer than I was when you left," my father apologized.

"Where are my mother and brothers?"

"Your mother died many years ago and your brothers left, leaving me alone."

I must have had a heart of stone because I didn't feel the slightest sorrow for my mother's death. Affection and care were conspicuous by their absence in my family. We were like a group of strangers who had the obligation to live together due to different circumstances.

"But you don't even know where they went?"

He made a nonchalant gesture.

"Some went north, others went south, and others boarded a ship… I don't know."

"Are you trying to tell me that you don't know where your children are?"

"They're old enough to fend by themselves, I have other problems."

The old woman took a seat on an old and lame footstool. She kept licking her lips and rubbing her hands as she watched us closely.

254

"This is Clodia, my wife," he said, gesturing at the old woman dismissively.

I looked at the woman, she was probably under sixty years old but she looked one hundred. She had the appearance of the old prostitutes who frequented the Circus Maximus and who, despised by most men, looked for their clients among the beggars and rags. Calerus and I greeted her with a slight gesture.

"He's Lucius Calerus," I said, introducing my friend.

My father and his wife nodded silently with puckered lips.

"How do you earn life?" I asked my father, looking away from the squeaky old woman.

My father nodded at the old woman. Unfortunately, the old woman not only had the appearance of a whore, but she was also one.

"If it weren't for this!" exclaimed the old woman, touching her genitals. "We wouldn't have anything to eat here!"

Her high-pitched voice was even more unpleasant than her presence and it penetrated our ears like a chisel on stone. Calerus couldn't help a gesture of disgust. Embarrassed, my father pounced on the woman and beat her so brutally that he threw her off her footstool.

"You old whore, treat my son and his friend with more respect!" he blurted her out furiously.

The old woman got up without complaining: My father's blows seemed to be something common. Calerus and I made the gesture of helping her, but my father made a gesture of preventing us.

"She's a bitch who only learns through blows," he muttered, looking at the woman with contempt.

"But your bread depends on her," I said, embarrassed. "We should go," I added, heading to the door.

"Wait son!" I stopped my step.

My father looked at the money bag greedily, the old woman from a safe distance, did the same.

"I don't know if it would be possible..."

I picked up the bag and dropped a handful of silver siliquas onto his bony hand. His eyes glowed with greed and his face lit up with a toothless smile. The old woman, with a surprising and agile movement, pounced on my father trying to snatch the coins, which fell crashing to the ground. And there I left them, sticking, fighting each other, pulling each other's hair, scratching each other, biting for some sad coins. I turned my back on them and walked away from that place, leaving far behind the echo of the unequal battle.

On the way back to the *castrum* I didn't open my mouth and barely looked at Calerus, who remained in respectful silence digesting the grotesque spectacle that he had just witnessed. The shame and humiliation of finding my father living off an old whore was beyond my strength. I didn't feel love for him not even something close to appreciation. But it was one thing to be indifferent and quite another that my father to be a ruffian. I bit my lip in anger and clenched my fists in frustration.

"Don't feel guilty, we don't choose our parents," Calerus said, looking at my irritated and sullen face.

"I have never loved my family: my father worked from sunrise to sunset and I hardly saw him, my mother was always busy taking care of her five children or secretly drinking wine. As for my brothers, they were nothing more than savage brutes who did nothing but beat each other. In my family there was never love, we just lived together. It's a shame, but that's how my childhood was."

"I'm sorry, friend," Calerus said sincerely, grabbing my shoulder.

"Seeing my father like this... living off the work of an old prostitute," I felt a lump in my throat.

It was definitely not a good idea to visit my family in Saguntum. I felt devastated and humiliated. I took one last look and saw my father enter the house followed by the woman, who kept fussing and screaming like a distraught. I shook my head and tried to forget that sad memory forever.

On the way to Carthago Nova we checked the defenses of the most important cities that were on the Via Augusta. So we stopped in Valentia, Dianium and Lucentum. I was pleased to see that these cities, not depending on a decaying and useless port, weren't only not in ruins, but also, and according to what I was informed, had progressed under the government of Majorian. In the absence of legionaries to protect them, they had armed themselves with well-armed and equipped divers. The Gaul senator Magnus had a great responsibility in the good disposition of the defenses of the main cities, by providing them with the necessary economic resources in exchange for his firm adherence to the Empire.

During the trip, I was pleased to see the peasants working the fields carelessly, the shepherds confidently guarding the flocks, and the merchants selling their trinkets in villages and towns. There was nothing that suggested, that, a few years before, the Vandals crossed our *limes* and landed on our beaches looting, killing and leaving a trail of ruins and destruction in their wake. Prosperity was returning to the fields of Hispania and a feeling of happiness and hope was breathed in our hearts. It was a shame that Saguntum, the once great port city and base of Hispanic commerce, had been left out of that wave of progress and well-being. The decline of the city must have infected its inhabitants, or at least that is how it happened to my father.

We arrived in Carthago Nova on a hot summer day and camped outside the city walls greeted by the shouts of joy and joy from its inhabitants. We set up our tents and, accompanied by Arcadius, Calerus, Ajax and Cassius Belenus, I crossed the wall in search of some tavern where to quench my thirst for wine. Carthago Nova made a pleasant impression on me. Its buildings were in good condition, the market bustled with activity and there weren't too many inhabitants marked by misery, as was the case in the wretched Saguntum. We walked along the *decumanus* via and arrived at the forum. Despite the evident Christianization of the city, there were not few pagan temples still standing. Of all of them, the one that most captivated me, for its beauty and its good state of preservation, was the temple dedicated to the Capitoline triad, that is, to the ancient Roman gods Jupiter, Juno and Minerva. My good friend Arcadius, tired of walking and as always, much more pragmatic, asked a passerby where he could find good wine and enjoy the most beautiful women and he replied that we should go along the *cardus* via towards the port. And there we went. The streets were crowded with people wandering around aimlessly. Merchants shouted their merchandise, children scampered among the adults and women gossiped at the door jambs. Carthago Nova was a lived city and what was even more important, with a desire to live.

"Another Rome is possible," Calerus observed, as if he had read my thoughts.

"This city is an example of that," I confirmed.

"Julius Valerius Majorian will make the Empire rise from its ashes and be feared once again by its enemies," a distracted Arcadius intervened, looking at the door jambs in search of the sign that distinguished the brothels. "Look, there's one!" he exclaimed victoriously, and ran towards the building without even waiting for us.

"He looks like a bull in heat," Cassius Belenus said watching Arcadius push his way through the crowd.

"Does he only look like one?" Calerus asked with a smile.

We were joking about Arcadius, whom we had already lost sight of, when I saw her. It was barely an instant when she crossed by my side, looking indifferently at the merchants' stalls. I stood still, petrified, spellbound. I saw her get lost in the crowd and my mind began to react. I managed to push my way through the crowd and head towards her, leaving behind the shouts of my friends who called out to me without understanding where I was going. I looked up in search of her and noticed that she was going into an alley, I accelerated my pace and with it, the number of pushes and elbows I gave to anyone who stood in my desperate way. My heart was pounding in my chest and my mind was beginning to distrust what my eyes had seen. I reached the alley. More and more people were getting in my way. A real wave of people going up and down indifferent to my anxiety. I looked around for a shortcut and found a small archway leading to a parallel street. I ducked and ran down the street in fear of losing her. I turned the corner and found myself back in the same alley crowded with people and stalls. I looked up and my heart leapt with joy when I saw her. She had black eyes and full lips. As beautiful as a goddess. I approached her, screaming her name like a demon.

"Alana! Alana!"

But she didn't hear me, even though I was almost beside her. I roughly pushed aside a merchant who was offering her his products and grabbed her by the shoulders.

"Alana, my love."

I hugged her tightly, with the irrepressible desire to never separate us. My glassy eyes were veiled by an immeasurable emotion, and my heart leapt in my chest filled with joy, happiness and exhilaration, like that of a wild foal that has just been released from its reins. After so many years, we were meeting again...

"Excuse me... but my name is not Alana..." The woman denied with a trembling voice, gently pulling away from me, fearing that, in my madness, I might hurt her.

She looked at me strangely, surprised, as if she had never seen me before, as if I were a stranger, a stranger who had mistaken her for someone else.

"Alana..." I mumbled.

"I'm sorry..." she whispered, shaking her head as she took my hands off her shoulders.

Her eyes, her mouth, her face were those of my beloved. How was it possible for that woman to deny being Alana? My soul collapsed in the most merciless disappointment. The petty goddess fortune threw again the dice of disenchantment and frustration and, once again, I was the object on which she poured her immense cruelty.

"What are you doing, legionary?" a *bucelarius* spat at me.

Immersed in my crazy musings, I didn't notice that several *bucelarius* had surrounded me and, grabbing me, they separated me abruptly from her. I couldn't take my eyes off those deep and radiant black eyes, they were Alana's, they had to be hers! The woman looked at me questioningly, uneasily and shook her head before losing herself in the crowd.

"Have you gone mad, soldier?" the one who seemed to be the leader of the *bucelarii* shouted at me again.

The officer's loud voice brought me back to reality and I found myself surrounded by *bucelarii* threatening me with their swords under the gaze of the onlookers who had stopped their wandering through the stalls to watch a legionary being held back by a patrol of soldiers.

"What on earth did you intend to do?" he spat an inch away from my face. He was a giant of almost seven feet of pure muscle and with a very unfriendly face.

"I had mistaken her for someone else," I stammered, still not understanding what had happened.

"Someone else? He asked?"

A crowd gathered around gossiping, eager to satisfy their unhealthy curiosity. The *bucelarii* began to have difficulty controlling them.

"Who is that woman?" I dared to ask.

The *bucelarius* face relaxed.

"What are you looking at? Come on; get back to your business, pack of gossips!" he shouted to the onlookers, who scattered, frightened by the giant's energetic reaction. "Put your weapons away, this one is harmless," he ordered his men.

The giant grabbed my shoulder and we walked away from the hustle and bustle and the stalls. Five men at-arms followed us at a distance.

"I can see from your uniform that you are *ducenarius*. I was also a legionary many years ago, but we were discharged when the legions of Hispania stopped being profitable. There were no more territories to plunder and Rome refused to pay for our salary," he said, looking up at the sky, searching his mind for old, almost forgotten memories. "You come from Tarraco, don't you?"

"Yes, my name is Salvio Adriano.

"I'm Tadius Ursus; head of the personal guard of the *civitatis comes* Valerius Aquilius. You are not from around here that explains why you don't know the young woman."

"Who is she?

"She is Valeria Aquiliaris, the only daughter of the *comes*."

I stopped my step and looked at him puzzled.

"Is what you're saying true?"

"Of course!" he exclaimed. "Everyone knows her in Carthago Nova. She is extremely beautiful…"

Suddenly I was overwhelmed and found a seat on a stone bench. The hopes of seeing Alana again had vanished like smoke after a gust of wind. But a strange unease welled up inside me. I wanted to see her again, to scrutinize her features, her smile, the brightness of her eyes, the warmth of her hands … That woman was not Alana, but she had awakened in me a feeling that was asleep, forgotten, lethargic after spending long years lifeless in a dark and sad corner of my heart.

"If you had mistaken her for a little friend, I have to congratulate you," said the *bucelarius,* who had taken a seat next to me. "She must be a very beautiful woman."

"I'd like to see her again."

The giant gave me a look that I couldn't interpret, but he made it clear that my suggestion was not to his liking.

"She is the only daughter of the *comes* and he feels a true devotion for her. Let me give you some advice," he said, as he got up. "Don't get near her; it could be detrimental to your health," he concluded, patting me on the shoulder.

The *bucelarius* got lost in the alleys of Carthago Nova, accompanied by his men.

I was lying on the pallet. It had been several hours since the sun had set behind the horizon, but I was unable to sleep. I was confused by the disconcerting appearance of Valeria and couldn't stop thinking about her. Her enormous resemblance to Alana, the way she looked at me when they pulled me away from her... My heart roared with the desire to see her again. My mind was buzzing with wild ideas and I couldn't sleep. In addition, the snoring of Arcadius and company, who had returned well into the morning completely drunk, didn't help to clarify my confused thoughts. I got up and decided to go for a walk. I left the *castrum* with the intention of entering the city. At the gate of the wall I asked the *circitor* where the ambassador house was located. The *bucelarius* looked at me suspiciously, but he finally gave me the information. I followed his instructions and walked along lonely and silent streets, crossing on my way an occasional disoriented drunk, a couple of lonely lovers and the usual night patrols. The house where the *comes* and his family resided was very close to the theater and was built of limestone and marble. The door was guarded by two indolent *milites*, bored on a quiet night. I hid behind a corner and remained there for several hours, waiting to meet the *comes'* daughter.

I felt a fervent desire to see her again and reaffirm whether her resemblance to Alana was real or just a product of my imagination. But, above all, I wanted to clarify my feelings. I loved Alana; I had no doubt about that. Long years had elapsed since the last time we had been together, but my love for her had not waned one iota in all that time. But Valeria's appearance had been a whirlwind of conflicting sensations. I needed to see her dark eyes again, to hear her sweet voice, to smell her intoxicating perfume. Only then would I be able to sort out my emotions and discover if the uneasiness she had aroused in me had been due to her resemblance to Alana, or if it was another feeling...

The sun was peeking over the horizon, illuminating the roofs of the tallest buildings in the city with a reddish-orange color. The barking of a stray dog and an occasional early bird neighbor emptying the chamber pots in the corrals attached to their homes announced that Carthago Nova was beginning to awaken from its slumber. I wasn't tired; impatience and uncertainty would grant me enough energy to continue my wait indefinitely.

Fortunately, it was not long before I saw her leave accompanied by a slave girl. I followed them at some distance to make sure that they were not escorted by the *bucelarius* or his men. She crossed the theater and ascended the *decumanus* via, it seemed that she was heading to the forum. I looked behind me several times fearing that I would meet the giant, but it seemed that the *comes* had assigned him other responsibilities. In the market, the laziest were still setting up their stands and few were the customers who had awakened early in the morning to make the first purchases of the day. Valeria and her companion entered a bakery, and that was the moment I chose to approach her. Nervous, I ran to the door and waited for them to come out. It didn't take long for the two women to leave the bakery carrying two loaves of bread in a basket.

"I greet you, Valeria Aquiliaris; daughter of the *civitatis comes* Valerius Aquilius," I said behind them as soon as they left the store.
The girl was wearing a sky-blue tubular tunic and covered her shoulders with a white shawl. I was completely bewildered in front of her, since I would have bet my soul that it was Alana who was looking at me with astonishment and surprise at my audacious attack.

"Allow me to apologize for my behavior with you yesterday," I continued. "My eyes betrayed me and mistook you for someone else."

Valeria's look calmed down and a shy smile appeared on her lips.

"My name is Salvio Adriano," I introduced myself with a nod, "*ducenarius* of the armies of Rome."

"I'm delighted," said Valeria, immediately resuming her walk.

"We may not have had a good start," I began to say, hastily following in her footsteps. "But your eyes tell me that I'm not stranger to you."

"I'm sorry, but I don't know you," she replied without stopping.

"Wait a second, please." I begged.

Valeria stopped at the slave's urgent gaze. I looked her in the eyes and smiled. She smiled back and her eyes lit up.

"Do we know each other?" she asked.

"Now we do," I answered boldly.

"But..."

"But you have the feeling we've known each other for a long time, don't you?"

She nodded.

"So do I," I said and stroked her cheek.

A strange sensation ran through my body. It was a kind of tingling, a powerful energy that crossed my spine and flooded my mood with almost forgotten feelings. For a few moments we looked at each other without saying anything, we didn't need to. In her shining black eyes I noticed the same thing I had seen in Alana's eyes years ago.

"*Domine* please, we must go," the slave urged.

"I don't understand," Valeria murmured "I have the feeling I've known you for years."

I nodded; I understood perfectly what she meant, as I was experiencing the same sensations. Suddenly I felt a hand pressing my shoulder as if it were an eagle's claw. I turned around and a huge fist hit my face making me fall to the ground.

"You damned legionary! Didn't I tell you to stay away from her?"

Disoriented, I looked for Valeria but couldn't find her. I got up and another blow brought me to my knees, I reached for my *spatha* as someone kicked my stomach. I curled into a ball while several legs were treating me brutally.

"Stop it, that's enough!" the voice commanded.

My bruised body ached terribly and I couldn't get up. I looked up and found myself surrounded by *bucelarii*. I recognized one of them at once. The chief of those men bent down and grabbed my hair.

"Pay attention legionary, I like you and that's why I warned you." Get away from Valeria or the next warning will be the last," Ursus threatened.

"Do I have another option?" I stammered my lips bloody.

The *bucelarius* smiled.

"Yes, ask her hand to the *comes*," he answered, sitting up. Maybe he will even grant it to you," he added, at the laughter of his companions.

In pain I got up and watched as Tadius Ursus got lost in the streets accompanied by his men. Despite the beating I had received, my heart was pounding and it wasn't exactly due to the blows suffered. I smiled and my broken lip hurt. I could be wrong, but in Valeria's eyes I had recognized the same love that Alana's eyes radiated. There was a magic between her and me, a spell, a link as invisible as it was real. It had only been an instant, but I was persuaded that I was not indifferent to her but… what about me? What were my feelings towards Valeria? Had I betrayed Alana? It had been several years since the last time we were together and I wasn't sure that I would see her again. Was it time to rebuild my life? Doubts made my head dull, but of one thing I was sure,

I wanted to, I needed to see her again and by God, I would do anything to get it.

I barely returned to the *castrum*. My colleagues, seeing the state in which I was, accompanied me to the *valetudinarium*. There, I related my two encounters with Valeria and, of course, with the seven-foot giant.

"Well, there are no women in Carthago Nova and you have a crush on the daughter of the *civitatis comes*!" Arcadius exclaimed laughing.

"You must be careful; the *bucelarius* isn't one of those who think twice before using his fists," Calerus intervened.

"I'd like to face him," Ajax grumbled, hitting his hand with his fist.

"Easy friends," I said with a smile. "I think she has feelings for me and that is the important thing."

"Have you already forgotten Alana?" Arcadius asked.

The memory of Alana came back to my mind and my heart saddened.

"I love Alana madly and will always love her, but I can't live only on her memories. If fate has a future meeting for us, so be it, but in the meantime, I must continue living without asking myself anything else."

Besides, in Valeria's eyes I saw the love and tenderness that only Alana knew how to give me. I had barely seen her couple of times and I had, we had the feeling of knowing each other for many years. Without a doubt, something beautiful and wonderful had sprung up in our hearts. The daughter of the *comes* was a new opportunity to be happy and this time I wasn't going to let it escape, no matter how many druids, *comites* or *bucelarii* stood in my way.

Sometimes Fortune takes our side and three days after receiving the beating, I was summoned, as *ducenarii* of the *palatina legio*, to a campaign meeting at the house of the *comes*. Dressed in my well-burnished coat of mail, with my red *sagum* hanging from my shoulders and my nerves on the surface, I went to Valerius Aquilius's house. There were the most illustrious and influential personalities of the city and even of Hispanic Rome.

It was a limpid and crystalline night where the stars illuminated the sky with their entire splendor. The sweltering heat of the day had given way to a light breeze that carried with it the scent of jasmine and violets. I took a deep breath of the sweet scent of flowers and smiled. It was a beautiful summer night and the hope of seeing Valeria again filled me with joy and happiness. Nervous, I reached the entrance portico of the house. I presented myself to the guards and they cleared my entrance. I

264

crossed the *vestibulum* and a servant escorted me to the *atrium* and indicated the *triclinium* that I would occupy during the meeting. The *comes* had not a bad idea, it was a wonderful night and having a meeting in the central courtyard of the house, under the light of the stars and the aroma of the flowers, would make it more pleasant and, possibly, more fruitful.

Due to my impatience, I was the first to arrive and sat on the *triclinio* waiting for the rest of the guests to come. The diligent servants showered me with attentions, constantly offering me wine and trays of fruit. One of them, a young ephebe of about twelve years old, insisted on offering me a tray with grapes, portions of watermelon and dates. I took advantage of one of his multiple approaches to ask him a question:

"Do you know if *domine* Valeria Aquiliaris will be at the meeting?"

"The *domina* never participates in her father's meetings, she prefers to watch them from the window," he answered, turning and looking at a window that outlined a female figure.

I looked away there and the shadow disappeared, hiding behind the wall. A few moments later, Valeria's head emerged, peering curiously through a half-open window. I greeted her and she hid again.

"Can you tell the lady that I want to talk to her?"

The servant raised his eyes in fear.

"*Domine...*"

"I think she wants to do it too, tell her to show you a place where we can talk and then sent you back to accompany me."

The young man hesitated, he wasn't very clear if he should do it.

"I assure you that I'll be eternally grateful to you and the lady, too."

Not very convinced, the servant left and entered through the door that led to Valeria's rooms. It was still early and I hoped I would have enough time to be able to speak to her, even if it were only a few seconds, before the attendees began to arrive at the council. In a few minutes the figure of the servant appeared. He gestured at me in the distance and urged me to follow him.

I crossed the *atrium* and entered through a door on one side of the inner courtyard. We climbed a stone staircase and came to a long corridor.

"The second door on the right. *Domine,* you have very few minutes before the guests arrive," he warned me pleadingly.

"Don't worry," I said with a smile.

"I'll be waiting at the corner in case anyone shows up."

265

I thanked with a gesture with my head and headed to the indicated door. My heart was beating so hard that I thought it would betray my presence to the guards of the *comes*. I knocked carefully and the door opened. There she was, dressed in a white linen robe. Beautiful, radiant, like a divine Venus emerged from the foam of the sea. I was absorbed, enraptured by such beauty and she had to take me by the arm to make me enter.

"You're crazy," she whispered to me.

"Crazy for you."

And without saying anything else, I kissed her holding her in my arms. I felt the warmth of her fleshy lips, caressed her soft neck and felt her body brushing against mine.

"I just want to know if you love me like I love you," I said boldly as soon as our lips parted."

"Me…"

Confused, she pulled away from me with her back to me.

"It's something very strange," she began to say. "I have the feeling that I've known you forever and that we've hardly seen each other. Maybe… maybe I've seen you in my dreams… maybe you're a childhood memory… I don't know…"

"Do you love me?" I insisted.

She was looking out the window. She touched her arms as if a chill had gone through her body. She was undecided, puzzled. She didn't understand why she was carried away by such powerful feelings towards a man she didn't know.

"I can't understand it, but I think, I think I've loved you all my life…" she replied, turning around with wet eyes.

A big smile crossed my face. I headed toward her, but the sound of hinges stopped my step.

"I'm sorry, *domine*, but the guests are coming," the servant urged me uneasily. "You must come down as soon as possible."

I looked at Valeria and she nodded at me.

"I love you," I told her.

She smiled at me and nodded sweetly. Happy, blissful at last, I descended the stairs like a flash and returned to the *atrium*, where already were several of the illustrious guests. Accompanied by the servant, I took a seat on my couch.

"I'll always be grateful to you for what you have done for me tonight," I told him.

"It's a pleasure serving the lady."

"What is your name?"

"Libius."

I took some siliquas out of a bag and gave them to him. He tried to reject them but I insisted.

"Friend, this is a pittance in exchange for how happy you have made me, accept them, I beg you."

For an officer of the legion to beg a servant wasn't very usual and my words must have caused him a great shock, since he took the coins and left with tears in his eyes.

I loved her. That's what I had confessed to her, I loved Valeria. And she loved me too. Her eyes and the blush on her cheeks revealed it. But how was it possible? We had barely seen each other... I remembered my first meeting with Alana and my lips formed a goofy smile. Immediately I was captivated by that enigmatic Suevian as I was now enraptured by this beautiful Carthaginiense. Love doesn't require any explanation, it is only necessary to let yourself be meekly carried away by it, to surrender to her designs in order to enjoy her immense favors. The bustle of greetings and the bustle of servants running around carrying jars of wine and trays of food woke me from my reveries and I observed that several Roman officials were in the *atrium*.

"Are you fine?"

I looked up and found Severus Nasus, the tribune who commanded my legion. Dressed in his best clothes, he carried a silver goblet and looked at me confusedly.

I feel fine, *domine*," I said, jumping to my feet.

"I'm glad. Come," he said, taking me by the shoulder. "I want to introduce you to some of the people attending the meeting.

A dozen Roman officers were standing around me. I already knew some of them: they were *ducenarii* of the first regiment of their respective legions, others were *primicerii* and I recognized a couple of tribunes. The *magister militum* Nepotianus greeted Severus Nasus raising his glass sullenly and continued his conversation with one of the *primicerii*. We joined a group of officers who were chatting animatedly, laughing a few times. Among them was the head of the *civitatis comes* guard, who was easy to recognize thanks to his height. I deduced that Valeria's father wouldn't be far away. And so it was. I noticed how Tadius Ursus whispered something in the ear of Valerius Aquilius who looked at me with curiosity.

"Greetings, gentlemen," said Severus Nasus as soon as he reached the group.

The *dignitaries* saluted and raised their glasses.

"Allow me to introduce Salvio Adriano, *ducenarii* of the first regiment of the *palatina legio* and veteran of the wars against Attila.

"Were you in Maurica?" Valerius Aquilius asked me with interest.

"That's right, *domine.*"

"I have heard about you," he said, looking at Ursus. "You look strong and, no doubt, you are brave. I hope that the goddess nature has also granted you the intelligence and prudence necessary to prevent you from embarking on fruitless ventures."

The officers looked at him without understanding what he meant, but I knew perfectly well.

"I have faced and defeated Attila himself. An honor few of us here present are in a position to claim. I have a steely determination and I can assure you, *domine*, that none of the enterprises I embark on is unsuccessful," I replied, looking him straight in the eye.

His face contracted and he clenched his fists.

"I see that the message that Tadius Ursus conveyed to you hasn't made you reflect. Perhaps other, more forceful methods should be used."

"The bruises on my body will heal with time, but what my heart feels is so beautiful and pure that no one," I looked at Tadius Ursus, "no matter how big his fists are or how sharp his *spatha* is, will be able to dominate.

"Do you think you are worthy of her?"

"Why am I not? Because my origins are not illustrious, because I possess neither land nor wealth? I love her and she loves me, that's what matters."

Everyone looked at each other surprised by the direction the conversation was taking, and several officers approached our group intrigued. The *comes* glared at me.

"How can you dare to say that Valeria loves you when she barely knows you!" he shouted at me with fire in his eyes.

"*Domine,* I'm just asking for a chance. Ask your daughter if she loves me, if she doesn't, I'm willing to never see her again. On the other hand, if I'm reciprocated, I ask you to grant me the opportunity to court her. My lord," I said conciliator, avoiding tightening more a rope that was threatening to break. "I lack riches and I can only offer my courage

268

and sword to Valeria, but I'm a good *miles* and I'll prove to you in the battlefield or in front of any enemy, that I'm worthy of her."

"If you are so sure that Valeria doesn't love him, ask her." Severus Nasus interjected.

The Roman officers watched the scene with amusement. Valerius Aquilius was puzzled and looked at those present in search of some support or alternative to get out of the impasse he had gotten himself into. A couple of voices were heard supporting Severus Nasus's suggestion.

"Valeria can't be in love with him. It's impossible," said an officer.

"Let's put an end to this farce, let Valeria speak and punish the daring soldier," said another.

The *comes* turned his gaze towards his daughter's room and noticed her translucent shadow behind the glass: Valeria was already aware of the discussion. Valerius Aquilius stroked his beard and ordered a servant to look for her.

With her head lowered and overwhelmed with shame, Valeria descended the stone staircase and stood in front of her father. We formed a circle around her and looked at her expectantly.

"Valeria, my dear," her father began. "This *miles* has asked my permission to woo you. According to what Tadius Ursus told me, he has assaulted you a couple of times and he has the audacity to claim that you love him. Well, tell me that it's false and let's settle this awkward situation once and for all."

Valeria breathed anxiously, her cheeks flushed and her eyes moistened. For a few moments she said nothing, enveloping us all with her eloquent silence.

"My daughter, you can speak freely," he said with a nervous smile. Tadius Ursus gave me an unsettling look that, on this occasion, I soon recognized.

Valeria looked up and staring at the *comes* said:

"Father, is it true that I can speak freely?"

Valerius Aquilius looked at her in bewilderment. The gazes of those present converged on him. After a few brief moments of indecision, he nodded.

"Yes, I love him."

A murmur that soon turned into an uncontrolled uproar burst into the silent night, filling it with laughter and amazement. The officers raised their glasses and toasted the new couple. The *magister militum*

Nepotianus patted me on the back several times, congratulating me on the pleasant news. Valerius Aquilius was petrified and looked at his daughter with astonishment without understanding anything. Tadius Ursus was frowning and his fists were tightly clenched. Valeria, embarrassed, ran crying to her room. Ursus whispered something in the *civitatis comes'* ear and he came to himself.

"Silence! Silence! Must I remind you that you are in my house?" he commanded angrily, raising his hands and all fell silent.

The *comes* began to walk among the officers with his hands behind his back. From the window of a room the beautiful silhouette of Valeria could be seen. For a few moments Valerius Aquilius remained silent in order to attract the attention of those present. Then, accompanied by Tadius Ursus, he addressed me.

"You have no wealth, no land, but you have your sword," he continued. "You say that with it you will make yourself worthy of Valeria... fighting against any enemy, don't you?"

I nodded, foreshadowing the trap his words concealed.

"I'm willing to grant you my daughter's hand," several officers broke into shouts and cheers, and the *comes* raised his hand asking for silence. "But first I must be sure that you are the right person. If you're going to feed my grandchildren with the blade of your *spatha* you'll have to prove that you know how to use it."

"What do you suggest?"

"You will face Tadius Ursus."

A sea of protests erupted unrestrained in the atrium. I looked up and looked for Valeria, but I didn't see her.

"Duels for honor and gladiatorial fights are forbidden!" my tribune exclaimed wrathfully.

"What you are trying to do is illegal!" cried an officer.

"It would be murder," said a *ducenarius*.

"I agree!" I exclaimed, and a deep silence extinguished the fire of protest. "I will fight Tadius Ursus, whenever and wherever you wish. The love I feel for Valeria will give me the strength to defeat him."

"But..." Severus Nasus tried to protest, but I interrupted him with a gesture.

A smile of satisfaction appeared on the fearsome face of the giant Tadius Ursus and he said:

"*Domine,* it is best that this absurd joke ends as soon as possible. If you give us your permission and the legionary agrees, we will engage in single combat right now."

He looked at me and I nodded.

"It will be that way, make a circle," ordered Valerius Aquilius.

"The whole thing is ridiculous; the purpose of this council was to devise a strategy against the Vandals, not to witness a fight to the death!" Severus Nasus exclaimed impotently.

"We'll talk about that later," replied Valerius Aquilius. "Now you are my guests, you are in my house and I'm the highest authority in the city. If Nepotianus has no objection, the combat will take place this very night."

The *magister militum* consented with a hand gesture and looking at us he said:

"If both contenders agree," Tadius Ursus and I nodded. "In that case, they can fight, but not to the death. We don't have enough soldiers to kill each other in a mad duel for honor or to win the love of a woman... therefore, whoever inflicts the first bloody wound on the adversary will be the winner."

"Great «*Prima sanguinis*» [first blood]" acceded the *comes.*

Tadius Ursus and I nodded again, accepting the conditions of the combat, but on the lips of the *bucelarius* a perfidious and cunning smile appeared, suggesting that he would not be satisfied with just wounding me.

Valeria, terrified, watched the scene from the room. With her heart shrinking with worry, she rushed down the stairs like an exhalation and, submerged in a sea of tears, threw herself on her father, begging him to impede the fight.

"Father, I don't love him, I don't love him!" she cried out between sobs. "Stop this madness!"

Valerius Aquilius looked into his daughter's pleading eyes and hugged her tightly. Then he understood what he had to do.

"You have been willing to fight against my best soldier," he began to say, still hugging his daughter. "To be worthy of Valeria's love, who has denied that she loves you to avoid great danger for you," he took his daughter by the shoulders and smiled, then approached me and offered me Valeria's hand. "Take her hand; you are totally worthy of it. I'm sure that with your sword you will conveniently support my grandchildren."

271

"Good for Valerius Aquilius!" cried a *ducenarius,* and cheers and salutes burst noisily from in the *atrium.*

The greetings, blessings and congratulations spread like fire in a wheat field, and not a few shouted «long live the bride and groom» as if we were already at a wedding feast. I felt blissful and happy. I looked at Valeria; her cheeks were streaked with tears of happiness.

Suddenly, a heartrending scream distracted us, and we looked away to the head of the guards.

"Do not!" Tadius Ursus exclaimed. The captain of the *bucelarius* drew his sword and made a menacing gesture toward me. "Valeria must be mine!"

"Ursus, what are you doing?" asked the *comes,* annoyed, getting in his way.

The giant gave him a strong push and threw him on several *milites,* who grabbed the *comes* to prevent him from falling to the ground. He attacked and lunged furiously at me which I was hopefully able to dodge. An officer jumped on him and Ursus skewered him with his *spatha.* They called out to the guard who swiftly surrounded him. We officers watched the scene in puzzlement. We couldn't believe that the most loyal *bucelarius* had attacked his *domine.* With bloodshot eyes, he attacked and defended himself against the guards, who one by one fell at his feet, staining the pristine marble of the pavement in vermilion.

"Stop!" I ordered, staring at the ground strewn with corpses. "It's okay Tadius Ursus, if you want it that way, it will be."

"Do not!" Valeria yelled, running towards me.

We melted into a strong hug at the look of hatred from Tadius Ursus, who remained surrounded by several guards. I kissed her and pushed her away from my side. Severus Nasus approached her and comforted her in her arms.

"Do what you have to do," my tribune said.

I nodded and drew my *spatha.* The *bucelarii* made way for me and I found myself facing the giant. Several soldiers removed the wounded and the dead, leaving a trail of blood in their wake. Tadius Ursus was looking at me with bloodshot eyes. He was breathing hard and his powerful muscles were tense, ready for combat.

"So that's it," I said. "You love her too... but hidden under the fearful shadows of silence. It must have been hard for you. You have spent hours, days, months and years with her without daring to reveal your feelings, did you never have enough courage to confess it?"

The giant, enraged by my words, pounced on me brandishing his sword and uttering a terrifying cry. I blocked his blow and with a feint managed to counterattack. Tadius Ursus looked at me surprised, without a doubt, he had underestimated me. More prudent and without lowering his guard he attacked me again and again. I managed to stop his onslaught several times, but he moved fast and with extreme agility preventing me from counterattacking. Our bodies gleamed with sweat and we breathed with difficulty, taking deep breaths with the intention of sucking in all the air that our lifeless lungs demanded. For a few moments we look at each other in search of a weak point, a low guard or a loophole where we can launch a deadly attack. We were panting exhausted. So, I decided to attack. I lunged at him, then another. I was possessed by a supernatural energy. The giant looked at me in surprise, wondering where I had gotten those strengths from. He defended himself with difficulty by delaying his step until his back met the cold marble of a wall. Cornered, he launched a desperate attack and lowered his guard. It was my chance. Furious, my eyes veiled with excitement, I defended myself from his last onslaught and lunged at him in a final onslaught. In his desperation, he had neglected his side and I thrust my *spatha* through him until the point hit the wall. He arched his eyes and looked at me in surprise, realizing that he would soon be reckoning to The Almighty. His sword fell to the ground and his clang echoed through the atrium, a tragic clatter that heralded the end of the fight. I stepped away from him and drew my sword. A stream of red blood gushed out from his body. Tadius Ursus, still puzzled, touched the mortal wound and then looked at his bloody hands. His legs, unable to support his weight, buckled and he fell limp to the ground.

Valeria ran to me and hugged me tightly. Panting, excited, and most of all, exhausted, I threw my sword to the ground and hugged her. Valerius Aquilius approached me and took me by the shoulder. He was looking at me with pride. Soon I was surrounded by Roman officers who congratulated me on the victory.

The council was canceled. After that bloody spectacle, there was no meeting of any kind. Finally, a few days later, the *comes* and the *magister militum* Nepotianus met.

As tribune Severus Nasus later told us, our spies had informed them that Genseric, the *Vandalorum rex*, had given up on his intention to attack Carthago Nova. Undoubtedly, the presence of the *limitanei* of Tarraco, backed by the *palatina legio* of Lugdunum, had deterred him.

Rome was no longer as weak as before. Nevertheless, and to avoid possible temptations of the Vandal, Valerius Aquilius urged Nepotianus to leave part of his troops garrisoned in Carthago Nova, to which the latter agreed willingly because he was persuaded of the risk posed by the nearby and always threatening presence of the Vandals. I received the news that my regiment would remain in Carthago Nova with great satisfaction, since it would allow me to be with Valeria, whom I had been courting for days with her father's approval.

The sun was at the top of the sky. A blue sky, very clear and beautiful, watched us from the heights while we, two lovers oblivious to everything that was not our love, remained lying on a blanket on the fine, warm sand of the beach.

The murmur of the waves submerged us in a pleasant lethargy. We looked at each other without saying anything, our bright eyes and our sincere smile said it all. I looked at her and couldn't help but remember Alana. If I didn't know that she was the comes' daughter, I would conclude that I was in front of her. But I had no doubts. I loved her because she was Valeria, not because she reminded me of Alana, even if their resemblance was incredible.

"What are you thinking about?" she asked me distractedly.

I hesitated to tell her my story, but if I intended to spend the rest of my life with her, I considered that it was fair that she knew it.

"Do you remember the first day I met you?"

"Yes, you mistook me for another woman…"

I lay on my back and looked up at an unblemished blue sky.

"Have you never wondered who she was?" I asked, turning my head.

Her eyes clouded with worry.

"I don't think I want to know," she mumbled, turning her face away.

"Don't worry my love, there's nothing to be afraid of. You are the one I love," I said to reassure her.

She turned her beautiful face and smiled at me.

"Who was she?"

I lay on my back again. I needed to confess everything to Valeria, but I was unable to look at her as I did so. Then I began to talk about

Alana without omitting a single detail: the extermination of her people, Walder's attack, the appearance of the druid... our son... the painful separation and, finally, his resemblance to her. When I finished telling the story, I looked at her and saw that her eyes were glazed over.

"So you have a son?" she asked between sobs.

"Yes, but as is the case with his mother, I don't know where he is. My presence endangers them and it is better that I remain separated from them."

"Did the druid tell you that?"

"I know it is an incredible story and, in many ways, fantastic, but that is how it happened. I must be apart from them or they will die. So, it is written."

"What if you see her again?" she asked me worriedly. "What will you do?"

"I loved her madly, it's true, but now I only love you and I will always love you. There isn't and there won't be any other woman in my life but you."

She wiped her tears with her hand and smiled, not very convinced. Then she kissed me softly.

"Is she as much like me as you say?" she asked me.

"Like two drops of water."

She sat up and sat on the blanket. She gazed thoughtfully at the sea, enraptured by its soft murmur.

"I have a story to tell you, too," she suddenly confessed.

I sat on the blanket and looked at her puzzled and curious at the same time.

"Nobody in Carthago Nova knows it, since it is something that happened a long time ago and far away from here," she continued. "My father was stationed in the cohort of the Lucensis..." she said.

"I know the region," I interrupted her.

"There was a small *castrum* there that protected the area from barbarian attacks. Since it was a stable position, many officers married and started families. My father married, but my mother gave him no children. My father's long absences, military campaigns, uncertainty about his possible return and deep loneliness caused great homesickness in her. She felt guilty for not having children and scratched her face in despair. My father loved her and comforted her day and night, but the barbaric attacks were more and more usual and so were his absences. It happened one long winter night. The wind was

275

blowing hard against the windows and the snow prevented us from traveling on the roads. My father had been on campaign for more than three months and possibly would not return until spring. My mother was alone, in front of the fire, drinking her tears when the door burst open. Then my father came in, carrying a bundle in his arms. My mother looked at him in rapt attention, since she wasn't expecting him. She rushed towards him to give him a hug but my father stopped her. Then he carefully placed the bundle on the bed and showed it to my mother. He pulled the blanket away from her, revealing the face of a little girl of about three or four years old. My mother wept with happiness and they both melted into an embrace. The little girl... was I."

Her eyes were excited and she wiped away a tear that ran down her cheek. I stroked her hair and smiled sadly.

"Do you know where your father found you?"

Valeria shook her head.

"One day, when I was old enough to understand, he told me that he wasn't my real father, but he never said anything more. Only that he found me and treated me like the natural daughter he never had. I never asked him, since I didn't need to know. For me, my father and mother were my real parents and it never mattered to me that their blood didn't run through my veins. The only thing he told me was that my real name was Elena." She paused for a moment and continued with her eyes veiled by tears. "I was twelve years old when my mother died due to a long illness, since then, my father has gone out of his way for me and we have never been separated."

"I met Alana in a village near Asturica Augusta, a few miles from Lucensis...."

"If she is as much like me as you say she is, she might be... my sister," she said the last words in a soft whisper, as if she feared she had said something foolish. But her supposition didn't lack some hint of certainty.

I watched her more closely, scrutinizing her face for some mark, some sign that would confirm our suspicions, but I found none. Their resemblance was striking, but that didn't mean they were sisters, though neither did it deny the contrary.

"Alana, Elena... your names are very similar..." suddenly, a name awoke in my mind: Lughdyr. I was persuaded that the druid would know the truth. But I shook my head. That Alana and Valeria were sisters was unimportant. Fate, again capricious fate, for unfathomable reasons, had separated them. Just as the *fatum* had taken me away from Alana's arms, now, without knowing the reason, it joined my path to Valeria's. "I love you" I told her, disdaining futile conjectures. "For me, the important thing is to be with you and to live the rest of my days with you. Anything other than you is unimportant." And I kissed her, ending the conversation.

They were wonderful months where the good news followed one after the other and seemed to have no end. Valerius Aquilius, lacking a chief to command his personal guard, was kind enough to let me take the position. Not in vain, I had defeated the giant Tadius Ursus in single combat.

A few weeks after my appointment, Valeria and I got married and moved to a small house near the amphitheater. It was a beautiful house consisting of a large atrium surrounded by fruit trees and with a refreshing pond in its center. Through the *atrium* one had access to the two rooms, the *tablinum*, the kitchen and the *triclinium,* which was the place where we received our visitors. It was the home I never had and there I lived the happiest years of my life.

I remember with great joy and happiness the day Valeria announced to me that she was pregnant. I took her in my arms and we spun around screaming with joy. My eyes got excited and she cried with happiness. Suddenly, I was afraid.

I was so happy that I was afraid it was all just a beautiful dream. I put her down on the floor and held her tightly for a few moments. I wouldn't let anything, or anyone, ever take me away from her. I loved her with all my heart. Now that a new life was germinating in her womb, she was more beautiful and radiant than ever in my eyes.

But I decided to live that moment with great intensity, since «*saepe ne utile quidem est scire quid futurum sit...* »[14] [sometimes it is better not to know what will happen].

---

[14] *Cicero quote*

CHAPTER XII

The campaign against the Vandal.

Romani hanc adepti victoriam in perpetuum se fore victores confidebant.[15]

But the sound of drums and war tubas reached Carthago Nova and black clouds like an evil omen hovered over the city when Julius Valerius Majorian, commanding a powerful army from Liguria, arrived in the city. The emperor had reestablished the foedus with the Visigoths and the Burgundians and defeated the Vandals in numerous battles. He was acclaimed and loved by the Roman people, and now he had the strength and support to avenge the humiliating sack of Rome by Genseric's army six years earlier. The Augustus had landed with part of the imperial fleet in Carthago Nova with the purpose of attacking the Vandalorum regnum of Africa. He longed to exterminate them as punishment for the sack of Rome and the outrageous kidnapping of the empress and her daughters. With their destruction he would send a strong message to all those barbarian peoples who had the unfortunate intention of taking up arms against the Empire, resurgent and glorious once again.

We were at the very beginning of summer when Majorian arrived at our shores. Black and threatening clouds escorted him. The easterly wind gave the day a most unpleasant aspect. In the port the dignitaries of the city were waiting for him, together with several hundred *bucelarii* and legionaries, among whom I was the chief of the personal guard of the civitatis comes.

The admiral ship, a beautiful *dromon* powered by three triangular sails and capable of holding two hundred soldiers, arrived at the dock and the *palatinae scholae* deployed the walkway. Majorian, dressed in

---

[15] *The Romans were confident that they would be victorious forever if they achieved this victory (phrase extracted and adapted from the Latin Grammar book by Santiago Segura Munguía).*

military uniform, saluted the large crowd that had gathered to greet him, and crossed the walkway escorted by several members of his personal guard. He was accompanied by a high-ranking officer whom I soon recognized; he was the bald-headed man I had met at the baths of Rome, Methylius Seronatus was his name, the egregious *praefectus classis Ravennatium*. Several *decurions*, *quaestors* and *censors* swirled around the Augustus, whom they entertained with greetings and signs of devoted obedience. Valerius Aquilius approached the emperor and offered his respects.

"I greet you, Julius Valerius Majorian, *nobilissimus* emperor of Rome. It is an immense honor to receive you in Carthago Nova."

"It is a pleasure for me to come to such beautiful and peaceful places," said the emperor looking around. "I notice with pleasure that the city has progressed a lot since the last time I visited it, even the people seem happier," he added smiling.

"Thanks to you, great Majorian. You have put an end to the danger posed by the barbarians and you are fair to the people. The Romans adore you."

"The barbarians haven't ceased to be a danger; in fact, I have undertaken this campaign to eliminate one of them."

"Genseric is vermin and, as such, must be exterminated," Valerius Aquilius said, informed of the emperor's purpose.

"Indeed, but we'll talk about that later."

A boy approached and handed him a beautiful laurel wreath. Majorian took it with a smile and raised it to the black sky for all to see. The crowd began to shout enthusiastic salves. The emperor knew how to win the favor of the common people.

"Well," said Majorian, noticing me. "I see you have Salvio Adriano under your command."

"I greet you, domine, I thank God for seeing you again after so long," I said.

"Not only that," Valerius Aquilius interjected. "He is also my son-in-law."

My father-in-law's words embarrassed me, I hated to give the impression that my promotion was due to my relationship with him.

"I think we have a lot to talk about," the emperor smiled, not missing a detail of my tight lips. "Allow me to introduce Methylius Seronatus, *praefectus classis Ravennatium*," he said, pointing to the bald-headed man who stood at his height.

The fleet commander looked at me and undoubtedly recognized me, but immediately looked away, ignoring my uncomfortable presence.

"I greet you, Valerius Aquilius, *comes civitatis* of Carthago Nova. The welcome offered by your people has been much warmer than the one offered by your climate," said Methylius Seronatus, just as the rain began to fall.

"I greet you, Methylius Seronatus commander of the fleet of Ravenna. I trust that your stay in our beautiful city will be pleasant."

A couple of flashes of lightning flashed across the sky and the thunderous thunder that followed drove away the crowd, who tried to take shelter from the waterspout under awnings and arcades.

"If I were superstitious, I'd say this was a bad omen," joked Majorian, climbing onto a wagon covered with a tarp.

Although he tried to hide it, I could see a malicious smile spread on the navy commander's lips. I had to speak with Majorian as soon as possible and reveal to him the conversation that he had with Methylius Seronatus shortly before his appointment.

The emperor, accompanied by his entourage, went to the imperial villa, the residence of the nobilissimus during his few stays in the city. Majorian was tired after such a long and tiring journey, and he went directly to his chambers. I escorted Valerius Aquilius to his house, but I didn't share my concerns with him. The comes was exultant with the presence of the emperor and I didn't want to make his day bitter.

It didn't stop raining all night. The strong wind opened the windows that beat furiously on the wall. Several times I had to get up to secure them and prevent them from reopening. But it was the restlessness, and not the force of the air, that kept me from falling asleep. I didn't comment on Valeria either, after all, it was just a conversation, and nothing seemed to indicate that Methylius Seronatus was disloyal to the emperor. However, four years had elapsed since his proclamation and no one had dared to attempt or conspire against him. He tried to relax, think about other things, fight to conciliate a dream that didn't come. Suddenly, there was a dry noise. Reluctantly, I got up considering it was another open window. I went out to the atrium protected by a blanket. The sky, completely black, had opened, dropping all its contents. I walked around the atrium looking for the open window, but couldn't find it. Jets of water fell from the roof, simulating waterfalls. Thinking that my ears had betrayed me, I returned to the room. I was opening the door when a ray struck a shadow on the wall and it wasn't exactly mine. I quickly turned around and saw a man dressed in dark robes pouncing on me carrying a dagger. I managed to dodge his attack by protecting myself with my blanket, but I slipped and fell to the muddy ground. Another flash of lightning illuminated the atrium and I saw with horror that my attacker was not alone: two sinister figures appeared behind him, each carrying daggers that reverberated in the light of the lightning. I feared for Valeria and managed to stand up. Then the three men threw themselves at me with his daggers raised. I took a flowerpot near the door and smashed it on the head of one of them, who fell inert to the ground. The other two, seeing their partner badly injured on the ground, hesitated and stopped. The water continued to fall on our bodies in waves and the rays followed one another without pause one after another, always followed by their tireless companions: the thunder. The two assailants exchanged indecisive glances, but finally continued their attack. Luckily they weren't very skilled at handling the knife and I managed to disarm one of them, stabbing his own dagger into his leg. He let out a gut-wrenching cry of pain and limped away through the door that had been forced open. The only remaining assailant looked at me, not knowing what to do. Then, he took the companion, who was lying inert on the ground, and dragged him towards the center of the atrium, then he threw him on his shoulders and without turning his back on me, he left through the forced door of the atrium.

After the storm, calm always comes or, at least, that is assured. In this case it wasn't so. Although it is true that it no longer rained with the same intensity and that the thunder and lightning had disappeared, a fine but persistent rain greeted a new day, preventing the sun's rays from drying the flooded streets, which woke up covered by dirty puddles. I confessed to Valeria my concerns and more, after the attack suffered. I ordered half a dozen milites to protect my house and went to the house of the civitatis comes in order to share my fears with him. My worried face changed in amazement when I entered the tablinum, and sitting on a footstool next to my father-in-law, I found Majorian. They both looked at me with amusement and invited me to take a seat next to them. A servant offered me a bowl of milk with some bread, raisins, and cheese.

281

"I greet you, Julius Valerius Majorian, emperor of Rome." and looking at him I added. "I greet you, Valerius Aquilius; you *civitatis comes* of Carthago Nova." Valerius Aquilius gestured for me to sit next to him, and I did so. "I have to admit that I'm surprised to see you here," I told the emperor. "I haven't seen an imperial guard at the gate."

"I greet you, Salvio Adriano," Maybe it's because I came alone.

I looked at him without understanding, and the emperor rose from the footstool.

"Times are hard in Rome," he began, as he paced with his hands clasped behind his back. "It's increasingly difficult to know who you can trust. You met yesterday the commander of the fleet, or did you already know each other?"

I was about to respond when he stopped me with a gesture.

"I know, I know, don't worry, I don't doubt your loyalty."

"How do you know I know him?" I asked curious.

"We all have informants and spies everywhere. It's a shame, but it's the only way to anticipate the movements of your enemies. Now I need you to tell me what you were willing to reveal to your father-in-law," he said maliciously.

I smiled at the emperor evilness and shook my head. So, I told him about my encounter with Methylius Seronatus four years ago without omitting any detail. Majorian was watching me attentively, stroking his chin.

"Honestly, I wouldn't have given the trivial conversation big importance if it weren't for the fact that I was attacked last night," I finished.

"Did they attack you? Is my daughter fine?" the comes asked uneasily, jumping up.

"Don't fear for Valeria, she didn't suffer any harm," I have ordered my best men to guard the house day and night.

My father-in-law looked at me calmer and nodded.

"What happened?" asked Majorian.

"There were three; they assaulted me in the middle of the night under the cover of darkness. I managed to wound two of them and they finally fled."

"Do you think they could have been sent by the fleet commander?" the emperor asked, stopping his step.

"I don't know, but I've never been attacked at home and I don't believe in coincidences."

"Methylius Seronatus has always been faithful to me. It is true that I have heard rumors and that he doesn't hide his sympathies for Ricimero but his behavior, so far, has been faultless."

"But this is precisely when you need him most," Said the *comes*. "So far, most of your campaigns have been on land. It's now when the commander has you at his mercy."

"In case he wants to betray me," Majorian interrupted. "I have achieved important victories over the enemies of Rome," he continued without stopping his pace around the table. "The Empire has prospered remarkably in recent years, and my generals are loyal, why would Methylius Seronatus betray me?"

For a few moments we were silent, pondering the answer.

"What does Ricimero think of your reign?" asked the *comes*.

"He doesn't like me. The Suevian would have preferred an emperor who was more manipulative and sensitive to his requests. A puppet he could handle as he pleased. But with me he was wrong."

"Maybe that's where the problem lies," Valerius Aquilius pointed out. The emperor frowned in confusion. "*Domine,* we must be extremely prudent, the hand of the Suevian is very long and he can take advantage of any mistake or any carelessness, to destroy you. He doesn't need to make an attempt on your life to strip you of your imperial insignia."

The words of the comes took their toll in the fragile confidence of the emperor, who sat on the footstool thoughtfully. His mind was working quickly connecting the dots, looking for solutions and finding different possibilities.

"I will follow your advice, my good friend," Majorian said to Valerius Aquilius. "Now let's talk about the campaign against the Vandals."

I got up interested and asked:

"What is the plan, my lord?"

Majorian got up from the stool and began to pace the tablinum, stroking his chin thoughtfully.

"From Liguria I have crossed the Tarraconense and Carthaginiense with my armies with the purpose that the Hispano-Romans understand that, during my government, Rome is not going to abandon them as it has done until now," he began to say. "And that I'll send my legions to protect their fields and cities when necessary. I have visited the main towns of Hispania such as Barcino, Tarraco and Caesaraugusta, and in all of them I've found nothing but joy and hope in the face of a new era of prosperity and peace. But for the Empire to resurface with new vigor, even more powerful and fearsome than before, it is essential to finish off Genseric and his horde of Vandals."

"I completely agree, *domine*," Valerius Aquilius intervened. "Genseric is the greatest danger looming over Rome."

"And for that reason I'm here, my friend," Majorian said. "To exterminate once and for all that miasma that comes from Africa and threatens to destroy the Empire," he continued vehemently, adding. "From Caesaraugusta I went to Valentia, and from there to Ilici, where Methylius Seronatus was waiting for me with the Ravenna fleet, the vanguard of what will be a colossal armada that will lead us to Carthago, the capital of the *Vandalorum regnum*."

Majorian approached the comes and placing his hand on his shoulder said:

"In a few days, your lookouts will scan the horizon for more than three hundred Roman ships. Meanwhile, the rest of my legions will reach Carthago Nova by land. Here we will embark for Africa and destroy the Vandals, making up for the infamy suffered by the sack of Rome and by the kidnapping of the imperial family."

"It's a bold plan," I said.

The emperor smiled.

"It can't fail," he added. "And to avoid the harassment of the Suevian, I've sent to Gallaecia an army under the command of the *magister militum* Nepotianus, supported by a contingent of Visigothic foederati commanded by the *comes* Suneric. His mere presence will persuade them to cross our limes and plunder the Hispanic provinces while the bulk of my troops invade Africa."

The *comes* and I nodded in astonishment. The emperor's stratagem was ambitious and risky, but if carried out successfully, the Vandals would be destroyed and southern Hispania would be free from their persistent harassment.

"By the way, I have a gift for you," said the Augustus, pointing to a small wooden box on the floor beside the table, which I hadn't noticed before.

I arched my eyebrows in surprise and Majorian authorized me to open it with a wave of his hand. I bent down and placed it on the table. I looked at Valerius Aquilius for an explanation, but he just shrugged his shoulders.

"What is it?" I asked before opening it.

"You will know soon," the enigmatic emperor answered.

With nervous hands I lifted the lid of the box and, to my amazement and astonishment; I found a rotting, foul-smelling head. It belonged to a stocky, bearded, blond-haired man with rough, angular features. It was in a deplorable state, but I still thought I recognized its owner.

"Walder?" I asked, uneasy.

"It was he, who killed Optila, and Theodoric, a faithful ally of Rome, has offered me his head. The German has paid for his crime."

I looked at the remains more closely, trying to scrutinize if it was really his head what rotted in that filthy box. But it emanated a repugnant odor and I closed it, taking for granted the words of the Augustus. I must admit that I felt a great relief and nodded gratefully. Optila could rest in peace while his murderer would languish in hell until the end of days. And I had one less problem to worry about.

"Thank you, *domine*."

The emperor nodded with a smile, pleased with the wisdom of his gift.

"Now I must leave, there is much work to do and very little time," he continued, smiling as he noticed the gleam of pride and admiration in our eyes.

"I'll escort you, *domine*" I said.

I left the house and accompanied by several of my milites, I escorted the emperor to the imperial villa. We didn't say a word on the way; everyone was immersed in his own thoughts and concerns.

Informed of the presence of the powerful Levantine fleet, Genseric, *Vandalorum rex*, sent several embassies requesting an audience with the emperor. All were rejected. Majorian felt strong and powerful. He concluded that there could be no negotiation with the perfidious Vandals: their fatal destiny was to succumb to our *spatha* and spears.

The summer clouds and storms, as they came, faded. The heat soon dried up the puddles, and the scent of roses and violets impregnated the sweet breeze with their intoxicating scent.

Majorian's legionaries reached Carthago Nova by land, and we were only waiting with impatience and uncertainty to see the ships coming from Ilici on the horizon to undertake the definitive battle against the Vandals. The emperor was restless and was considering sending a messenger to Ilici, worried about the unexpected delay of the fleet. But Methylius Seronatus reassures him by claiming that the winds were not favorable and that he should have a little patience. Nothing and no one could prevent our legionaries from landing in Africa and annihilate the barbarians of Genseric. Victory was certain, and all the glory of the emperor. Those words soothed the Augustus, who limited himself to gazing out at the sea, yearning to see the sails and flags of the Roman ships.

I was walking with Valeria along the dock observing the Ravenna fleet. The sea was calm and several children, using rough sticks to which they had tied fine ropes at one end like a fishing pole, were catching small fish with rudimentary hooks. One of the children gave me his rod, and I tried to catch some of the fish that curious, suspiciously examined the bait of bread with oil without daring to give it a bite. Shrugging my shoulders, I handed the rod back to the boy, admitting my defeat.

"Will you go with them?" Valeria asked me, looking at the warships.

"No, my duty is to protect the *comes*, your father," I answered. "And his daughter as well," I added, touching her growing belly.

"I'm very happy," she said, giving me a kiss.

I watched the admiral ship and saw that Methylius Seronatus was arguing with several *magistri navis*. One of them, who was sitting on a barrel, jumped up, shook his head vehemently, and, visibly angry, withdrew from the conversation. At full speed and without noticing me, he crossed the runway and got lost in the city. I couldn't follow him, since I was afraid to leave Valeria alone, especially considering the attack she suffered recently. Something was wrong and I had to find out as soon as possible what it was about.

The sun had set behind the horizon and a sky full of stars took its place. All was quiet at the harbor, where I had gone accompanied by a dozen legionaries. I was about to inspect the ships, since the discussion I had witnessed that morning had greatly disturbed me. I reached the dock and noticed with uneasiness that the admiral ship had disappeared. I asked the sailor that was on watch and he only knew that, shortly before nightfall, Methylius Seronatus had embarked and departed on the last tide.

"Where are the *magistri navis*?" I asked.

"I suppose that at the camp that the comes has made available for them."

"Are there legionaries or sailors on the ships?"

"Just a couple of sailors on duty in case any problem arises on the ships during night."

"The *dromons* are totally unprotected in case of attack and the admiral ship has disappeared..."

I didn't finish the sentence, since a loud noise of broken wood distracted us. We looked out to sea and realized with horror how one of our ships had been attacked by an enemy ship. There was another loud crack, and then another. We immediately understood that our *dromons* were being attacked by the spurs of the enemy ships. A dark moonless night had veiled the barbarian ships, which were now fully visible thanks to the fires they had lit on deck.

"Inform everyone about this," I exclaimed out of myself. "They are attacking our fleet!"

Dozens of fireballs from the enemy ships crossed the black sky in a parable as beautiful as it was destructive, falling on our defenseless ships while the few sailors who watched them jumped into the water in panic, sinking into its dark waters.

"Look for the *magister navis*, look for the captains!" I roared. Not quite sure what to do, I drew my *spatha* and ran along the dock accompanied by my legionaries.

Helpless, we contemplated how, one by one, our *dromons* were shipwrecked, consumed by fire or rammed by enemy spurs.

"Bring catapults, wake the sagitarii!" I ordered.

A group of archers arrived at the dock and, smearing their arrows with tar, fired incendiary darts at the enemy ships but without success. The distance prevented them from reaching them and the few arrows that reached their target were quickly neutralized.

"What the hell is happening?"

I turned around and met the emperor's wild eyes, unable to believe what I was witnessing.

"How is it possible...?"

"Treason."

"Methylius Seronatus..." Majorian whispered. His eyes reflected the fire that devoured our ships.

I nodded.

"Send horsemen to Ilici, I fear for the fleet." And hiding his face in his hands he mused. "This is my end; bitter is the taste of treason."

Our ships were sinking in the dark waters of the harbor and with them, the emperor's hopes of conquering Mauretania and destroying the Vandals.

The worst and most disheartening omens were confirmed when the horsemen sent in haste to Ilici returned: the armada had been attacked and destroyed by the Vandals. The shadows of treachery were once again hanging over the Empire, withering with their miasma the green shoots of prosperity and hope.

Lacking ships with which to return to Rome, Majorian was forced to return on horseback and cross Hispania during the summer. As we feared, Methylius Seronatus had fled in the admiralty ship accompanied by almost all the *magistri navis*, only one captain refused to betray the Augustus, and his body was found covered with stab wounds and dried with blood on a beach days after the disaster. The fleet, lacking commanders, was easy prey for the Vandals, who sank the ships before our helpless eyes. I still remember the emperor's eyes veiled in despondency and discouragement on the day he began his voyage. Betrayed, defeated and sunk, he marched to Rome with the uncertainty of not knowing what awaited him there. No one doubted that Ricimero would use the relentless defeat of our fleet as a pretext to overthrow him. Unfortunately, and just as it happened to the *magister utriusque militiae* Aetius, great men are followed by a trail of envious, opportunistic, flattering and treacherous men who crouched like vermin, await the opportune moment to attack their unsuspecting prey and devour it without the slightest compassion. Once again, the enemies of Rome had to be sought not in distant and frozen lands but, on the contrary, within its walls.

CHAPTER XIII

A long summer night.

Spemque metumque inter dubiis.[16]

Restlessness gnawed my insides and the unbearable heat didn't help to soothe my flaring nerves. Valerius Aquilius tried to reassure me but his eyes betrayed him since he was more worried and terrified than I was. In the room, I could hear Valeria's screams of pain, unable to get the creature out of her entrails. I tried to enter several times. I wanted to console her, kiss her, make her feel better in some way. I wanted to tell her in her ear that I was there, next to her; to support her as much as necessary, but the midwives prevented me one and another time. Childbirth was something exclusive and restricted to the female sex and only women could attend the parturient. This was the refrain repeated over and over again that I was forced to listen to every time I opened the door. But she was dying, I knew it and so did Valerius Aquilius. Almost two days of pain, sweating, screams and blood carried on her tired back my sweet Valeria. I was waiting at the door, moving from one side to the other, biting my fingers at the lack of nails, hoping to slip through the crack in the door, taking advantage of the exit to get water or clean clothes from a midwife. A group of mourners approached the house, tearing their clothes and scratching their faces, as they cried inconsolably. I kicked them out of the house of Valerius Aquilius. My wife wasn't dead and neither was the child inside her.

Night came and Valeria continued fighting with stubborn integrity to save her life and that of the child. I was sitting on a stone bench in the *atrium* with Valerius Aquilius. In the sky, the sickle of the moon allowed us to contemplate millions of stars that pulsed with a magical and unreal glow. The hours passed slowly, indolent, apathetic, as if time had stopped, refusing to move on. Time... Valeria... my life... my world... My eyes were red from crying and exhaustion. I got up and went to the door. Helpless and hopeless, I heard Valeria's plaintive moan. My wife was exhausted after her titanic effort. I wiped away my

---

[16] *Among the doubts are hope and fear (Publius Vergilius Maro).*

tears and looked at the sky. I watched as a star scratched the skies with a faint white line and then disappeared. Instantly another star fell from the sky. They were like beams of light, a ray of fire that was extinguished as quickly as it arose. Fleeting tears from a troubled sky that also cried for the tragic fortune that hung over my family.

"They are the Perseids," Valerius Aquilius explained.

For a few moments we both looked up at the sky, fascinated by the spectacle we were seeing.

"They are so called because they arise from the constellation of Perseus. There are those who say that today is a magical night and that if you make a wish it will come true," he looked at me with tear-soaked eyes.

"Pagan superstitions," I growled, wiping my tears away.

"Sometimes we have nothing left but faith and hope, be it God or the Perseids..." he whispered, and closing his eyes tightly, he added: «Dum vita est spes est.» [while there is life, there is hope]."

Tears ran down his cheeks as he moved his lips, whispering a prayer, a wish, a dream. I clenched my fists, looked up, and closed my eyes. Offering my soul as a pledge, I prayed to Almighty God, to Jesus Christ, to all the Saints, I prayed to the Perseids... in short, I prayed to everyone who wanted to listen to me. I opened my eyes and looked at the *civitatis comes* who smiled at me through tears. The squeak of hinges startled us, we looked away toward the bedroom door, and saw the midwives come out with lowered faces and wet eyes. One of them shook her head and walked towards us.

"We're sorry," she said, breaking into tears. "There is nothing else we can do. The child can't get out of her and she is getting weaker and weaker. She will die soon, go say goodbye to her," she finished, before getting lost in the darkness of the night along with the rest of the midwives.

Desolate, we entered the room. There was Valeria, lying inert on the bed, pale, her eyes sunken from lack of food and fatigue. We were afraid we were late, but a slight movement of her chest revealed that she was still breathing. I knelt next to her and wiped her pearled forehead. Valerius Aquilius, unable to bear the pain any longer, left the room with his soul broken.

"I'm here, my love," I whispered in her ear.

She opened her eyes heavily and turned her head. I caressed her cheek and felt a burning fever consume her. She smiled at me before closing her eyes. Shattered, I rested my head in her lap and burst into tears. Valeria, my love, my life, was gone, to never return. I cried out broken with pain and sank my face into the sheets as I caressed her cheeks.

"Don't suffer Adriano, she is still alive. I'm here to free her from the icy breath of death," said a voice behind me.

I turned startled and found Lughdyr. I rubbed my eyes in disbelief. The druid, looking serious but determined, approached the bed and tapped me on the shoulder.

"Get out of the room," he ordered me, not taking his eyes off Valeria.

"Can I help you?" I stammered.

"No, just get out and close the door."

"Will she survive?" I asked hopefully.

The druid touched her forehead and opened her eyelids.

"Leave us alone please."

Without hesitation, I left the room and closed the door. Outside, sitting on a stone bench, with his face sunk in his hands and with shuddering convulsions caused by deep pain, was Valerius Aquilius. I sat down beside him and touched his shoulder. He looked at me, and in his eyes I saw the indescribable pain of someone who has lost what he loves most in the world.

"Is it all over?" he asked in a trembling voice, fearing the answer.

I shook my head.

"There is still hope."

He wrinkled his eyebrows, obviously not understanding my words.

"An old friend has arrived from a place far away. He is with her at this moment."

"Will he be able to save her?" he asked, still not understanding how someone had crossed the atrium without being seen.

"If there is anyone in this world who can do it, it's certainly him."

He nodded unconvinced. He looked towards the door of the room, and clenched his fists tightly, whispering a prayer.

These were moments of anguish in which we didn't take our eyes off the room where Valeria was fighting for her life and that of our son. The heat was suffocating and sweat ran down our foreheads as if it were a river overflowing after the rain. I looked at the *comes* and a bitter smile came across his tired face. The hours passed and the room remained silent. I sat up and began to walk from one side of the atrium to the other. The *civitatis comes* was looking at the floor with a dejected gesture without stopping rubbing his sweaty hands. The sun was just beginning to timidly appear over the hills surrounding the city and we were still waiting. With my heart pounding, I headed to the door; I couldn't stand the tension any longer. Suddenly, the hopeful cry of a child stopped me in my tracks. Valerius Aquilius and I looked at each other for an answer. My heart raced: the little boy's cry vibrated in the air with the sweet song of nightingales in springtime. The door opened and the solemn figure of the druid appeared with a child in his arms. A ray of sunlight illuminated him, giving him golden hues, he looked like an old Angel come from heaven carrying the most precious of treasures. Lughdyr was smiling. We ran to him nervously, fearing for Valeria's health.

"All right, now rest," the druid went ahead to say, noticing the fear in our eyes.

I looked at the little one, who was sleeping peacefully in the old man's arms.

"He is a boy," he said, and a smile came over his face.

I caressed his soft cheek, he was a handsome boy. I slowly entered the room accompanied by the *comes,* fearing to make the slightest noise. Valeria was sleeping soundly. Her face was still very pale and the dark circles under her eyes betrayed the horrible sufferings she had endured. Valerius Aquilius, after confirming that his daughter was in better condition, hurriedly left the room and collapsed on a footstool. Unable to bear so many hours of anguish and pain, he burst into tears and had to be comforted by the druid.

I left the room and Lughdyr handed me Salvio Alexandros, since this is how Valeria and I say that our son would be called. I cradled him for a few moments and a strong emotion ran through my body. I approached the *civitatis comes,* who was a little more recovered, and showed him the little one. He smiled with tears in his eyes and kissed him.

"You're both exhausted," the druid interjected. "You'd better leave the child in the care of a servant and rest."

"What about Valeria?" Valerius Aquilius asked.

"Don't worry, I will watch over her," answered the old man.

Valerius Aquilius called a servant girl and handed her the child. We entered the room for the last time and kissed Valeria, who was breathing more calmly and had regained some color. We were leaving the room when the *civitatis comes* stopped in front of the druid.

"I don't know who you are and where you come from, but you have saved the lives of my daughter and my grandson, I will always be deeply grateful to you. In me you have a friend, a brother, ask me for whatever you want, and I'll gladly give it to you," he said gratefully.

"There is no greater reward for me than to have saved the lives of Valeria and her son."

"My house is your house, please, I beg you to be my guest all the time you need," said the *comes,* shaking his hand.

"I thank you for your hospitality; I'll remain in your house until Valeria is well again."

The *civitatis comes* nodded excitedly and marched exhausted to his quarters.

"I hope that someday you tell me how you manage to appear and disappear at the most opportune moment. I said to the druid."

"There is a powerful bond between Valeria and Alana."

"They are sisters, aren't they?" I asked.

The druid leaned his staff against the wall and sat down on a stone bench next to Valeria's bedroom.

"A few days ago, Alana had a vision in which she saw a woman very similar to her suffering an unbearable suffering," the druid paused and looked me in the eyes. "She also saw how the black hand of the Grim Reaper clung to her soul trying to snatch it from her body. But the woman was very strong and fought desperately to defend her life and that of her little boy. Then she asked me to use my magic to save the woman and free her from its claws."

"And you succeeded," I said gratefully.

The old man nodded.

"Valeria is very weak now, but she will have recovered in a week. She is an extremely strong woman; she has fought like a beast to defend her life and that of her son.

"I don't know how to thank you."

"You should thank Alana, she gave the alarm."

I felt my heart shrink, I still didn't stop loving Alana and now, thanks to her, my wife and son were alive.

"She knows it, doesn't she?" I asked.

"Yes."

I looked down in shame and looked at the floor, absurdly feeling like an unfaithful husband.

"Don't worry, she wants the best for you and she is sure that with Valeria you will be very happy."

"So, she already knows she has a sister?"

"I told her who the woman in her vision was."

"Why didn't you tell her before?"

"I had to wait for the right moment," he answered hermetically without much interest in providing more information.

"How are Alana and Adriano?" I asked, respecting his reservations.

"They are healthy and happy. Alana takes care of the sick and helps the needy. Adriano is growing fast and is as strong as a steer," he said, unable to hide the pride he felt for them.

The memory of Adriano surfaced in my mind and I smiled with emotion. Our separation, although necessary, caused me great pain that I could never get over.

"You are exhausted," the druid pointed out, waking me up from my reverie. "Go to bed and don't be afraid for Valeria, I'll watch over her."

I gave up and after giving Valeria another kiss, I went to my room exhausted, but happy. Lughdyr had saved my family from certain death. I took a last look back and saw how the old man, sitting on the stone bench, was looking towards an indeterminate point on the horizon. I smiled, wondering where his mind was flying to at that moment. Probably he was hugging Alana and Adriano, telling them the good news: her sister and the newborn were alive.

I was walking along the beach accompanied by the druid enjoying a beautiful summer day. Valeria, although she still remained in bed, was out of danger and little by little, she was recovering from the tiring labor. Lughdyr, always accompanied by his faithful staff, walked morose, immersed in his thoughts and practically didn't open his mouth. I was happy, but exhausted. The night of my son's birth was so intense that I think I became ten years older. In fact, from that day on, my temples showed overcrowded white hair. The druid, weary from the trek, sat on a rock and gazed out to sea, vigorously sucking its salty breeze. He closed his eyes abstracted as he breathed in and out the healthy sea air. After taking several breaths he looked at me.

"The sea air has the property of comforting us. There is nothing more pleasant than walking barefoot on the sand and feeling the coolness of the water caress your feet. It's like going back to the origins of man," he said enigmatically, as always.

"As far as I know, only the pagan goddess Venus was born from the foam of the sea," I said, not understanding his words.

"Look at the horizon," he pointed to the sea with his staff. "The sea is the origin of everything, including us."

"You mean the man came out of the sea?" I asked skeptically. "I think Christian monks won't entirely agree with you."

The druid shook his head.

"Human knowledge is still in its infancy, perhaps one day man will understand."

I didn't say anything; after all I didn't understand what he meant. I sat next to him and gazed out at the wide sea for a few minutes. Then I looked at him and dared to ask him something that had been in my mind since the warm summer night of my son's birth.

"I'd like you to tell me what happened to Alana and Valeria and why they had to separate. I have the impression that you know it, don't you?"

Lughdyr nodded almost imperceptibly. He rested his hands on the staff, and without taking his eyes off the horizon, he began to say:

"It happened many years ago in a village near Legio. The two girls lived with their parents in a secluded hut. They were happy and loved by the people. Hirso, the father of the girls, was a great doctor and traveled to distant lands to cure the sick. Iliana, his wife, was extremely beautiful. Alana and Valeria are her living image. Not a few times Iliana accompanied and assisted her husband during a cure. One day, Hirso was summoned by the servant of a nobleman from Legio, and Iliana accompanied him. The nobleman was seriously ill due to a hunting wound that had become infected. Hirso healed him, but the nobleman, after meeting Iliana, became infatuated with her and swore that she would be his. He sent spies to Hirso's8 house to monitor his movements and follow him wherever he went. After a few weeks, Hirso, accompanied by Alana, who was about three years old, went to the forest to collect medicinal plants. He was unaware that at that time he was being closely watched by several men. When he was several miles from the house, he was attacked and killed in front of his daughter."

"What happened to Alana?"

"The girl was crying inconsolably over the inert body of her father. The assassins weren't able to end the life of the creature and left her abandoned in the forest confident that some vermin would finish their work."

"So, you found her, right?" I asked.

"Distant cries caught my attention, I closed my eyes and I could see her. The little girl rested her head on her father's chest with her cheeks pierced by her tears. Then her aura confirmed to me that she was someone special."

"A druid-girl."

"Possibly."

"What happened next?"

"I approached her and she stopped crying, I wiped her tears away and pulled her to her feet. Then I realized that the body on which the little girl was crying was Hirso's, the doctor whom I knew and with whom I had talked about different diseases and medicinal plants. I put her body on my shoulders and we marched towards my cabin. It was getting dark and there was no time to drive Alana to her house."

The druid stopped his speech. He clenched his staff and his brow furrowed. Remembering that story caused him great pain.

"I stoked the fire and after providing the girl with a sedative, I marched to her house to inform Iliana of the death of her husband. But when I arrived, the door of the hut was open and there was no one inside. Everything was scrambled, as if thieves had entered. I closed my eyes and tried to focus. Then I saw it."

A single tear ran down Lughdyr's cheeks.

"Shortly before dark, someone knocked on the door of the hut. Confident, Iliana opened it and two *bucelarii* broke into the house with their swords drawn. Behind them emerged the figure of the noble Suevian. He ordered her men to wait outside and pounced on her. Little Valeria or Elena," he specified. "who was sleeping at the time, woke up frightened and began to scream. The nobleman looked at her with despise and gave her a strong blow, knocking her senseless. Iliana grabbed a dagger and threw herself at him, wounding the nobleman in the leg. The cries of the Suevian alerted his *bucelarii*, who entered the hut. He then ordered them to kill her. Iliana protected herself with her dagger but it was useless. The sword of a *bucelarii* pierced her stomach, leaving her badly wounded. Staggering, with his eyes full of anger, the nobleman left the house with his leg bleeding. One of his soldiers asked what to do with the girl and he answered that they could do with her whatever they wanted.

The druid closed his eyes and began to breathe more slowly.

"Iliana managed to take a few steps out of the hut with the intention of following those who had taken her daughter, before she fell dead to the ground. That's how I found her."

"Cowards," I muttered, shaking my head, unable to believe what I was hearing.

"Several weeks later, I was told that the *bucelarii* who had taken the girl had sold her as a slave to a Roman officer."

"Valerius Aquilius."

The druid nodded and said:

"It was the best thing that could have happened to little Elena, now called Valeria Aquiliaris."

"They don't know what really happened to their parents, do they?"

"Luckily, both Valeria and Alana didn't remember anything about those horrendous crimes until now, when nightmares surfaced in Alana's mind. She is already conscious and Valeria will soon know. You must tell her, since it is fair for her to know her origins.

"I'll do so," I agreed. "After all, otherwise it would be very difficult to explain your sudden appearance." I looked him in the eyes and continued. "Then, the *civitatis comes* took care of Valeria while you took care of Alana."

"She was a special child. At the time, I wasn't aware of the magnitude of her powers, but soon after, I understood that she was a druid-girl and as such had to be instructed."

"Did Valeria lack such powers?"

Lughdyr nodded.

"Sometimes Nature is capricious, and in this case, she favored Alana, granting her admirable gifts."

"Honestly, I'm glad Valeria lacks them."

I stood up and stretched my muscles, somewhat numb from being sitting on a wet rock for several minutes. The druid, looking tired, also stood up.

"Valeria no longer needs my care; the time has come for me to leave."

"I'll always be grateful for all you have done for me and for the women I love most," I said, without trying to convince him to delay his departure, since I knew that the decision had already been made.

"Perhaps our paths will cross again."

"I hope so, my good friend. Kiss my son for me and tell Alana that I love her and that she will always be in my heart."

"She knows," he said with a smile.

A soft mist emerged from the sea and began to surround us, becoming denser and denser until it enveloped the druid and me. I was quiet; I knew that the old Lughdyr had something to do with this strange phenomenon. A moment later, the fog dissipated and the wizard had disappeared.

"Thank you Lughdyr," I whispered with glazed eyes, looking out to the endless sea.

CHAPTER XIV

Genseric besieges Carthago Nova.

Quicumque mortem in malis ponit, non potest eam non timere.[17]

The news, though expected, fell upon us like a bucket of cold water. All Carthago Nova was shocked. The man who had granted a few years of peace, tranquility and prosperity to the Empire was dead. Once again, Rome was in deep chaos. The misgovernment, the vacuum of power and the confusion had emboldened the ever-rebellious barbarians, who crossed our *limes* with the intention of taking advantage of the prevailing disorder.

Valerius Aquilius was sitting on a footstool in the *atrium* of his house. In his face one could notice the weariness of someone who lacks hope. He was looking at the ground with his hands clasped. Surely, he was thinking, or rather fearing, for the future of Rome. The sun was setting behind the hills, illuminating the sky with a beautiful orange color.

"A beautiful sunset." I said, approaching him.

With a gesture he invited me to sit next to him. I took a footstool and did so.

"They have confirmed that Majorian has been killed," he said almost in a whisper.

"It was expected, he had become a disturbance to Ricimero."

"Bastard," he snarled, clenching his fists.

"Is there any more news of what happened?"

He shook his head.

"Little more than what is already known. When the Vandals destroyed our navy, Majorian was forced to leave on horseback for Rome, but in Placentia he was apprehended by the *praefectus praetorium Galliarum,* who had orders to arrest him. He was vilely stripped of the

---

[17] *Whoever considers death as a misfortune cannot but fear it (adapted from the Latin Grammar book by Santiago Segura Munguía).*

imperial insignias, maltreated and executed on the seventh day before the idus of August."

"What was he accused of?" I asked.

A bitter smile appeared on his lips and he answered:

"Treason."

I shook my head in disbelief.

"An execrable crime masked behind a big lie," I said.

"Any pretext was a good one for Ricimero to attack him, and the defeat of our fleet was an excellent opportunity that he didn't let slip away."

"Even if the traitor was someone else."

"Methylius Seronatus will pay for his betrayal; don't have the slightest doubt about that."

I shook my head not very convinced of his words. Disloyalty is a more devastating and damaging scourge than the plague and Rome was infested with conspirators and traitors who sold their dignity for just a handful of solids. The memory of the emperor came to my mind and my face twisted with a grimace of pain.

"Majorian could have fought and defend himself with his legions…" I whispered.

"That never. Our emperor chose to die rather than raise his sword against a legionary again. Seeing so much Roman blood spilled in the war against Marcus Mecilius Avitus shocked him," he replied. "After the failure of the campaign against Genseric, he lost the favor of a large part of the army, very well manipulated by Ricimero, and decided to surrender, even if this meant his death."

"And now who will take his place?" Who will be the new emperor of Rome?

Valerius Aquilius got up with difficulty. The stress suffered during the last months had greatly affected his health.

"I don't know, I suppose someone whom Ricimero can handle at his whim and who doesn't cause him excessive setbacks," replied the *comes*, before heading towards his chambers.

His name was Libius Severus and he held the position of senator. He was invested with purple on the fourteenth day before the calends of December, three months after the execution of Majorian. Elder,

300

skittish, cowardly and condescending, he was the perfect candidate for Ricimero. But no one liked his proclamation, not the Visigoths, not the Vandals, not even Leon, the Emperor of the East.

Messengers rode down the roads bearing increasingly confused and disturbing missives. In one of them, it was reported that Egidius, *magister militum* of Gaul, had rejected Libius Severus as emperor, rebelling against the Empire and proclaiming the independence of Gaul. The Visigoths, faced with the evident weakness of Rome, crossed our *limes* and headed to the Mediterranean. Due to the lack of a strong army to support him, Ricimero was forced to hand over the important city of Narbonne to the *Gothorum rex* in exchange for granting his support to the new emperor and the cessation of hostilities. Theodoric, against the opinion of his bellicose brother Euric, accepted the agreement and marched with his armies towards Gaul ruled by Egidius with the approval of Ricimero.

Meanwhile, in the south, the raids of the Vandals were becoming more frequent and the city of Carthago Nova was no longer a safe place. We managed to repel several attacks, but our walls were increasingly damaged and the number of legionaries and *bucelarii* wounded or killed kept increasing. If we didn't receive reinforcements from Rome, the city would fall into Vandal hands inevitably.

The barbarians burned our fields, destroyed the aqueducts that supplied the city with water, and razed nearby villages. Every day, hundreds of peasants wounded, hungry and exhausted from long walks, crossed the walls in search of a safe place to shelter their families. But there was no place for everyone. With burned crops, ransacked livestock, and useless aqueducts, hunger, thirst and disease beating down on us was only a matter of time.

Going along the dilapidated streets of Carthago Nova meant traveling through a hell of despair and anguish. In the alleys the peasants crowded with their families. They were dirty, hungry and grieving. In their eyes sunken by hunger, the plea of those who don't want to see their children die was reflected. Newborns died from lack of milk and parents abandoned their little ones at the doors of the houses in the hope that some kind soul would take care of them. Thefts and murders were on the rise, in many cases as a result of a paltry crust of bread or a half-rotten apple to be thrown into the mouth.

In this hostile and inappropriate environment, our second son or rather daughter was born. Thank God, the birth of Aquilia Annia wasn't as complicated as that of Salvio Alexandros, and the little girl came into the world one spring night. Her older brother, barely two years old, gazed at her with devotion. Valeria, her face still sweaty from her effort, was smiling happily with the girl huddled in her arms. She was more beautiful than ever. I took little Alexandros so he could see her little sister up close and he gently caressed her cheek. Valerius Aquilius watched the scene excitedly. I left the little boy next to Valeria's bed and went out of the room accompanied by the *comes*.

The midwives left shortly after, satisfied and relieved by the easy delivery, surely they remembered with concern the arduous and tiring birth of Alexandros.

"A beautiful baby girl," said my father-in-law, smiling gratefully at the midwives. "Congratulations," he added, giving me a big hug.

"She looks just like her mother," I replied proudly.

The *civitatis comes* waited for the women to leave the *atrium* to reveal his concerns to me.

"But I fear for her and for Alexandros. Valeria and you are strong, but the children could get sick at any moment and the city is running out of medicines. The situation is untenable," he continued. "If food doesn't arrive soon, we'll be forced to abandon the city."

The wrinkles on his forehead revealed his deep concern. Earlier that day, three corpses had been found dumped in the street, possibly dead from starvation. The city's physicians were working tirelessly and the fear of a plague decimating Carthago Nova was as real as it was alarming.

"Is there any news about the messenger you sent to Libius Severus?"

"None and I don't think there will be. Frankly, I fear that the concerns of the emperor and Ricimero are focused on maintaining only the Italian peninsula."

Valerius Aquilius was right. Ricimero not only gave Narbonne to the Visigoths, but encouraged them to fight against the rebel Egidius with the promise to grant them all the lands they conquered. The Suevian intended to ingratiate himself with the Visigoths and, by giving them practically all of Gaul, concluded that he would succeed. But Egidius defeated the barbarians in the battle of Aurelianum and they had to retreat again behind the Loire River.

"You are right, Gaul is considered lost and we will be next."

"Egidius managed to stop the Visigoths in Aurelianum, but the death of the Visigothic prince Frederic during the battle could represent a serious setback for the future of Rome," said the *comes*.

"Euric took part in the battle. It's said that it was he who, during the heat of the battle, killed his own brother Frederic…"

"One less obstacle in his ascent to the throne," Valerius Aquilius interrupted.

A dense silence took hold of us, since we were well persuaded of what his possible coronation as king of the Visigoths meant for the Empire.

"He has only to eliminate his brother, King Theodoric, to proclaim himself *Gothorum rex*, and it's known to all that the ambition of the prince is immeasurable."

"If his troops cross our *limes,* Rome will be destroyed."

"That has always been his dream: to seize the remains of the Empire," added the *comes* with his face flushed with worry.

We walked slowly along the *atrium*. The night was cool, and a breeze loaded with the scent of jasmine and geraniums softly caressed our faces, taking our minds off such dark omens.

"But our problems are others," he continued, stopping his step. "We will have time to worry about the Visigoths. Now, it's the hunger of our people what keeps me awake at night."

"As you know," I began to say, resuming my walk. "The Vandals have made numerous incursions into the interior, plundering towns and villages. Now, according to the latest reports, they are heading towards the coast to load the ships and return to Africa."

"The last village they have sacked is Ilorci…"

I nodded. He looked at me with attention.

"They are several dozen wagons loaded with grain and hundreds of sheep and goats?"

"Enough to feed the village for months."

"That's right."

"What is your plan?" he asked me interested.

"Ilorci is about four days from here, and the route to the coast will force the Vandals to pass very close to Carthago Nova."

"Do you want to attack the caravan?" he asked incredulously. "It will be escorted by hundreds of soldiers. It would be suicide." he added, shaking his head.

I stopped and put my hand on his shoulder.

"They are confident, they don't expect our attack. I only need a hundred soldiers."

"I can't authorize this attack, losing so many men... you included, is an excess I can't afford."

"Is there another option?" I asked. "Valerius Aquilius, the children are starving and the sick are multiplying day by day. If we don't get food, the city will succumb. Don't be afraid, I'll be back," I assured him with a smile.

Crouching on the hill, we watched the dozens of fires that the Vandals had lit to warm their meals and shelter from the coolness of the night. The new moon protected us with its dark cloak, allowing us to distinguish, through the bonfires, the shadows of the hundreds of soldiers guarding the caravan. We were only a hundred soldiers, but hunger, despair and fear for the future of our families multiplied our number. With me were Arcadius, Calerus, Cassius Belenus and Ajax. From the privileged watchtower, we didn't lose detail of each of the barbarians' movements.

"They must be about five hundred soldiers." Arcadius whispered.

"I think so."

"I have counted more than thirty carts of grain and the heads of cattle can be counted by hundreds," Cassius Belenus intervened.

"The plan is as follows" I whispered, without looking away from the barbarian camp. "Ajax, you and twenty men, will reach the sheepfold and release the cattle and the horses," Ajax nodded "Arcadius, you and ten men will attack the guards who are near the carts," I said to him, pointing to the East Area of the camp, where the carts with the grain were located. "Cassius, have your archers prepare incendiary arrows and aim at the tents," the *ducenarii* nodded. "Calerus, you will attack the northern area of the camp together with fifteen *milites*. I will attack from the South."

"What will be the signal of attack?" Cassius Belenus asked.

"When each of you is in position, I'll make a signal imitating the howling of an owl. Then Cassius will order his archers to empty their quivers over the tents. When the arrows fly over the sky, Arcadius will release the animals and immediately, Calerus and I, making as much noise as possible, will attack them."

"When my archers have emptied their quivers, I'll go down the hill to support you," Cassius Belenus said.

"Chaos will take over the camp and the Vandals won't know how many soldiers are attacking them," Calerus observed.

"That's what I intend to achieve. There mustn't be a single barbarian left, everyone must die or we'll run the risk of them fleeing for help. Go ahead," I ordered.

With the utmost stealth, my officers called their men and headed to the indicated positions. A few minutes later, a howl broke the silence of the night and a rain of fire fell on the unsuspecting Vandals. Ajax and his *milites* opened the sheepfolds and the animals ran in fear, trampling everything they found in their path. The incendiary arrows reached their target and the tents began to burn spreading the fire rapidly throughout the camp. Smeared in black and bursting with eerie cries we charged against the confident barbarians, who looked at us in terror, believing that they were facing creatures fleeing from the deepest depths of the abyss.

"*Roma invicta est*!" I exclaimed, with my *spatha* drawn, and thirsty for Vandal blood.

"*Roma invicta est*!" my soldiers roared, drowning the cold night with the howl of our war cry. "¡*Roma invicta est*!"

Around us, fire and smoke enveloped everything. The cries and orders of the Vandals followed one another. The barbarian officers were unable to bring any order to the chaos that had engulfed the camp. More interested in fleeing than fighting, the Vandals ran in fear intending to hide in a nearby forest. But Cassius Belenus and his men did their job very well, annihilating every Vandal who tried to escape that hell.

The sun was shining on the horizon and we were still finishing some barbarian soldiers. The fires that devoured the tents began to die out and the dawn lit up the scene of death and destruction that the Vandal camp had become. Tired and exhausted due to the effort, I looked around looking for some enemy who still remained alive, but found none. A dark silence overwhelmed the battlefield, only broken by the whining and wailing of the wounded barbarians. Without any remaining strength, I fell on my knees to the ground and my men did the same.

Soon I felt like a hand was resting on my shoulder, I looked up and saw that it was Calerus. In his wet eyes I noticed that he was a bearer of bad news.

"Adriano," he said, with a lump in his throat. "Ajax is dead."

I clenched my fists and stood up. Calerus made a gesture for me to come with him. All around was destruction. Hundreds of dead bodies lay on the scorched ground. The animals, scattered around the camp, grazed peacefully next to the corpses, oblivious to the horror that surrounded them. The *milites*, looking tired and dirty with mud and blood, were regrouping while I counted the dead and wounded. We arrived at the place where the body of Ajax, was located, around him were gathered the corpses of more than fifteen barbarians.

"Here was the bulk of the Vandal troops," said Calerus, pointing to the inert bodies of several legionaries and *bucelarii.*

"There are dozens of dead in this area. If it had not been for him and his men, we would have failed. They fought like heroes," Arcadius interjected, looking at the smoldering remains of the sheepfold.

I knelt in front of Ajax and took his cold, lifeless hand. His face reflected a deep serenity and stillness, as if he were satisfied after having successfully consummated his last mission. The brave soldier had sacrificed his own life to preserve ours. My eyes got wet and tears pierced my dirty cheeks.

"Rest, my friend," I whispered, my throat tight with emotion. "You have fought like a hero and so you will be remembered. We could never be grateful enough."

I ordered the bodies of the dead *milites* to be collected and placed in the wagons. With our eyes still veiled by tears, we left that cursed place and departed for Carthago Nova carrying the valuable food that would satiate, even if only for a few months, the hunger that was pressing the desperate population. Twenty *milites* had died, among them my good friend Ajax, but dozens of Vandals littered the burned camp with their inert bodies, leaving it at the mercy of the vermin.

Miles away and mounted on a grain wagon drawn by two sturdy oxen, I heard the jubilation shouts. From the city walls, men, women and children greeted us and cheered happily as they saw us arrive laden with provisions. The city gate opened and a regiment of horsemen escorted us to Carthago Nova. Valerius Aquilius was among them.

"I congratulate you! I see that you have succeeded in your mission!"

"Twenty men have died, among them Ajax," I replied sadly.

He nodded regretfully.

"These are difficult times that require painful sacrifices. Keep in mind that his death was not in vain. Thanks to you and the twenty deceased soldiers, the people of Carthago Nova will be able to alleviate their hunger."

"How are Valeria and the children?" I asked, trying to get the image of my friend Ajax, lying limp on the ground in a pool of blood, out of my mind.

Valerius Aquilius smiled.

"I was looking forward to your return, as it could not be otherwise."

A crowd came out of the city and ran towards us. Happy that they could fill their empty stomachs, they rushed towards us, showering us with kisses and hugs. The memory of the deaths of my companions, and especially that of my friend Ajax, prevented me from enjoying such a day of jubilation. Arius Sidonius, Optila and Ajax had already died... who would be next? I tried to dismiss from my mind the harmful thoughts and crossed the walls under the deafening joy of the jubilant crowd.

Genseric must not have been excited about our bold attack, because a few weeks later, his ships landed on our shores and the city was besieged by a powerful army. With our stomachs full, we now had other worries, like preserving our lives, among others. The barbarian king himself commanded the attack, which meant that his raid was not a simple punitive action.

Two days after the Vandals arrived at our shores and set up camp, a Vandal delegation led by Genseric headed for Carthago Nova. They were attended by the magistrate Flavius Protus, a gray-haired old man with a weathered face and an affable look, and the *civitatis comes* Valerius Aquilius as the highest military and judicial authority of the city. I had the privilege of accompanying them as captain of the guard. Four legionaries, mounted on war horses, escorted us.

Genseric, escorted by six horsemen, was waiting for us halfway between his camp and our walls. Summer was beating hard, and our coats of mail were burning hot under the blazing sun. We were nervous;

the future of the city and, therefore, the future of thousands of people, including our families, depended on this negotiation. We rode slowly, watching the enemy camp in order to sound out the number of regiments that made up the invading army. The Vandal king was impatient and was urging us with his eyes. Surely he was also wasting away under his coat of mail and iron helmet.

"I greet you, Genseric, king of the Vandals. My name is Valerius Aquilius; *civitatis comes* of Carthago Nova."

"I greet you, Genseric, *Vandalorum rex*." interjected Flavius Protus. "My name is Flavius Protus, magistrate of the curia."

"I greet you, illustrious citizens of Carthago Nova."

Genseric's eyes reflected coldness. His lips were tightly pressed together and the wrinkles between his brows revealed that he wasn't in a very good mood. He was an old man of more than seventy years, but the strength he radiated eclipsed the vigor of the boldest of the legionaries.

"I pray by Jesus Christ that you leave our lands and go in peace, too many men have already died." said the magistrate.

"A few weeks ago, you cowardly attacked a group of soldiers, and robbed the provisions they were carrying. We'll leave if you hand over the criminals who committed such an atrocity and the stolen provisions."

Valerius Aquilius couldn't help but look at me sideways. I remained silent, alert to any suspicious movement of the king or his guards.

"The supplies came from Carthaginian villages. Your men killed the peasants, ravaged the fields and stole our food. Not Genseric, those provisions weren't yours, but ours. We simply took back what belongs to us," replied the *comes*.

The king turned red with anger. He clenched his jaws tightly and waited a few seconds before replying.

"I could raze your city to the ground right now and put the entire population to the sword. Don't abuse of my generosity and hand me over to the bandits, or is it that you refuse my outstretched hand?" he asked, holding out his gloved hand.

"Your outstretched hand?" Valerius Aquilius said suspicious of the Vandal's intentions. "You have burned our crops, razed our villages and slaughtered our people. Is that the meaning of your outstretched hand? We don't trust you, King Genseric, and of course we won't hand over to you the heroes who recovered our supplies. If you want to capture them, you will first have to break down our walls."

Flavius Protus looked at the *comes* in surprise and smiled in satisfaction. The magistrate was a brave man who would not pay obeisance to a barbarian king. Genseric, on the other hand, didn't like the hostile tone of Valerius Aquilius's words. Wrathful, he clenched his fist and pulled his hand away. But a sly smile broke out on the lips of the Vandal, who raised his eyes and looked carefully at the hundreds of men and women who watched us anxiously from the wall. And with the look of a wild beast ready to pounce on its prey, he said:

"So be it."

And without adding a word, he turned his horse and rode towards the Vandal camp, accompanied by his personal guards, ending his brief speech.

The air echoed with the thunderous thundering of the Vandals' swords as they struck fiercely against the shields. Thousands of barbarians were slowly advancing towards our walls without ceasing to hit their defenses while uttering terrifying cries. A spectacle that shook even the boldest of our soldiers. Some carried ladders; others pulled heavy battering rams and high assault towers. From the walls, the *milites* watched as the powerful enemy army moved inexorably towards us. Valerius Aquilius commanded us. Serious, but self-confident, he gave clear and concise orders to archers, legionaries and *bucelarii*.

"They are very numerous, but we fight for our lives while they do it for a meager booty. If we resist a couple of attacks their morale will falter and Genseric will have to return to Africa with his tail between his legs," Valerius Aquilius said, staring at the advance of the Vandals.

The barbarians stopped beating their shields and stopped. Behind them were arranged catapults, siege towers and battering rams. We watched them, ready to repel any attack. They, settled behind their shields, looked at us defiantly forming several rows. The loud sound of a Vandal war tuba broke the silence, and dozens of fireballs emerged from the enemy field and roamed the sky threatening our walls.

"Watch out!" yelled the *comes*. "They are attacking us with catapults!"

The fireballs clattered against the walls producing a terrifying noise and spreading flares of fire everywhere. Some of them crossed the walls, falling on the roofs of houses. In the absence of water, men, women and children struggled to stifle the fire with sand, blankets or by beating it with simple brooms. For several minutes the flaming shells flew over us, but luckily, their damage was less.

The call of a second tuba preceded a shower of arrows. We hurriedly protected ourselves behind the battlements and shields, from the darts that our enemies threw at us. A third sound was the warning for the great Avalanche. With fierce shouts, thousands of Vandals hurled themselves at our walls carrying ladders and siege machinery.

"*Sagitarii* take your positions!" Valerius Aquilius ordered.

"Roma invicta est!" I screamed furiously, raising my *spatha* to the sky.

The *comes* smiled and yelled at me:

"Roma invicta est! Roma invicta est!

It didn't take long for our war cry to spread among our ranks and even among the civilian population like the roar of a raging storm, infusing them with renewed impetus and hope. The cry of "Roma invicta est!" became a determined prayer, a relentless howl that gave them courage and decision, urging them not to falter, to continue fighting while in their hearts still beat a breath of life.

Dozens of *sagitarii* settled behind the battlements and fired their weapons, but the barbarians were too many and didn't take long to reach the walls with the ladders. We began to throw pitch, stones and burning sand at them, and managed to suffocate the first attack.

"Come on soldiers, we have to prevent them from climbing the walls again!" shouted the *comes*.

The Vandals retreated and a new rain of arrows fell on us killing many of our men.

"Protect yourself with your shields!" Valerius Aquilius ordered, moving from side to side of the wall without ceasing to issue orders.

The rhythmic sound of a few drums warned us of the imminence of a new movement on the part of Genseric's troops. I peered through the battlements and with horror; I could see how several siege towers were dragged by dozens of slaves who pulled them by means of thick ropes.

"They'll use their siege towers!" I exclaimed. "*Sagitarii*, prepare the incendiary darts!"

The wooden wheels of the towers creaked as they advanced, making a noise similar to the lament of a hundred mourners. A dark omen of what would happen if they reached our walls. From those menacing watchtowers, the barbarian Archers could hit their targets more easily.

"We must prevent the towers from moving forward or it will be our end!" I said to the *comes*.

Valerius Aquilius nodded and ordered the crossbows to be prepared. Four of them were placed on their tripods and armed with their powerful javelins just in front of the siege towers.

"Set the javelins and fire at the towers!"

Two men tightened the rope of the fearsome weapon and another prepared the javelin, smeared it with pitch and set it on fire with a torch. Then he aimed at one of the towers and fired. The projectile was launched at high speed and hit its target noisily, scattering the burning pitch over part of the tower, making it unusable. The shouts of jubilation followed, giving new strength to our exhausted army.

The impact of three more javelins on the siege towers persuaded the Vandal king, who ordered their retreat to a safe area in the rearguard. Then, dozens of small rocks, launched by the catapults, fell on our heads causing a great number of casualties and damage, including a crossbow. Genseric, skillfully, had ordered the catapults to be loaded with stones, which were launched as projectiles reaching great speed and scattering everywhere, making it very difficult to get protected against them.

We were forced to take shelter behind the battlements and walls, as our shields were completely useless. More concerned with protecting our integrity than the city walls, we neglected the advance of thousands of Vandals who pounced on us again with ladders and battering rams. Fortunately, the stone throwing ceased and we were able to defend ourselves from the assailants who were already preparing to ascend our walls.

We defended ourselves fiercely. We *milites* had our wives and children in mind. We were persuaded of what would happen to them if the Vandals managed to conquer the city. Valerius Aquilius was bravely defending himself against several barbarians who had managed to go beyond the wall. I went to his aid and we were able to get rid of them. I looked at the *comes* and noticed that his coat of mail was stained with blood, but I didn't know if it was his or that of a barbarian. Valerius Aquilius looked at me and noticed the concern in my eyes. He smiled and shook his head.

"Stay quiet Adriano, I feel better than ever." he lied.

"Maybe you should rest; you have fought during many hours." I suggested.

"Carthago Nova needs each one of us."

"But..."

"No, this is my place!" he interrupted with an authority that left no place for a reply.

I nodded, kept quiet and continued fighting. From time to time I looked at Valerius Aquilius and noticed that he made ostensible gestures of pain. I was worried about his health.

The enemies' onslaughts followed one after another during hours, and we, exhausted and wounded, repulsed their attacks bravely, defending our lives. Thus, nightfall came and the Vandals stopped their siege, retreating to their camp. The streets of Carthago Nova were strewn with the corpses of hundreds of *milites* and as many civilians who fell, struck down by enemy projectiles and arrows. We had resisted the first Vandal attack: a meager victory stained with the blood of hundreds of men and women.

We watched the enemy retreat from the walls. I looked for the *comes* with my eyes and located him a few steps away from me. I went towards him and found him completely pale: his coat of mail was soaked in blood. Concerned, I took him to his house and ordered a physician and Valeria to be summoned.

The physician was attending to Valerius Aquilius when Valeria arrived at the house. Concerned, she entered the room and found her father pale but conscious. He had lost a lot of blood but none of his wounds were life-threatening. She looked at me with tear-blurred eyes and I smiled at her; the *comes* was out of danger.

"Father!" Valeria exclaimed, falling on his lap between sobs.

"Calm down daughter, it was just a scratch; tomorrow I'll be ready for battle again."

"You must rest tomorrow, since any sudden movement could cause the wound to open up." advised the physician, a mature man with a kind look who had taken care of the family for years.

"But someone must organize the troops." protested the *comes*.

"Father, tomorrow you must rest, let someone else take care of that task," Valeria begged.

"Valerius Aquilius, the troops are very well trained and we know Genseric's strategy. You'd better rest for a few days, Carthago Nova needs you in full strength," I suggested.

The *civitatis comes* gritted his teeth in pain and nodded. He was aware that if he commanded the troops the next day, he would die without remission.

"Adriano, I appoint you *praepositus* of the army of Carthago Nova, you will lead the defense of the city," he muttered. "I only ask God to grant me enough strength to contemplate the defeat of our enemy."

"I promise you that you will see it," I told him, totally convinced.

"We'd better let him rest," the physician intervened.

We said goodbye to the *comes* and left him alone in his bedroom. I accompanied Valeria home, kissed the children and returned to the *castrum* to organize the defense. I was convinced that the sunrise would bring not only the sun's rays, but also a new Vandal onslaught.

We withstood the barbarian attacks for four hard days. Nevertheless, the more Vandals we killed, the more they appeared on the horizon. If we destroyed a siege tower, they came back with two, three, four... Their resources were inexhaustible, while ours dwindled at every instant.

It was sunset and the indefatigable barbarians returned to their camp. The *milites* were looking exhausted at heaven, thanking God for remaining alive. The appearance of many of them, mine included, was quite regrettable. Our eyes were red and sunken because of lack of sleep, our faces were hungry skulls from the little food we ate and our uniforms were dirty with blood and dust.

"Inspect the walls and warn the masons if necessary," I ordered a *circitor*. "I'm going to the hospital to count today's casualties."

I headed to the *valetudinarium* after each fight to know the number of wounded and dead, then I went to the house of the *comes* and inform him of the development of the battle. I arrived at the hospital and met dozens of physicians and assistants, among whom was Valeria who was busy going from one wounded to another with the intention of alleviating their ills. I spoke to the physician in charge who informed me that three hundred wounded and one hundred and twenty dead had arrived at the *valetudinarium* during the course of the day. It was a very hard day. I was about to leave the hospital when something caught my eye in the chapel attached to the building. I approached and found Calerus praying fervently in front of an image of the crucified Christ. I watched him for a few minutes until he got up, sanctified himself and prepared to leave the chapel. Then our eyes crossed and smiled. His eyes were streaked with tears.

"Complicated day, right?" he asked me, as we left the hospital and got some fresh air.

"We have no more than about two thousand soldiers in good condition, the rest are wounded or dead. I don't know how many more attacks we will be able to resist."

We were heading to the house of the *comes*. Along the way we observed the devastation that the fireballs and stones thrown by the catapults had caused in the city. In the hospital not only the wounded were legionaries and *bucelarii,* dozens of citizens also suffered in their flesh the rigor of the fighting. Around us followed the cries of those who had lost a family member or suffered the loss of their properties destroyed by the fatal action of the catapults.

"Will we get some backup?" Calerus asked.

"We are alone" I replied, nodding.

"You're wrong about that. We're not alone."

"What do you mean?"

Calerus stopped and stared into my eyes.

"Jesus Christ is with us," he said, touching my shoulder. "Have faith, we'll get out of this."

His glassy eyes gave me an unwavering confidence. It was evident that my friend was convinced that divine mediation would free us from the desperate situation in which we found ourselves. I smiled and looked at the ground doubting his words.

"I assure you that I wish with all my heart that I could have your faith, but unfortunately, against the barbarians only this serve," I replied, drumming with my fingers the grip of my *spatha.*

We continue our way and arrive at the house of Valerius Aquilius.

"Pray friend Adriano, pray with all your strength and have faith. The Savior is with us, I feel it. He will rid us of Vandals."

He grabbed me tightly by the arms and stared into my eyes. From his lips sprouted a sincere smile.

"Rest my friend, it's been a very hard day," I just said.

"Will you pray?" he asked me, still holding my arms, as if he intended not to let me go until I answered him.

"All right," I said. "I'll pray a couple of Lord's Prayer before bed but with a lot of faith."

"Ha, ha, ha! You'll see how you don't regret it."

We said goodbye to each other. Calerus went to the *castrum,* while I entered the house. Valerius Aquilius was in his bedroom, lying on the bed. He had improved ostensibly from his injuries, but he was still very weak. Valeria, along with the children, was accompanying him. I sat on a footstool and transmitted the war report to him, always exaggerating the casualties of the enemies and minimizing ours, it made no sense to worry the *comes* more than is strictly necessary. I accompanied my family during several minutes. I beheld the blind devotion that Valeria felt for her beloved father, little Annia who remained asleep in bed next to him, and Salvio Alexandros who didn't stop playing with a wooden soldier that his grandfather had carved for him.

"What are you thinking about, honey?" Valeria asked me, waking me up from my reverie. "You've been staring at the floor for several minutes without saying anything."

"Nothing, my love," I answered, getting up from the footstool. "I must return to the *castrum,* I have to organize the defense of the city."

"You are doing very well son," intervened the *comes.* "With God's help, Genseric will leave soon."

"I hope he hears your prayers," I said skeptically.

I said goodbye to my family and headed to the *castrum.* I organized the night watches and went to rest in the barracks. Although I was not sleepy, I lay down on my bunk hoping that rest could provide a little respite for my exhausted spirit. I looked at the ceiling and remembered Calerus's words: «pray my friend Adriano, pray with all your strength and have faith.» I smiled as I also remembered the words of the *comes*: «With God's help, Genseric will be gone soon.» I have never been much of a believer, my faith in God was relative but... what did I have to lose? I thought of Valeria and the children, and pressed my palms together. I closed my eyes and prayed for them, for Carthago Nova, for Hispania... for Rome.

Dawn came and with it the punctual Vandals. Behind them, the rising sun reflected their long, reddish shadows, giving them the stature of mythical giants. Once again, they advanced accompanied by the shrill sound of war tubas, by fierce shouts and by the wrathful blows to the shields: indefatigable and immune to the strenuous fighting days they carried on their backs. My *milites* looked at them with resignation. One of them snorted.

"Don't they ever get tired?" asked a young legionary who was watching the enemy advance right next to me.

And he was right. The Vandal captains were haranguing their soldiers by beating them on the back, or shouting loudly, raising their threatening swords. One or another daring barbarian ran towards us and after showing us his naked ass returned to the formation amidst the laughter of his comrades. They were in high spirits, while we were exhausted and hopeless.

"We'll kick their hairy asses and they'll go back to Africa, you can be sure of that," I assured the legionary, with all the conviction I could gather.

"I think someone has not prayed with enough faith."

I looked towards the soldier who had pronounced those words and found Calerus. He was looking at me with a cynical smile.

"You look very happy even though the barbarians are still attacking us; perhaps the good Lord hasn't been kind enough to listen to our prayers," I replied mockingly.

"Don't blaspheme my good friend and next time pray with more faith."

I was going to answer him, but he headed to his position on the wall.

It was the wildest attack and lasted well into the night, but we resisted. The wounded could be counted by hundreds and the dead too.

The walls were very weakened, they would hardly withstand another day the rush of the catapults. Puddles of blood strewn the streets while the fires ravaged the few buildings still standing. The hospital was crowded and there was no room for any more injured. I reviewed the troops, counted the dead and wounded, organized the guards and, dejected, prepared to transmit the war report to the *comes*.

I couldn't deceive him; he noticed fatigue and defeat in my eyes. The city would not resist anymore. Valeria took the children and went out to play in the *atrium* with them. Despite being quite young, they were aware that something horrible was happening.

"Maybe we should surrender the city," suggested Valerius Aquilius after I informed him of the situation.

"I witnessed the plundering of Rome. Genseric, as he had agreed with the pope, respected the temples and the properties of the church, but they wiped out everything else."

"But he respected the lives of its inhabitants."

"Sort of. They killed someone who had tried to deceive them by hiding his valuables but, in general, the *Vandalorum rex* kept his word."

"So, what do we do?" the *comes* asked me.

Thousands of lives depended on my response. If Genseric accepted our surrender, Carthago Nova would be plundered and the population, though poor and hungry, respected. If we continued our bitter resistance, we would be at risk of dying behind the walls once they were destroyed by the barbarians.

"We aren't sure that Genseric will accept our surrender. Carthago Nova has a very important strategic value and its possession would allow him to have the south of Hispania under his control," I said.

"Well, we'll have to ask him what he wants, what's the price we must pay to save the lives of our citizens."

"Remember that the first thing he requested was the heads of those who had attacked his soldiers…"

"Don't be foolish," he said. "You know that even if I had put you in his hands Genseric would have besieged Carthago Nova anyway. Moreover, I won't sacrifice one of my soldiers to save the city," the *comes* added convinced, reading in my eyes what my intentions were. "If it is God's will that Genseric destroy us, so be it."

The room's door was half-open and I saw as, in another room, Valeria cradled little Annia, while Alexandros ran from side to side wielding a small wooden sword. So, I decided: if I had to offer my life to save that of my family and my countrymen so be it. Yes, that's what I decided to do, give my life and allow the sack of the city, as happened in Rome. It would be nothing more than a meager sacrifice that I would carry with pleasure. Carthago Nova and its inhabitants would survive, that was the important thing. But I would only surrender my life, since they had no intention of immolating the rest of the *miles* who bravely stormed the food caravan. They didn't deserve to suffer the consequences of my firm decision.

"I'll go to the Vandal camp tonight and talk to Genseric."

I got up and left the room leaving the *comes* with his words in his mouth, I didn't want to hear any reply.

On horseback and carrying torches, Arcadius, Calerus, Cassius Belenus and I, set off to the barbarian camp. The sentinels on guard looked at us suspiciously, but they cleared our path and a dozen horsemen escorted us to the king's tent. Along the way we watched the barbarian troops, intending to find out how many soldiers Genseric had at his disposal, as well as scrutinizing by their countenance what their mood was. In battle, morality is more valuable than numerical superiority. And they were thousands and looked untouched and rested. I looked at Arcadius and nodded worried.

"These barbarians are indefatigable" he whispered.

We arrived at the tent of the *Vandalorum rex* and noticed that he was very busy issuing orders to several of his officers. A soldier informed him of our presence and Genseric looked at us interested. The king asked him something and the Vandal pointed his finger at me.

"He probably asked him who's in charge," Calerus said.

And it must have been so because Genseric gestured to me to get closer. I dismounted and escorted by two members of his personal guard, entered the Vandal's tent once I was duly disarmed. The *Vandalorum rex* was sitting on a footstool, his elbows resting on a wooden table. He had an angular face, dark eyes, and a brushy beard with some silver strands on his chin. Despite his age, his bearing was strong and robust, the same as that of a warrior king.

"I salute you, Genseric, king of Vandals. My name is Salvio Adriano, *praepositus* of the armies of Carthago Nova," I said, with a slight inclination.

"I have to admit that I'm completely surprised," he said, as he gestured to me to take a seat on a footstool.

I sat without opening my mouth.

"We have besieged you during several days, and as far as I know, no one has been able to enter or leave the city."

I continued in silence, I didn't understand his words.

"Can you explain to me how you knew of the emperor's death?" he asked me. "I just got the news!" he exclaimed incredulously with a half-smile.

Had the Emperor Libius Severus died? I tried to keep my composure and convey the impression that I already knew the news. The king seemed confused, I had to seize the opportunity, I didn't know very well what for, but I had to seize it.

"That's right, *domine*," I replied. "We know that and that's why I'm here now."

Genseric rolled his eyes and looking at me more carefully, he said:

"I remember you... You escorted the *comes* Valerius Aquilius and the magistrate in our previous meeting."

I nodded.

"I understand that if you are here, instead of such high personalities, it's because in Carthago Nova things aren't probably very well…" the Vandal king was cunning as a Fox. "Fine," he agreed at last, aware of his power. "If you have something to say, say it then."

I got up from my footstool and wandered around the tent. What the hell was I going to tell him, that I intended to offer my life to save the city? Suddenly an idea arose in my mind that, although far-fetched, might work.

"As you well know, four years ago the elderly senator Libius Severus was invested with the purple thanks to the mediation of Ricimero, and your candidate, Anicius Olybrius, was rejected in a totally unfair manner."

Genseric looked at me attentively.

"Olybrius is married to Placidia, one of Valentinian's daughters, and deserves to be crowned…"

"My son Huneric is married to Eudoxia, Placidia's sister," the Vandal interjected. "If Olybrius is proclaimed emperor, my son would be his brother-in-law and who knows if in the future… That's why I proposed his coronation four years ago, but Ricimero got his way again!" he exclaimed indignantly, hitting the table hard.

"Ricimero must have already moved his pieces to anoint some magister or senator faithful to his interests, while the legitimate emperor remains in the shadows without claiming what, in justice, belongs to him."

The barbarian king rose from his footstool and addressed me.

"What do you want?" he asked, squinting at me with distrust.

"Ricimero hates the Vandals; if he can clothe any of his acolytes with the purple, he won't cease his efforts until he destroys you, using even his German allies if necessary. But if you succeed in having Olybrius crowned, then Rome's relations with Carthago would be entirely different." The Vandal looked at me with interest. "Let me suggest that you send a legation to negotiate his candidacy."

"What do you get of all this?"

"Peace with you, protect our cities from your attacks and who knows if a future alliance against other nations."

"Like the Visigoths or the Suevians, right?" he asked more confidently.

"That's right."

The Vandal poured a glass of wine.

"I have to think about it all," he said, before taking a long drink.

"Think about it, but remember you don't have much time. Ricimero is very astute and surely he hasn't wasted his time in sterile discussions."

The Vandal king wrinkled his brow, pondering my words.

"Go back to Carthago Nova," he ordered, ending the conversation. Then he dismissed me with a disdainful gesture, as if I were an annoying fly hovering over his food.

I bowed my head and accompanied by my friends, I returned to the city hoping that my words had had an effect on the barbarian king.

The sunrise announced the Vandal's reply. Watching over the wall, I observed the dawn and how the solar rays were preparing to illuminate the fields, which were soiled by the blood spilled and by the war devices that were piling up after the constant attacks. At my side were my companions Arcadius, Calerus and Cassius Belenus, whom I had already informed of my conversation with Genseric. We looked expectantly at the horizon waiting for the attack of the barbarians. But it was not to be. That day, the Vandals weren't punctual for their appointment. The sun was rising over the horizon, but our enemies showed no signs of life. Hopeful, I ordered a rider to inspect the enemy camp. Minutes turned into hours waiting for his news.

"It's weird that they haven't yet attacked, perhaps they have left..." wished Arcadius, without taking his eyes off the horizon.

We all hoped it was so.

"Look, the scout!" Cassius Belenus said, pointing to a horseman galloping at full speed towards our walls.

We descended in haste from our watchtower and made our way to the city gate. There we waited anxiously for the arrival of the horseman. He dismounted as soon as he crossed the gate, which was immediately closed behind him. Without a breath, he came towards us smiling.

"They have left!" he exclaimed incredulously. "It's as if the earth had swallowed them up. They've disappeared!"

"Well!" Arcadius exclaimed, clenching his fists tightly.

"We did it!" Cassius Belenus shouted, bringing out all the tension accumulated after long and painful days of siege.

"Praise the Lord," whispered Calerus. He knelt down and prayed a prayer of infinite gratitude.

I nodded and placed my hand on his shoulder. Tears were running down his cheeks wetting the dry earth. Something inside me warned me that that would be the last day Calerus would wear the uniform of legionary, and so it was. That same afternoon he requested his license from the *civitatis comes*, who willingly granted it to him, since in the unexpected retreat of the Vandals the *comes* glimpsed the Hand of the Almighty. And it was well worth losing a great soldier in exchange for gaining a devoted servant of God. So, Calerus entered the monastery and decided to dedicate his life to prayer, study and meditation.

The news about the retreat of the Vandals quickly spread throughout the city, and men and women danced, laughed and cried happily, since they were freed from the barbaric siege. However, in order to avoid surprises, I organized the guards and ordered the weakened walls to be rebuilt. Around us congratulations and displays of joy followed each other. The grim darkness that had gripped the city over the past few months had faded under the bright light of unexpected hope.

I went to the hospital, where Valeria was helping the physicians. The good news was faster than me, and as soon as she saw me entering the room, my beloved wife threw herself at me giving me a strong hug.

"You got it, you got it," she whispered.

"We have achieved it among all of us," I said before kissing her.

"We're saved."

«Just for now,» I thought. How long would peace last? Who knew it? If it weren't the Vandals who attacked us next time, it would be the Visigoths, the Suevians or perhaps the Ostrogoths or the Franks... the retreat of the Vandals was nothing more than a small truce of fixed duration. But it wasn't time of bad omens but of happiness; we had withstood the barbaric attack and it was time to celebrate it.

"I'll inform your father," I said.

Tears of happiness ran down her soft cheeks. I stroked her face and kissed her again before leaving the hospital.

When I arrived at the house, I found the *comes* accompanied by a young soldier who had informed him of the good news. When the *miles* noticed my presence, he greeted me and said goodbye. Valerius Aquilius remained lying on the bed still convalescing from his wounds.

"I see that you have already been informed," I said, looking at the legionary that was leaving the room.

"Good news the sooner you know it the better, don't you think?"

"The Vandals have retreated. Maybe Genseric reflected on my suggestion and eventually headed to Ravenna or Rome to claim the throne for Olybrius. With his powerful navy close to Italy, his arguments will be much more persuasive."

"You were very bold," said the *comes*, satisfied. "You met with the Vandal to surrender the city and got him to leave without claiming any kind of reward or loot."

"We had a stroke of luck," I said, sitting on the bed. "And now... who will be proclaimed as new Augustus?"

The *civitatis comes* was tearing his beard and remained thoughtful for a few moments.

"To be honest, I have no idea. I see no one in Rome prepared to take on such a responsibility. Perhaps the next emperor will come from Constantinople..."

"Constantinople?" I asked confused.

"The Eastern Empire is still strong and Leo, its emperor, is a skilled strategist. If there is no capable man in Rome, he will propose one..."

"And it will have to be ratified by Ricimero," I finished his sentence.

Valerius Aquilius nodded.

"And what about Genseric's candidate?" I asked.

"Olybrius?" the *comes* denied with his head "Ricimero will never tolerate Huneric, the future king of the Vandals, to be the brother-in-law of an emperor of Rome. It would have to be above his body."

"Then the Vandals will return."

"And more furious than ever."

CHAPTER XV

The Eastern Empire comes to the aid of Rome.

Turpitudo peius est quam mors.[18]

Tranquility prevailed in our city for months. We rebuilt the walls which were badly damaged by the catapults, we built and rehabilitated the *insulae* and the *domus*, and we harvested the crops and milked our cattle. Carthago Nova was like a small Hispano-Roman island lost in a vast sea of barbarians. It seemed that both Rome and Carthago had forgotten about us, letting us live in peace without fear of spotting enemy soldiers on the horizon.

Calerus finally became a monk and wore religious robes. He got tonsured and dressed in a brownish tunic of untanned wool. He said mass every day in a dilapidated old church he headed, which he had determined to restore.

We left our backs during several weeks, picking up large blocks of granite or heavy wooden beams. Arcadius and I helped him when we could and, little by little, the rickety church began to show some dignity.

"If we keep working like this, it'll soon become a beautiful Cathedral," said Arcadius, drinking from a wineskin.

"I'll be satisfied if we manage to repair the leaks," Calerus replied with a smile.

I looked at the church and felt proud of my friend. It was sober and sturdy, built with large stone ashlars and a beautiful wooden gable roof.

"I hope to see more of you in my church when it's properly tidied up," he said with a slightly reproachful tone.

---

[18] *Dishonor is worse than death (adapted from the Latin Grammar book by Santiago Segura Munguía).*

"Phew! I'll try my friend, but I can't promise anything, you know that Adriano demands a lot from his officers and I'm almost always on duty…"

"Don't use me as an excuse; the truth is that you usually get up quite late on Sundays due to the fondness you have developed for the taverns of Carthago Nova," I interrupted him. "Listen to him and go to church more often, it'll do you good."

"And you too," Calerus replied, tapping me on the shoulder.

"Well… yes, you're right… me too."

We continued our tireless work amid laughter and put new jambs on the church door, since the old ones had been eaten by woodworm. We were so concentrated on our task that we didn't notice the arrival of the comes.

"You're doing a great job," said Valerius Aquilius, accompanied by two guards.

"I greet you, civitatis comes," Arcadius said martially.

"God Save you many years, Valerius Aquilius," Calerus said, shaking his hand. "I hope the results will be to your liking."

"Recently, this place wasn't even useful for housing pigs, and soon it'll look like a cathedral," the comes pointed out, looking with satisfaction at the work.

"That's what I said," Arcadius interjected.

"I greet you, Valerius Aquilius," I said, striking Arcadius. "Were you looking for me?

"That's right. I asked Valeria and she said that I could possibly find you here. I have important news to share with you. Let's take a walk."

I got rid of dust and dirt by washing myself in a bucket of water and said goodbye to my friends. They'd have to place the heavy jambs without me.

"Is there any news from Rome?" I asked, as we strolled through the streets of the city.

"No, we still don't know who will be appointed emperor," the comes replied.

"Many months have elapsed since Libius Severus died; negotiations have probably been very tough."

Valerius Aquilius nodded.

"There are many barbarian kings involved, and they don't want to miss the opportunity to present their own candidates."

"So, what's going on?"

The *comes* stopped and cooled in a fountain. It was half a day and it was very hot. He dried his hands in his uniform and sought refuge on a stone bench protected by the shade of a palm tree. Valerius Aquilius wasn't the same since he had been wounded by the Vandals. Now he got tired easily and sometimes, he had trouble breathing. The years didn't pass in vain in the brave soldier.

"This morning a Jewish merchant from Toulouse arrived in the city. He brought with him woolen fabrics, some trinkets and disturbing news."

I looked at him carefully.

"As he told us, Theodoric, the king of the Visigoths, has died and his brother Euric has been proclaimed new king."

I sat next to him. I was immediately aware of the magnitude of the news. Euric hated us for years. He had always been against the policies of his brother Theodoric, a faithful ally of Rome and now, once he had died, he had a free way to cross our limes with his armies and increase his territories at the expense of our Empire.

"That means that the war against the Visigoths is imminent," I mused, as if afraid to hear my own words.

"That's right, and more so now that we still lack an emperor."

Euric had achieved his purpose of being anointed king of the Visigoths, now a colossal empire was opened in front of him to plunder and conquer, an irresistible treasure with which to satisfy his obscene greed. Once again, dark omens hovered over a dying Rome determined to survive, like the fish that snouts and picks caught in the fisherman's net, but that finally dies after a long and barren agony.

That same night I had a terrible nightmare. Dozens of ships engulfed in flames appeared in it. The sailors, made a fireball, threw themselves tormented into the dark waters in the hope of alleviating their ordeal. I was on one of the ships, defending myself painfully from demons with red blood eyes, which attacked me with strange sickle-shaped swords. I was surrounded everywhere. My legionaries fell one after the other at the unbridled thrust of the enemy, who finished them on the ground without showing any mercy. Desperate, I threw myself into the sea trying to escape. For a few moments I swam under the dark waters and contemplated the corpses of dozens of soldiers with empty

325

glances and emaciated faces. I managed to climb to the surface and breathe. Exhausted, I reached the beach and fell deadbeat. Dozens of ships were burning in front of me, and the shadows of the demons were heading, slowly but inexorably, towards a city that I recognized as Carthago Nova.

"You must flee; get out of this cursed city," a voice said.

I turned and beside me, leaning on his staff, appeared the figure of the druid, who watched undaunted the advance of the demons.

"When the boats swim at the bottom of the sea and the demons threaten the city walls, you will march with your family to the north," he continued. "Otherwise, they'll die."

"Is there no way to avoid disaster?" I asked him, joining in.

"It's written. The end is near and nothing, nor anyone, can help it. As the fortune-teller predicted, for twelve sublime centuries Rome has dominated the world. The Empire of a thousand years has come to an end and must now disappear. Its armies will be destroyed, its cities conquered, but its legacy, the promise of civilization and prosperity that it has always embodied, will be eternal and will never die. Rome will be praised and glorified for centuries."

"Will this ever end?" I asked, covering my face down with my hands.

"Rome has prospered based on blood and fire, destroying peoples and subduing its people. Now, all the blood shed will fall upon her and a mighty army will emerge from the realm of the dead and cry out for revenge." Lughdyr replied.

With grim expression I watched the demons overcome the city walls destroying everything in their path. Carthago Nova had become a heartbreaking hell.

"So, is this the end?" I asked.

"It'll be the end."

The druid's figure dissipated until it finally disappeared into darkness.

I woke up discouraged, bathed in a puddle of sweat. I joined in and sat on the bed. My heart hurriedly struck my chest, threatening to run away from my body. Next to me was Valeria, who slept peacefully oblivious to the horrible nightmare that had haunted me. More serene, I set out to resume my rest when on the pavement of the room I observed a small object that gleamed illuminated by the silvery moonlight. It was mistletoe.

The winter was very severe and took its toll on our *civitatis comes*. Bedridden, he became increasingly pale and wiry. The physicians who treated him were not very hopeful and commented that at any moment death would knock at his door. Calerus visited us regularly, since his presence comforted him. Valeria didn't leave her father's bedside for a single moment. She fed him, wiped the cold sweat from his forehead and cleaned him every day. I visited him often and tried to cheer him up with good news about the progress of the reconstruction of the city or how good the harvests and the fishing had been, but above all, I tried to keep the ghosts of the war out of his mind.

One extremely cold night I went to visit him. There was Calerus sitting on a footstool, reading an old book. To his right, caressing his forehead, was Valeria.

"I greet you, *civitatis comes* how are you feeling?" I asked, before giving Valeria a kiss.

"I've been your father-in-law for years; will you ever stop addressing me so solemnly?" he answered in just a whisper with a smile. "Well, well, my old bones refuse to abandon the world of the living."

"You'll overcome this as you have already overcome so many other situations." said Valeria with more confidence than she really had.

I approached Valerius Aquilius and took his hand; it was cold and extremely thin. His eyes were sunken and his fragile bones supported a haggard skin, which showed thin blue veins. The thinness of the comes was alarming. Trying to push the bad thoughts from my mind, I sat down on a footstool.

"I see you are in good company." I said, looking at Calerus, who smiled at me and invited me to take a seat.

"I'm telling him the legend of the origins of Rome."

"I heard that old story a long time ago," I said, trying to remember it, "but it's not a bad time to hear it again."

Calerus was a great speaker, his voice was deep and pleasant, and the cadence of his tone was calm and soothing. He smiled and reached for a page in the book.

"Well, our friend Adriano has arrived a little late, but since he is interested in refreshing his memory, if it's all right with you, I'll retell the story from the beginning."

The comes and Valeria nodded with a smile and Calerus prepared to narrate the legend of the birth of the Empire.

"Many, many years ago, there lived a king named Numitor, who reigned in the city of Alba Longa. This king had a younger brother named Amulius who managed to wrest the throne from him and banished him. Not content with this and fearing that one of Numitor's sons would take the throne from him, he ordered that they be killed. Only the daughter of Numitor, named Rhea Silvia, managed to escape from death, but Amulius, to ensure that she would not get married or have children, forced her to become a priestess of the temple of Vesta. But one fine day, she fell asleep on the shore of a river and the god Mars, bewitched by her beauty, possessed Rhea without her being aware of it. As a consequence of this act, Rhea Silvia gave birth to two twins. Fearing for the lives of her children and before Amulius found out, she put them in a basket and let them run downstream of the Tiberis in the hope that someone would take them in and free them from certain death. The basket ran aground on Mount Palatine and the children were picked up by a she-wolf who took them to her den. There they were nursed and cared for by her until one fine day, a shepherd who was tending his sheep in a nearby field heard the cries of a child. He carefully approached the entrance of the cave and, in the darkness; he found the two little ones.

I watched the comes, who listened attentively to the legend. His face showed a placid smile and his eyes shone with emotion. Calerus, with his story, was soothing his pains, relieving the comes of the illness that afflicted him.

"The shepherd, whose name was Faustulus, took the children and brought them to his hut, where he cared for them as his own. And he named them Romulus and Remus. The little ones grew up and discovered their origins. They returned to Alba Longa and killed Amulius, crowning their grandfather Numitor as king. The two brothers then headed south with the intention of founding their own city. Remus wanted to found it on Aventine Hill while Romulus intended to do it on Palatine Hill, where the basket had run aground years before. They decided to ask the gods and climbed to the top of a hill waiting for a sign from them. Remus saw six eagles fly while Romulus saw twelve. The gods had manifested themselves and their designs were interpreted by an augur: if the city was founded on Aventine Hill, six glorious centuries awaited it, while if it was founded on Palatine Hill, twelve centuries of long and prosperous life awaited it. But Remus didn't understand it that way. He argued that he had seen the birds before his brother and that the city should be founded where he had decided. Both brothers fought and in the end Romulus killed his brother, pronouncing the following words: "*sic deinde, quinqumque alius transiliet moenia mea.*»[19] He then satisfied his pretensions and founded the city on the Palatine Hill, calling it Rome in his honor. And he, Romulus, was the first king of the *Caput Mundi*, the greatest city that has ever existed."

"So, the Empire would live for twelve centuries?" I asked.

"That's right," Calerus answered, closing the book.

The druid's words came to my mind: «It is written. The end is near and nothing and no one can prevent it. As the fortune-tellers predicted, for twelve sublime centuries Rome has dominated the world. The Empire of a thousand years has come to an end and must now disappear. Its armies will be destroyed, its cities conquered, but its legacy, the promise of civilization and prosperity it has always embodied, will be eternal and will never die. Rome will be praised and glorified forever.»

"My faith prevents me from believing in fortune-tellers and false prophets," Calerus said, as if he knew what I was thinking. "Rome is undergoing a complicated situation, but not worse than it was fifty years ago and is still alive."

"But very weak," specified the *comes*.

Valerius Aquilius watched the roof of the house with his gaze lost, as if his mind were traveling to remote places or distant times. Like Rome, the old man was gradually dying, lengthening his agony, clinging reluctantly to a breath of life that seemed willing to abandon him.

"Rome is dying and so am I...." he lamented in a bitter sigh.

Valeria came out of the bedroom holding her cry. Calerus approached him and prayed a Lord's Father I got up and left the room to comfort Valeria, who was despondent sitting on a stone bench.

---

[19] *This is how anyone else who jumps over my walls will end from now on. (Titus Livius)*

Several months remained the *civitatis comes* wasted away by fevers and weakness, until one day in late spring, he left us to join the God he so worshipped. Calerus was present at his last exhalation and carried out the last rites. Valeria was swimming in a sea of tears and I tried to ease her pain by holding her in my arms. My eyes wept bitterly, I felt great sorrow for Valerius Aquilius's death.

He was buried in Calerus's small church, who officiated the funeral himself. The whole city went to the burial and the bells, which rang out for two weeks, reminded us that the protector of Carthago Nova had left us.

I comforted my beloved Valeria during several days, until she could finally overcome the death of such a loved one. The laughter of little Annia, who was now four years old and the antics of Salvio Alexandros who was six, helped her get over it and the smile re-emerged on her beautiful lips.

Carthago Nova's *civitatis comes* had passed away, and the dramatic situation of the city, harassed by the barbarians and forgotten by the Empire, pressed for the appointment of a new imperial agent. No message came from Rome and we were getting information about the new Augustus, assuming that one had already been proclaimed. It should be the curials who decided in assembly who would hold such a position and send a missive to the emperor to ratify his appointment. In the meantime, it would be the magistrate Flavius Protus who would deal with the most urgent and priority issues concerning the administration of the city.

The curials gathered for this purpose in the *ordo decuriorum* or curia. The Senate of Carthago Nova was a building of large stone ashlars and very few ornaments. Its interior consisted of a large room surrounded by seats where the decurions or curials sat. As I was subsequently informed, they discussed during long days who would be the best candidate to rule the city. Each curial considered that he was the most appropriate person and since the *ordo decuriorum* was made up of a hundred curials, it was not surprising that the deliberations lengthened worryingly over time. In the meantime, I was in charge of training young *bucelarii*, reinforcing the city's defenses, and protecting crops and livestock from the few bandits who proliferated in the area like mushrooms after the rains.

Oblivious and indifferent to the angered discussions that were settled in the *ordo decuriorum*, I walked through the walkaway inspecting the reconstruction of the wall with Arcadius, when a *bucelarii* approached and almost without breath said.

"*Domine*, the curials have made a decision, the magistrate Flavius Protus is waiting for you in the *castrum*."

Arcadius looked at me surprised and asked:

"Why would he want to inform you personally?"

"I don't know, but we'll know soon who the chosen one is."

Flavius Protus was a respected personality in the society of Carthago Nova. Of illustrious birth and ancient ancestry, he had held the position of *civitatis Defensor*, legal defender of the city, and censor. At present, and after having been elected for five consecutive years by the *ordo decuriorum*, he held the rank of magistrate. We entered the *castrum* and found the *clarissimus* seated on a footstool. He was a man of an advanced age, with clear temples and intelligent, crystalline eyes. He wore the *toga praetexta* and the *calcei senatorii* distinctive of his noble status. As soon as he noticed our presence, he stood up.

"I greet you, Salvio Adriano," he said with an affable smile.

"I greet you, clarissimus Flavius Protus."

Arcadius nodded and left discreetly.

"Let's get out of the castrum and take a walk, this day is too beautiful to stay cooped up in here," I suggested.

Flavius Protus agreed with a smile and we went outside. We walked in silence for a few minutes. People who crossed our path greeted us with kindness, even a woman carrying a basket of apples offered us one. The people were happy and confident, several months had elapsed since the last appearance of the barbarians, and the dream of a world without war and death didn't seem so far away.

"I've been informed that you have already chosen a new *civitatis comes*," I said, breaking the silence.

"As long as the new emperor doesn't have another candidate in mind," replied the magistrate. "Remember that it's a position appointed directly by him."

"But, as far as I know, Rome still lacks an Augustus, and whoever holds the purple in the future will have more pressing problems to deal with than appointing the imperial representative of a city in Hispania," I replied, not hiding my dismay at the indifference with which Rome treated the provinces beyond the Alps. "I suppose that your election will be respected and ratified by the new Augustus."

The magistrate nodded regretfully persuaded of the certainty of my words and pointed to a stone bench beside a fountain. We took a seat. Flavius Protus silence was beginning to disturb me.

"It has been many days of discussions and negotiations," he began in a deep and determined voice. "Many of us curials have worked hard to bring common sense into a sea of nonsense and foolishness, and finally, I believe the right decision has been made."

"I'm glad," I said indifferently.

The magistrate looked at me in confusion.

"Don't you care who will be appointed as the new imperial representative in the city?"

"Honestly, it's the barbarians who really worry me. I trust the Senate and I'm convinced that they'll have made the most appropriate decision. The chosen one will be the right person."

"You have so much confidence in the Senate; it's evident that you haven't participated in the negotiations."

"What do you mean? Are you saying that the Senate should not be trusted?"

"Don't misunderstand me, but the Senate is made up of a hundred decurions, each one of them with very different purposes and ambitions."

"I don't understand that, the civitatis comes should only have one goal: the prosperity of Carthago Nova."

Flavius Protus looked at me as if I were a child who had just said something foolish.

"Politics is more complicated than it seems. Naturally all decurions seek the prosperity of the city, but what differentiates us are the proposals we suggest to achieve it," he explained to me, as if he were teaching a child.

"I know that," I said without hiding my irritation. "That's why I'm a *miles*. I only have one goal, which is to protect Carthago Nova from all its enemies, whether internal or external."

"Thank God you only have to worry about our external enemies; I'll take care of the internal ones!" he exclaimed, bursting into thunderous laughter.

I joined the magistrate in laughter.

"It hasn't been easy, many curials had solid arguments to be appointed as civitatis comes and because of this, the process has taken so long," he continued, returning to the topic of the election. "But some of us think that in these troubled times, our comes must have leadership qualities and be respected by the army. He must be a civilian and military leader."

The magistrate looked me straight in the eyes, I was beginning to sense what he was trying to tell me, but I didn't want to rush and waited for him to finish his speech.

"We curials lack military experience, we are nobles, bureaucrats, mere civil servants, not very skilled with the sword...."

"What are you trying to tell me?" I asked, looking him in the eyes.

Flavius Protus rubbed his chin, holding his gaze at me. After a few moments he smiled.

"I think you're the right person to hold that position, and that's how I passed it on to the Senate."

"But... I babbled, but Flavius Protus silenced me with a gesture."

"And, after lengthy deliberations, this is how it has been decided: friend Adriano, you are the new *civitatis comes* of Carthago Nova, pending your ratification by the emperor, of course."

I couldn't give credit to his words. I was confused, nervous, overcome by circumstance. It was true that during Valerius Aquilius's illness I had led the defense of the city and that since then, as praepositus, two thousand milites were under my command, but it would be very different to rule the most important city in southern Hispania. I knew nothing about politics and I didn't know how to handle myself in those environments where excessive greed, betrayals and revenge ran with impunity like mice for an abandoned barn. I just had to remember how the last emperors had lost their lives.

"I don't think I'm prepared to occupy such a position," I refused, denying with my head. "Please pass it on to the curia."

"I knew that might be your answer, and that's why I wanted to inform you of your appointment personally and privately. You're the right person, the people love you, the soldiers respect you, and the decurions and nobles of the city value you. You're the best candidate, don't doubt that, and you'll always have my support and advice whenever you request it," he said, touching my shoulder.

"I'm but a mere legionary. I don't come from noble birth, nor do I possess the brilliant rhetoric of the curials. Leave me with my soldiers, let me patrol our lands, rebuild our walls, instruct the young tires. Give me a sword and I'll faithfully serve Rome and Hispania, Carthago Nova. Allow me to continue wearing the military robe and the coat of mail,"

I pleaded. "A *toga praetexta* is useless to drive barbarians out of our limes. I'm not worthy to rule this city, only to defend it." I looked into his eyes with serenity, and with firm determination, I added. "My voice must be heard in the *castrum*, not in the curia. Speeches and politics are the weapons used by curials, and spatha and spears are the equipment that soldiers brandish. And I'm a soldier not a senator."

A shrewd smile appeared on Flavius Protus' lips. I feared I had fallen into his trap.

"That's precisely what Carthago Nova needs for its survival: a general, not a politician," he replied. "You defended the city from the barbarian onslaught and got them to leave without offering them any kind of perk in return. Well, you may lack the eloquence of a decurion, but your persuasion capacity is unquestionable. Moreover, you are highly respected by the troops, and not without reason the population has set you up as their savior. Wear your military tunic and coat of mail, and arm yourself with your spatha if you wish. My intention is not for you to change your attire," he continued ironically with a laugh. "Terrible battles are fought in the Senate, and although they don't leave the fields barren and strewn with corpses, they're no less bloody. I'll teach you how to handle yourself in that hostile environment. I'm sure that, accustomed as you are to draw your sword skillfully, you won't be less skilled when it comes to unleashing your tongue with arguments no less sharp and forceful." He showed me again a confident smile. "Forget about political intrigues," he insisted with a smile, grabbing me by the shoulder. "Just worry about administering justice and protecting us from foreign attacks; I'll take care of the petty people who wear toga praetexta," he threw the last words into the air, loaded with bitterness.

I took a deep breath and smiled at his solid arguments. Well, if being named *civitatis comes* didn't prevent me from being at the head of my troops, and if I also had the invaluable support of the veteran senator, nothing prevented a ducenarii named praepositus of the army of Carthago Nova by a convalescent Valerius Aquilius, from accepting such a high privilege. My heart beat uneasily in my chest, doubting if I would be worthy of the enormous tasks that the Senate and the people of Carthago Nova would demand of me. Suddenly, the image of Valerius Aquilius came to my mind and, a new fear, welled up in my mind. Would the old civitatis comes agree with my appointment? Yes, I suppose so, I concluded. He appointed me head of the army when he was in his house healing from wounds suffered during the barbarian siege. He trusted me, making me responsible for the defense of the city against enemy harassment. And we repulsed them, as God lives that we managed to make the Vandals leave. I'll never be grateful enough to Valeria's father.

"Well?" asked the magistrate, pulling me out of my reverie.

I read in his eyes that he wouldn't accept a negative answer.

"I hope I can count on your help," I accepted with resignation.

"You only have to ask for it."

The ratification by the new emperor was pending, but one clear morning in late spring, in the *ordo decuriorum* and surrounded by a hundred curials, I was named *civitatis comes* of Carthago Nova. I couldn't but feel extremely proud. Valeria wept with joy, Arcadius, whom I soon promoted to head of my guard, was overjoyed, and Cassius Belenus and Calerus congratulated me heartily. Soon the news spread throughout the city and at the door of the *domus* neighbors, friends and onlookers crowded around, handing out gifts, hugs and congratulations. For days we did nothing but receive in our house curials, merchants, officials and representatives of the people. The life of a civitatis comes was more tiring than I thought, and many days I ended up lying in bed exhausted after a hard-working day. Thank God, Flavius Protus, along with some trusted senators, helped me in my arduous task. I delegated much of my military responsibility to Arcadius, who worked with total diligence and professionalism, as could not be otherwise. Weeks went by until one fine day, a fleet from Rome brought with it the long-awaited message.

Several Roman warships arrived at our port. They were commanded by an old acquaintance, the *praefectus classis Ravennatium* Methylius Seronatus, the traitor who had abandoned the fleet to its fate six years ago, in front of the coasts of Carthago Nova, leaving it at the mercy of the Vandals. I was surprised that he was still alive, since I thought he had been executed for committing treason. But the fleet-commander was clever as a weasel and slippery as an eel and managed to get away unscathed from the betrayal claiming that the fleet had been attacked in surprise, and given the Vandals' huge numerical superiority, considered putting the admiralty ship to safety rather than sacrificing it in a hopeless battle The Senate of Rome believed his fallacious speech and, surprisingly, reinstated him in his previous responsibilities as commander of the Ravenna fleet.

I received him dressed in my military uniform, I hadn't yet been appointed civitatis comes by the new Augustus and it wasn't the time to flaunt a position that didn't belong to me. The Senate of Carthago Nova was the place chosen for the reception, I wanted to show the traitor that I had the support of the Senate and, therefore, of the people. Methylius Seronatus arrived escorted by a *magister navis*, another traitor like him, and several personal guards. He was wearing his full-dress uniform and entered the Senate with his characteristic smugness and arrogance. As soon as he entered, he fell upon me and was surprised to see me seated, wearing my legionary uniform, in the seat that corresponded by right to the civitatis comes.

"I greet you, *clarissimi*," he said as soon as he entered, looking at all the decurions without knowing exactly whom to address. "I'm the bearer of an important message for the senators of Carthago Nova."

"Well, as you can see, this is the right place," I told him without hiding the irritation that his presence alone caused me. "You already know me, I'm Salvio Adriano, *civitatis comes* elected by the Senate, waiting to be ratified by the future emperor," I added.

"Well, you've come a long way since the last time we met," he said mockingly. "I suppose the Augustus will have no objection to ratify what the Senate has so decided."

"What news do you bring us?" I asked him directly, wishing to lose sight of him.

"Congratulations Hispano-Romans!" he exclaimed with theatrical pomposity. "Rome has a new emperor!"

A murmur began to go through the seats. The traitor was silent for a moment, increasing the impatience of the decurions.

"After long negotiations between Ricimero and Leo, emperor of the East, it was resolved that Anthemius, general of the armies of the East, should be invested with the purple."

Few were those who knew him, and murmurs broke out. The curials looked at each other, shrugged their shoulders or asked those who claimed to know something about him.

"Our Augustus," continued Methylius Seronatus, "has arrived in Italy with a powerful army commanded by Marcellinus, *magister militum per Illyricum*." We knew Marcellinus, since he served under Aetius and Majorian command, but after the latter's death he went to

Constantinople and put his sword at the service of the emperor of the East. "A new era is rising over Rome! Our enemies will bite the dust and be slaughtered, I'm proof of that!"

"What do you mean?" asked a decurion.

"The Eastern and Western empires have united in the defense of Rome and are preparing to arm a formidable fleet to attack the Vandals in their own lands." he replied, as he paced excitedly through the senate. We'll raze their cities in Africa and then it will be the turn of the Visigoths, Burgundians, Ostrogoths and the rest of the barbarian peoples who question our power....

"How did you do six years ago, when you abandoned our fleet to its fate and allowed it to be destroyed by the Vandals?" I asked angrily, getting up from my seat.

He gave me a murderous look and I noticed one of his guards reaching for his hilt. Red with anger, he approached me.

"The Senate of Rome didn't find a hint of treason in my heroic behavior, but on the contrary, congratulated me for saving the admiralty ship," he said, pointing his finger at me. "I'm the *praefectus classis Ravennatium*, I've have always served Rome faithfully, and I won't tolerate anyone questioning my loyalty to the Empire," he added, spitting out of his mouth.

"Your flight caused the execution of Majorian," I growled, getting down from my seat and approaching him. "as well as the destruction of our navy and the death of hundreds of citizens of Carthago Nova during the siege of the Vandals. I warn you, Methylius Seronatus, give rise to the slightest suspicion of treason, and it won't be the Senate of Rome that will ask you for explanations, but my sword," I added, clutching the hilt tightly.

The traitor reached for his spatha, but I saw in his eyes that he lacked the courage to unsheathe it. Frustrated and ashamed by the affront, he left the Senate escorted by his guard and the *magister navis*. Flavius Protus approached me and shook my hand.

"I knew I wasn't wrong when I choose you," he said to me with a smile.

The rest of the curials approached me, congratulating me for having put the traitor where he belonged. The fleet-commander departed the next day filled with hatred and a burning desire for revenge. He wouldn't easily forget the scorn he had suffered in the *ordo decuriorum* of Carthago Nova, but neither would I forget his perverse felony. I only longed to meet him again, and to be able to settle our differences with our swords. And the capricious fate saw fit to make it happen; a few weeks after his departure, the *magister militum* Marcellinus, commanding more than three hundred Roman ships, landed on our shores. Methylius Seronatus as *praefectus classis Ravennatium* accompanied him.

As Majorian had intended six years before, the aim of the powerful fleet was to attack the Vandals where they could suffer the severest damage: in their capital Carthago. The city received such a contingent of troops with rejoicing, since it was a huge source of revenue. Some ships required minor repairs, the warehouses had to be filled with food, water and wine, the legionaries would have to eat and spend their wages in the taverns, and many swords had to be sharpened by master blacksmiths. The dock was a hive of wagons loading goods and provisions, the longshoremen worked from sunup to sundown but returned home with a bag full of silver siliquas. Perhaps the traitor was right, and a new and promising dawn would illuminate the eternal Empire.

I received such illustrious personages in my *domus*, the information they possessed was somewhat reserved and the less people knew about it the better. It was a night in June and I had ordered dinner to be served in the *atrium*, taking advantage of the coolness of the night. Only the *magister militum* Marcellinus and the fleet-commander Methylius Seronatus would be present. They arrived punctually to the appointment wearing their best clothes. Marcellinus was a middle-aged man with white but abundant temples, dark eyes and a clean and crystalline gaze. We introduced ourselves and took our seats. The servants filled our glasses with watered wine and brought trays of lamb, cheese, roast pigeon and salt fish.

"I bring the document signed by the emperor ratifying you as *civitatis comes* of the city of Carthago Nova," said Marcelino, handing me a rolled-up bundle.

I knew the news since they arrived two days ago, but it was necessary to make it official. I unrolled the document and read it with pleasure. Then I turned a victorious and satisfied glance at Methylius

Seronatus who was trying to conceal his discomfort. You could smell the hatred we felt for each other.

"Thank you Marcellinus, it's a great honor that the Augustus considers me the right person to hold such an important office," I said, nodding my head gently.

The *magister militum* drank some wine and looking sideways at the traitor said:

"I've been told about you. I know that you served under Aetius orders in Maurica and fought against the Suevians and the Vandals. I've also been informed that you are doing a great job in Carthago Nova reinforcing its defenses and reconstructing the buildings..."

"He's been in this position a short time" the fleet- commander intervened. "The merit must be granted to Valerius Aquilius, the previous *comes...* and his father-in-law," he added with acrimony, without hiding his contempt.

Marcellinus looked at both of us and in our gazes he read the bitter bitterness we felt towards each other.

"It is time to be united," he said seriously. "For the good of Rome, you must forget your quarrels."

We looked down at the table, but without saying a word. It would take much more than the good intentions of the magister militum for the traitor and me to discard our resentments.

"What's the plan?" I asked, sipping some wine.

"We have expelled the Vandals from Sardinia and Sicily. Basiliscus, the general of the East, will go with more than seven hundred ships from the east to Carthago. He'll wait for us in Cape Mercury, a few miles from the Vandal capital. Once we join our forces, we'll disembark and attack the city by land. Without a safe harbor to shelter their ships, the barbarians will wander lost and will eventually be exterminated," replied Marcellinus.

"We're talking about more than a thousand ships and about thirty thousand milites," the praefectus intervened. "The expedition can't fail."

I was about to add that I wouldn't fail unless the wicked hand of a traitor intervened, but I held back.

"I've been told that you courageously defended the city from the Vandal siege and that you know their tactics very well," Marcellinus said, sitting up at the table. "We need people like you in this campaign. With the Vandals defeated, Carthago Nova will be out of danger."

"What do you need?" I asked.

"Just good soldiers, braves and experienced. We don't need many, if you come with several men you trust; it will be more than enough."

"You can count on me and my *milites*, but I'd like to ask you for two perks that I think you'll have no problem in satisfying," I said with a half-smile. "They are insignificant, just a few minor details."

Marcellinus narrowed his eyes suspiciously, but made a gesture for me to continue.

"I'll board the admiral ship of Methylius Seronatus."

My first request was completely humiliating, as it meant that I didn't trust the commander of the Ravenna fleet and that I intended to remain close to him to keep an eye on him. The traitor clenched his fists and turned red with anger. The magister militum nodded.

"I'll only obey your orders and at the slightest suspicion of the existence of a traitor in the fleet," I continued, looking into his eyes, "I'll order him to be captured and thrown into the sea."

"This is too much!" shouted Methylius Seronatus angrily, rising to his feet and banging furiously on the table. Several plates and glasses crashed to the floor.

"Shut up, Methylius," Marcellinus ordered. "And sit down!"

Methylius had foam pouring from his mouth, and he was breathing fast with bloodshot eyes, like a raging animal. He shot me a defiant look that reflected the sick hatred that gnawed at his gut. He took a deep breath and then, between spasms of rage, sat back down.

"I'm the *praefectus classis Ravennatium*, your admiral. At sea I'm the one who gives orders and I demand to be obeyed. On land you can do whatever you want, but on my ships I'm the one in charge," he mumbled between gasps, looking at me with contempt.

"Do I need to remind you that Emperor Anthemius has appointed me commander-in-chief of the West-troops?" Marcellinus asked him, keeping his calm. "That means whether we're sailing on the waters or marching on dry land, I'm the main responsible for the armies."

Methylius Seronatus clenched his jaws and nodded without taking his eyes off the table. On his forehead, a vein swollen with rage throbbed alarmingly, threatening to explode.

"Your terms are quiet reasonable, get ready since we are leaving in three days," agreed the *magister militum*.

CHAPTER XVI

The navy lands in Africa.

Quo plures eramus, maior caedes fuit.[20]

I said goodbye afflicted to Valeria and the children from whom, up to that moment, I hadn't separated for a single moment, and embarked on the admiral ship along with Arcadius, Cassius Belenus and several dozen of my best men. The admiral ship was a powerful *dromon* with three triangular sails and two rows of rowers. It was equipped with a ballista and two little catapults. It was a formidable ship. I still remember the look Methylius Seronatus gave me when I crossed the runway. Arcadius warned me to be careful with him and not to separate from my *spatha* for a second. My brave friend was right. Unaccustomed to sailing, it didn't take long for me to suffer from sea swings and the fish began to feed on the food I threw up as soon as I ingested it. Pale as I was, I used to sit on the ship-bow in the hope that the freshness of the wind cleared me and help me get used to the tireless swell. The fleet-commander watched me rejoiced, wishing that in one of those dizziness he would find my bones in the depths of the sea. Luckily, his wishes were truncated and in a few days I had become accustomed to the persistent swell and even began to enjoy the journey.

Without further setbacks, we arrive in Cape Mercury and join General Basiliscus' fleet, who was the commander of the navy by order of Leon the Eastern Emperor. It was a colossal spectacle. The coast didn't have enough space to moor such a large number of ships, and we had to build floating walkways by joining with thick ropes one boat with another. The endless beach was dotted with tens of thousands of shops, fires, stables and even corrals, where we kept the live animals that would

---

[20] *The more numerous we were, the greater the mortality (phrase extracted and adapted adapted from the Latin Grammar book by Santiago Segura Munguía).*

341

feed us. As the traitor said, more than a thousand ships and approximately thirty thousand legionaries were preparing to exterminate, once and for all, the fearsome Vandals.

The sea was calm and a clear blue sky announced a beautiful day in late June. The milites sharpened their weapons, the hostlers brushed the horses and the cooks prepared the food. Every legionary knew exactly what his task was. After mooring our ships, ordering the landing of troops, equipment and tools, setting up tents and organizing legionaries on the ground, Marcellinus, Methylius Seronatus and I went to Basiliscus's tent, who awaited us impatiently. On the milites' faces, I noticed the optimism of those who feel safe of victory.

The legionaries stood firm as we passed, and Marcellinus responded by haranguing them, slapping them on the back, or greeting them with a confident smile.

We reached General Basiliscus' tent. The imperial guard who watched the entrance informed him of our arrival and shortly after, a huge officer escorted us into his presence. Basiliscus was reclining on a triclinium eating some pieces of meat from a nearby tray. He was a bit fat; his ring-filled fingers were.

as fat as ropes, his skin was very pale, and his hair was scarce and with a certain coppery hue. He wore an entirely white *toga virilis* and leather sandals. More than a general, he looked like an indolent senator. His image made me uneasy; I doubted that this man was sufficiently qualified to lead such a powerful army.

"Please sit down," he gestured, and we sat down on comfortable cushions. "Pour wine for my guests," he commanded with a fluty voice to one of his servants, a young ephebe whom he didn't stop seeing.

"I greet you, Basiliscus general of the Eastern Empire. Allow me to introduce Salvio Adriano; *civitatis comes* of Carthago Nova and veteran legionary in the wars against the Vandals. His experience will be very useful to us in this campaign. You already know Methylius Seronatus," Marcellinus said.

Basiliscus greeted us disdainfully almost without looking at us and drank a generous gulp of wine. I noticed that the tent was adorned with beautiful silks and expensive cedar furniture. The cups were made of silver set with precious stones. In spite of being in the middle of a campaign, the general avoided depriving himself of any kind of luxury.

"I was looking forward to seeing you," said Basiliscus, with his unpleasant voice. "I thought you were no longer coming to the appointment."

"We have had more hardships than expected in Sicily and Sardinia, but finally the Vandals have been defeated. Now they only have Carthago left as their last bastion in the Mediterranean," Marcellinus explained.

I was surprised that Marcellinus, a military veteran and winner of a hundred battles, had to excuse his delay after conquering two islands, when Basiliscus had arrived in Cape Mercury directly from Constantinople. I shouldn't underestimate him; there was no doubt that he was a man of immense power.

"Well, the important thing is that you are already here," Basiliscus agreed with a condescending air.

"Genseric will be aware of our presence; we must act immediately and leave for Carthago tomorrow if it were…"

"That's impossible," Basiliscus interrupted.

"Why?" Marcellinus asked in confusion.

"I have sent a message to Genseric and I'm waiting for his reply."

Marcellinus gazed at him with wild eyes. I looked at Methylius Seronatus, who was watching the generals sullenly without showing any emotion, as if he already knew the news.

"Did you send him a message?" he asked, rising from the cushion in bewilderment.

"I have demanded that he surrender the city and give us all its treasures. In return, I'll allow him to flee to southern Africa with his hosts. In those remote and distant lands, he won't cause us any trouble," Basiliscus replied in his fluty voice, indifferent to the anger of the magister militum.

Marcellinus began to wander around the tent trying to organize his thoughts.

"Genseric won't surrender, he'll use this valuable time to rebuild his ships and attack us. With the fleet destroyed, we won't be able to return to the mainland for at least six months," he said anxiously.

"Attack more than a thousand ships?" Basiliscus asked sarcastically. "He's not that crazy. He is barbarian but not stupid."

At that time, an officer of the Imperial Guard entered the shop, bringing with him the answer of the Vandal king.

"Wow, what a nice coincidence!" Basiliscus exclaimed, unfolding the scroll.

"We all look forward to it," I noticed that Methylius Seronatus was overly calm. He drank small sips from his glass and then played distractedly with it. Marcellinus stopped and didn't look away from the plump general.

"Genseric is requesting me for five days to discuss our proposal carefully with the nobles of the city," Basiliscus finally said.

"Can you see?" Marcellinus asked beside himself. "He wants to buy time! The wind blows from the east, it's certain that he is waiting for a change in its direction to attack us," he added vehemently, "Carthago is no more than two days from here, let's leave tomorrow at dawn."

"No," exclaimed Basiliscus, without giving rise to any answer. "I'll grant him the five days. The Eastern-Empire has financed this campaign with six thousand gold modius, we have recruited more than twice as many troops and ships as the Western-Empire, and in addition, Anthemius and Leo have agreed to be their commander. Whatever I decide will be done and if you don't agree with my orders, get on your ships and get the hell out of here.

Marcellinus was furious. His nose swelled when he breathed just as the lips of a sorrel widen after an exhausting effort. For a few moments he stood still, obfuscated, bewildered. But after pondering it, he came to the obvious conclusion that Basiliscus was right. The Greek was the Chief General of that immense army and the magister militum was his subordinate and owed him obedience. Marcellinus snorted angrily but eventually gave up and took a seat again on the fluffy cushions. Basiliscus looked at him with satisfaction and drank a sip of wine.

"What's the plan?" Marcellinus asked, without hiding his anger.

"We must wait," replied the effeminate general. "Simply to wait for the Vandal's response. It's that simple. If he accept my proposal he'll leave Carthago and march south, straying into some scorching African desert and disappearing forever. One less problem that Rome should worry about. And if he doesn't accept it, he'll be exterminated by our army. Whatever his decision, his end is near. You can go," he added, turning around in the *triclinium* and turning his back on us. He gestured to the youth, who approached his master to satisfy God only knew what lustful desires.

Basiliscus finished the meeting and we left the tent. Marcellinus was furious. We walked hastily with the intention of getting away from the tent as soon as possible. The image of the plump and depraved general caused me great disgust and restlessness. Any army however large or powerful, in the hands of an inept commander, was destined to the most shocking of failures.

"Methylius, I want our three hundred ships ready for combat," Marcellinus ordered, without stopping his quick pace.

"Do you think Genseric will attack us?" he asked incredulously. "It would be a suicide."

"Suicide is to stay here waiting for his answer. Obey and anchor part of the fleet with the bow facing southeast. In case they attack us from the northwest, we'll have time to escape, avoiding the attacks of their stems."

"Then we'll be in a counterattack situation. If we remain with the ships tied to each other, they'll tear us apart."

"In these seas, the wind always blows from the east during summer," he pointed out with a half-smile, as if the *magister militum* had said something foolish. "In addition, the ships are already moored and the crew has disembarked."

Marcellinus stopped his pace and fulminating him with his gaze mumbled:

"Do what I say and never question my orders again."

The commander swallowed saliva and nodded.

"At your command, domine. I'll take care of it personally," he accepted, heading to the ships.

We watched how he got lost in the legionaries' tents. Marcellinus had his lips contracted.

"I don't trust him." His sincerity surprised me. "I know that six years ago he left the fleet to its fate causing its destruction. And most disgusting of all, the corrupt Senate of Rome believed his lies. That's why I left the Western-Empire and went to the East. I was disgusted with the vileness, greed and nepotism that poisoned the foundations of Rome. I refused to serve a new emperor named by Ricimero. But unfortunately, the Easter-Empire doesn't differ excessively from its brother from the West. Watch him and keep me informed," he ordered me.

The sun was breaking over the horizon and I headed to the coast to see if Methylius Seronatus had obeyed the *magister militum's* order. Confused, I observed that the boats were still tied to each other as they had been the day before. Enraged, I crossed the walkway of the admiral ship.

"What do you want?" the *magister navis* snapped at me, getting in my way.

I looked at him with contempt and disgust. He was a man with a sinister look, rotten teeth, and greasy straight hair. The stench he emanated could be smelled miles away.

"I want to talk with Methylius Seronatus. Get away or you'll start the day bathing in the sea, which from what I can see, would suit you very well," I replied.

"You can't get on this ship, neither you nor any of your men," he replied, shooting me a challenging look.

"Who gave that order?"

"General Basiliscus," a voice behind me answered.

With a triumphant gesture, the *praefectus classis* passed by my side and got into the ship. The two men smiled haughtily.

"Has he ordered anything else that Marcellinus or I should know about?" I asked him with my lips pursed.

He began to walk smugly on the ship's walkway, the magister navis followed him like a faithful dog. He waved his hand at me and I got on the boat.

"Yesterday, Marcellinus ordered me to do something really stupid. Anchoring three hundred ships with the sails oriented to the northwest awaiting an attack that won't occur in any way, demonstrates the little naval knowledge that our *magister militum* possesses. Late at night, I decided to meet the Greek General. Basiliscus is a reasonable man and naturally, he suggested that I not obey Marcellinus's order and leave the ships as they were, since it is impossible for Vandals to attack us."

"And you also advised him that only your men could get on the ships, didn't you?" I asked him.

"Your legionaries can get on the ship," He replied with a gesture. "But I have to authorize it first," he added, looking into my eyes.

"You're still the same traitorous bastard who abandoned us in Carthago Nova," I snapped, reaching for my hilt.

"Easy, Adriano," said a voice behind me. "I come from Basiliscus' tent and I have already been duly informed."

I turned around and notice that it was Marcellinus. His brow was furrowed and his fists were clenched so that his knuckles looked white. He sneered at Methylius Seronatus and his captain. He took me by the shoulder and we descended the gangplank. I glanced back and noticed that the fleet commander and the *magister navis* were laughing loudly pointing an insulting finger at us.

"I don't understand why Basiliscus has questioned your order," I sputtered red with anger, tempted to turn around and skewer those two bastards with my spatha.

"This is the most important military campaign that Rome has embarked on in centuries. Basiliscus is an extremely ambitious man and he won't ignore any opportunity that could help him get the support of the Greek Senate in order to get, at the right moment, the East imperial insignia. If he succeeds in getting Genseric to accept the deal and hand over Carthago, the general will return to Constantinople full of glory and riches without having lost a single ship. On the other hand, if there is a battle, the victory will grant him the sympathy of both Senates the Greek and the Roman, who will recognize him as the savior of the Western Empire, but his triumph will have to be shared with the rest of the officers. And Basiliscus wants us far away, acting in the background where we cannot steal prominence from him. Neither Rome nor Constantinople should have any doubt as to whom to thank for this victory."

"And what does Methylius Seronatus obtains with all this?"

"Who knows, perhaps the *praefectus classis* sold himself out to the Greeks in exchange for gold, land, or being appointed commander of the Eastern fleet, I don't know."

"But the truth is that our ships are in danger."

"Just as they're moored and if there is a change in the wind's direction, with only two hundred ships, the Vandals would devastate our fleet. Basiliscus and Methylius Seronatus are belittling Genseric and putting the campaign in serious jeopardy. They are fools."

"Dangerous fools," I added, with the assent of the *magister milites*.

We would remain garrisoned in Africa for five days awaiting the message from the Vandal king, and Marcellinus ordered a campaign *castrum* to be erected. We had to be prepared to avoid any kind of surprise. The milites cut down trees, cleared the ground and dug a deep moat around the entire perimeter. They piled up all the earth to make an embankment and stakes, javelins and spears were stuck in as a palisade.

Methylius Seronatus, together with some of his captains, officers and trusted sailors, watched our work placidly from the admiral ship, seated comfortably on a footstool, while a servant gave him food and drinks, and another one relieved him from the unbearable heat by moving a large fan of ostrich feathers. The behavior of the army-commander and the sailors didn't go unnoticed by the rest of the troop, who looked on with resentment while they dug the earth and built the palisades.

"The sailors should be more prudent," Arcadius told me, wiping the sweat that ran down his forehead after carrying a heavy log. "We must all work as one or the success of the campaign will be seriously jeopardized."

"I agree with you, but there's nothing we can do about it. Basiliscus, in gratitude for having brought us this far without the slightest mishap, has granted them rest by burdening us pedes with all the work," I said, also wiping my sweat, since I had accompanied him in such a strenuous task.

We took axes and chopped down the huge log. The wood would be used to heat the meals or light the castrum at night.

"I'm seeing too many strange things in this campaign and that worries me," said Arcadius, shaking his head.

"What do you mean?"

"We aren't a united army: Basiliscus and Marcellinus hate each other, the sailors and the legionaries are suspicious of each other..." he answered, shaking his head. "During the battle I don't know whether to worry more about the barbarian in front of me or the legionary behind me."

"Be patient, we only have four days before Genseric sends us his answer. In the meantime, keep your morale and confidence strong. Keep in mind that both, sailors and legionaries from the East and West are seeking the same goal: to eliminate the Vandals. This is what is really important. When we engage in battle, the quarrels will be forgotten."

Arcadius nodded without much conviction, and not without reason. While we legionaries, Marcellinus included, left our skin to build a real fortress, Basiliscus remained under the protective shade of his tent, still being fanned by his favorite ephebe, while Methylius

Seronatus and his sailors enjoyed drinking wine and playing dice, comfortably seated on the deck of their ships.

Four days had elapsed since we arrived in Cape Mercury and we still hadn't received Genseric's answer. Basiliscus, according to what Marcellinus informed me, was secure and confident. The Greek general was convinced that the Vandal would surrender the city and head to remote lands in southern Africa. But I doubted it and so did Marcellinus. Unfortunately, our fears were confirmed shortly before dawn on the fifth day of the campaign.

The sentries gave the alarm. I dressed in my uniform as soon as I could and hurried out of my tent. The legionaries were forming up hurriedly on the beach, in their respective numeri. In front, the centenarii, with shouting voices, didn't stop giving orders and whipping anyone who arrived late to the formation. The *castrum* was immersed in dreadful confusion.

"What is going on?" asked Arcadius, running towards me, accompanied by Cassius Belenus.

"Where are the rest of my men?" I asked.

Arcadius turned his head and I noticed that the hundred men he commanded were running towards us.

"Cassius Belenus make the men fall in and inspect them; they must be perfectly equipped for battle. Arcadius come with me to the beach, let's go see what the hell's going on."

Dawn hadn't yet come, but an incipient orange sky was appearing on horizon announcing its proximity. Something caught my attention, and I stopped at the watchful gaze of Arcadius, who looked at me confused. I looked up at the sky and watched the clouds, then looked up at the flags and banners waving in the northwest wind.

"Damn it!" I exclaimed. "The wind's direction has changed!"

We restarted the race to the beach, where hundreds of officers were already piling up along with Marcellinus and Basiliscus.

"What's going on? "I asked a *ducenarius*, though I was already afraid of the answer.

"The Vandals, *domine*. They are attacking us," he replied, pointing to a fleet of ships heading towards us boosted by the northwest wind.

"Officers of Rome, Genseric's army is heading towards our ships, line up your numeri and prepare for battle!" Marcellinus exclaimed addressing the legionaries and looking at the magistri navis he continued: "*Magistri navis*, the enemy ships have the wind at their backs!"

he glared at Basiliscus and added: "Get out to sea and escape to the southeast, regroup protected from their spurs and counterattack!"

The officers and the *magistri navis* beat their chests with their fists and ran ready to carry out the orders of our general.

"I'll embark on my admiral ship and command the Eastern- fleet." Basiliscus stammered in terror.

"Stupid!" the *magister militum* blurted him out. "The fleet is immobilized and at the mercy of the Vandals!"

Basiliscus stumbled and fell to the ground, but managed to free himself from the *magister militum's* grasp and fled to his *dromon*. Marcellinus watched in wrathful how the plump Greek ran terrified towards his ship escorted by his personal guard. Over a thousand ships and thirty thousand soldiers, the most formidable military campaign in centuries, was now in serious danger because of his negligence and foolish pride. I'd gladly have skewered him with his own sword, but now Marcellinus had other, more pressing problems to worry about.

"Assault Methylius's ship; chain him or rather kill him in the case he resists. Go against the Vandals, and attack them, make them chase you, distract them until we can free all the ships that are moored," the *magister militum* ordered me.

I gestured to Arcadius and he hurriedly ran to my men. Marcellinus, without wasting a second, gave orders to his officers and directed the embarkation of hundreds of soldiers onto the moored ships, in the hope that they would go to sea before being attacked by the Vandal spurs.

On a diffuse horizon, still shrouded by the gloom of the languid night, the menacing outline of hundreds of Vandal ships could be made out. Their sails were swollen by the northwest wind and their terrible bronze spurs pointed insatiably towards our ships. If those sharp stingers successfully completed their task, not only hundreds of ships and thousands of men would be dragged to the depths of the black sea, but also the future of thousands of Romans who awaited with hope the favorable outcome of the battle.

I didn't wait for Arcadius or my legionaries and, with my sword drawn; I headed to the admiral ship. There, I noticed that Methylius Seronatus with a calm gesture was ordering the walkway to be removed, just when I was about to embark. Once again, like a cowardly and treacherous dog, he was about to abandon the battle.

"Stand still or you'll be eaten by the fish!" I shouted to the sailor, who had already raised the walkway.

"Throw it into the sea!" the *praefectus classis* ordered him. "That bastard is not authorized to embark!"

The sailor hesitated long enough for me to cross the walkway and board the ship.

"If you value your life at all, don't touch the walkway." The sailor, aware that I wasn't joking, turned away.

"Kill him, he wants to take control of the admiral ship!"

Several sailors came towards me with their swords drawn.

"In the name of the *magister militum* Marcellinus, I take possession of this ship and order it to attack the enemy fleet; those who don't obey me will be punished because of treason!"

Our commander-in-chief is Basiliscus, not Marcellinus. Soldiers, I order you to kill him!" Methylius Seronatus replied

The wind from the north-west intensified driving the sails of the enemy ships vigorously. I couldn't waste time in vain discussions. I looked around me and saw how some of our ships set sail propelled by the effort of the oarsmen, since the wind was against us. If I didn't take control of the admiral ship soon, all would be lost. I took the pugio hanging from my *cingulum militare* and threw it to Methylius Seronatus. The sailors followed the direction of the dagger with their eyes until it stuck in the neck of the fleet-commander, who fell to the ground amidst frightful guttural noises, drowned in his own blood.

"We are here!" exclaimed Arcadius behind me, accompanied by Cassius Belenus and a twenty of my legionnaires. "Is everything ok?" he asked between gasps, turning his gaze to Methylius Seronatus's body lying lifeless on the deck.

"Raise the walkway" I ordered.

We took the ship without further bloodshed. I threw the traitor's body into the sea and addressed the sailors, who fell in in front of me as a sign of obedience. The *magister navis* with rotten teeth and a pigsty odor was steering the ship. Unfortunately, neither I nor any of my men knew how to do it. That swine was a necessary evil. Just as Marcellinus ordered me to do, we turn to the unequal encounter with the Vandals. Our rowers made heavy efforts to give speed to the heavy *dromon*, but the wind was blowing from the northwest making our march difficult. The Vandal ships, illuminated by the reddish and fledgling aurora, were already completely visible, and their sharp spurs emerged on the waves like gigantic arrows ready to get brutally skewered against our defenseless fleet.

"They're burning their ships!" Cassius Belenus exclaimed, watching a group of boats with their bows wrapped in flames.

"No!" the *magister navis* shouted in horror. "They're fire-ships, they'll be thrown at our fleet!"

Cassius Belenus looked at him without understanding.

"The fire-ships are loaded with tar, sulfur and any combustible material. After being set on fire, they're thrown on enemy ships in order to set them on fire and destroy them," the *navis magister* explained.

"We must intercept them before they collide with the ships that are still moored!" I exclaimed.

In a deft maneuver the captain managed to position the ship downwind, and it developed a higher speed. But it was too late. Pushed by the northwestern winds, the fire-ships collided loudly at our ships burning them instantly. Since, the ships were tied to each other, it was easy for the fire to spread and the entire coast was engulfed in a fireball, a real hell on earth. The sailors threw themselves into the sea trying to escape the flames, but died when they were crushed by the hulls of the ships or drowned in the deep waters.

"We must escape!" Tullas shouted, since that was the *magister navis'* name.

At that moment, a fire-ship hit us hard, causing us to fall to the ground. The flames engulfed the ship quickly and although we tried to quell the fire, it was an impossible task. The sun rose over the horizon illuminating with its rays dozens of enemy ships whose purpose was to conclude the good work that the fire-ships had done. We heard dozens of whistles and concluded that we were surrounded by Vandal boats. From the turrets, the archers fired their certain darts at us, causing a large death toll. Then there was a loud, secluded, heartbreaking noise. The boat swayed and we rolled down the ground. I managed to get up on the sloping deck and found that our ship had been ramming by an enemy spur. The Vandals, shouting terrifyingly, approached us and, brandishing their swords, set out to conquer the admiral ship of the Western fleet.

"Let's leave the ship!" a sailor shouted before jumping into the sea.

Several followed him and suffered the onslaught of the arrows that were thrown from the barbarian ships. I looked towards the coast and watched our invincible army engulfed in flames and hidden behind a cloud of black smoke. Several ships saved from burning, but instead of heading towards the Vandals they fled east, taking advantage of the downwind. Basiliscus's admiral ship was one of them. The Greek general had lost the battle and fled abandoning the rest of the army, seeking refuge in the safe Constantinople.

Around us, legionaries and Vandals fought fiercely, and it didn't take long for the ground to turn the vermilion color of blood. A Vandal attacked me, but I was able to get away from him with ease and sliced his neck with my spatha. We defended ourselves bravely but our enemies were more numerous. The fire and the hole in the hull that was pierced by the ram of the Vandal ship, threatened to sink the ship. There weren't many options: either die on the ship, drowned at sea or assaulted by the barbarians. Then I noticed that the ship that had rammed us was unprotected. Defending myself boldly, I approached the *magister navis*. Tullas was fighting fiercely against a barbarian. I got rid of his rival by cutting him on the ribs, and the smelly captain smiled gratefully at me, showing a string of rotten teeth.

"Do you think you can get us out of here?" I asked, pointing to the enemy ship.

"Do we have another option?" the captain understood the question.

I shook my head and he shrugged.

"Legionaries of Rome!" I yelled, trying to get the attention of my soldiers in that horrible disturbance. "Follow me!"

I ran putting away every barbarian that got in my way; I climbed the spur of the enemy ship accompanied by the smelly one and several of my men. The Vandals, surprised by our audacity, were slow to react, and ran behind us, shooting flaming arrows at us. Like wild beasts they pounced on the straggling milites pouring on them their frustration for the lost ship. A Fierce carnage raged around the spur. My legionaries sacrificed their lives as heroes, so that a few of us could escape from that hell.

The *magister navis* smelled worse than a sewer, but he was a skilled navigator. With two movements of the rudder, he managed to detach himself from the admiral ship and, pushed by the downwind, we headed northeast. During our escape, we ran into a couple of enemy ships, but thanks to the skill of the captain, we left them behind. Some other ships tried to chase us, giving up a few minutes later: their captains weren't enthusiastic about the prospect of being late to distribute the large loot.

The silhouette of the enemy ships and the smoke screen of the burning ships faded, until they got lost on the horizon. Exhausted, wounded, and most of all, defeated, we flopped onto the deck.

"I can't find Cassius Belenus."

I opened my eyes and hiding a blue sky, I found the face dirty with blood and soot of Arcadius. I got up, drawing strength from where I didn't have it, and started looking for Cassius Belenus among the survivors. Few dozen legionaries and sailors had survived, and many were seriously injured. I walked around the deck and saw some young milites sobbing. There were others, with amputated arms or hands, screaming in pain while inexperienced hands cauterized their bloody stump. A couple of soldiers who had died during the flight were thrown overboard. The spectacle was bleak, covered in sweat, blood and bitter defeat, the remains of the invincible imperial army were scattered on the deck.

"I've looked everywhere for him, but he's not there," Arcadius said.

"Did you go down to the cellar? Maybe he is resting..."

"Yes, there are only a dozen wounded there," he interrupted.

We persisted for several more minutes until finally, convinced that it was useless, we gave up the search. I mourned for a long time the death of my friend Cassius Belenus, hugging Arcadius. We both felt deeply the loss of our partner, our friend... our brother. Shared tears are a valuable consolation for grieving and defeated souls. Our spirits languished in disgust with a war that seemed to have no end, and that had already claimed the lives of many friends and hundreds of thousands of Hispano-Romans. A war unleashed not by the conquest of new territories, or the subjugation of other nations. Its purpose was quite different and certainly discouraging: we were fighting for our very survival. I mourned Cassius Belenus's death as well as that of so many other legionaries who were sacrificed due to Basiliscus's negligence and incompetence, more interested in achieving glory and power than in his own soldiers. I remembered Methylius Seronatus, at least he had paid with his life for his betrayal, but Basiliscus sailed unscathed towards Constantinople, leaving behind him the most humiliating of defeats. The spoils of the imperial fleet lay sunk in the depths of Cape Mercury, and with them, the last hopes of Rome.

We reached the Sicilian coast before nightfall, and I was pleased to see that we weren't the only ones who saved our skins. Anchored near the beaches, several dozen ships appeared in front of us. I prayed to God that among the survivors was Marcellinus. The trickle was incessant and during the night several dozen more ships landed on the island. The dawn illuminated almost a hundred Roman ships, most of them from the Western Empire, since the ships from the East had fled eastward to seek refuge in the safe harbor of Constantinople. I could only distinguish half a dozen Greek *dromon*, all of them badly damaged by fire or by enemy spurs, and which had sought refuge in Sicily unable to reach the Greek coasts in that pitiable state. Many of our ships were in no better condition and some of them had to be sunk not without first seizing whatever they possessed of usefulness.

We boarded a boat and headed to the beach. Thousands of soldiers appeared scattered on the fine sand in search of rest, or seriously wounded, abandoning themselves to death. The few physicians who remained alive were busy relieving pain, cauterizing wounds or amputating limbs. The pierced cries of pain and the pitiful cries followed one after the other at the indifferent gaze of the rest of the legionaries, immune to the suffering of others.

The neighbors of the nearby town of Agrigentum turned to us and relieved some of our agony by providing us with food, water and some wine. I searched everywhere for the magister militum until a physicist informed me that he was on one of the Greek ships. Accompanied by Arcadius, I boarded a boat and headed to the ship where Marcellinus was, hoping that he was in good condition. We went up the walkaway and I asked a Greek imperial guard, who confirmed that the magister militum was on the ship. I was surprised that it was the imperial guard from the East who was guarding the ship, but at that moment my concerns were different.

"But he cannot attend to you now, he is resting." the guard pointed out, with certain nervousness.

His face blushed, while beads of sweat trickled down his forehead and he licked his lips uneasily. The soldier was hiding something.

"You belong to the Eastern troops, don't you?" I asked him and he nodded. "Why a soldier of Basiliscus's imperial guard is protecting Marcellinus?"

"His men are dead and Basiliscus…"

355

I didn't let him finish, we ran across the deck and went down the hatch to the chamber where Marcellinus was. In the cellar we passed another imperial guard who stopped in confusion at our unexpected presence.

"Where is Marcellinus?" I asked.

The soldier pushed me and tried to escape, but Arcadius, as agile as he was forceful, gave him a strong punch and the imperial fell unluckily on a step, breaking his neck.

"Arrest the other guard, I don't like this," I ordered him, fearing what was happening.

Arcadius nodded and I, spatha in hand, headed to the magister militum's chamber. The door was locked. I had to kick it several times until it gave way and I managed to enter the room. Then, my worst omens came true. On the bed, wrapped in blood, Marcellinus' body was laying. I approached him, and after verifying that he was dead, I closed his eyes.

"Why?" I asked, full of anger. "Why?"

"He escaped!" Arcadius exclaimed, entering at that moment. "Good God..." he whispered, looking at the *magister militum's* bloodied body.

"Basiliscus' imperial guards have taken his life."

"But why did Basiliscus want Marcellinus dead?"

I covered the magister militum's body and we left the ship. The imperial guard fled, getting confused with the legionaries scattered on the beach or embarking on some other ship.

We walked among the soldiers to get an idea of what we had on our hands: Save the lives of hundreds of men and dozens of ships. The news of the crushing Vandal victory would spread like wildfire and would soon reach the ears of the rest of the barbarian kings, who, aware of our weakness, would pounce on us like vermin. A terrible and black horizon loomed over Rome and it was imperative that we return to our homes as soon as possible.

"Basiliscus' negligence and vanity have caused the destruction of our fleet," I began to say, answering the question that Arcadius had asked on the Greek ship.

"I understand, and that is why he has ordered his assassination," Arcadius said, shaking his head still not understanding the infinite vileness of the powerful.

"Dead cannot defend themselves."

"But we're still here," Arcadius said, taking me by the shoulders. "We know what really happened!"

I shook my head.

"Constantinople is far away and now we have more pressing problems to worry about," I replied, pointing to the legionaries who wandered the beach aimlessly, shocked by so much devastation and death.

With Basiliscus fleeing to Constantinople and Methylius Seronatus and Marcellinus dead, we searched among the survivors for another high-ranking officer, but they were all dead or had been captured by the Vandals.

And I, as *civitatis comes* of Carthago Nova, became the commander of the defeated army. We had to evacuate the beach and return, some to Carthago Nova, others to Constantinople and the rest to Rome, as soon as possible. The first thing I did was to meet with the *ducenarii* and the *centenarii* who were still alive, and organize the troops in numeri according to their legions of origin. Then I met with the physician to find out what condition the injured were in, and what medications and supplies they might need. Then I spoke to the magister navis, among them was the toothless and smelly Tullas. It was essential to know the exact number of ships we had, as well as their status. So, I knew that, of the more than a thousand ships that made up the fleet, only one hundred and ten remained stranded on the Sicilian coast. The rest had either been destroyed or fled to Constantinople. But, without a doubt, more than half of the ships were now submerged under the waters that bathe Cape Mercury.

I talked with the magistrate of the small village of Agrigentum, and he very generously offered us all his help and collaboration. Thus, several carpenters from the city helped us with the reparation tasks of the ships and we didn't lack cloth and bandages for the wounded, neither a crust of bread to alleviate our hunger, or a sip of wine to refresh our parched throats.

They were days of tiring and hard work, but we were aware that we didn't have a single minute to lose. Finally, one hot summer day, we had everything ready to embark and return to our homes. The ships anchored off the coast with their sails down. On the beach, perfectly grouped in numeri, were the soldiers. The wounded and sick, who weren't few, had already been embarked on the ships and were impatient to rejoin their relatives, and alleviate their wounds in their company. Most of the ships would return to Rome, only a few would depart for Constantinople and only one would do so for Carthago Nova. The breeze turned into a gentle wind, announcing that the time to depart was near. Up on a catwalk and accompanied by the magistrates and the few officers still alive, I addressed a troop that was watching me expectantly.

"Legionaries! Legionaries! Heroes, pride of Rome!" I exclaimed. "In Cape Mercury we haven't been defeated by the barbarians, but by the vanity of a miserable and cowardly general. It was Basiliscus who led us to defeat, not our *spatha* or our courage. Keep this in mind and never forget it. You are heroes not defeated soldiers." I looked towards those men, in the hope that my encouragement words would overcome the shield of shame and failure they had barricaded themselves in. "We have survived hell and if God has granted us his favor, it's so that we can return to our homes and prepare to defend our families. Legionaries of Rome, difficult times are predicted for the Empire. Our enemies are strong and numerous, but we must not be discouraged and defeated. We are Romans, children of a glorious Empire with more than a thousand years of existence. It's up to our swords to save our civilization and that our world doesn't fall into the hands of the savage barbarians." The soldiers watched me carefully in deep silence. "Legionaries!" I yelled, raising my sword. "¡Roma invicta est! ¡Roma invicta est! ¡Roma invicta est!"

The *milites*' shouts resounded on the beaches of Sicily like the roar of a raging and wrathful sea, like a storm clamoring for vengeance and honor, like the blast of a thousand thunders in a black storm. The legionaries unsheathed their weapons and challenged the blue firmament with their spatha. In the nearby bluffs thundered the echoes charged with dignity and pride of an army ready to face all sorts of misfortunes. *Fortis cadere, non potest cedere*» [the strong fall, but cannot yield]. Our legions had been defeated off the coast of Africa, but we would not surrender to the relentless onslaught of the enemy. We would not yield to the barbarian hordes. The dream of a lasting peace was as unattainable as a star, but as God lives, we would shed every drop of our Roman blood to achieve it.

With moist eyes, and overcome with a deep emotion, I ordered the troops to embark. We were returning home.

CHAPTER XVII

A bitter farewell.

Amicus, adiuta me, quo id fiat facilius.[21]

I was very grateful to Tullas, since without his amazing skill we wouldn't have escaped the disaster of Cape Mercury, but it was another *magister navis* who guided our ship to Carthago Nova, so that we could avoid his fetid odor and repulsive breath. We docked the ship at the dock amidst the joy and surprise of our people, who already thought we were dead. Unfortunately, it wasn't all tears of happiness for our arrival, since there were many companions who left their lives in Africa. Men and women approached us insistently asking for their loved ones, obtaining negative answers in most of the occasions. Thus, the joy of those who could embrace their father, husband or brother was overshadowed by the sadness of others who, with broken hearts, tore their clothes torn with pain, being difficult to console. It was a day of desired encounters and sad confirmations. I went down the walkway and looked for Valeria, whom I soon found accompanied by our children and Calerus, who crossed himself as soon as he saw us. I ran to meet her and we embraced.

"I thought you had died," she sobbed, hugging me tightly.

"I'm here, honey," I said, before kissing her.

"Dad! Dad!" cried Annia and Salvio Alexandros in unison, raising their arms, demanding cuddles and caresses.

I bent down and held them in my arms. Tears ran uncontrollably down my cheeks. Wrapped in the warmth that only a deep and devoted love can grant, I remained for a few minutes, trying to disdain from my mind the scenes of death and blood that germinated uncontrollably in my memory like the green sprouts of a wheat field. With my eyes veiled by tears, I looked at Valeria. Her lips drew a mournful smile. Her face was still punished by the anguish that comes with a tormented wait.

---

[21] *Friend, help me make this easier (phrase extracted and adapted from the Latin Grammar book by Santiago Segura Munguía).*

"Thank God you're back," said Calerus, hugging Arcadius. "Where is Cassius Belenus?"

Arcadius shook his head.

"God rest his soul." the monk wished sadly and crossed himself.

"It's been a living hell, we survived almost by a miracle, but most of them are dead." I said, sitting up with the children in my arms.

"Adriano!" Flavius Protus exclaimed addressing us, pushing his way through the crowd. "What a joy that you are alive!"

"I think so too!" I exclaimed.

I left the children on the ground and hugged the magistrate.

"It must have been horrible," he said regretfully.

"It was a hell. The beach in Cape Mercury will be stained with blood for years to come."

The magistrate nodded regretfully.

"We'll talk about that and other issues later... Now, join your family and rest. When you are ready, come to the Senate," he said seriously with his eyes veiled with concern.

"I'll do so."

We embraced and Flavius Protus got lost in the crowd. Although he hadn't participated in the campaign, he looked tired and alarmingly worried. Something wasn't right in Carthago Nova.

"Adriano, I leave you. My throat is dry and needs urgent attention. If you need anything from me, you know where to find me." said Arcadius.

"At Calerus's church?" I asked him mockingly.

"Ha, ha, ha, see you, my friend!" he exclaimed, walking away accompanied by a beautiful young woman.

"This man will never change," Calerus interjected with a smile.

"God will forgive him all his sins, don't you think?"

Calerus shrugged his shoulders unconvinced and said:

"I must go. Unfortunately, there will be many who will seek comfort in church today, and pray for loved ones who are no longer with us. I'm so glad you're back," he added sincerely, grabbing my forearms.

"Thank you, my friend."

Cassius Belenus' memory came to my mind. I felt tightness in my throat, and my eyes watered. We hugged goodbye and I went with my family to our house.

I stayed cooped up at home during two days, enjoying the company of Valeria and my children. I longed to forget the wars, the dead friends, the mutilated limbs floating in a red sea of blood... I was jaded, tired of so much death and misfortune. I hated that my children were growing up in such a cruel and wretched world. But alas, there was nothing I could do about it, and the relentless defeat against the Vandals would only bring more trouble and hardship.

One night I woke up in cold sweats. I had had a recurring dream but no less frightening. In it, I was surrounded by ships engulfed in flames and was attacked by demons with blood-red eyes. Ever since I got back from Sicily, I had the same nightmare every night. I remembered the druid's words: "When the ships swim at the bottom of the sea and the demons threaten the city walls, you'll march with your family to the north. Otherwise, they'll die."

"Are you fine honey?" Valeria asked me, leaning into bed. "Was it the same nightmare?"

I nodded in panting.

"The first part of the druid's prophecy has been fulfilled; Cape Mercury was a hell of fire and death. Hundreds of boats now rest at the bottom of the sea..."

"And who are the demons that threaten the walls?" I had made Valeria a participant in my nightmare for a long time.

"I don't know, maybe it's the ultimate attack by the barbarians."

The next morning, unable to delay my duties as *civitatis comes* any further; I headed to the Senate where an impatient Flavius Protus awaited me. I found him sitting in his seat accompanied by several curials. Everyone had a serious and worried countenance.

"I'm glad you're already fully restored," the magistrate told me. "Let's go outside and take a walk, autumn is coming and I don't want to waste a day as beautiful as this."

We left the Senate and walked along the city-streets.

"The defeat against the Vandals will have unimaginable consequences," He began to say. "Now, we're weaker than ever, and the barbarians know it. You can swear by god they know it. But that's not the most serious thing."

"What do you mean?"

"They aren't few the Spanish-Roman dignitates who have crawled to Euric's court with expensive gifts, paying tribute to him."

They complain that they don't accept a Greek emperor imposed by the Emperor Leo, and that in addition, has led them to a disastrous defeat against the Vandals. They assure that it's he, Euric, who must take the first step and separate his territories from Rome.

"But that is high treason!" I exclaimed indignantly.

The magistrate nodded.

"They fear losing their dignity and wealth, and sell themselves to the highest bidder. Rome is weak and Euric is the most powerful king among the barbarians. Many nobles have already decided to whom to dispense their allegiance when the time comes."

"Do we know who they are?"

"There are many, but the most hideous and aberrant case is that of Arvandus, the *praefectus praetorium Galliarum*. The traitor has been arrested and is in the dungeons of Ravenna. He is accused of preparing the partition of Gaul between Visigoths and Burgundians. If he has betrayed the Empire, what will the rest of the provincials and dignitaries not do?"

"They'll crawl like slugs at the feet of foreign kings," I admitted regretfully.

We took a seat on a stone bench. It was sunny but a gentle breeze refreshed our tired faces.

"Do we have any news from Genseric or Euric?" I asked.

"It's just a matter of time for Euric to cross the Loire, and attack the Roman cities on the other shore. Then he probably heads south and cross the Pyrenees. As for Genseric, we expect to see his troops threatening our walls at any moment."

"It doesn't sound like very flattering news."

"No, they aren't."

I got up from the bench and stood up.

"We might not resist another Vandal attack," I admitted.

"I know. In addition, Genseric won't be satisfied with looting the city; he'll want to annex it to his territory. We are in a race against time. It's like a game," The magistrate explained, rising from the bench. "There is a big cake on the table and five children are running towards it with the intention of eating all they can. What one does not eat, the other will."

"I understand."

"The cake is Rome, and the five children are the Visigoths, Vandals, Ostrogoths, Burgundians and Franks. What one of them doesn't take from us, the other will. It's an infamous game in which everyone wins and only one loses: Rome."

"The Empire will be preyed upon by five packs of hungry wolves. What pleases me..." I added with a crooked smile, "is that once they have satisfied their stomachs, they'll rush at each other like rabid beasts. The infinite ambition that invades the entrails of the greedy barbarians will destroy them."

During winter the military campaigns come to a halt since the roads are flooded by the rains, making it difficult for the troops and carriages to march. We spent the long cold winter days, sheltered by the fireplace and preparing our defenses for a future attack. It was just a few weeks of tranquility, where we managed to forget about wars, deaths and destruction. But peace was nothing more than a wish; an ephemeral dream that ended with wakefulness and, a few weeks before the plants bloomed anxiously awaiting the flight of the indefatigable bees, disturbing news reached our city: the Vandals had landed with thousands of soldiers in the Pillars of Hercules and taken the cities of Carteia and Malacca. In their wake, they didn't leave a trail of fire and destruction, but quite the contrary. The messengers, completely perplexed, informed us that King Genseric had offered them the opportunity to surrender. If they accepted, the city wouldn't be looted or burned and the lives of its inhabitants would be respected. But the Vandal's prerogatives weren't free. Their Senate was to publicly discard Anthemius' authority and, therefore, of Rome, rendering him total submission and obedience. The decision was very simple: destruction and death, or surrender and life.

The arrival of spring was the beginning of the end. Of our end. The barbarian hosts took up positions and crossed our *limes,* snatching the cities from us with little resistance. In the north, Euric had finally detached the false mask of an erratic ally of Rome, by seizing the cities of Avaricum and Tours. The Visigothic king had invaded Gaul, devouring an important piece of the appetizing cake, anticipating the Franks and Burgundian onslaught. In the south, it was Genseric the one who claimed his part of the feast, by invading the Carthaginian.

Meanwhile, in the *ordo decuriorum* at the Senate of Carthago Nova, we found the curials arguing about the dramatic spring that awaited us, overcome by an overwhelming sense of discouragement and fear.

"They are advancing very fast; they have already seized Gades, Anticaria and the town of Iliberri. They're heading to Abdera right now." Said, the curator Flacus Mutius; a man with a lean face, a clear forehead, and an aquiline nose. A man of unquestionable honor and lack of courage.

"But they aren't destroying cities or towns, or burning crops or murdering peasants," added a censor.

"Indeed, Genseric only demands that they swear loyalty to him and renounce to Anthemius' command, which he considers a usurper of Greek origin," Flacus Mutius explained in an excessively condescending tone, as if the requests of the *Vandalorum rex* were a trifle, a totally acceptable trifle.

"And what is your opinion regarding the Vandal's *good manners?* Flavius Protus asked the curator rising from his seat.

"What do you mean?" the questioned man asked somewhat confused. "If you mean..."

"No, you don't need to answer me," Flavius Protus interrupted with a gesture. "Many of us here are afraid of what will be your position as soon as the invader's signs are glimpsed in the distance. No, I don't want to listen to you; it would be extremely painful for me that a *clarissimus* from Carthago Nova said certain words." The magistrate began to walk through the Senate, shaking his head sadly. Flacus Mutius was staring at him with tight lips and red with anger. "Genseric doesn't intend to enrich himself with this campaign," he continued "his objective is another; conquer the Carthaginian and annex it to his territories. Therefore, it's very likely that he will grant us the privilege of surrendering. An unconditional, humiliating, servile surrender... Well, if in return he respects our life and our possessions... right?" he looked at the curials, intending to scrutinize their thoughts. It didn't take long for him to realize what the minds of many of them were hiding. "Some of you will conclude that Genseric is a generous, magnanimous, fair barbarian..." he continued. "Perhaps the idea has even crossed his mind that Carthago Nova would be richer and more prosperous under his patronage. After all, his armies are closer to our borders than the legions of Rome. So... do we accept him as king and deny the Greek?" he asked rhetorically. "I have the impression that in this room, there are senators who don't look down on the barbarian's invasion... after all, he hasn't destroyed cities, he hasn't enslaved the Hispano-Romans, he hasn't burned the fields." He stared at Flacus Mutius, who, unable to hold his gaze, fixed his eyes on the pavement. "But I insist, do we want to remain Romans or do we kiss the Vandal's hand and become one of them? What are we going to do, Senators from Carthago Nova?" Some curials started to reply, but the magistrate raised his hand. He hasn't finished his speech yet. "I only ask one thing, just one. Think well your answer, because the future of our citizens and our families will depend on it."

Flavius Protus returned to his seat, and was congratulated with encouragement words and pat on the back by the most like-minded curials.

"Rome has abandoned us; we have no chance of surviving a barbarian attack!" an old and fearful *decurion* exclaimed, rising from his seat. "Better to live like a barbarian than die like a Roman," he whispered, taking his seat again.

"We must surrender!" another exclaimed, supporting his words.

"You talk about giving up when you haven't been given that chance yet?!" exclaimed another one vehemently. "You are so cowardly that you flee just by hearing the name of the enemy."

"Indeed, we are speculating," I snapped, trying to put some order in that hornet's nest. "arguing about a circumstance that hasn't yet happened. We don't know if Genseric will negotiate peace or send his soldiers to our walls. This is a pointless debate; let's focus on the facts and not the guesswork."

A thunderous murmur echoed through the room. The curials were divided and many of them, truly scared. I don't blame them. Many of us had wives, children, and some had grandchildren. Our life mattered very little to us, but it was very different to think about the fate our loved ones would suffer if Genseric took the city with blood and fire.

"After conquering Abdera. After conquering Abdera!" I continued, trying to make myself heard in the hubbub. The murmur faded, and though it didn't die off completely, at least its appeasement allowed me to continue my speech. "The Vandal king is sure to head to Carthago Nova. If it's true that he is accompanied by tens of thousands of soldiers, defending our walls will be a colossal endeavor of very improbable success." Several decurions nodded, convinced of my words. "The *ordo decuriorum* is the maximum responsible for the protection of our citizens and we must act prudently and wisely. Well, we shouldn't digress on assumptions and conjectures. It's a futile effort and, as your faces reveal, exhausting. We will discuss this topic later. But I'm going to express my opinion, so that no one, absolutely no one in this Senate, has any doubt about what my determination will be when the time comes." The room was plunged into a deep silence. "I'm Hispanic… and Roman and I'll be until the end of my days. I can't interpret one without the other. Can you?" my rhetorical question was followed by a brief pause, for my words to settle in the curials' minds. "If so," I continued, "I don't think you deserve one name or the other." A new murmur began to run through the room. I raised my hands and continued. "No, Carthago Nova curials, you don't deserve it. You don't deserve to call yourselves Hispanic, because being Hispanic entails the duty to defend our lands from our enemies, and you don't deserve to call yourselves Roman because if you deny the emperor, if you deny Rome, you must also deny everything that Rome represents. Starting with your names, origins and ancestors!" The murmur turned into a fierce gale, and several curials shouted insults and raised their fists threateningly, but I wasn't intimidated. I hadn't finished yet. "If you despise Rome, you despise yourself!" The roaring shouts of the senators must have been heard from the very doors of the Urbs. I raised my arms again and continued, once tempers had subsided slightly. "You reject your emperor and submit yourself meekly to the arms of a barbarian king," I continued, my voice was calm but determined. "And, I tell you, I tell you senators of Carthago Nova that I don't distinguish any difference between you and the prostitutes who change clients at will, guided only by greed. Or is it your fear that drives you to behave like cowards?"

"This is intolerable; I won't consent to this outrage!" a curial yelled, reaching for a dagger hidden in his robe.

"Put your knife away," I said, pointing at him, "or else, use it against the Vandals who are at the gates of Carthago Nova, but never dare to raise it against a Hispano-Roman who pretends to be faithful to his principles. If you are bold enough to brandish a weapon in this sacred place, I have no doubt that you will find yourself by my side, in the front line of battle when Genseric storms our walls. I trust you will. You'll be well received."

My words aroused some laughter and the curial, embarrassed, hid his dagger and sat down again.

"Good, very good," I continued, once the fire of anger that threatened to scorch the *ordo decuriorum* faded. "I'm satisfied with what today here, in the Senate of Carthago Nova, where we litigate the representatives of the people, I have seen. Yes, *domini,* I'm very satisfied." I looked away from the confused faces of the curials. "Well, I have witnessed how honorable and worthy curials have been seriously outraged by some words that many have interpreted as grave insults. And they have yelled with raised fists and even displayed weapons," I added, looking at the decurion who drew his knife. "Well, I'm very satisfied because... if you, noble curials, have responded with unusual fury to my words, unleashing your anger, your rage, your obfuscation... what will you not do against the barbarian swords? All those who raised your threatening fists against me, against a Hispanic-Roman like you, what won't you raise against an invader who threatens to destroy everything you believe in? I hope, I wish, that you unleash all your anger against the Vandals, the true and only enemy, and not against your *civitatis comes*. Otherwise, as I have told you before, you'll be as trustworthy as the prostitutes who sell their services in the sordid brothels."

I took a seat leaving the Senate submerged in the most formidable of storms. I remembered the words of Flavius Protus when he assured me that the battles that were fought in the *ordo decuriorum* didn't leave the pavement strewn with the dead, but they were no less bloody for that. Until now, I hadn't been aware of how right I was. After long minutes, in which the discussions, insults and threats followed one another in a hurried way, perhaps due to the fatigue of the decurions or to the certainty that said tidal wave led nowhere, silence, a pleasant and comforting silence, was taking over the room. Then I spoke again:

"I have sent horsemen to inform us about the number of Genseric's troops and confirm if it's true that the Vandal respects the cities and the lives of those who pay homage to him," I began. "However, we still don't know if Genseric will be as benevolent towards us as he is being towards the rest of the conquered cities. Remember that we have already resisted his siege. Perhaps now his intentions towards us are very different and it is not enough to open the doors of Carthago Nova and kiss his filthy Arian barbarian feet to save our lamentable and cowardly lives," I said, glaring at the curial in favor of surrender. A murmur laden with imprecations, insults, and recriminations ran through the room. "Now," I went on, gesturing for silence. "Now, we must act calmly and prudently. First of all, we will wait for the arrival of the horsemen and their reports. In the meantime, we'll reinforce the walls and train new tires. It's useless to argue for any longer about the future of Carthago Nova until we have more information and know for sure what the barbarian's intentions are. Flavius Protus has asked a question," I continued, looking at the magistrate. "I'm not asking you to answer it now. It's not the moment. What I do beg of you, what I implore you from the depths of my heart is that you meditate your decision at length, since our future as Romans will depend on it," and to conclude, I added: "If the curials agree, I'll raise this session, and I'll summon you to a new one when our riders have returned. It'll be the moment to express your opinion."

The curials accepted my suggestion and left the Senate immersed in a confused lullaby of conflicting opinions. In the eyes of many of those *clarissimi* I read that, despite my harsh words, they would not doubt what their decision would be when Genseric found himself at the gates of the city.

I arrived home with the concern highly marked on my face. My daughter Annia jumped on me as soon as I opened the door, while Salvio Alexandros was reading a scroll, helped by Valeria. I kissed the little girl and laid her on the floor entertaining with a rag doll. My wife looked at me and approached me leaving the little boy immersed in the reading of a hexameter of Virgil's Aeneid. It was an extremely complicated book for an adult and Salvio Alexandros was reading it without understanding anything at all, but as a reading learning tool it was invaluable.

"What is happening?" Valeria asked me worriedly.

For a few moments I doubted whether to confess the truth or not, after all, it wasn't worth worrying her.

"The Vandals have seized several cities and will be heading to Carthago Nova soon, but don't worry, we'll get reinforcements from Rome and we can deal with them." I lied with a smile, trying to be as convincing as possible.

Valeria frowned; it was evident that I hadn't succeeded.

"Tell me the truth, don't try to hide anything from me or I'll be even more worried."

I looked into her eyes. She was more beautiful every day. I approached little Salvio Alexandros who stopped his reading to give me a big smile. Little Annia pretended to feed the rag doll with a wooden spoon. They were my family, I loved them more than anything in the world and I would not allow them to be in any danger. I looked at Valeria, who remained with her beautiful black eyes fixed on me, waiting for an answer. I sighed and told her everything that had happened at the senate.

"What are you going to do when the Vandals are in front of our walls?" she asked.

"The Senate will have made a decision before that happens."

"Then?" she insisted.

"I don't know," I admitted, sitting dejected on a footstool. I grabbed the pendant instinctively and pressed hard the silver mandrake that hung from my neck.

"Maybe the druid can give you the answer," Valeria told me, touching my shoulder. She thought the pendant had been given to me by Lughdyr. I don't quite know why, but I never told her it was Alana who did it.

"Lughdyr is far from here," I pointed out rising from the footstool. "But you're right, I need advice, and I know who can give it to me."

In a church nests a peace that can hardly be found elsewhere. The smell of incense and wax, the silence, the images depicted on ceilings and walls, the crucified Christ and the sobriety and hardness of the ashlars, give temples a magic, a spell capable of sharpening the mind and awakening sleeping feelings. With such a hope I took a seat on a cold stone bench with the desire to meet Calerus. A few minutes elapsed until the monk, formerly a warrior, made his appearance. My presence surprised him and, smiling, he approached. It was dark and the church was empty. Better so, I preferred to talk to Calerus and ask him for advice alone in that spiritual environment.

"I salute you, friend Adriano. I have to admit that it's quite a surprise to see you at this hour in church, is everything okay?"

"I need to talk to you."

"I understand," he said, sitting next to me. "My friend, if you need to talk and be heard, I can assure you that there is no better place than this," he added with a smile.

I nodded and began to tell him about the discussion we had had in the Senate. Calerus watched me carefully, without losing a single detail of my words. When I finished the monk rose, and with a gesture invited me to accompany him for a short walk through the corridors of the church.

"I need your advice."

"You don't know what to do when the time comes for the Vandals to besiege us do you?" he asked me.

"One part of me wants to fight, to die with the sword in my hand defending the Empire, but other fears for Valeria and the children. I don't want any misfortune to happen to them," I replied with my eyes tarnished.

The monk nodded, wrinkling his lips.

"We must live to honor God; we aren't useful to Him dead."

"You mean we should kiss Genseric's hand and live like barbarians? Like Arian heretics?" I asked him confusedly.

"They are Arians, it's true, but the basis of their beliefs is the same as ours: they believe in the existence of the Unique God and his son Jesus Christ, with the only but not least important caveat, that they deny their divinity. For them Jesus Christ was created by God to fulfill his plan; the redemption of the world. Jesus Christ can be called God because of his relationship with the Creator, but he is still just one more creature. There's nothing divine in him, he's just a man. They also deny the Holy Trinity and believe only in God the Father. Both Jesus Christ and the Holy Ghost were created by God to serve as intermediaries with men and help him fulfill his sacred plan. This is the big difference between Arians and Catholics."

"Do you think we should surrender to the Vandals?" I asked him, more interested in learning his opinion of barbarians than in receiving a theology class.

"You are *civitatis comes,* and a member of the *ordo decuriorum,* your decision depends on the lives of thousands of people, including your family."

The monk stopped and looked me straight in the eye.

"How long have we been fighting the barbarians? How many good men have died in this endless war?" I remembered Arius Sidonius, Optila, Ajax, Cassius Belenus and so many more… "Sooner or later Rome will fall; does it make sense to prolong the agony any longer? Is there any hope of victory, however remote it may be?" I shook my head. "Then does it make sense to have more bloodshed?"

"But we would no longer be Romans."

370

"We are only men, sons of God. If you can raise your children in peace, if you can harvest crops without fear of them being burned or raise a house without fear of it being destroyed, what does it matter whether your lord's is called Genseric, Euric or Anthemius?

"Are you giving a lesson in Christian resignation?" Are you suggesting that we be condescending and turn the other cheek, since we will enjoy our reward in the kingdom of heaven?"

I could see in his face that my words had hurt him.

"You must think with your heart, not with your guts," he replied.

I began to walk down the corridor accompanied by Calerus. For several minutes I meditated on his words. My friend was asking me to give in to the enemy and humiliate my head in order to save it. I didn't know what kind of future awaited us if Carthago Nova was conquered by the Vandals. Who could assure me that we wouldn't be enslaved or killed? Who could be sure that we wouldn't be forced to convert to the Arian faith? I was a Roman, my family was Roman, and if Rome fell, perhaps it wasn't worth living.

"No," I said almost without thinking, still deep in thought. Calerus looked at me with a confused expression.

"What do you mean?"

I sighed deeply.

"I have made a decision."

"I hope the good Lord has enlightened you and your decision is the right one," my friend wished with his eyes veiled with sadness.

The horsemen returned a few weeks after the senate had gathered in assembly, confirming the words of Flacus Mutius: the cities, municipalities and villages that knelt at the feet of the Vandals were respected, but those that refused to recognize Genseric as their lord were exterminated, and their inhabitants sacrificed. Shortly thereafter an officer of the *Vandalorum rex* arrived in the city. He brought with him a message with his terms. A new meeting of the *ordo decuriorum* was called and after several hours of visceral and exhausting discussions, an agreement was reached.

The sound of drums and war tubas preceded the Vandals' arrival. The sun was setting behind the horizon and the twilight was hovering over our languid city, dying it in red. From my vantage point, I watched how the barbarians, in formation, slowly but inexorably approach our walls menacingly. They carried flaming torches, whose flames reflected in their breastplates, helmets and eyes, dressing them with the color of blood. Lucifer's army emerged from the depths of the hells. The cadence of the drums penetrated our ears, shrinking our hearts, while the ground groaned because of the march of the invincible troops. They stopped a few hundred paces from the walls, far from the range of our archers. They were tens of thousands of soldiers who, as a humiliating sample of obedience, had been joined by hundreds of *bucelarii* from the subdued cities. The sun disappeared, and a silvery full moon emerged over the horizon behind the enemy, now reverberating with its silver rays. The wind blew, making the flames of the torches ripple, as if it were a sea of fire. The sound of drums and tubas ceased, and an ominous silence enveloped the shadowy night. From our elevated position, we watched the scene, aware that we wouldn't have had any chance. Next to me, Arcadius looked at the barbarians with a serious and worried gesture.

"The time has come," I said, and descended the stairs of the wall accompanied by my friend.

The druid's words came to my mind: "When the ships swim at the bottom of the sea and the demons threaten the city walls, you'll march with your family to the north. Otherwise, you'll die."

I had no doubts; I knew I was doing the right thing. I went to the house, where Valeria and the children were waiting for me. They were ready. We climbed into a wagon with our belongings and marched in silence in front of the tearful eyes of several neighbors. From the narrow streets, as if they were tributaries, dozens of citizens began to appear, either on foot, on horseback or in carts, joined us forming a human river. Flavius Protus joined with his family, other *decurions* did the same. Flacus Mutius watched the sad procession from the roof of his house. Our gazes met and he nodded goodbye. His eyes shone excitedly. We passed near Calerus's Church. The monk blessed us with water, praying a Lord's Prayer Father. His eyes were clouded, and tears were running through his cheeks. I said goodbye to him without getting out of the cart, I had a lump in my throat. We waited at the city gate until we were all ready. Gradually, we were joined by more fellow travelers. Arcadius, on his mighty warhorse, made the decision, along with a handful of legionaries and *bucelarii*, to accompany us on our diaspora. Although hundreds of people piled up in the streets, the silence was almost total, being only broken by the bark of a lone dog and the cry of a child. None of us wanted to leave Carthago Nova, but we had no choice. I waited for the arrival of some straggler and finally gave the order:

"Open the doors!"

The dry creaking of the wood preceded the terrifying sight of the Vandal soldiers carrying their menacing torches. Many women and children broke into tears and men instinctively lay hands with our grips. Would Genseric keep his word? The lives of my family and so many more Hispanic-Romans depended on it. I led the procession up in a cart. Next to me were Valeria and the children, who looked in terror at the barbarians. Annia, panicked, sank her face into her mother's chest trying to take the image of those demons out of her mind. The procession was slowly following me. Genseric, riding his horse, watched us closely. I stopped in front of him. He nodded and made me a gesture to go our way. I spurred on the oxen and we started on our journey. When I was several dozen steps from the ramparts, I stopped and looked back. A senator emerged from the city gate, approached Genseric and kissed his hand. It was Flacus Mutius.

In the dark and lit by torches, just over a hundred families and fifty soldiers left Carthago Nova and, following the Via Augusta, we headed north towards the city of Tarraco, hoping that the capital of Tarragona would remain safe from barbarian attacks. After several hours of silent march, we took a rest in a small clearing near the road. It wasn't yet dawn, but we were already at a safe distance from the Vandals and we didn't have to worry about their attack. Genseric had kept his word. We lit some fires and heated up some food. The reflection of the flames played capriciously with the faces of the fugitives, making their excited eyes shine.

"*Domine*," said a boy of about twelve who stood in front of me. "Do you think we have done well to leave the city?"

Ten faces lifted their distracted gazes from the fire and directed them at me. I remembered the meeting in the Senate shortly after the arrival of the horsemen and the messenger of the *Vandalorum rex*. The atmosphere was tense and after several hours of bitter debate, it was time for the unpleasant vote. My mind flew, evoking that moment:

The curials came to the Senate in deep and eloquent silence. They seemed to be more at the funeral of an illustrious and beloved person than at a session of the *ordo decuriorum*. Little by little and with a rhythmic and defeated step, they took their seats in their respective seats. I looked at those men. Many of them exuded nervousness and fear, their eyes revealed it. But, on the other hand, there were others whose looks and gestures showed an iron determination. Their eyes were not poisoned by fear and doubt, but rather conveyed an unwavering loyalty to Rome. Among the former was Flacus Mutius, the *curator*, and, among the latter, the magistrate Flavius Protus. The rest of the senators were divided. In that session of the Senate the future of Carthago Nova would be decided. The decision wasn't easy, since the lives of thousands of people depended on that vote. It was hot in the Senate, unbearable and sweltering. Our hearts were fluttering wildly and our faces were disfigured with worry and anguish. Be that as it may, from that day on, our lives, our world would change irreversibly. The Senate was silent and the senators looked at me impatiently for the ill-fated conclave to begin. So, I got up from the bench and began to speak:

"*Clarissimi* senators of Carthago Nova, a few days ago an assembly took place in which I made you participant in Genseric's advance through Spanish lands, as well as his conduct with the conquered cities. At that time, we made the prudent decision to wait for such information to be verified to incline our vote towards one of the only two possible alternatives. Well, as many of you already know, the explorers have returned and with them the confirmation that Genseric doesn't destroy the cities that humble at his feet. Instead, he is relentless with those who persist in his determination to remain loyal to the Empire. In addition, we have received a visit from a messenger of Genseric with his terms." In the eyes of the curials I read that they were also aware of this fact, as well as the content of the letter. So, I decided to be brief to open the discussion as soon as possible. "The *Vandalorum rex* offers us peace in exchange for the unconditional surrender of the city, asserting that if we agree to submit to his royal authority, he'll respect the life and possessions of each of the Carthaginians."

A low rumble followed by nods and puckered lips spread through the room. I shifted my gaze to those clarissimi in order to scrutinize their spirits and intentions, but in them I only recognized the fear of those who contemplate helplessly as his world crumbles, devoured by the insatiable jaws of greed and ambition.

"The *Vandalorum rex* is at the gates of Carthago Nova. In a few days or even hours we will glimpse their ensign waving on the horizon," I continued. "These are the facts; this is the infamous reality that haunts us. Now, the people, our people, trust the criteria of this *ordo decuriorum*

374

to wisely resolve this situation and prevent misfortune from beating our beloved city."

The senators looked at each other. They were scared, confused, bewildered. Some, abandoned to defeat, others, the least, kept their gaze firm and dignified, ready to sacrifice their lives and that of their loved ones rather than submit to the barbarian.

"In the last session of this noble Senate, the magistrate Flavius Protus asked us a question," I continued, looking at the *decurion*. "This assembly has been called to respond to it. I remember you, *clarissimi decurions* that the magistrate asked us if, at the imminent arrival of the barbarians, we would surrender the city or fight for it. We all know what our choice would entail. In that session I asked you to think deeply about your decision, because our future will depend on it. Well, I trust that it was that way. I'm not going to delve any further into the consequences of our determination, since this assembly has been convened for this. In this Senate there are two opinions, two very different opinions on how to face Genseric's arrival. Both currents are totally opposed: one pleads to bow to the barbarian, while the other chooses to fight. Flacus Mutius will defend the first option; the surrender to the invader, and Flavius Protus, the second; defense of the city. Now we will listen to the arguments of both clarissimi and then we will proceed to the vote. I reiterate, Senators of Carthago Nova, that you reflect on your opinion and that you don't let yourself be carried away by confused or visceral feelings. The life and future as Hispano-Romans of thousands of citizens depend on what this wise conclave agrees. May God enlighten us."

"May God enlighten us," the senators repeated in barely a whisper.

"Clarissimus Flacus Mutius, whenever you want, you can proceed," I said with a gesture to the curator.

Flacus Mutius nodded, rose heavily from his seat, and walked to the center of the room. His lean face was blurred with concern and deep regret. He licked his dry lips and after clearing his throat a few times, he started his arguments.

"Thank you very much *civitatis comes* for revealing the situation with bleak accuracy," he said, pacing the room, his voice strong, deep, and confident, strikingly in contrast to his weak, defeated countenance. "It's good to know what we are dealing with, without masking it with confusing and delicate words. It's good not to ramble on conjectures or assumptions, if not on confirmed realities, however adverse they may be. And the facts that our *civitatis comes* has told us cannot be more dire, they cannot be more hopeless, they cannot be more painful," he paused and looked at the curials, who were staring at him in tense silence. "But behind every ruin, hidden under the rubble of every disaster, a hope always arises. Life, the future, invariably breaks through after misfortune. It always does noble *clarissimi*. Always. But I won't deny that it's easy. No, it's not easy. And life will make its way in Carthago Nova after the arrival of the Vandals, whatever our decision. And here, in this sacred room, what we are really discussing is the tribute that Carthaginians will have to pay for Carthago Nova to last beyond our existence. And, I only manage to distinguish two kinds of tribute: sacrificing our fidelity to the Empire, or," he stopped his walk and looked sternly at Flavius Protus. "the lives of our citizens."

Flacus Mutius approached his seat and a servant brought him a glass of water. Meanwhile, the Senate was engulfed in a murmur of confused conversations, but from the gestures of some and others, it was evident that the curator was winning the favor of the majority of the *decurions*.

"In ten, fifty, or even a thousand years, Carthago Nova will continue to exist. It may have other name, perhaps it will be ruled by other peoples, but it will survive. I have no doubt about that," he continued. "But I digress. Excuse me, senators; I have drifted too far back in time. What we are dealing with now, is not the Carthago Nova of ten, fifty or a thousand years from now, but the Carthago Nova of now. But..." The *curator* stroked his chin and narrowed his eyes thoughtfully. "But what will become of our city if today it's devastated by the Vandals? How long will it take to recover from the spilled blood? How will history judge the curials who decided to undertake a foolish resistance even though they were persuaded that victory was impossible? No, *clarissimi*, I refuse to stain my hands with the blood of my people, of my family." The curial looked down at his palms and shook his head. "Rome, our beloved Rome, has been defeated," he continued, pacing the room again. "For many years the battles fought by our legionaries have been counted as defeats. The barbarians cross our *limes* without encountering resistance, the Hispanic cities surrender in their wake, many dignitaries and even senior army officers now serve under the orders of the barbarian kings. The legions have left Hispania years ago. What happened to Legion VII Gemina? Where are the second Flavia Pacatiana cohorts, the Lucensis cohorts, the first

Celtiberorum cohorts, and the first and second Gaul cohorts? I'll tell you: years ago they were discharged, dissolved because they weren't profitable for Rome. They involved a high cost that the emperors were unwilling to bear. The defense of Hispania wasn't relevant to Rome!" he exclaimed with fury, with rage, with pain. "Since then," he continued, shaking his head. "We have been preyed upon by the Suevians, by the Visigoths, by the Vandals... and what has Rome done? What has *Urbs* done to protect us? I'll tell you: nothing. Absolutely nothing. Moreover, when Requiarius invaded the Carthaginian and Tarraconense, Emperor Avitus didn't send the Roman legions stationed in Gaul, but ordered Theodoric to cross the *limes* of Hispania with his horde of Visigoths to restore order. And we all know of the destruction that the *Gothorum rex* caused in Hispanic lands. Yes, it's true that Majorian arrived in our city accompanied by a powerful army. I won't deny that it was a bold attempt, together with the colossal army erected by Anthemius, to exterminate the Vandals, but we all know that both campaigns ended in formidable disaster; an undeniable reflection of the impetuous decline in which the Urbs is plunged."

Most of the senators nodded and murmured convinced of his words. Flacus Mutius drank a drink of water again and continued:

"Genseric is at the gates of the city and in his generosity..." His address was interrupted by a succession of insults and expletives. "In his infinite generosity, he has offered us peace in exchange for denying a Rome that has abandoned us!" he exclaimed, trying to make himself heard in that storm.

"¡¿Are you insinuating that the invader is generous?!" a curial snapped angrily.

"You are a traitor!" yelled other curial.

The echoes of the boos and the curses of the *decurions* cracked on the walls of the Senate. Some outraged and others vehemently supporting the curator's speech.

"Silence! Silence!" I screamed, and little by little, the oaths, insults, and laments, vanished. "Flacus Mutius has the floor and for the sake of this session and the momentous decision that we must take, I beg the *clarissimi* senators to refrain from further interruptions."

And, with a gesture, I exhorted Flacus Mutius to continue:

"Thank you, *civitatis comes*," said the curator with a slight nod. "As I was trying to point out before my impetuous companions interrupted me..." a new rumor spread through the room but was quickly put down.

"Years ago, Genseric besieged our city and thanks to a clever ruse of our *civitatis comes*," the curial dispensed me a clever smile, "we managed to prevent our walls from being stormed by his troops. It was a great triumph, there is no doubt, but also an affront to the *Vandalorum rex*, who was tricked into going to Rome in support of Olybrius, his candidate for emperor, renouncing the siege to which he had subjected us."

"What is it you want Mutius?" Flavius Protus exclaimed angrily. "Are you suggesting that we should have allowed Genseric to conquer the city?"

This time it was a fierce murmur what thundered through the Senate. The curator's insinuation was quite petty and despicable. Even some of his most staunch followers looked down in shame.

"Silence!" I yelled again. "Silence, senators! Let Flacus Mutius explain himself properly."

"I've been accused of being a traitor in this room," the interpellated began to say. "Just for stating that Genseric is a generous king. And, he certainly is so."

I was forced to demand silence again. The spirits were quite inflamed and I feared that, finally, that session would conclude with some badly wounded senator. After a few moments, the curator was able to continue with his speech.

"Despite the affront, he has granted us the same privilege granted to the rest of the Hispanic cities: total surrender in exchange for our dedicated submission. If, in addition, we take into account that he has assured that he will respect our lives and properties, even the most reluctant to give up will understand that the offer is rather generous. There is not a hint of resentment in his heart and he could, very well he could, I must add, have vented all his anger on our city, avenging for the deceit he suffered. But he hasn't..."

"Silence please!" I interrupted. The Senate was once again abuzz with foul phrases.

I couldn't hide the irritation his words were causing me, but as *civitatis comes* of the city I had to act accordingly, and allow the senator to express his opinion freely. Flacus Mutius inclined his head in thanks and continued:

"No, he hasn't. He has offered us peace, a generous peace, and we must accept it, because we would be foolish if we rejected his outstretched hand." He looked away at the curials, assessing followers

378

and opponents, and continued. "Senators of Carthago Nova, Rome, whether we accept it or not has abandoned us. This is the dramatic reality. We can fool ourselves believing that there is a future under the aegis of the Empire, we can dream that one day a hero, a general or a victorious emperor will emerge, annihilating our enemies and raising the Empire once again, elevating it to pass and almost forgotten glories. Yes, friends, we can dream. I also want it with burning and despair. But the reality is tenacious and insists on manifesting itself again and again with inclement harshness. Rome, our mother, has abandoned us, she has abandoned her children. This is the only truth. And now we must decide whether it is worth dying as Romans of a dying Rome, or just living. And not as Romans, or as Vandals, but as what we are: Hispanic. Ponder your position, *clarissimi* senators of Carthago Nova, for my part the decision is more than evident."

The curator took a seat in the bench, concluding his intervention. There was no applause; no words of support or adhesion only silence, an abysmal silence enveloped the Senate with the cloak of fear, defeat and failure. As was mandatory, I allowed a few moments for the senate to assimilate Flacus Mutius' speech before giving the floor to Flavius Protus.

"Well, we have listened with great interest to the motives and reasons of the *clarissimus* Flacus Mutius, I now give the floor to the magistrate Flavius Protus. Please. I made a gesture and Flavius Protus nodded and went to the center of the Senate."

The magistrate walked around the room with his hands clasped behind his back, with a slow pace, his eyes fixed on the pavement and his gesture blurred with worry. The *decurions* watched him in silence, many with sweat beading on their foreheads, others with gall rising bitterly in their throats, and the vast majority with fear gripping their hearts and wills. Flavius Protus stopped his pace and turned his gaze towards the seats filled with uneasiness and restlessness.

"*Clarissimi* senators of Carthago Nova," he began, "today I have listened with astonishment as an eminent member of this council has defined Genseric as a generous man in whose heart dwells no rancor," he paused briefly before continuing, "I remind you that this generous and charitable man, five years ago depredated our region, stealing our livestock, plundering our crops and ravaging the villages. I remind you that he besieged our city and that his kindly army murdered hundreds of Carthaginians. It's evident that the dignitate Flacus Mutius and I have opposite criteria on the concept of generosity." The lips of some of the senators showed smiles. "We can deny all those who have sacrificed their lives for Hispania and for Rome," he continued. "we can forget our ancestors, with whose effort and sweat our walls, our homes, our Senate was built. We can forget our culture, even our religion. Fine, let's forget. But... then? What is left for us, senators? If we forget our origins, if we repudiate our past... What or who will we be?" he paused and looked at the senators. "We will be Hispanic, simply Hispanic. That's what our honorable curator assures us. But... what is a Hispanic who ignores his Roman origins, who denies the blood that runs through his veins, who accepts to live in chains? What would differentiate us from the savage barbarian tribes? Indeed, in the eyes of many of you I see the answer: it would not differentiate us at all. If we forget our ancestors, if we don't honor all those who have offered their lives to defend Hispania and Rome from their innumerable enemies, we'll be nothing more than unworthy savages incapable of calling ourselves men."

"What are you trying to do?" a senator interjected. "That we fight in spite of the fact that victory is impossible!"

"*Dulce et decorum est pro patria mori.[22]*" he replied. "We'll all agree that it's a brilliant phrase uttered by Horace, but unfortunately, I see few Horaces in this room..."

A furious clamor arose in the Senate, and the expletives and insults returned to the council with unusual virulence. For several minutes we remained enveloped in shouting, howling and bellowing, until at last sanity broke through the maddening uproar.

"Don't confuse sanity with cowardice!" yelled Flacus Mutius. "God knows that if there was even the slightest hope of victory we would fight, as we did five years ago!"

His words were followed by the applause and nods of a large number of *decurions*.

"Is it you who speaks or is it the fear that eats away at your meager courage?" asked the magistrate, squinting his eyes. The *curator* stood up threateningly, but Flavius Protus raised his hand demanding silence. It was his turn and he had to be heard. "Fear... always fear, an indefatigable friend of flight, of surrender, of dishonor. The speech of the *clarissimus* Flacus Mutius oozes fear, enormous quantities of terror with which he has infected the integrity of those present here. *Quicumque mortem in malis*

---

[22] *It's sweet and honorable to die for one's country (Horace).*

ponit, non potest eam non timere.[23] And I don't fear death, and if I have to choose, I'm inclined to an honorable death rather than an unworthy life."

"To die for a Rome that has forsaken us?!" exclaimed a senator with a cynical smile.

"Flacus Mutius has defined Rome as a mother who has abandoned her children," the magistrate continued, raising his arms in order to appease spirits. "Our mother has abandoned us; our distinguished *curator* has assured us." Silence dominated the room again. "And, I wonder, *clarissimi* senators of Carthago Nova, I wonder if it is natural for a mother to neglect her children." He looked at the *decurions* and asked them: "What is it that leads a mother to neglect her offspring? Is there anything she loves more than her children? Wouldn't she give her own life to defend that of her descendants? So... why has Rome, our mother, abandoned us?" The senators looked down at the pavement or glanced at each other with no response. "I'll tell you, I'll open your cowering minds infected by the fearful words of the curator: Rome, our beloved Rome, is ill, seriously ill. This is the only way to explain the abandonment to which she has relegated us. And what should we do? What does the son do when his mother lies dying in bed? Flacus Mutius, our pragmatic curator, suggests that we abandon her, that we let her die consumed by illness and oblivion. On the other hand, I propose that we take care of her, fight for her and, when the time comes, we die for her. Yes, we are children of Rome, and it's our obligation to take care of her, since the *Urbs* took care of us while it had vigor and strength. Surrender means giving our mother to the barbarians, to sacrifice her in exchange for our mean lives. And I refuse, I must refuse. I can't live, if it can be called life, to live in chains, to live at the cost of denying my own mother. I beg this illustrious Senate that we fight, that we passionately defend our lifeless Rome, and if we are defeated, if the Grim Reaper reclaims our souls, that it be admired, when they find us with a blood-stained chest, with our *spathe* in hand and with our face showing a gesture of pride and confidence, since we'll have sacrificed our lives with dignity and honor. I trust that the panic that poisons your hearts won't drag you to commit the most despicable of crimes: abandoning a dying Rome that needs, more than ever, our help. Don't

---

[23] *Whoever considers death as a misfortune cannot but fear it (Latin Grammar by Santiago Segura Munguía).*

be afraid to face the Grim Reaper, *clarissimi* senators of Carthago Nova, since disgrace is the most heinous of deaths."

With his eyes veiled, the magistrate took a seat in his seat, concluding his speech. The Senate was plunged into a soft, tremulous whisper. Flavius Portus' words had pierced the wall of fear behind which many of those senators had hidden, now torn between reason and feelings.

"Well, *clarissimi* senators of Carthago Nova," I started to say after a few minutes. "Both the curator Flacus Mutius and the magistrate Flavius Protus have vehemently and clearly stated their positions regarding the surrender offer proposed by the Vandal King Genseric. Flacus Mutius has vigorously defended the stance of surrender" I said, diverting my gaze to the *curator*. "reasoning in its favor with solid arguments. Flavius Protus, on the other hand," I added, looking at the magistrate. "has insisted that we must fight the enemy, manifesting an unwavering loyalty to Rome and the Empire, offering his life to remain faithful to his ideals. Now, the time has come for this Senate, in representation of the city, to decide on one or the other dilemma."

I looked at those senators with the purpose of scrutinizing in their eyes which way they would lean their choice, and in their eyes, in addition to doubt, I read a deep fear. But there were also those who exhibited a cold and determined look. Possibly they were persuaded that there was no life outside of Rome. Either way, the Senate was very divided and it was impossible to discern what would be the final decision.

"*Clarissimi,* let's vote. Please raise your hand the senators who are in favor of the surrender of the city…"

And the senators voted, elected and decided that we should accept Genseric's surrender conditions. It was discouraging. The vast majority raised their trembling hands driven by fear and cowardice. The *Vandalorum rex* had defeated us without fighting. Flavius Protus and several curials looked away to the pavement, shaking their heads sadly. The rest, those who voted in favor, remained in eloquent silence, unwilling to celebrate their victory, as there was nothing to celebrate. Then I remembered my conversation with Calerus. At that moment I needed his advice, his help and, perhaps, his support, a support that he denied me. And there, in his church, I made a decision, and it was time to reveal it at Carthago Nova's *ordo decuriorum.*

"We senators have decided: Carthago Nova will open its gates to the Vandal's hosts," I proclaimed. "The majority of you, *clarissimi* curials, have so resolved. I have nothing to say, the votes of the Senate must be respected and so it shall be. But..." I got up from my seat and walked towards the center of the room. The decurions were looking at me attentively. "but there is another option."

"What do you mean?" asked one of the curials who voted in favor of surrender.

For a few moments I walked around the room with my eyes absorbed in the pavement, increasing the expectation of the senators.

"It won't depend on us; it's true, but on the Vandal's generosity," I answered at last, looking with narrowed eyes at the curator. "I, in the same way than some of those present here..." I said, turning my gaze to Flavius Protus. "refuse to kneel at the invader."

"But so it has been decided in...!" exclaimed an elderly curial, known for his manifest inability to show the slightest hint of courage and valor.

"And so it shall be, as I said before." I interrupted serenely, raising my hand. "The gates of the city will be opened to the Vandals. Moreover, you have my most sincere blessings if you also wish to open the doors of your houses to them and lead them to the bedchambers of your daughters. Anything to save your own vile skin." The curials looked down in shame, unable to reply to my merciless insult. But I insist: there is another option."

"Then expose it!" exclaimed a *decurion* who had voted in favor of fighting. "There is still a handful of curials in this Senate who yearn to remain loyal to the Empire, whatever the sacrifice."

I nodded and unveiled my determination without further ado:

"If this Senate approves it, and I understand that it must be so, I'll go to the Vandal camp and ask King Genseric for his consent, so that all of us, who don't wish to be chained and subjugated by the invader, may leave the city unscathed. This is my proposal: those Carthaginians, who wish to surrender, let them do so, and those others who wish to leave, let them do so freely."

"It seems fair to me," the *decurion* agreed with a nod.

"But it must be Genseric who finally accepts your proposal and not this Senate," Flacus Mutius interjected.

"True," I admitted "For that reason I'll meet with Genseric, and afterwards, I'll duly inform the *ordo decuriorum*."

"I'll accompany you," the *curator* offered. "I want to be present at the negotiations."

I smiled bitterly at the unfathomable distrust that reverberated in his eyes and said:

"So be it. And if the curials think it wise, Flavius Protus and Lucius Calerus will also accompany me on the embassy." I turned my gaze on the curial, who accepted my suggestion without hindrance, and added: "Tomorrow we'll leave for the Vandal camp, and afterwards I'll duly inform the Senate of the arrangements agreed upon." The session was concluded.

Genseric's troops were half a day from Carthago Nova, and I went to meet them escorted by half a dozen *milites*, and accompanied by Flavius Protus as representative of the senators who decided to remain faithful to Rome, Flacus Mutius as delegate of those who were in favor of surrender, and Lucius Calerus as defender of the Catholic faith.

The spectacle was imposing. The Vandals appeared in front of us encamped in an immense esplanade. Tens of thousands of soldiers and horsemen, perfectly organized, equipped and trained along the lines of the Roman legions, were dismantling their tents and preparing to march. Flacus Mutius looked at me with a serious look on his face and tight lips. We stopped a few dozen paces from the camp and a Vandal patrol came to meet us.

"Who are you?" the barbarian officer asked, drawing his sword.

"I'm Salvio Adriano, *civitatis comes* of Carthago Nova, and I'm accompanied by the curials Flacus Mutius and Flavius Protus, and by the monk Lucius Calerus. We want to talk with King Genseric."

The Vandal looked at us with superiority and with a disdainful gesture, indicated us to accompany him.

Genseric's tent was guarded by half a dozen soldiers. The horseman who escorted us dismounted and addressed the officer of the guard. After informing him who we were, the officer entered the tent to inform the king. He came out after a few minutes and beckoned to us. We dismounted and entered the tent escorted by the royal guard. Genseric was seated on a footstool guarded by two burly soldiers. We were truly in awe of the exceptional presence of the *Vandalorum rex* who, at eighty years of age, maintained an enviable physical shape and an indestructible glow in his eyes.

"I greet you, Salvio Adriano. I see with pleasure that our paths meet again." said Genseric with a smile, recognizing me immediately.

"I salute you, Genseric, *Vandalorum rex*. The designs of the good Lord are inscrutables." I began to say with a slight bow. "Allow me to introduce you to the curials Flavius Protus y Flacus Mutius, and to the monk Lucius Calerus." The Vandal king nodded and my companions did the same. "I'm sorry that your candidate Olybrius wasn't the one chosen to wear the purple. I'm convinced that if it had been, we wouldn't find ourselves in this awkward situation," I said, nodding.

A half-smile spread on the king's lips, after almost five years, he hadn't forgotten the stratagem I used to free the city from its siege.

"I'm not quite sure «uncomfortable» is the right word" he muttered dismissively. "However, now the situation is similar to that of then. My hosts will soon besiege you, and this time there will be no ruse you can cling to, to avoid the inevitable. Fate has insisted that Carthago Nova be subdued by my troops and, against fate, nothing can be done except bow."

"The news of your victories precedes you and with them, your generous indulgence with the subjugated cities," Flacus Mutius intervened, slavishly humiliating the head.

I shot him a murderous look and the curator slowed his pace and returned to Flavius Protus and Calerus.

"What is it that you have come to offer me?" asked the king.

"The surrender of the city, as you demanded in your letter," I replied.

"Well, such surrender will be accepted as long as you deny the Greek emperor and agree to be subjects of a… barbarian."

Flacus Mutius couldn't suppress his smile. His skin was safe.

"Not all of us are willing to kiss your hand," I replied, at Genseric's disgruntled gaze. "But we don't want the city to be punished because any of us wish to remain faithful to Rome."

"What do you propose, then?"

I looked at Flavius Protus and he nodded.

"Those of us who are unwilling to accept the barbarian yoke, will leave the city and march north."

"Do you swear never to return?" Genseric asked, interested.

"Not while Carthago Nova is under Vandal rule," I replied.

"All right," he agreed. "I'll allow you to leave the city when my armies reach the walls. Leave if you wish, but each family will only take with it the belongings that it can carry on a team of oxen. Your furniture and belongings will be sold to pay for my soldiers. I'm sure that more than one neighbor of yours will be happy to get them for a low price. This includes cattle and slaves of course, who obviously stay."

I nodded, accepting his demand and said:

"There is something else."

"What is it?"

I gestured for Calerus to come closer to me.

"You Vandals are Arians, and as you well know, in Carthago Nova they profess Catholicism," the monk intervened. "I beg the noble Genseric, *Vandalorum rex,* to respect our beliefs and not force our citizens to fall into apostasy."

"I was wondering what a monk was doing accompanying the great men of the city." He said, rising from the footstool. "Now I understand why."

The Vandal king began pacing the store with his hands clasped behind his back.

"Until now, we Vandals were considered by the Romans little more than pirates. We plundered cities, returning to a safe harbor to enjoy our riches, leaving destroyed cities, raped women, and murdered men in our wake. But I have ambitious plans for my kingdom. Rome is sinking and it is our chance to be great, powerful and... feared. The Roman emperors have underestimated us, for them, we are nothing more than a minor kingdom. But things have changed; we'll take away the Roman cities of southern Hispania, but not leaving a trail of destruction in our wake, or by burning the fields, looting cities and killing peasants. If I want to build a prosperous kingdom, a formidable empire, I have to surrender the cities without causing their destruction. They must swear allegiance to me and increase my troops with their *bucelarii.* Moreover, they must pay taxes to me instead of to the emperor and grow and prosper. I want a rich and powerful kingdom, and destroying walls and burning villages is impossible to achieve."

We watched him closely. Genseric wanted his kingdom to rival that of the Visigoths, Franks, Ostrogoths, or Burgundians. All of them barbarian kingdoms that would fight to take the place of Rome once it was annihilated. The Vandal king, like the rest of the barbarian kings, considered the Empire extinct and that its collapse was a matter of time. The Vandal would dispute his piece of cake.

"I'll respect your beliefs," he stared at Calerus, stopping his walk. "I'll respect your lives and let go of all those who don't wish to obey me. This is what you wanted, isn't it?"

"Yes, *domine.*"

"Well, there you have it; tomorrow I'll arrive in Carthago Nova. When my troops are in front of your walls, those of you who wish so could leave. The rest will live in peace. You may go."

We left the Vandal camp escorted by the royal guard until they allowed us to continue on our way alone, once we were at a prudent distance. Flavius Protus and Calerus were worried, their lips were pursed and their foreheads furrowed with wrinkles. On the way, they hardly opened their mouths. Flacus Mutius on the other hand, was very satisfied with the outcome of the meeting and couldn't suppress the triumphant smile that appeared on his lips. We were near the city walls when Calerus, riding his mule, approached me.

"Adriano, I have to talk to you."

"Tell me."

For a few moments he hesitated, what he had to say was very hard for him.

"I won't leave the city," he said at last.

"I understand."

"I have built a beautiful church and it's my obligation to remain with my parishioners in these difficult times. Genseric has committed to respecting our beliefs and I must take care that this is the case."

"You don't have to explain yourself to me," I recited, not hiding my disappointment.

"Adriano!" he exclaimed, stopping his mount. I looked at him and approached with my horse.

Flavius Protus and Flacus Mutius continued on their way leaving us alone.

"We've always been together, but the time has come for our paths to part. You must understand that wearing the habit of a monk is more than just saying mass every day. I respect your decision to leave the city, now you must respect mine to protect my parishioners."

"You will no longer be a Roman."

"I'm a Catholic monk. Being Roman, Visigoth, Vandal or Frank doesn't matter if Jesus Christ is by my side."

Calerus had made an irrevocable decision and I had no choice but to accept it. I remembered the friends I had lost along the way, and my heart shrank at the thought that now I would lose one more. I nodded sadly, and we continued in silence on the road that led to Carthago Nova. My eyes were blurred with tears.

"*Domine,* are you all right?"

The boy's question brought me back to reality, fading my memories.

"*Domine?*"

Around the campfire, the runaways watched me with interest. Valeria tenderly touched my hair, while the little ones slept peacefully in the wagon. The flames crackled, breaking the deep silence. The boy looked at me with a sorrowful expression; his young spirit was overwhelmed by the uncertain future that awaited him.

"We have embarked on an exodus with a confused horizon. I don't know the situation of the cities we'll pass through and, above all, that of Tarraco, our objective." I began to say sincerely, looking into the eyes of those present. "But we have made a decision; to continue being Hispano-Romans and die as such. Possibly the most comfortable decision would have been to kiss the Vandal's hand and accept to be his servants, but those of us who are here today, those who have been forced to leave the city we love so much together with our loved ones, think that another world is possible and that Rome, in spite of all adversities, will survive."

I raised my voice and the people who were at other bonfires approached us.

"I promise you that I'll lead you safely to Tarraco.

"And once there, what will happen?" Helvius, the baker, asked. He was with us along with his sister, his wife and his son, who was only a few months old. "You said yourself that you know nothing about Tarraco. It's possible that by now the city has been destroyed by the Visigoths or other barbarians. What shall we do then? Where shall we go?"

"I share your fear; I'm also traveling with my family," I said, gesturing to Valeria and the children, who were in the wagon. "Our decision wasn't easy and all of you who are here have come voluntarily."

"Don't misunderstand me; I'd rather be with you under the shelter of this bonfire, than in Carthago Nova humiliated in front of a barbarian," the baker interrupted me.

"We'll reach Tarraco and if its Senate is willing to defend the city, we'll defend it."

"And what if it is against it?" another neighbor asked.

"I'll leave with my family in search of a place to settle down, far away from wars and deaths," I answered.

The conversation became animated and a soft whisper, full of hope and renewed illusion, flooded the black night. Finally, and by the fire, we, the diaspora companions, gathered together.

"Where is that place?" Fraucus, a mason with a wiry face who had helped in the reconstruction of the wall, asked.

There was a sudden silence, no one knew the answer.

"I would march west," Flavius Protus put in, throwing a twig into the fire. "To the highlands of Gallaecia. The Visigoths hate those cold, poor lands, and the Suevians are quite busy feeding their families, as to worry about a handful of exiles. Life there will be hard, but we would only have to worry about feeding our children or grandchildren, and not about listening to the sound of war tubas."

Many looked at him and nodded. A rumor of agreement and approval spread among those present. Gallaecia didn't seem to interest the Vandals, since it was too far north, nor the Visigoths, since it was a territory crowned by steep mountains and deep valleys. Those were barren and greedy lands that demanded a high price in sweat and blood in exchange for the meager fruits they offered. The Suevians, after being massacred by Theodoric fifteen years ago, would welcome a group of healthy and strong Romans who are ready to repopulate and cultivate their rugged region.

"We'll go to Tarraco and I hope we can live there in peace," I said. "But Flavius Protus' suggestion is not at all contemptible."

We were still sheltered for a few hours of darkness and the men and women retired to their beds amid murmurs and words of encouragement. I said goodbye to my bonfire companions and went to rest accompanied by Valeria. Due to the emotions of the last hours, we were exhausted and we urgently needed to rest. A long journey awaited us.

We continued our march following the Via Augusta. Along the way, dozens of peasants who fled terrified from the barbarians joined our caravan. So, we crossed the town of Lucentum, where we got some supplies. The magistrate of the city was called Verinus Quintus. He was a young man in his early twenties with an intelligent look and affable expression. He belonged to a wealthy family of merchants and landowners. As I later knew, his father died fighting the pirates who looted the coastal villages of Levant with impunity. He welcomed us with open arms and helped us in everything we needed, but he didn't follow us. He possessed immense properties and had no intention of parting with them. He didn't confirm it, but in his eyes I warned that he would kiss the hand of any barbarian king who guaranteed and protected his heritage. The same thing happened in Dianium and Valentia. Their *limes* were still far from the barbarian presence, so they felt protected. But in the eyes of their committees and their curials, I read that when the moment came, they would make the same decision as Verinus Quintus.

We were heading to Saguntum and, the black clouds that had accompanied us since dawn, had decided that it was time to unload all their content on our tired bodies. We protected ourselves from the incessant rain on the side of a butte. We set up the tents and I decided we should rest. The march was over for that day. I built a fire and we heated up some fish that the inhabitants of Valentia had kindly provided us. Valeria was lying in the cart, she had been coughing for two days; she had a fever and was exhausted. I put some stones to heat on the fire, then I wrapped them in some cloth and put them near the bed. Although it was not overly cold, she was completely freezing and shivering in freezing spasms. I was grateful that the children, during her illness, were in the care of Flavina Aelia, Flavius Protus' eldest daughter. I left her asleep and went over to the fire. My friend Arcadius was there, roasting a freshly caught rabbit.

"How are you feeling?" he asked, handing me a piece of meat.

"She's still the same as two days ago," I answered, saddened. "If only there was at least a physician among us…"

"Soon we'll get to Saguntum, you'll find one there."

"I hope so."

"Will you visit your father?"

Since we left Valentia I had asked myself that question on countless occasions. I still remembered the painful scene he had played with an old prostitute, who was also his wife, for a handful of coins. I was grateful that that day it had been Calerus who had accompanied me and not Arcadius, otherwise, the embarrassment would have been overwhelming.

"I don't know," I answered, throwing a rabbit bone into the fire.

"I'm not one to give advice to anyone, but I think you should go see him. He is your father, after all."

A loud cough distracted me. I got up distressed and went to the car, where Valeria was coughing uncontrollably. I stroked her hair and whispered in her ear to calm her down. After several minutes, she stopped coughing and got slept again. I moved my face closer to kiss her and noticed a stain on the blanket that covered her. My heart fluttered in my chest full of worry when I realized that the dark, wet stain was blood.

I arrived in Saguntum in the hope of finding a good physician to relieve her of the ailments that were tormenting her. During the last few days she had not improved from her illness, but on the contrary, she was in worse and worse condition. In the mornings she woke up in cold sweats, coughed blood assiduously and had lost a lot of weight. I asked Flavius Protus to speak with the civitatis comes of the city, while I looked for a doctor accompanied by Arcadius.

The city was still in the same decadent state in which I found it nine years ago. At least it had not worsened. When looking for the physician, I arrived at the door of what had been my childhood home. I stopped in front of the house, which from its neglected appearance seemed abandoned. The door was locked with a rusty chain and the floor was littered with leaves and dirt. The little lime that once covered the walls had disappeared, exposing small ashlars of mud worn by the action of the rains and wind. I approached an old woman who remained attentive to our movements and asked her about the owner of the house.

"Who is asking?" she asked suspiciously, before answering.

"I'm his son," I answered.

The woman frowned as if she doubted that a man dressed in the war uniform of a *civitatis comes*, could be the son of the pariah who lived in that house.

"He died two years ago."

I wasn't surprised by the answer, nor did I feel any regret for the death of my father. In fact, after so many years, I expected it.

"And what about the woman who lived with him?" I asked, more out of curiosity than out of any real interest in the old whore's welfare.

"She died before him."

"Where is he buried?"

The woman shrugged her shoulders.

"He was poor. I suppose his bones are now resting in some mass grave in the cemetery."

"Thank you for the information. May God protect you."

I said goodbye to the old woman and directed my steps towards the real reason for my return to Saguntum. It did not take me long to locate the house where one of the few doctors who still worked in the city lived. I knocked on the door and it was opened by an older, bald man with bushy gray sideburns and a pungent odor of rancid wine.

"What do you want?" he asked me with acrimony. The sight of a military uniform did not impress him in the least.

"My wife is sick and needs a doctor."

He looked me up and down reluctantly; the physician had no interest in leaving the house. Surely we had interrupted him while he was gulping down a delectable jug of wine.

"What symptoms does she have?" he asked.

"She has a bad cough, cold sweats and has hardly eaten anything for the last few days."

"Is she spitting up blood?"

"Yes."

"She's got consumption, so consider her dead." he said, closing the door.

Arcadius kicked the door hard, shattering it into a thousand pieces. The physician watched, with his eyes arched in dread, as the wrathful legionary entered the house, grabbed him from behind and, with a shove, pulled him out into the street.

"You'll come with me and see my wife! Take everything you need and don't tempt your luck anymore!" I said, lifting him up by the collar.

"All right... all right." he mumbled, once released from my grip, dusting off his pants. Wait a moment while I get my saddlebag.

We took the lazy and drunk physician to the camp almost on the fly. When we arrived, Valeria was prostrate on the pallet. The doctor, somewhat more clear from his drunkenness, got into the wagon and found her in a sleepless night caused by fever. He opened her eyelids and checked her pulse and temperature. Then he took a handkerchief from Valeria's hand and studied her spit. He got out of the wagon shaking his head.

"What I was afraid of."

"The consumption?" I asked alarmed.

He nodded his head.

"As I have told you before, she is already dead. And it wasn't necessary that you had dragged me here, disturbing my rest, or that you had smashed the door of my house to confirm my suspicions." he protested.

"Is there no hope? Are there no medicines or some treatment...?"

"She is in her final stage," he interrupted. "It's only a matter of hours, days, or at the most weeks for her to die. Now, I want my money."

The despicable doctor stretched out his bony hand demanding payment for his services. Red with rage, I was tempted to vent all my rage on that lean and disgusting doctor, but Arcadius approached him and threw several coins, ordering him to leave as soon as possible. The old man tried to protest by demanding a higher payment for the shattered door, but my friend shot him a murderous look and muttering curses, he returned to Saguntum.

I got in the wagon and saw that Valeria was sleeping. Her beautiful face bore the dark marks of the disease that mercilessly consumed her. Her eyes were sunken into prominent, haggard cheekbones, her skin hung from her bones, and she was terribly frail and weak. I kissed her tenderly on the forehead and got out of the wagon with my eyes veiled by her tears.

Unable to bear it any longer, I cried long and softly begging for Valeria's life. My friend Arcadius hugged me and we both plunged into a deep, heartbroken cry. My wife, my sweet and loving wife, was dying of a relentless disease. The cry turned into a shout of pain and despair. Hugging my friend, I cried bitterly until my eyes went dry. I felt how my withered heart was eaten away by regret and anguish. The elusive and capricious luck showed me with merciless glee the most cruel and ruthless side of her.

We left Saguntum the next day, leaving its despicable physician in it. Arcadius pulled the reins of our chariot while I watched day and night for Valeria. Flavina Aelia had kindly offered to take care of the children for as long as it was necessary. I watched her play with Salvio Alexandros and feed Annia; it was evident that she had become very fond of them. God hadn't blessed her marriage with children and both she and her husband Velius enjoyed their presence and cared for them as if they were their own.

We marched towards the city of Dertosa, the last great city that we would find on our way before reaching Tarraco. The further north we went, the cooler the days and the more intense the rains. Our step was slow, tiring and sad, tremendously sad.

It was beginning to dusk and we camped near a small stream with crystal clear waters. The men set up camp, while the women went to the stream for water for dinner. Valeria was sleeping. She remained in a candle sleeper most of the time, from which she rarely woke up. Her fever was punishing her soul, causing her nightmares and delusions. I wiped her sweat and after wetting her lips with a little water, I got out of the wagon and asked Arcadius to watch over her. I grabbed my quiver and my bow, and headed towards a nearby forest. There were still a few hours until the sun set over the horizon and I needed to distract my mind and loosen my seized muscles. I walked along a small path of weeds crushed by the action of wild boars and rabbits. The forest was very lush and shrouded in shade, since the tops of the tall oaks and ash trees blocked the passage of light. Although I tried, I couldn't get out of my mind the image of Valeria devoured by her fierce illness, and inconsolable tears ran down my face. Then, I remembered Salvio Alexandros's death. On that occasion he would have died had it not been for the miraculous intervention of the druid. I stopped and threw my bow and quiver to the ground. It was my last hope.

"Lughdyr!" I called him with all my might, in a heart-rending cry of pleading and anguish.

A flock of birds, frightened by the unexpected cry, burst into the skies.

"Lughdyr!" I shouted again, clenching my fists. "Lughdyr!"

For several minutes I screamed the druid's name until, tired and voiceless, I fell defeated on the ground wrapped in a sea of tears.

"Lughdyr, please, she needs you." I whispered, kneeling on the cold leaf litter.

The squawk of a bird woke me. Exhausted in my despair, I must have fallen fast asleep. I opened my eyes and found myself enveloped in a milky mist. I picked up my bow and quiver and sat up. I heard another loud squawk and a crow, black as night, crossed in front of me and perched on a branch. The bird looked at me defiantly and squawked again.

"Lughdyr?" I asked in a whisper.

Out of the mist emerged the old man's white figure. Leaning on his everlasting staff, he approached with a sorrowful face.

"Hello, my friend Adriano," he greeted me with a sad smile.

"She is dying," I said with my voice cracking.

"I know."

"I need you to help her," I begged.

"There's nothing I can do for her." he said, shaking his head. "Nature is claiming her and must come to her call."

"You saved her one day!"

"Her time hadn't come on that occasion."

Shattered and hopeless, I fell to my knees on the ground and burst into tears. I felt my soul slipping away and my heart breaking into a thousand pieces, oppressed by an abysmal anguish.

"Go back with her," the druid whispered. "She'll leave this world soon and you must stay by her side."

I wiped away my tears and looked at the druid.

"Go with her," he insisted, touching my shoulder.

In a dejected mood and helped by the old man, I stood up and nodded.

"How are Alana and Adriano?" I asked.

The druid smiled gently.

"They are fine, you don't need to worry. Now go with Valeria. Soon, very soon everything will come to an end."

"What do you mean?"

The crow cawed and got lost in the fog, accompanying its master, who disappeared without answering my question.

I ran back to the camp with the fear that it was too late. Panting, I reached the wagon and saw that Valeria was awake. A fragile smile came from her lips and she held out her hand to me.

"Where have you been?" she asked me, faintly.

"In the forest, hunting."

"You've been with him, haven't you?"

I ducked my head, not knowing what to answer.

"Bring me the children, I want to say goodbye to them."

Without being able to utter a word, I went to the fire where Flavius Protus and his family were warming their exhausted bodies. Salvio Alexandros and Annia were with Flavina Aelia and Velius.

"Children, come with me, mom wants to talk to you."

The little ones, as if they sensed the tragic misfortune that was about to happen, accompanied me docilely, plunged in a deep silence. Flavius Protus looked at me and I shook my head. Flavina Aelia hid her face in her hands and Velius consoled her with an embrace. The light of the bonfire betrayed the emotion in his eyes.

I went to the carriage accompanied by my children. Arcadius was next to it, dressed in military uniform. With the helmet covering his head, the coat of mail well burnished and vigorously holding the *spiculum*, he watched over the funeral of a queen or a mythological goddess like an ancient hero. We climbed into the carriage and the children saw their mother. No longer holding back their tears, they threw themselves on her chest in a tight embrace and wept bitterly, while calling her "mommy, mommy..." Valeria smiled and kissed them, still hugging and caressing them.

"I love you, my children, I love you..." she said in a whisper, wrapping them in her wiry arms. The Grim Reaper was snatching her soul, but she resisted with unusual determination. Before leaving, she needed to feel the warm embrace of our children, appreciate their sweet smell, listen to their soft voice, be filled with their infinite love. All of them would be happy memories that would accompany her in her last transit. The black death would have to wait a few moments before claiming its trophy.

But she was exhausted, faint, defeated. She looked at me and in her eyes I read that she had to separate the little ones from her lap. A child's eyes must be prevented from contemplating such cruel and sad farewells.

"Children, mom needs to rest. Kiss her good night."

"I don't want to!" the little girl protested.

"I want to stay with mommy." replied Salvio Alexandros.

It wasn't easy to separate the little ones from their mother. I gave them to Arcadius, who held them in his strong arms. They were submerged in a sea of tears and kept weeping quietly on his armor, seeking shelter and comfort in the lap of the great warrior. With misty eyes, I climbed into the chariot and found Valeria's bitter smile.

"I have loved you even before I met you," she whispered to me.

I approached her and kissed her feverish lips.

"I have met Alana and... your son, Adriano, in my dreams," she continued. "I have talked to them and I have recognized in their eyes the same love that our sons have for each other," she said.

"Say nothing, rest..."

"Alana loves you and she'll watch over you when the time comes."

"Please…"

She cut me off with a wave of her hand.

"I have also spoken to the druid. I saw him today, a few hours ago... He told me that I shouldn't be afraid... death is the force that frees us from the chains that bind us to this world, allowing our soul to travel free and merge with Nature. Death is not the end... but the beginning."

"Dear…"

"Please, when I die, I want to be cremated. Don't bury me in an unknown graveyard. My ashes will be scattered by the wind and my soul will fly free like sparrows in spring."

"Don't think about that."

"I must and you know it." She smiled at me and caressed my face gently.

She spoke barely in a whisper, her voice faded, choked with disease, and every phrase, every word was uttered with colossal effort. Her eyes were losing the luster of life.

"I love you, my life," I whispered in her ear.

A placid smile appeared on her lips and her gaze revealed that she no longer suffered.

"Don't go, don't go," I begged her with a hug.

"I love you."

I felt her chest stop. She was no longer breathing. Her eyes closed and her face reflected the peace of someone who has freed her soul, abandoning all suffering. I kissed her on her lips and cried on her chest. Valeria, my life, my love, she had died.

I got out of the wagon and hugged my children. Broken by the pain, we remained embraced until, exhausted by crying and exhaustion, they fell asleep in my arms.

I watched over her and did not leave her side for an instant until the funeral pyre was prepared the next day. The sun was beginning to set behind the oaks when Valeria was meekly lying on the pyre. She was dressed in a beautiful white linen robe. Her death had restored all the beauty that the disease had tried to take from her. Everyone was watching the pyre with excited eyes. In the shadows of the forest, I seemed to discern the figure of the druid Lughdyr. Arcadius clenched his jaws trying to hold back the tears that struggled to flow, Flavius Protus watched me with his face disfigured by pain, while Flavina Aelia took care of the children away from that sea of tears and suffering. Unable to bear the emotion anymore, I kissed her lips.

"I love you my love and I will always love you," I whispered.

I raised the torch and lit the litter that covered the pyre. In an instant, a gentle wind fanned the fire, enveloping Valeria in its sacred mantle.

"Fly free, my love." I said, while the flames rose mightily in the sky, "soon our souls will unite and we'll never part."

I watched over her until the flames were consumed. The first light of dawn illuminated the remains of the pyre. I was still vigilant. My eyes were dry and unable to shed any more tears.

"Adriano, we must go," said a voice behind me.

I turned to find Arcadius' weary face and sunken eyes. I approached the pyre, knelt down, and said one last prayer for Valeria. I took a deep breath and with a broken soul, I accompanied my friend.

My discouragement must have spread to the rest of the members of the diaspora, since for days hardly anyone opened their mouths. We wandered like ghosts following the road without looking back, but with little hope of what we would find ahead. I treated Salvio Alexandros and Annia as best I could, but it was Flavina Aelia who finally took care of them. I was immersed in a deep nostalgia and not even the children were able to cheer up my downcast spirits. Flavius Protus informed me of the news that got to the caravan, as well as about the refugees' morale, who were increasingly pessimistic and dejected. I remember how the old man spoke to me while he warmed my chilled body in the fire of a bonfire. I barely listened to him, discouragement had taken hold of me and nothing mattered to me anymore.

"Adriano, the news that comes to us from nearby towns is quite disturbing," I remember him telling me during a frigid night.

"These are bad times," I said.

"The Hispanic nobles are swearing eternal fidelity to the Visigoth king, and many of us wonder if it makes sense to continue with the march."

"Well, they can go back to Carthago Nova; I never forced them to come with me."

The night was cold and the fires multiplied on the side of the road. A deep silence enveloped us, only broken by the cry of a child and the occasional cough. I was heating a piece of meat on the fire, next to me sat my faithful friend Arcadius and opposite, a disheartened Flavius Protus. The children, as usual, met Flavina Aelia.

"Don't be unfair to them, Adriano, they don't deserve it," the magistrate grumbled.

I shrugged my shoulders indifferently. Valeria had died and with her my soul. The future of the caravan, of Hispania, of the Empire was unimportant to me.

"Adriano, your children need you, we need you, come to your senses or you'll find your own ruin," he insisted.

"During my life I have done nothing but lose loved ones. I'm tired and I want all this to end at once. There is no point in dragging out this horrible agony any longer. Nothing is worth it."

"Not even your children?" a female voice asked behind me.

I turned and saw Flavina Aelia. The magistrate's daughter was flanked by the children, who were sadly holding her hand.

"Don't be selfish Adriano, they have lost their mother, don't make them lose their father too." she concluded, and gently pushed the children to come closer to me.

My children ran and hugged me tightly. Then I realized how stupid and mean I had been. I felt the warmth of the little ones and squeezed them in my lap. Flavina Aelia looked at me with moist eyes. The magistrate's daughter was right, overwhelmed by grief, I had forgotten my own children, ignoring their suffering. No, they weren't guilty of their mother's death, and they had already suffered enough with her loss, as to lose also the affection and the love of their father.

"Forgive me, my children, I'll never abandon you again," I promised them, with my cheeks wet with tears, fused in an eternal embrace.

The children smiled while the tears ran down their soft cheeks. Flavius Protus nodded with emotion and Arcadius touched my shoulder before disappearing into the darkness. He was a warrior not very used to showing certain emotions in public. I took a deep breath and exhaled sharply, trying to rid my soul of all the anguish and pain that afflicted me.

The next day we awoke with the sound of the thunder. The morning had just peeked over the horizon and black clouds threatened to unload all their contents on us. The darkness was almost total and we decided that it would be best to wait for it to clear. And we did well, because in a few minutes it began to rain heavily and the lightning and thunder followed one after the other with extreme speed, scaring not only beasts and children, but also more than one seasoned soldier. The Via Augusta followed the path of a small stream that flowed a few miles further on into the Iber River. Due to the force of the rain, the stream became a torrent, carrying logs, stones and everything in its path. Some horses, terrified by the sound of thunder and the swelling of the stream, broke loose from their reins and rode wildly, getting lost in the thicket of a nearby forest. I protected the children in the wagon and covered them with a blanket, then harnessed the oxen and whipped them to reach a nearby hillock. But the wheels got stuck in the mud and the oxen pulled with difficulty the cart, which moved at an excessively slow pace. The rain did not stop, and a sea of water fell on us, preventing us from seeing more than a few steps. In desperation, I took the children in my arms and we climbed the small hill. Some followed me and were able to get to safety. I left the children in the care of Helvius' wife and returned to the camp.

"Adriano, come this way!" shouted Arcadius.

With some difficulty, I noticed that my friend was making hand gestures to get my attention. I walked towards him and found him lifting, with strenuous efforts, the wheel of a cart. The stream had overflowed and the water was up to my ankles, but as I descended the hill and approached the camp, I saw that the situation there was even worse.

"He was trapped by the wagon," Arcadius said, lifting the wheel.

The face of a child was peeking out from under the wagon and was submerged in the murky waters of the overflowing stream. The water was already up to our knees.

"Terrified by the thunder, he hid under the wagon, but the flood of the stream surprised him, and a movement of the wheel imprisoned him. If we don't free him soon, he'll die drowned," Arcadius explained to me, while we tried to lift the wagon that had been obstructed by the mud and the stones dragged by the stream.

The boy's head appeared and disappeared, sinking into the water, and the level of the stream kept rising. I dived under the water to try to free him. Feeling with my hands, I found that the wheel had imprisoned the little boy's ankle and that a large part of it was sunk in the mud, making it impossible to lift it.

"It's going to be impossible to lift the wheel; it's sunk under the mud!" I shouted, trying to make myself heard in the midst of the gale.

"What can we do?"

The water level was rising and the current was getting stronger and stronger. The boy could barely stick his head out and raised his arms in anguish. We had to find a solution as soon as possible. I looked around for something to help us and on a wagon, I saw a shovel. I picked it up and dived back into the water. The mud, thanks to the force of the current, had softened which facilitated my purpose. It was risky and there was a possibility of severing the boy's ankle, but there was no other option. I put the paddle next to the wheel, and taking advantage of the current, I pushed the paddle enough to move it over his ankle to free it. At first the wheel didn't move. I surfaced to get some air and squeezed with all my strength on the paddle until I felt the wheel move slightly, but enough for the boy to free his leg. I held on to him tightly and we surfaced.

"He's alive!"

Arcadius shouted as soon as he saw us emerge from the murky water. He was holding the child in his arms, who was coughing up the water he had swallowed.

"What about the ankle?" I asked him anxiously, fearing that it was broken.

"It's swollen and sore, but it doesn't seem to be broken," he replied, touching the little boy's ankle.

I nodded happily, and with the water up to our waists, we reached the shelf where the rest of the refugees were.

"My son!" the boy's mother exclaimed, running towards us with her face broken with worry.

"He's fine," Arcadius soothed her, handing her the boy. "Only his ankle is a little bruised."

"God bless you," the woman thanked him in tears.

Lucretia, since that was her name, climbed the hill with the child in her arms and was attended to, by the women who were there. She was a young and willing woman, who earned her living by helping in the housework of several women of the city, since her husband had died of a long illness a few months before. Lucretia was strong and thanks to her work and effort, she managed to take care of both her son and her sick husband, without having to sell her body in some sordid brothel, as unfortunately was not uncommon. Because of her courage and dignity, she enjoyed all our respect and affection.

Exhausted, Arcadius and I lay down in the mire. The force of the water had subsided, but the deluge persisted. After a few minutes I sat up and saw that our camp was submerged under the water. Most of the wagons, together with our belongings, were sunk in a river of mud and debris. The oxen had fared no better, and many were bloated, dead, still tethered to the wagons, or stranded among the branches and trunks on the bank, swept by the current. The desolation and helplessness were branded on our faces. We had lost everything.

The waters returned to their course, leaving a trail of mud and destruction in their wake. The Via Augusta was hidden under the mud and brush, making our way difficult. Our clothes were wet; we had lost our oxen, our carts and all our belongings. The women sobbed quietly before the terrified gaze of their children, who looked at them wondering what was going to become of them. But there was no time for lamentations, winter was stalking us and we had to cross the river Iber as soon as possible and reach Dertosa. There we would find refuge before reaching our goal: Tarraco. With the children in our arms or on the few horses we managed to save, we resumed our march once the clouds got tired of emptying their contents on us and the sun's rays timidly warmed our soaked bodies.

Fortunately, the Iber, although swollen, wasn't overflowing, and we were able to cross the colossal seven-eyed stone bridge that gave access to the city of Dertosa. Exhausted by the effort, with our clothes in tatters and mud up to our ears, we were pleasantly attended by its citizens, who provided us with warm clothes, food and shelter for the night.

Dertosa was a beautiful city. Although it displayed the typical decadence of the cities of the Empire, it still preserved beautiful stone and marble buildings and a formidable river port, although it was evident that the flow of ships and goods was not what it had been in the past. Its people were pleasant and attentive, and even more so when we revealed our origin and the reason for our departure. Its walls were stout, but the city had practically no army. Only two hundred *bucelarii* guarded its defense.

Nelius Varus was the *civitatis comes*. From an illustrious family, he had extensive military experience and had fought along with Marcellinus a long time ago. He was about sixty years old, but he was a stout man with an angular face and a gray beard. During the days we stayed in Dertosa, I could see that he used to ride for hours, and was a master of the *spathae*. He had been a wealthy landowner and sold his crops to merchants from distant lands. But the commercial decline of the Empire also affected its most illustrious citizens and now, Nelius Varus, had serious problems to feed his own family.

I was in his *domus* along with Arcadius and Flavius Protus. It was dark and Dertosa's *civitatis comes* had invited us to dinner. The house exhibited a bit of its former splendor and was adorned with sumptuous marble sculptures, beautiful stone fountains, and beautiful mosaics depicting all sorts of scenes. But the inexorable passage of time left its mark on the cedar furniture, the couches and part of the pavement. Dinner was arranged in the couch and Arcadius and I took seats on two footstools while he and Flavius Protus did the same on the worn *triclinia*. Nelius Varus gestured to a servant who, shortly, returned to the room carrying a tray with roast pork and vegetables. We spoke at length about Rome, the barbarian advances and the economic and social situation of the Empire.

"There are many *dignitates* and wealthy landowners who are being sold to the barbarians," Flavius Protus said, while he enjoyed a piece of tasty pork. "We hadn't had a good meal in weeks and we were enthusiastically thanking the food that he was giving us."

"They consider the Empire lost and will fight to maintain their possessions and privileges. Poor wretches" Nelius Varus pointed out.

"What do you mean?" I asked.

"The Visigoths have their own nobles, officers, and advisers to satisfy. How do you think Euric will pay for their services?"

We agreed, persuaded of what he meant.

"They may allow them to keep their possessions for a few years, but in the end, they will be taken from them and given to their trusted men," he continued.

"What will you do?" Arcadius asked.

"I'm faithful to Rome and will always be. But Dertosa is a small town, and I only have a handful of *bucelarii* to defend it. I suppose when the moment comes, I'll be forced to do what you did; abandon it and go to Tarraco."

"We are concerned that Tarraco's *civitatis comes* will surrender the city and we will have to leave again," Arcadius said.

Nelius Varus burst out laughing.

"That's because you don't know him!" he exclaimed, still laughing. "Not him, not his curials. They will never surrender the city to the barbarians."

Flavius Protus and I looked down in embarrassment. Although it was so decided by the Senate, the memory of our departure and the humiliating surrender of Carthago Nova to the Vandals embarrassed us. Nelius Varus looked at us and immediately perceived our embarrassment.

"Forgive me if I have offended you, it was by no means my intention."

"Don't worry," I said, raising my hand. "After all, we left the city, leaving it in barbarian hands."

"There was little more you could do. You had the senate against you, if you had tried to defend it, surely some *decurion*, soldier or simple citizen, would have betrayed you. I, in your place, would have done the same. Unfortunately, you had no other choice."

"The curials feared for their families, the defense of the city would have been a sterile sacrifice that would have cost thousands of lives," Flavius Protus argued by way of justification.

A servant entered the room and filled our glasses with wine. The *civitatis comes* got up from his couch and began pacing the *triclinium,* glass in hand.

"That's why I tell you that Tarraco will never surrender; it will have to be conquered by force. The *civitatis comes* is a veteran who has served under the great Aetius. He is faithful to Rome and he would rather die than kiss the hairy hand of a barbarian."

"He must be an exceptional man," I said.

"Indeed, Traustila..."

"Traustila?" Arcadius and I asked in unison.

"Do you know him?"

"Well of course!" Arcadius exclaimed, rising from the footstool. "We fought together against Attila in Maurica…"

"Did you fight in Maurica?" Nelius Varus interrupted admiringly, taking his seat again on the *triclinium*.

"We were just children, recruits full of wishes and hopes." I answered. For a few moments I remembered that moment, that battle, those great men with whom I shared blood and suffering: Optila… Aetius… Distant memories, anchored in the depths of my memory and that now flourished fueled by the name of the city that witnessed of the most formidable and bloody battle history had ever witnessed. "But tell us about Traustila," I commanded him, returning to ruthless reality. "Glad to hear that he's still alive."

"Years haven't been wasted for him. He must be my age, but he is still strong as a bull and skilled in swordsmanship."

Knowing that Traustila was still alive and, furthermore, that he was Tarraco's *civitatis comes,* filled me with joy. Now I was convinced that we would be well received in the city and, above all, that we would die rather than surrender it. I was impatient to resume our march and get to Tarraco as soon as possible; I burned with the desire to see my friend again.

"You have given us excellent news," I told him.

Nelius Varus got up from the *triclinium* and with impatient eyes told us:

"Although Traustila himself has described to me on countless occasions the battle of Maurica, if you want to make this poor old man happy, I ask you, or rather, I beg you, to relate to me, according to your own experience, how the battle of Maurica developed. And please, do not be greedy and tell me all the details. We have all night…"

We burst into thunderous laughter and toasted the ancient Roman victories with glee. For hours we talked about Attila and his defeat in Maurica, and told stories of the former Gaul officer and now *comes* of the most important Roman city in Hispania. We laughed, ate and drank well into the night. When fatigue took its toll on us, we gathered in a room that Nelius Varus had prepared for us. I slept peacefully on a straw mattress, covered with a blanket, remembering the day when, accompanied by Traustila, I presented myself before the *magister utriusque militiae* Aetius. Many years had elapsed since then and the memory of loved ones fallen along the way came to my mind filling me with sadness and nostalgia. Finally, I fell asleep under a deep and restful sleep.

The walls of Tarraco looked imposing from a distance. Traustila had done a great job and they weren't few the *bucelarii* patrols that we encountered on our way. The soldiers were well uniformed and better equipped, but we were surprised by the age of many of them, as most of them had probably not reached the age of eighteen. The capital of Tarraconensis was the last Roman relevant stronghold in Hispania and the Gaul *comes* had spared no effort to protect it. We walked slowly but hopefully: Traustila would deny us neither shelter nor food and Tarraco would resist the barbarian onslaught with blood and fire. We, the refugees, didn't ask for more. We were Hispano-Romans, and as Hispano-Romans we wanted to die. In the last weeks there were many reports of deserters, apostates, renegades and traitors who had even sold their souls to the Arian faith of the barbarians, in exchange for keeping their meager possessions or the little money they had in their pockets. Roman Hispania was threatened by the Visigoths in the North and by the Vandals in the South, but there were still a few of us who believed that order would defeat chaos and light would defeat shadow. We dreamed that the mighty and eternal Rome would rise from its embers, as it had always done.

It was a clear but cold day. The sky was clear of clouds and the birds were flying south in their unique arrowhead formation, flying away from the cold winter that was predicted. I walked along with Arcadius and my children. The little ones missed their mother terribly and hardly opened their mouths since she left us. Flavina Aelia made tireless efforts to coax a smile from them, but to no avail. They were usually assaulted by nightmares at night and not infrequently they woke up in tears amidst spasms and convulsions. I wished that the arrival in Tarraco would give them some peace of mind, and that time would diminish the deep pain that their mother's death had caused them. I looked at Salvio Alexandros, who was walking only a few steps away from me, looking at the ground and kicking at the pebbles in his path. It had little to do with the Salvio Alexandros who ran after dogs, fought thousands of imaginary enemies with his wooden sword, or fell asleep reading Virgil.

I felt great compassion for him. Annia walked beside me. She held tightly to my hand and didn't leave me in the sun or shade. When I had to separate from her because of my duties, she looked at me with eyes full of terror, wondering if she would ever see me again, and she jumped on me, submerged in a sea of tears when she saw me coming back. They were nine and seven years old, a very difficult age, and they needed their mother more than ever. I approached Salvio Alexandros and ruffled his hair. He smiled bitterly at me and my heart broke into a thousand pieces. The joy for the closeness of Tarraco was overshadowed by the sadness conveyed by the eyes of my children.

A chant behind me caught my attention. I turned and met the smile of Lucretia, the friendly greeting of Fraucus and the smiling nod of Flavius Protus. The one singing was Helvius, the baker, who with his little daughter sitting on his shoulders, was humming an old Carthaginian melody. They looked very happy. After long weeks of tiring march, we had made it. Unbidden, Valeria's memory came to my mind and I clenched my jaws tightly. The children were grieving for the loss of their mother, and I was grieving for the loss of the woman I had loved most in my life.

We were a few hundred paces from the city when some horsemen came to meet us. The one who commanded them was a *bucelarius* who didn't look more than twenty years old.

"Who are you?" he asked us disdainfully, looking us up and down as if he were in front of a group of ragged and tattered people.

Arcadius was about to intervene, but I held him back with a gesture. We were going to request asylum and it wasn't a matter of facing the first soldier we met.

"We come from Carthago Nova, my name is Salvio Adriano and I'm…" for a few moments I hesitated. "I'm its *civitatis comes*. I want to talk to Traustila, he knows us."

The *bucelarius* frowned not very convinced of my words. I understood him, even though we were wearing clothes donated by the citizens of Dertosa that, on many occasions, didn't correspond to our sizes.

"Follow me," he agreed reluctantly, without getting off his horse.

Arcadius approached me.

"Insolent child. You have identified yourself as *civitatis comes* and he hasn't even gotten off his horse to offer you his due respects. This one is going to find out as soon as I put on the *centenarius* uniform," he whispered in my ear.

I smiled at him and touched his shoulder to reassure him.

"Arcadius, there is another thing you should be worried about."

"His age," my friend said immediately.

"Indeed."

"But you were much younger when you were named *centenarius.*"

I smiled remembering those long-ago times.

"Yes, but remember the circumstances."

"It's true, you saved the life of the *Hispaniarum comes* in the battle of Maurica and you defended yourself bravely from the Hun attacks. What times!" he exclaimed, laughing loudly.

We laughed for a few moments while we looked more closely at the horsemen who escorted us to Tarraco. The *bucelarius* was probably the oldest and wasn't even twenty years old, but the rest of them were no more than sixteen or seventeen. Where were the veteran soldiers?

We crossed the main gate of Tarraco escorted by the soldier and went through its solid walls. The city was unrecognizable, very different from the one where I was trained as a legionary more than twenty years ago. The buildings were in good condition and there were no signs of misery or poverty in the form of malnourished children or beggars lying in the streets. We crossed a small market that was crowded with merchants and customers, exchanging gold and silver coins with alacrity. The blacksmiths worked briskly, giving air to the forge to heat the iron that would become solid swords or burnished scale armor, a baker showed in his stall the effort of long hours of insomnia and a goldsmith cajoled a wealthy-looking old woman showing her an amber necklace set in gold thread.

"*Domina,* with this necklace your husband will be captivated by your beauty, and tonight he'll irremediably surrender to your charms," the goldsmith said with a lascivious look.

"How insolent!" the old woman exclaimed, pretending to be offended. "Besides, I have no husband."

"It's probably because you don't want to," replied the goldsmith with a big smile.

The woman laughed demurely at the merchant's witticism and willingly paid what had been agreed. She put on the necklace and proudly strolled down the busy street, showing off like a rooster in a henhouse.

"The city swims in abundance," I said to Arcadius.

"It seems so, but its soldiers are very young," he replied, pointing to the walls.

Arcadius was right. We came across dozens of hairless *bucelarii* who hadn't yet left puberty, either guarding the walls or patrolling the city. Inexperienced young boys were protecting the rich and prosperous Tarraco.

We stopped at the gate of the *castrum*. It was a fortification inside the city itself. A sturdy stone wall surrounded it, and it was protected by a barbican and several watchtowers. The *bucelarii* announced our arrival to the *circitor*, one of the few legionaries that probably existed in the city, and the latter went to the *praetorium*. After a while, he returned accompanied by a high-ranking officer dressed in war uniform, whom I soon identified.

"Adriano and Arcadius: My good friends!" Traustila exclaimed in the distance, stretching out his arms.

"My dear friend!" I exclaimed, heading to him.

"Traustila!" Arcadius cried with a smile, unable to believe that he was in the presence of the Gaul.

We embraced in a big hug and smiled with joy. Time had taken its toll on the Gaul, since he was well into his sixties. His hair had turned gray and dozens of wrinkles furrowed his worried forehead. Even so, he was still in excellent physical shape and appeared to be in good health.

"I've been informed that you are Carthago Nova's *civitatis comes*." said the Gaul.

"I was, but the *ordo decuriorum* decided to prostrate itself before the Vandals and surrendered the city. Those of us who refused to kiss Genseric's hand were forced to flee."

"I understand, I think we have a lot to talk about."

"Traustila," I began to say, looking him in the eyes. "We've had a very long journey, my companions need rest and..."

"You can count on that. For the time being, we'll put you up in the *castrum* until we find a more appropriate place. From today, you are citizens of Tarraco and you'll be taken care of as such. Now let's go to the *praetorium*, I can't wait for you to tell me the details of your odyssey."

I looked at him gratefully and accompanied him to the camp, followed by the rest of the refugees.

"Who are these children?" he asked, noticing Annia and Alexandros, who, impressed by Traustila's martial bearing and height, had stuck to me.

"My children," I answered.

"We certainly have a lot to talk about." he said with a smile, touching my shoulder.

Traustila settled the exiles in a military barracks and ordered food and clothing to be brought to them. Once settled, they were able to rest comfortably on straw mattresses. A physician, assisted by an assistant, consulted the sick and observed the condition of the old men, women and children. Most of them were somewhat malnourished, but their health condition was acceptable. They were happy and satisfied after the long journey. The calamities they had endured had not been few and they were finally in a place they could call home. The Gaul *comes* met all our needs and was there for us at all times. He himself accommodated several families in their respective cubicles and asked the physician about the health of the elderly and children. He was sincerely concerned about them, and this earned him their admiration and respect. More than a few kissed his hands gratefully.

The sun had set behind the horizon and most of the refugees were wrapped in their blankets when Traustila and I came out of the barracks to get some fresh air.

"They are good people," said the Gaul as soon as we came out.

"They are heroes."

We took a short walk around the barracks. It was cool and we covered ourselves with the *saga*. Although I was exhausted, the cold of the night and, above all, the presence of Traustila, gave me renewed energy. The Gaul walked slowly and, despite the darkness, I noticed that concern veiled his gaze.

"I want to thank you for everything you are doing for my people," I said.

"It's the least I can do for them, there are few who are willing to give up everything to remain Romans, to tell the truth, they are fewer and fewer."

"What are you worried about, my friend?"

The Gaul felt a shiver and adjusted his *sagum*.

"What do you think of Tarraco?"

410

I didn't understand the question, and concluded that he intended to change the topic, as he didn't feel like digressing into sterile discussions about the future of Rome.

"It's prosperous and the people seem to live in peace."

"True, but the price we have to pay is very high."

"What do you mean?"

"Some years ago, the Visigothic hordes came to our walls. They besieged us for days, launching terrible attacks with catapults and ballistae. Most of my legionaries and *bucelarii* were killed, and a tide of barbarians surrounded the city. I didn't want to surrender Tarraco, but it was only a matter of time before it fell into Euric's hands. Then I came up with a crazy idea: dress the young men in helmets, chain mail and coat of mail, and place them behind the shield. The idea worked, and although the attacks lasted several more days, our walls held. Euric, in despair, watched from his horse as, despite their wrathful onslaughts, our troops didn't dwindle, quite the contrary. I then led a delegation to negotiate a truce.

The cold was biting and we resumed our way back to the barracks.

"We reached an agreement and I managed to save the city, but it was a humiliating agreement," he continued, stopping his pace. "Since then, we have been Euric's tributaries; I pay him and he doesn't burn our crops, plunder the villages or attack the city."

"But with the money you pay him he buys mercenaries, equips troops and launches his hosts against other less docile Roman cities," I replied, not hiding my indignation.

"I told you that the agreement was humiliating."

My face showed disappointment and the Gaul looked at me sadly.

"These are difficult times, Adriano, and they require decisions that are not always to our liking," he defended himself. "The city is prospering and lives in relative peace."

"The Visigothic king won't settle for a few crumbs when he can gobble up the whole cake," I remarked, recalling Flavius Protus' metaphor. "It's only a matter of time before he attacks Tarraco."

"I know, I know... that's why, when a young man is strong enough to hold a sword, he is instructed in its handling and dressed in uniform.

"An army of children."

"An army of Romans."

The conversation was tense, but I had no interest in offending and confronting the man who had given us shelter. I looked into his worried eyes and grabbed his shoulder.

"I hope you'll allow me to join your army along with the escapees from Carthago Nova," I said with a smile.

"Naturally, you'll be very well welcomed," accepted the Gaul and we embraced in a strong embrace.

We entered the barracks and took shelter by a fireplace. Accompanied by a jar of wine, we talked for hours about Valeria, my children, Carthago Nova, Tarraco, my promotion, his promotion... Thus I knew that Traustila, after the Visigoths' attack on Tarraco, the local Senate; grateful for saving the city, favored his proclamation as *civitatis comes* before the emperor Anthemius, and the latter ratified his appointment. We caught up on the vicissitudes and misfortunes suffered during the last years by one and the other. We laughed and cried remembering the old times, the friends, companions and loved ones we had lost along the way and, above all, we reflected on the uncertain future that awaited the agonizing Empire. It was well into the night when fatigue took its toll on us and Traustila left for the *praetorium*, and I lay down on my straw bed next to Salvio Alexandros and Annia.

Winter passed and Traustila found an occupation and a home for each of us. Arcadius was delighted to issue orders in his dazzling *centenarius* uniform and soon gained the respect and fear of the young soldiers, including the *bucelarius* who had given us such a sour welcome. Flavius Protus, as a former magistrate and curial of Carthago Nova, was willingly accepted in the Senate of Tarraco. There, before the curia he vehemently and passionately proclaimed speeches in favor of the Empire, rejecting any kind of surrender to the barbarians. Fraucus also had no shortage of work as a mason, Helvius worked in the most important bakery of the city and many others like Lucretia, Flavina Aelia or Velius found work easily. The truce with the Visigoths had been very productive and the harvests were abundant and the flocks of sheep numerous. Salvio Alexandros and Annia slowly regained their spirits and regularly attended classes given by an elderly teacher. The price Traustila had paid for the peace and prosperity of the city had been very high, but its benefits were evident.

Spring came and with it the military campaigns of the barbarians. Thus, we knew that Euric had conquered Arelate, the most important city in Gaul and that Anthemiolus, Emperor Anthemius' son, had died in battle. A powerful Roman army had been exterminated. The Empire was unable to stop the relentless Visigothic advance, and it was only a matter of time before Euric led his army south. But luckily, and in the absence of troops to protect us from the foreign onslaught, it was the winter with its rains, snows and icy winds, which protected us under its aegis. At least, for a few months and under the shelter of a generous fire, we forgot about the demoniac and persistent barbarians.

CHAPTER XVIII

The last battle.

Roma immortalis est, vivit victuraque est [24]

The winter elapsed sad, cold, lilting. Tarraco remained veiled by the cloak of concern and discouragement. An unfathomable terror flooded the souls of its inhabitants, who clustered in the churches begging for divine intervention to free them from the aberrant demons that harassed them. The women sobbed with their little ones in their arms and the men, in silence, sharpened their swords and knives, polished their mail coats and studded their shields, equipping themselves for a spring that was predicted full of blood and death. The news that reached the city through seasoned merchants, wandering monks or fugitives from conquered villages, was quite confusing and disturbing, and Traustila summoned the curia in assembly to transmit the details of the same. The Senate building was very similar to the one in Carthago Nova; it was built with large stone blocks and with the pavement and columns fluted in marble. Even though it was early spring, the heat was stifling inside the Senate, and even the coolness of stone didn't keep sweat from sliding down our pearly foreheads. The faces of the curials showed worry and concern. I took a seat in a seat next to Flavius Protus. The *ordo decuriorum* was in deep, agonizing silence. The sound of the Gaul's *campagi* broke the silence and Traustila appeared in the Senate hall dressed in uniform with the military tunic, the coat of mail and the *paludamentum* over his left arm. His lip curled in concern, he climbed up on the lectern and began to speak.

"*Clarissimi* from Tarraco, for days, I've been informed by messengers and by wandering travelers from all corners of Hispania and

---

[24] *Rome is immortal; it lives and has to go on living (phrase adapted from Plautus' «Trinummus»).*

Gaul of horrible news," he began to say. "I've waited sometime in the hope that it was wrong or misrepresented, but unfortunately most of it has been confirmed."

A frightened murmur ran through the Senate, the curials looked at each other with their faces contracted and disfigured by concern.

"Ricimero, after the defeat of Emperor Anthemius's son in Arelate, incited various legions to revolt in order to overthrow him. Not satisfied with it and to encourage rebellion, he accused him of being possessed or bewitched forcing him to abandon the throne.

"What a cheek. How can the Suevian dare to accuse the emperor of witchcraft when he is an Arian heretic?" a decurion whispered next to me.

"It's only a pretext to wrest power from him," said another.

"Naturally, Anthemius refused to abdicate the throne, leaving it in the hands of the Suevian, and marched to Rome to secure his authority," Traustila continued. "But Ricimero didn't give up and recruited six thousand German mercenaries. For months, Rome was besieged by Ricimero troops until; finally, the Germans crossed its walls."

The murmurs broke out and the *decurions* looked at each other in bewilderment, unable to believe that Ricimero was able to attack Rome with a horde of German savages.

"But the Suevian didn't limit himself to hiring the swords of the barbarians to attack the *Urbs*, but in addition, and for the purpose of paying his soldiers, he left it at the mercy of plunder…"

"It cannot be!" exclaimed an indignant curial rising from his seat.

"This affront can't go unpunished!" shouted another.

"Death to the Suevian!" cried one more, raising his fist.

The Senate was overwhelmed by a tumultuous storm of anger and indignation. The imprecations, insults and threats followed one after another in an ordo decuriorum grieved and afflicted by the ignominious affront.

"The dead can be counted by thousands," muttered the Gaul. "Including the emperor himself."

"Has Anthemius been killed?" asked a confused *decurion*.

"He hid himself in a building in the city, but was found by Gundobaldo, the prince of the Burgundians…"

"And nephew of Ricimero," a curial ended.

"He was killed on the fifth day before the Ides of July," Traustila Continued. "The emperor of Rome died in cold blood, pierced by the sword of a barbarian."

"Damn Suevian! His lust for power has ruined Rome!"

"Who is now the new emperor? In the case there is one," Flavius Protus replied.

The silence fell and we all awaited Traustila's answer.

"The news is coming in rapid succession," he began to say. "Olybrius was sent by Leo, the Eastern-Emperor, to mediate in the conflict between Anthemius and Ricimero, but the Suevian, cunning as a weasel, persuaded him to accept the purple even before the death of the Augustus."

Olybrius was Placidia's husband and therefore Huneric's brother-in-law, son of Genseric and natural heir to the Crown of the Vandals. A bitter smile peeked out on my lips remembering when, six years ago, I persuaded Genseric to favor his proclamation as emperor, but thanks to Leo mediation, it was Anthemius who was endowed with purple. Finally, after long years, the *Vandalorum rex* had attained his purpose.

"Olybrius was fostered by Ricimero and supported by the Vandal King Genseric," the Gaul continued.

"It can't be!" A *decurion* shouted.

"It will be our end," whispered other *decurion*.

"Euric is probably rubbing his hands, now he has his path expedited to attack our city," said other of them

The comments were overwhelming, causing a smothering murmur in the Senate. The news of Anthemius's assassination was nefarious, but much worse was the proclamation of Olybrius; Genseric's favorite, as new emperor. Ricimero considered Genseric stronger and more powerful than Euric and had favored the appointment of his candidate with the intention of ingratiating himself with him. How wrong the Suevian was. It was not good news for Roman cities, which suffered from the harassment of the Visigoths.

"Silence!" Traustila shouted. "Silence!" The calm took over an angry Senate until it was plunged into silence. "As I said before," he continued. "Events are unfolding hastily. A few months after Olybrius' proclamation as emperor, Ricimero died."

"May God punish him in hell," said a curial.

A new murmur of satisfaction flooded the *ordo decuriorum*. Ricimero death was met with fuss and more after tolerating the sacking of sacred

Rome by his German mercenaries. For years the Suevian had intrigued, proclaimed and overthrown emperors at will, according to his interests. Being of barbarian origin and professing the Arian faith, he could never be anointed with the purple, but there were many who considered that Ricimero guided the designs of the Empire during the last years.

The murmurs died down and the glances of the curials converged on Tarraco *civitatis comes*; his face indicated that there were still more surprises awaiting us.

"And, a few months after the Suevian's death," he continued. "on the fourth day before the ninth of November, Olybrius died."

"The new emperor has not lasted long," a decurion said sarcastically, arousing nervous laughter in the rest of the curia.

"So who the hell is the new Augustus now? What barbarian king has imposed his candidate?" a senator asked.

His jaded words reflected the indifference and exhaustion of those of us who considered that the crown of Rome was poisoned by the interests and ambitions of the barbarian kings, who were the ones who really decided who wore the imperial insignia. One more reflection of the decadence that corroded the bowels of Rome.

Traustila exhaled a long sigh and shook his head. The information he was about to convey was yet another humiliation to the reviled dignity of the Empire.

"After the deaths of Anthemius, Ricimero and Olybrius, it is the Burgundian prince Gundobaldo, who now stands as the maker of emperors…"

"Will the same one that killed Anthemius decide his successor?" a wrathful curial asked, before the astonishment of the *ordo decuriorum*, in disbelief of what they were hearing.

The senators shook their heads in a discouraging murmur. They were unable to accept the vexations, mockery and offenses with which the barbarian invaders were poisoning the land that had given them shelter and asylum a hundred years ago. I couldn't but recall the fable of the dog and her puppies.

"And who now rules the future of Rome?" asked a tired-looking curial.

"On the fourth day before the ninth of March of this same year, Glycerius, *comes domesticorum,* was proclaimed emperor of Rome."

Bitter laughter echoed from the walls of the Senate. A high officer of the imperial guard had been proclaimed Augustus; a new puppet in the hands of the barbarians would rule a doomed Empire. The curials' faces reflected with irreproachable cruelty that all was lost. The *Caput Mundi* was at the mercy of the foreigners, who played with it as a cat plays with a mouse before devouring it. If we intended to defend ourselves from the barbarians, we should do it alone, since opprobrium nested in a Rome plunged in rottenness and pestilence.

"The barbarians will pounce on our *limes* like wolves on an unprotected flock," Traustila continued. "We must reinforce our defenses and arm our citizens."

"And pray to God." a *decurion* interjected.

"We won't surrender Tarraco; we'll fight to the end even if it means death!" an *aedile* exclaimed, with the convinced assent of the rest of the senators.

What a scene so similar, as well as different, to the one I witnessed in Carthago Nova, when the future of the city was being decided in the face of the advance of the Vandals.

"*Clarissimi decurions*, a year of hard work and sacrifice awaits us. Let us gather the crops, strengthen the defenses and arm our citizens. There is only one way: victory or death," the Gaul Said.

We left the Senate crestfallen and dejected. Around us the curials whispered, and lamented for the uncertain future that loomed over Tarraco. I said goodbye to Flavius Protus and accompanied Traustila to the *castrum*, we had a lot of things to do and very little time.

"I must entrust you with one last mission," the Gaul Said, while we walked towards the *castrum*.

"Whatever you need."

"If Euric has already conquered Arelate, it's certain that he will tear down our walls."

"That won't happen," I replied, with more conviction than I really had.

Traustila smiled at me and grabbed my shoulder, shaking his head.

"If Tarraco falls, you must save as many citizens as possible."

"I don't understand you."

"There is a tunnel that starts from the *praetorium* and leads to a steep part of the coast. There, I'll moor several dozen boats. As soon as the first barbarian crosses the walls, you must get the population to safety."

"But you are the *civitatis comes,* you are the one who..."

"If the city falls, I'll fall with it," he interrupted me with a hand gesture, and without giving rise to the retort he added:

"I'll show you where the tunnel is. When the barbarians arrive, all civilians must protect themselves behind the walls of the *castrum,* and when their defense is impossible, you'll leave the city. Convey this information to Flavius Protus and Arcadius, the rest of the curials already know it."

It hadn't yet dawned, and accompanied by Arcadius, I entered the forest ready to enjoy a day of hunting to distract my tormented spirits. Although we walked slowly, the noise of the dead leaves creaking beneath our feet discouraged every living being in the vicinity. It was daunting. Still, we wandered crouched down, with our bows prepared in the hope that some good piece crossed our path. A noise to our right caught our attention, and towards its creaking origin we directed our steps. The dead leaves were wet and elusive and Arcadius, obsessed with chasing the alleged animal, slipped and fell badly on a log, banging his head and losing consciousness. Worried, I approached him and tried to revive him. He was unconscious but breathing. The squeal of a bugle urged me. Suddenly, a black bird flew over my head perching on a nearby branch.

"Don't worry, your friend is fine," Lughdyr said. "The old man was wearing an immaculate white robe and walked leaning on his eternal fall."

"I greet you, druid," I said, making a gesture with my head.

Lughdyr approached me and we embraced, with a bitter smile on his face.

"The end is near," he admitted, grabbing me by the shoulders. "Follow the advice of the *civitatis comes* and lead your family into the tunnel. They'll survive."

"Will the city be destroyed?" I asked.

"Sometimes the images appear confused and tumultuous, but I see with the clarity of a summer's day the horror of death and the black blood splashing on the coat of mail of the bucelarii and the quilted breastplates of the Visigoths. I can't assure you who will be the winner, but avoid unnecessary risks, and get Alexandros and Annia to safety."

"I will."

The druid nodded.

419

"You look bad, are you fine?" Lughdyr was exhausted and distressed, as if his days among the living were coming to an end.

"Years don't pass indifferently on this old man's burdened back."

"Druids are wise and powerful, but not immortal."

"That's right."

I have never seen the druid so sorrowful and dejected. His arcane aura was fading like the ochre leaves of a beech forest scourged by the furious autumn wind. I looked at him worriedly, persuaded that his visit had other motivations.

"How are Alana and Adriano?" I asked him.

"Well, very well," he answered with a smile, "away from the wars and devastation that ravage these lands, helping those who need it most."

"The prophecy...?" I asked, remembering the omen that more than twenty years ago separated me from Alana and that assured that my true love would free me when I found myself at the mercy of death.

The druid nodded and said:

"Soon, it will be fulfilled."

"Then..."

The old man had huge, haggard bags hanging under his eyes. He was breathing heavily and he moved slowly. It was evident that he had made a great effort to meet me.

"Feelings arise from the depths of our souls. Love is not a suspicion or an intuition. It's a pure and magical feeling that must not be reasoned. The prophecy will be fulfilled and your true love will tear you from the clutches of the Grim Reaper, when it intends to drag you into its world."

I looked at him confused, not understanding his words. The old man noticed the confusion conveyed by my gaze and said:

"You'll understand when the time comes."

I lowered my eyes, giving in to the incomprehensible riddle.

"Now I must leave, my friend. You've honored me with your friendship, and I sincerely hope that Nature will keep you for many years..." he said, but his eyes were veiled with the shadow of an overwhelming sadness, as if his words were nothing more than an unrealizable wish.

"This is a farewell, isn't it?"

"The Mother demands my presence: my mission is over," he answered, looking at me with somber eyes. "Goodbye, Salvio Adriano."

Suddenly, he was enveloped in a dense vapor as black as night, which oscillated in an enigmatic spiral stretching towards the sky. The crow uttered a piercing screech that echoed in the forest with the echo of torment and agony, and flew, plunging into the mist impregnated with the smell of farewell, faithfully accompanying his master to meet the Mother.

"Wait!" I exclaimed, holding out my hand.

But it was too late, the mist vanished, and with it, the druid.

A devastating fire was raging over the land of Hispania. A scorching and destructive fire fed by the ominous winds of betrayal and cowardice, since loyalty and dignity are two capricious harlots who sell themselves to the highest bidder. No one, not even the highest dignitates, or the most glorious generals, are dispensed from selling their favors if they find a good client who will pay the required price. And that client was Euric. The Visigoth king filled with gold and ambitions several illustrious Romans, who didn't hesitate to join his cause and take up arms against their own people, disavowing the Roman blood that flowed through their veins. Thus, Seronatus, vicar of the sub-Gaul diocese, was accused of connivance with Euric and condemned to death, Arborius, the *Hispaniarum magister militum* who replaced Nepotianus, didn't hesitate a moment to put his *spathae* at the service of the barbarians, and like them, countless curials, landowners and *civitatis comites* sold their souls and honor as soon as they saw the flags and insignia of the invaders on the horizon. But the most odious and execrable treason was that committed by Vicentius, the *Hispaniarum dux,* who, not satisfied with betraying the Empire, commanded a horde of barbarians and, together with the Visigothic *comes* Gauteric, crossed the Pyrenees and devastated the cities of the coast of Hispania on his way to Tarraco. Treason is a miasma that spreads rapidly over the spoils of defeated nations.

And it didn't take long for the refugees fleeing from the slaughter and desolation that the enemies of Rome left in their wake, to gather on our walls. The first to arrive were the residents of Dertosa led by the *comes* Nelius Varus, then refugees from cities or more distant villages arrived. The rumors of the barbarian advance kept happening and no one dared stay in their city to see if they were true or not. Tarraco gladly accepted all the refugees, since they supposed more arms to support shields, hands to throw stones, and legs to help the wounded. Over the past few months, Traustila had done a great job and instructed every young man over thirteen or woman who was willing to carry a sword and was not afraid of the moment to use it. The women protected their breasts with quilted linen breastplates, and helmets and *campagi* were made to their measure. They created a regiment and Traustila appointed a woman, the brave Messalina, its commander. At first several *decurions* protested. It wasn't to their liking that women dressed like men and, in addition, carried weapons. But they fell silent when they observed their agility in swordsmanship or their prowess with the bow. For weeks, we built moats and palisades around the walls, made catapults and ballistas, and filled our silos with grain in anticipation of a long siege.

The sun was breaking through the treetops, staining the diffuse line of the horizon purple and blood, when the «*barritus,*» the heart-rending battle cry uttered by the Visigoths, reached our ears, disturbing the entrails, and intimidating the hearts of the most intrepid warriors. It started out as a whisper, like a gentle swell, but turned into a stormy gale when the barbarians screamed, bringing shields to their mouths. The echo of their bellows resounded furiously, flooding the lands of Tarraco with a black omen of blood and death. Their purpose was none other than to terrorize the enemy, and by God they were succeeding. Sheltered behind the walls, we observe the advance of the Visigoths and their war machine. They were thousands, tens of thousands of soldiers driven by the determination to destroy Tarraco and continue on their way south, until they found themselves in front of the Vandals and, then, possibly, they would kill each other. They were commanded by the Visigoth King Euric, who rode on a beautiful war chestnut black as a raven's wing. I managed to distinguish two high officers that flanked him, one of them dressed in a military tunic, a coat of mail and a Roman helmet with a plume. Possibly they were the *comes* Gauteric and the perfidious Vicentius. But my heart leapt from my chest and the gall rose sour up my throat when, despite the distance, I thought I recognized the long hair and blond mustaches of a barbarian whom I had considered dead for years, since I contemplated his corrupt head inside a bloody box. Majorian demanded his execution as punishment for Optila's death. But King Theodoric deceived us, sending us the head of some wretch who had the misfortune to resemble the German. I smiled bitterly at our trusting foolishness. Walder was over sixty years old, but he still had the cruel, ruthless look of old times. A chill ran through my body and I instinctively adjusted my helmet. It was written: Walder and I would fight the final fight, and one of us would water the land of Tarraco with his blood. The Visigoths advanced without ceasing their terrifying cries, until they were at a safe distance from our walls. Then Euric raised his hand and his troops, fully trained, spread out in several attack columns. The last battle had begun.

I raised my sword and shouted:

"Rome invicta est! Rome invicta est!"

And the war-cry was uttered by thousands of throats and resounded in Tarraco like a prayer, like an inviolable oath that urged us to fight for our land, for our families, even sacrificing our lives, since we had taken the determination to die as Romans.

"Roma invicta est! Roma invicta est!" we shouted, raising our *spathae* to the heavens. A cry hurled to the winds with the clamor of pride and dignity, to be heard by the foreign hordes and, above all, by the conscience of traitors like Vicentius, who knelt obscenely to the barbarians, and now launched their hosts against their own people.

"Prepare the catapults!" Traustila shouted, trying to make himself heard amid the tumultuous shouting. "Are all the civilians in the *castrum?*" he asked me uneasily. I nodded and he smiled contentedly, he was more worried about his people than about the black future that awaited him.

The creaking of the wood and the tightening of the ropes warned us that the catapults were ready to throw the stones and rocks piled up on the ramparts. The Visigoths were still far out of range so we had to wait for them to advance.

"*Sagitarii,* get ready!" ordered the Gaul. The archers armed their bows and took cover behind the battlements.

Euric was watching us closely, scrutinizing our defenses for any chinks or weak spots where he could focus his attacks. Then he made a gesture and several hundred soldiers, carrying scales, were placed in the front line. He made another gesture and several horsemen came to meet him, who, by their clothing, must have been his captains. He spoke with them for a few moments and then the horsemen returned to their positions.

"Check that the cauldrons are ready, the Visigoth's attack is imminent" I ordered Arcadius.

The sound of a war tuba preceded the beating of hundreds of drums. In formation, with a cadenced step and beating their shields with their swords, the enemy advanced towards our walls. A fierce sea of Visigoths headed towards us carrying their fearsome catapults and siege towers. Soon huge stones and fireballs flew over our heads, which, impregnated with tar, stuck to the buildings and set them on fire instantly. The civilians ran from place to place carrying buckets of water, trying to quell a devastating fire that threatened to turn the unhappy Tarraco into black embers.

"Sagitarii, get ready!" Traustila shouted, raising his sword.

Our archers set their arrows and pointed their bows skyward. The Visigoths advanced until they were exposed to our darts. The time came for a response.

"Fire!"

A hail of incendiary arrows fell on our enemy causing fierce carnage. But that wasn't the only target. During several nights and protected by the darkness, we had dug a large ditch around the city and poured hundreds of modius of pitch into it. Then we covered it with leaf litter and dry branches, hiding it from the enemy's sight. The effect of the arrows on the pitch was immediate and a fiery stream of fire split the Visigoths, burning many of them alive. A tongue of black, viscous smoke hid the bulk of the invading army, leaving those closest to our walls helpless and exposed to the accurate arrows of our archers. The barbarians looked at each other terrified and undecided, persuaded that they had fallen into an ambush.

"Open the gates!" ordered Traustila.

While the *sagitarii* took charge of the Visigoths, hundreds of *bucelarii* came out of the city armed with *spiculae* and javelins and devastated the bewildered and trapped barbarians that, without possibility of fleeing, fought bravely for their lives. As the fire began to die down and the smokescreen that protected us was blown away by the wind, our soldiers returned to the city, leaving in their wake hundreds of Visigoth corpses scattered on the battlefield.

But Euric wouldn't give up easily, and while his slaves and auxiliaries put out the fire by throwing water or earth, he ordered the advance of his infantry, which marched supported by archers and catapults.

Hundreds of Visigoths had perished inserted by our arrows, burned by fire or pierced by the swords of our horsemen, but still they were thousands, and such a loss didn't seem to cause the barbarian king any displeasure.

The fire was extinguished and the enemy, prudently since they feared another ambush, advanced towards us without ceasing to hammer their shields. Arcadius and Traustila were at my side, and guarding the front of the wall, there were hundreds of *bucelarii* who watched in terror the attack of the powerful enemy army. One of them trembled with fear and held his sword with difficulty, another urinated in fright, staining his tunic, and yet another threw his bow to the ground, and ran into the city, quite possibly to protect himself in the arms of his mother. Unfathomable fear spread rapidly through our troops, drying their throats and churning their guts. Our brave battle cry was forgotten in a hidden corner of their terrified hearts. Traustila, attentive to the morale of the troops, didn't miss a single detail and looked at me with resignation.

"We can't require a boy to fight like a man," I told him.

"But we can ask him to die as such," he replied gruffly.

The Visigoths crossed the extinct tongue of fire and found themselves again within the range of our archers. Traustila gave the order and thousands of arrows fell on them, making it difficult for the Visigoths to advance while they protected themselves with their shields. But they were thousands of brave and fierce soldiers, eager for booty and to dirty their swords with Hispano-Roman blood, while we were only a handful of veterans accompanied by young boys.

Euric gave the order and thousands of arrows fell on us, forcing us to protect ourselves behind the battlements. The Barbarians advanced pushing the siege towers, while the catapults didn't stop firing projectiles over our heads.

"Fire the catapults!" ordered Traustila, protecting himself with his shield from the enemy's darts.

A *bucelarii* set fire to a bale of pitch-soaked straw and the catapult successfully launched it onto the enemy, burning several of them alive.

"Don't stop firing your bows, the catapults and the ballistae, we must stop their advance! Aim the catapults at the siege towers and fire incendiary arrows at them!"

A deafening shout from the enemy's side preceded the advance of hundreds of men who, with their shields strapped to their backs, ran towards our walls carrying ladders. Many of them died skewered by our arrows, but they were very numerous and did not take long to lean their ladders on our walls. Like ants climbing up a log, the Visigoths ascended the ladders protected by shields. We threw pitch, burning sand, and boiling oil on them, but we didn't succeed in stopping their advance. Many of our *milites,* persuaded of defeat, senselessly threw down their swords and ran to hide in the alleys of the city. Arcadius came across one of them, and didn't hesitate to run him through with his sword.

"Do you want to die in the hands of a Roman or a Visigoth! What do you want to do by hiding under your mother's skirt? Do you think you will be safer there? Protect the walls with your lives because if the Visigoths manage to climb it, it will be the end of your families and there will be no place where you can hide."

"We have the tunnel," one of the *bucelarii* replied in a trembling voice.

All the inhabitants of the city were informed of the existence of the tunnel, the issue was that there weren't enough boats for everyone, and many would have to sacrifice their lives so that the rest could escape.

"Only the elderly, women and children will be allowed to flee, we men will fight to the end. Our spilled blood will be the price we must pay to ensure their escape."

"No!" the soldier exclaimed.

"You should show that same bravery against the enemy," Arcadius said to him, advancing towards him with his blood-stained sword.

The *miles* tried to flee and ran towards the city, but was hit by an accurate arrow. Arcadius and the young *bucelarii* looked towards the wall and found Traustila, who was aiming with his bow at the rest of the fleeing men. The deserters, aware that they had no alternative, unsheathed their swords and returned to the wall followed by a relentless Arcadius.

The Visigoths managed to storm the walls and fought on the rampart alongside the young recruits who, aware that they would soon find themselves in front of the Grim Reaper's empty sockets, defended themselves with renewed vigor and heroic courage. Messalina and a group of women prevented the barbarians from ascending a ladder, and although they showed great courage and a total absence of fear, a valiant example for not a few recruits, they were overcome and many of them suffered the barbarians' atrocious slashes. The Visigoths burst into thunderous laughter when they realized that the defense of the city rested on the fragile shoulders of an army of bearded men and women. I came to their aid and killed two Visigoths by throwing them off the rampart. Messalina smiled gratefully at me and attacked a barbarian, who looked at her in surprise holding his intestines that were sticking out from under his breastplate, wondering how it was possible that a woman had pierced him with her sword. The Visigoth fell at the feet of the brave warrior and his guts spilled over the rampart like a sack of slippery eels. A shower of arrows fell upon us and the heroic Messalina received the deadly impact of one of them. She fell on her knees with the dart stuck in her chest, and blood stained her breastplate red. She looked at me with her eyes veiled by the eternal night but she had still the strength to cry out:

"*Roma invicta est!*" And her body fell defeated and lifeless on the rampart.

But there was no time for lamentations, since Euric ordered the advance of the siege towers. The veteran Visigoth archers, from such a watchtower, emptied their carcasses and numerous were the wounded or dead *milites,* wounded or killed by their accurate arrows.

"Protect the walls!" Traustila ordered, taking charge of a group of Barbarians who tried to climb up a ladder.

They say that certain predators smell the fear of their victims and that this smell stimulates them and drives them to continue attacking them. The same thing must have happened to the Visigoths. With bloodshot eyes, uttering horrible shrieks and persuaded of their infinite superiority, they threw themselves in waves on our walls with the desire and the hope that one of such attempts would be the definitive one.

Traustila, Arcadius and I, as the most veteran soldiers, took the lead in defending the city and protected the parapet from the barbarian assault. We managed to repel the first onslaught with blows, blows from the sword or by throwing stones and boiling oil at them, and prevented the enemy from continuing to climb up our defenses. But there were dozens of ladders that managed to lean on our walls and very few soldiers to protect them. Finally, they managed to overcome the wall and headed towards the city gate in order to open it. If they succeeded, Euric would enter Tarraco accompanied his cavalry. That would be the end of us. I poured the last cauldron of pitch on a barbarian who was trying to climb a ladder. The Visigoth was impregnated with the black and viscous liquid, and he stopped in terror, aware of what was going to happen to him, and it did. I picked up a torch and threw it at him. The barbarian fell to the ground engulfed in a ball of fire, bursting into terrible howls of pain. Several enemies fell to the ground dragged by him, burned or crushed to death. The ladder became useless by being devoured by fire and I went to another one that was being protected by a young soldier who was fighting bravely.

"They're going to attack us with a battering ram!" exclaimed a *bucelarii* pointing at the enemy troops.

I approached the battlements and saw how several soldiers, running at great speed, were heading towards the city gate pushing a huge wooden trunk whose tip was crowned by a bronze ball.

"Traustila, we must leave the walls and protect ourselves in the *castrum*!" I shouted.

The Gaul nodded and ordered the retreat.

We ran to get protection inside the *castrum,* the last defensive bastion of the city. A loud noise behind us warned us that the battering ram had hit our door.

"Come on, soldiers, run!" I shouted.

"They haven't knocked down the gate yet!" exclaimed Arcadius.

"That's great. So we'll have more time to reorganize our defense in the *castrum!*"

The *milites* ran towards the center of the city, while the Visigoths climbed the walls and hit the gate with the battering ram. Several soldiers protected the retreat by firing our bows, or with the edge of our swords.

"Adriano, they are too numerous and the last soldier has already entered the *castrum*, we must retreat!" shouted Arcadius.

"I haven't seen Traustila!" I exclaimed worriedly, looking towards the walls.

"We must retreat!"

Arcadius was right, the Visigoths were climbing the walls by hundreds and many headed towards the city gate, while others marched towards us. We got rid of two of our enemies and crossed the street that led to the *castrum*. We had blocked it with wagons smeared with pitch. I made a last glance in the hope of seeing Traustila appear, and as I was about to set fire to the wagons, I saw that the *comes* was running badly wounded, being pursued by several Visigoths. I gave the torch to Arcadius and ran to help him.

"Adriano, no, it's too late!" screamed Arcadius.

I reached the Gaul and noticed that he had a deep wound in his side. He could hardly walk so I threw him on my back. The enemies were advancing rapidly with their swords at the ready. Almost at a crawl we managed to get through the row of wagons, just when the enemy was about to catch up with us. Arcadius threw the torch on the wagons just when several Visigoths were climbing up them, and plumes of black smoke hid their bodies, but not their piercing howls of pain. One of them, turned into a burning ball of fire, managed to cross the wagons, falling to the ground engulfed in flames.

"We must hurry; they'll soon be able to put it out," said Arcadius.

We held the Gaul by the arms and, on our shoulders; we managed to cross the *castrum* gate, which closed immediately as we passed through. The spectacle in the camp was quite desolate. Hundreds of soldiers and civilians scattered on the ground in terror, moaning and sobbing, imploring divine intervention to free them from the barbarian hordes. The women wept quietly, cradling their babies, or searched in grief among the survivors for their loved ones. On the ground, dressed in military uniform, I found the lifeless body of Nelius Varus. His breastplate was soaked in blood and his lips, lips framed in a bloody and dirty face, were smiling. The brave *civitatis comes* of Dertosa had honorably sacrificed his life to preserve a wish, a dream as unattainable as the moon. I pressed my lips together in grief for such an immeasurable loss.

"We must flee as soon as possible or we will die!" cried a soldier suddenly, crying out of pure fear before the frightened gaze of those present. His words of dejection and defeat were followed by the terrified murmurs of hundreds of people.

We placed Traustila in the *valetudinarium* and left him under the care of a physician. Arcadius and I had to organize the defense of the camp and first of all, it was necessary to find out how many troops we had at our disposal.

"The *milites* that are still fit to fight! Line up!"

I ordered, but only Arcadius squared up in front of me. The rest looked away or pretended not to hear me. I turned to a group of *bucelarii*. Their eyes reflected the inconsolable fear of one who knows that he is going to die.

"Soldiers!" I shouted at them and they stood firm, as if they feared me more than the Visigoths. Perhaps they had witnessed the deaths of the *milites* killed by Arcadius or Traustila, and they were well persuaded that I wouldn't hesitate to inflict an exemplary punishment on the deserters either. "Tarraco is likely to fall into barbarian hands, but our duty as soldiers and as Romans is to protect it while we have a last

429

breath of life left. We must facilitate the escape of civilians, delaying the enemy advance, do you have a family?" I asked a young recruit.

"Yes, *domine,* they are safe in the *castrum.*"

"Would you give your life for them?"

"Of course, I would, *domine.*"

"Then why do you hide in the herd like a submissive lamb? Hoping to slip past the butcher's knife? Fight like a Roman soldier, fight like a man for Hispania, and if death surprises you, everyone will know that you have died like a hero and that you have sacrificed your life to save your loved ones. Then, your name will be remembered and praised by the descendants of Tarraco. Escape through the tunnel if that is what you want, but I assure you that the Visigoths will find you, and that they'll kill you as if you were a lamb. You'll die and your family with you. Death chooses the cowards and glory the fearless. Be brave, after all, we all die," I added, taking him by the shoulder. "the only thing that changes is when, where... and how. We cannot decide when or where to die, but today the Grim Reaper has granted us the privilege of choosing how. It's in our hands, that they remember us as cowards or as heroes. The choice is yours, young soldier."

The *miles* nodded convinced of my words and lined up behind Arcadius. The *bucelarii* looked at me in bewilderment, deep in their guts a furious storm of mixed feelings was unleashing, since reason was urging them to flee, but their hearts were urging them to fight. Finally, the love they felt for their own, was more powerful than the fear that oppressed them, and they got into formation, valiantly offering their lives in sacrifice in exchange for saving that of their loved ones.

"No soldier will accompany the civilians through the tunnel; it will be the curials who will," I said. "We'll leave the town when everyone is safe. Understood?"

The young *milites* nodded resigned to the uncertain future that awaited them and entrusted their souls to the Almighty. I reviewed and verified that I had under my command about five hundred soldiers, some of them women, and several hundred civilians, who had volunteered to fight against the Visigoths to facilitate the escape of their relatives. The prospects weren't very flattering; a handful of terrified soldiers couldn't face a horde of savage barbarians. I organized my defenses and headed to the hospital, since I was worried about Traustila. The Gaul was lying on a pallet wrapped in a pool of blood. I looked at the physician who was attending him and he shook his head.

"We will resist," I lied to him, getting down on my knees, trying to appease his torment.

"Order the civilian population to flee. For Tarraco to fall into Visigoth hands is only a matter of time," he said, with a bitter smile.

"I'll do so."

"It has been an honor to fight by your side and I feel tremendously fortunate to die as a legionary, as a Roman," he whispered. In his eyes, I read an invincible pride capable of facing all sorts of adversity by staying true to his principles.

"I'll never forget you, friend."

Arcadius approached us and knelt down.

"You are a hero," he said, touching his shoulder. "The bravest legionary I've ever met. Your name will never be forgotten."

"I've never sought glory, only the survival of Rome, and unfortunately I've failed in my mission."

"No, you haven't failed. There is no greater glory than giving one's life for the Empire, for the *Urbs*... for Hispania. No, friend Traustila, you've fought with honor and defeated the enemy in a hundred battles. Those guilty of the fall of Rome must be sought in the Senate, in the ostentatious palaces and rich estates, not in the *castrum* where the legionaries who have offered their lives to defend it are found."

"*Roma invicta est,*" he muttered. A tear ran down his cheek and his sight was lost in the confines of time. Surely his mind got immersed in pleasant and almost forgotten memories, but that granted him some last moments of happiness and peace, since a pleasant smile came to his lips. The brave warrior closed his eyes and exhaled his last breath. Traustila, Optila's inseparable friend, the legionary who had fought under Aetius command, the victor of countless battles against the enemies of the Empire, had died.

Arcadius and I mourned our friend's death quietly, but time was pressing and our duty obliged us to dispense little mourning for our fallen comrades. I went to the barracks where Flavius Protus was with his family and my children. The magistrate stood up as soon as he saw me enter through the door. His eyes showed concern and worry.

"What is it, Adriano?" he asked, grabbing me by the shoulders.

We left the barracks, what I had to tell him was important and only he should hear it or our families would panic.

"You must escape right now. You'll lead the escape; you know the tunnel and the cliffs. Embark with your family and my children and hide

431

in the bluffs. If I haven't joined you by nightfall, march westward toward Gallaecia."

"But..." Flavius Protus tried to protest, but I interrupted him with a hand gesture.

"There is no time, leave or it will be too late," I insisted.

"What will you do?"

"If I don't manage to join you..." a lump in my throat prevented me from speaking..." tell Flavina Aelia to take care of my children, they adore her. We'll defend your escape as long as a drop of blood runs through our veins."

"It's suicide!" he exclaimed, shaking his head.

"My duty is to protect Tarraco's citizens, and I'll do so. Organize the escape with the other *decurions*. We have no time to lose."

The magistrate nodded and we entered the barracks. Salvio Alexandros and Annia were sitting on a straw mattress looking worriedly at the floor. When they saw me enter, they ran to me and gave me a big hug. We stayed there for a few moments while Flavius Protus spoke to his daughters and sons-in-law.

"Sons, you must accompany Flavius Protus and Flavina Aelia."

"Why?" Annia asked suspiciously.

"We, the elders, must protect the city; you'll go to a safe place with Flavina Aelia. When all this is over, I'll join you."

"Promise it!" Annia exclaimed, hugging me tightly.

"That... promise it," Salvio Alexandros demanded distrustfully.

"Nothing will separate us; I love you more than my life. I pro... I promise that I'll join you and... and we'll never be separated again."

Tears flowed uncontrollably down the children's cheeks, and they hugged me tightly in a vain attempt to prevent me from detaching myself from them. They doubted my words, persuaded of the misfortune that was coming upon the city, convinced that this would be our last moment together.

"I promise you, my children. I'll come back," I insisted with my eyes blurred with tears.

Flavius Protus made a gesture to me, everything was ready to leave.

"Go with Flavina Aelia," I told them. The magistrate's daughter approached us accompanied by her husband. "She'll take care of you until my return."

"I love you daddy," said little Annia.

"I love you too," Salvio Alexandros said, putting his arms around me.

With the help of Flavina Aelia and Velius, I managed to free myself from the affectionate embrace of my children, who, crying desperately and stretching out their little hands towards me, left the barracks and headed to the *praetorium*. There was the tunnel through which they would escape from that hell.

"Take care of them, Flavina Aelia!" I exclaimed, watching how they entered the *praetorium*.

"Only until your arrival!" Cried Flavina Aelia with a lump in her throat.

I wiped away my tears, and took a deep breath. With my heart sunk because of Traustila's death and the separation from my children, I directed my steps towards the walls of the *castrum*.

The camp was in the eastern part of the city, near the gate that led to the port. It was accessed through four streets, two main and two narrower. All of them had been blocked with burning wagons. Our strategy had paid off and we were able to delay the barbarian advance, but the enemy had managed to put out the fires and thousands of soldiers were heading towards our walls.

I looked at the *praetorium* and saw hundreds of citizens clustered at the door, eager to get out of the city as soon as possible. The Visigoths beat their shields and shouted loudly, sowing panic not only among women and children. The curials tried to organize the escape, but with little success, since the citizens, driven by fear, rushed into the *praetorium*. The escape was turning into a total disaster, since panic had seized the terrified crowd. I feared for my children and prayed that Flavius Protus had already put them to safety, but unfortunately I couldn't run to the *praetorium* to corroborate it; the Visigoths advanced through the four streets carrying ladders and battering rams, and we had to defend the walls of the *castrum*.

"*Sagitarii*, get ready!" I exclaimed. "Shoot!"

The young archers fired their arrows at the human mob that wriggled through the streets, causing a great loss of life. It was impossible to miss and the archers fired their arrows in bulk with speed.

But the barbarians took cover behind their shields and reached the wall. They supported their ladders on it and began to climb it. I ordered pitch to be thrown at them, and a cloud as black as smut surrounded the camp. The Visigoths' screams of pain were confused with the *milites'* screams of rage and fear. But the enemy was much more numerous and they soon assaulted our wall.

"Now is the time to flee!" a soldier exclaimed, throwing his sword at the barbarians and running towards the *praetorium*.

"Not!" I exclaimed, shaking off the attack of a Visigoth. "For the sake of your loved ones, keep fighting!"

But it was useless. An irrepressible desire to escape, indefatigable friend of fear, seized most of the *bucelarii,* and they fled towards the *praetorium* throwing their swords and shields.

"Let's run or they'll kill us!" yelled a *miles*.

"Let's save our lives!" shouted another.

It was the end. Arcadius and I were surrounded by enemies, fighting with the desperation of a cornered and wounded animal. In the heat of the battle, we hadn't noticed that the Visigoths had managed to break down the door of the *castrum*, and hundreds of them entered on horseback, killing the fleeing milites trying to escape the massacre. Then I saw him.

"Arcadius go to the tunnel, everything is lost!"

"I'll fight alongside you to the end!"

"Not! Go and protect my children. Do it for Salvio Alexandros and Annia, they need you!"

"It's you whom they need, you are their father!"

"I must finish with something that started many years ago," I said, pointing to a giant barbarian with long mustaches and blond hair.

My friend looked at him puzzled and asked:

"But wasn't he dead?!"

"They tricked us," I replied. "They served us the head of another barbarian on a platter."

Arcadius immediately understood and said:

"Finish off the damn German, I'll protect you."

"Not!" I exclaimed, taking him by the shoulders. "Run away at once!

The bravest of the legionaries hesitated for a moment and shouted:

"Go get him and kill him!"

And Arcadius ran towards the *praetorium*, looking at his back several times with his expression disfigured by pain. I waved goodbye to him, persuaded that we would never see each other again. Seeing him run towards the tunnel calmed me down, my children would be safer if my good friend's sword protected them. I looked around and found myself surrounded by Visigoths. I think I was the last legionary left alive, and the barbarians amused with me doing feints and thrusts that I deflected with difficulty. They laughed out loud when a Barbarian threatened me with his spear and another showed me his naked, hairy backside. They had defeated us and conquered the city; it was time to have fun.

But while the barbarians entertained themselves with me, the population of Tarraco and my children fled. This thought comforted me: my sacrifice wouldn't be useless. A barbarian with curly and dirty beard approached me more than necessary, threatening me with his spear while still laughing like a madman. With a nimble movement, I grabbed his spear and sliced his neck, ending his moment of merriment. His companions abandoned their laughter and laughter. Suddenly, the circle that was holding me was broken and the Visigoths made way for three horsemen. They were Euric, Walder, and Vicentius the traitor, the *Hispaniarum dux*.

"You?" the German asked in confusion, and dismounting from his mount, he added: "Well, never mind, it will be a pleasure to kill you again."

"I'm not the only one who has come back from the dead," I replied.

The German let out a great laugh, and unsheathing his sword said:

"Theodoric wasn't so foolish as to hand over to the Romans the head of his *spathariorum comes*. It wasn't difficult to find in the dungeons of Toulouse a prisoner who enjoyed my lofty, godlike beauty."

Walder burst into laughter that was accompanied by the rest of the Visigoths. Then my eyes met Vicentius's.

"What has Euric promised you in exchange for your treason?" I asked him, "Land? Gold? Behold this Hispanic city shrouded in smoke and fire," I said, stretching out my arms. "Behold its citizens and its soldiers lying lifeless on the pavement. They have fought and shed their blood to be faithful to their homeland, their customs and their beliefs. And you Vicentius, *Hispaniarum dux*? For whom have you fought? Why is your sword stained by the blood of your people? For land? For gold?" I insisted, lengthening my speech with the purpose of distracting the attention of the barbarians. "High must be the price that Euric has paid you to put your *spathae* at his service, to devastate Hispania, the land of which you are *dux*, commanding the barbarian hordes. You swore allegiance to the Empire; instead you revolt against it with the ferocity of a rabid dog. If you have been promised land, you must know that in

435

the land that is watered with blood, only pestilence and misery germinate, and if it's gold what you have been offered, I'll tell you that there is no gold in the world with which you can buy the salvation of your damned soul. You are a traitor and you'll die as such."

"Enough! Rome no longer exists! Can't you see that? Everything is lost and only the boldest and bravest will survive the ruin of the Empire."

"Don't confuse boldness and bravery with treachery," I replied.

Vicentius unsheathed his bloody sword and moved towards me, but Walder stopped him with a gesture.

"It's been a long time since we don't see each other. It's a pity we meet in these circumstances. A pity for you, of course," Euric interjected, letting out a loud laugh. "Walder, finish him off quickly, I want to sack the city before it's consumed by the flames."

"I'll do so, my lord, I'm also impatient to enjoy the women of Tarraco. Are you married?" Walder asked me with full intention.

I didn't answer him.

"If so, I'll find your whore and she'll be the first who enjoys my charms."

The passage of time had left its indelible mark on the German's face, but his muscles were as strong and powerful as they had been twenty years ago. His face was wrinkled and furrowed with scars, his thick hair and long whiskers were still intensely blond and unbrushed by gray hair. And his yellow eyes were still those of a beast, inhuman eyes that knew no clemency or forgiveness.

The Visigoths formed a circle while they cheered their captain. Walder stopped a few steps away from me. I was breathing heavily, exhausted after the battle and uneasy about the black future that awaited me. At that moment I would not have bet a single bronze coin on my life. On the other hand, the German was fresh and confident. He scrutinized me in detail, looking for any wound or gap in my coat of mail. After a few moments he smiled.

"How many times must I kill you? I hope this is the last one!" he exclaimed, throwing a strong thrust at me, which I was able to block with difficulty.

He uttered a terrifying scream and attacked me again with his sword. I was able to block his thrusts with my shield, but his blows were powerful and I was exhausted after long hours of tireless battle. The

Visigoths harangued each of his attacks and he turned and raised his arms high in victory.

"Fight, Roman!" he spat at me. "Defend yourself like a man!"

I didn't fall for the provocation. I knew his fighting style very well, and I knew that his best blows came from counterattacks. My only option to defeat him would be to defend myself and wait for his excessive confidence in victory to cause the slightest mistake. If this didn't happen, my end would be near.

"You're an old man!" I shouted out loud for all to hear. "You are hardly strong enough to hold your sword, and you want to force yourself on the women of the city? Don't make me laugh, you old fart, I'm sure you haven't had an erection for years."

My bravado had an effect and the German rushed at me, bursting into a wrathful roar. I protected myself with my shield, deformed after enduring the barbarian's persistent blows. I threatened him with my *spathae* a couple of times, but all I managed to do was to arouse the hilarity of those present.

"Is that all you can do?" I asked with disdain.

"Walder, kill him at once, your fight will last longer than the conquest of the city," the king urged him.

If I had a chance, it was based on unsettling the German, and thanks to the king's intervention, I was succeeding. He launched an attack on me again, then another and another and another. Finally, he pulled away from me, panting from the effort and frustrated by the futility of his onslaught. I was at the limit of my strength, but I was doing my best to pretend otherwise. I could barely hold the sword and the rickety shield.

"Attack me, you damned coward!" he shouted.

"Come here, you old decrepit man, I'm in no hurry to die! If you don't kill me, they will!" I spat at him with a bitter smile, pointing my sword at the Visigoths around me.

"Come on, Walder, finish him off, damn you!" shouted an enraged Euric.

The German looked at his master and nodded. He threw down his shield, clutched his sword in both hands, and rushed angrily at me. He kept attacking me and I kept defending myself, hoping that his frustrated attacks would force him to take foolish risks and he would make a mistake. His beloved king was looking at him with a contracted gesture, and he was being ridiculed by an exhausted Hispano-Roman, defeated, but also obstinate in staying alive; an opprobrium difficult to digest for the brave captain of the *spatharii*. I only had to resist a little more his powerful onslaught. And so it happened. Red with fury, he neglected his defense while throwing blows left and right. But he was a great warrior and a great warrior dies killing. He launched a powerful attack that I managed to dodge with a feint. Then, I noticed a breach in his defense and threw a thrust. I felt my sword pierce his padded breastplate, tear his flesh and break a rib. A deep silence enveloped me and I didn't hear his howl of pain, but his disfigured face revealed that the wound was mortal. The German threw me a last thrust which I managed to repel, but with his left hand he drew a dagger hidden in his belt, and thrust it angrily into my side. A piercing scream, my own scream of pain, woke me up from the unreal state I was in, and I fell to my knees with my hands soaked in blood. I looked at the German waiting for his last and final attack, but he was standing, staring blankly into the horizon. He dropped the sword, then the bloody dagger and then fell limp on the ground, remaining hidden for a few moments, engulfed by a cloud of dust. The German had died.

I touched my side and felt the wet blood gushing from the wound. If the scar wasn't cauterized in haste, I would die. And I was persuaded that the Visigoths would have no intention of saving my life. Exanimated, I fell on my back with my eyes fixed on the firmament. It was dusk in the lands of Hispania.

The languid light of twilight faded before his eyes, engulfed by a milky mist. He could only listen to his breathing, weaker and weaker, more and more choked. The air refused to enter his chest. Life was inexorably slipping away from him, as water from a fountain flows between hands that try uselessly to hold it back. He was dying. But he was not afraid. A peaceful and unknown serenity overwhelmed him. That's when he saw her. Hidden behind a mournful black robe she approached him and placed her cold, emaciated hand on his forehead. She brought her face closer and Adriano beheld the grim and cadaverous smile of the Grim Reaper. She was trying to tear out his soul, to snatch his last breath of life and drag him into her world, the world of darkness. He knew he was going to die, but he didn't care, nothing mattered anymore.... He had shed all suffering and was captivated by an unfathomable sense of calm. So he acceded to Death's wishes and allowed himself to be swept away by it.

Then the vivid memory of some almost forgotten words welled up uncontrollably in his mind, and with his last strength he muttered:

"You'll find a pure and beautiful love, a love blessed by the Mother, a love forced to abandon you to return at the moment you need it most, when your body lies wounded and exanimated, when your last breath is about to expire and the Grim Reaper is about to tear out your soul, to drag it to its world of suffering and desolation, then, your beloved will return to free you from its clutches and you'll never be separated."

The druid's words...

His eyes were veiled in darkness and, meekly, he prepared to cross the dark frontier between the living and the dead. Then... she appeared. She was a goddess. She wore a white robe and her hair swayed capriciously, swayed by a gentle breeze. She approached Death and challenged it with her deep, arcane black eyes.

"You can't take him, he doesn't belong in your horrible world of shadows and torment," she said firmly.

The Grim Reaper looked at them in confusion with its empty, black sockets and hesitated for a few moments before vanishing with a terrible, unearthly scream of fury and frustration, taking with her the darkness that covered them.

The dusk hovered darkly and protectively over them. Stars twinkled in the sky and an immaculate freshness washed away the putrid smell of death that permeated every inch of the hapless Tarraco. The woman, illuminated by the flames that devoured the city, approached and kissed him.

"I love you, Adriano," she whispered in his ear. "We'll never part..."

"I love you... Valeria."

Invaded by an infinite feeling of peace, and sheltered by the black cloak of the eternal night, he closed his lifeless eyes. He felt Valeria's warm hands caress his pearly forehead, calming his deepest fears and uncertainties.

His lips sketched a last smile.

EPILOGUE

Countless plumes of black smoke rose mercilessly over Tarraco's dark night. The city was still consumed by flames and the devastation that the Visigoths had left in their wake. A shadow, a legionary, a defeated soldier, moved cautiously among the dead that covered the *castrum*, with his *spathae* drawn in anticipation of being attacked by some straggling or greedy barbarian who was still foraging his share of the loot in that city given to desolation and death.

The legionary looked at the corpses for one in particular. But his tear-stained eyes weren't helping him in his hard work. Then he saw him and, shaking his head, knelt beside him with the devotion of a faithful Christian to the relics of a saint. At least the barbarians had respected his corpse, and he wasn't stripped of his coat of mail or his military tunic. The *miles* couldn't leave his remains abandoned to the hungry vermin. He didn't deserve such an ominous ending.

"Adriano, my friend," Arcadius whispered with his heart sinking with the most horrible of sorrows. The tears stabbed his cheeks and his face was disfigured by indescribable pain. "I shouldn't have left you, I shouldn't have left you..."

"You had no choice."

The voice behind him startled him, and he leaped to his feet, ready to attack whoever had uttered such words. But he restrained himself when he realized that he was dealing with an enigmatic woman accompanied by a young man in his early twenties with well-drawn features. They both wore white robes and stared at him with bitter faces.

"A... Alana?" Arcadius asked, with his eyes narrowing in confusion.

The woman nodded and said:

"You must not fear for him, his true love freed him from the Grim Reaper's clutches and now he is in a beautiful place, away from wars and miseries."

"But... but I thought it would be you who..." the legionary said stammering.

Alana leaned down and kissed Adriano on his cheek.

"I loved him and he loved me," she replied, "and he gave me the most wonderful of gifts," she added, pointing to the young man. "But Valeria was the love blessed by the Mother, the worthy and pure love that would prevent him from being dragged into the world of darkness and desolation. They are together now and will never be separated again. We shouldn't mourn his loss, but rejoice, since now he is filled with happiness and peace, a peace that had been denied him for years."

She looked up and gave the legionary a beautiful smile. Her eyes shone sad and excited. She got up and said:

"You must tell his story to honor his memory."

Arcadius looked at her confused, but it didn't take long for him to understand her purpose.

"But I'm a soldier, not a *cornicularius.*"

"We'll help you," young Adriano intervened, gently placing his hand on the veteran legionary's shoulder.

Arcadius knelt down and placed his hand on his friend's chest. Alana and her son did the same.

"His story is the story of Hispania," Alana began, staring at him. "Don't allow his memories to be lost in the sands of time, nor his memory be blown away by the wind of oblivion and indifference. Tell his story friend Arcadius, and his heroic bravery will be remembered forever."

The brave legionary took a deep breath and squeezed Adriano's bloody, inert hand. He'd have preferred to die beside him rather than gaze at his body lying beside him. Yes, he owed him. To him and to so many Hispanics who decided to die as Romans rather than live as barbarians. Men and women who, driven by an iron determination, sacrificed their lives in the hope that another world was possible.

So, he decided that he would. He would write the story of Adriano, that of Hispania, that of the Hispano-Romans who watered the land of his ancestors with their blood. He will thus honor his memory. And his memory will never be forgotten.

In this land, the mountains and meadows are green and infinite, the coasts are cut by steep and misty cliffs, and the sky eternally veiled by leaden and threatening clouds. But the sound of the drums, the tubas and the screams of the barbarians are alien to us, almost strange, as if it were a distant nightmare that we would like to forget.

We set out on a long journey until we landed on the shores of Hibernia. There was only one reason why we decided to head to the island of the druids: Peace. Its shores are hidden behind an eternal mist and it remains protected by a thousand magic and spells. There were few who knew of it, and far fewer those who would venture through its thick, deadly fog. So, there we headed Flavius Protus with his daughters, his sons-in-law and grandsons, along with Alana, and my friend's three sons.

Long years have passed since the black death surprised Adriano. Salvio Alexandros and Aquilia Annia have married and God has blessed them with healthy and robust children. Adriano returned to the land of the Suevians to continue the work of his mother, establishing himself as a respected and beloved druid. And, Alana has remained by my side, helping me in the writing of these lines, the posthumous tribute to a great man. The druid-woman has given me the prerogative to experience Adriano's feelings and emotions, to relive his experiences. I have felt what he felt, I have loved as he loved and I have suffered as he suffered... I have become Adriano to be able to tell his story, because a story can only be told with passion, strength and intensity, when one has participated in it.

Spring has arrived and the gray clouds have granted an ephemeral truce to the sun's rays, which timidly warm my old and tired bones.

As for the Empire, just as the soothsayers predicted, it was devastated twelve centuries after its birth. Rome had prospered by blood and fire, and by blood and fire it was destroyed by her enemies, as Lughdyr told Adriano one day.

Three years after the conquest of Tarraco by Euric and his horde of Visigoths, a Herul prince named Odoacer deposed the last emperor; a thirteen-year-old boy named Romulus Augustus, and confined him to Campania, southern Italy. Ironies of capricious Fortune, the last emperor of Rome had the same name as the founding father: Romulus. Odoacer sent the imperial insignia to Constantinople. The message was clear: Rome would never again be ruled by an Augustus, and Zeno, the Eastern-Emperor fearful of his power, recognized him as lord and master of the conquered lands.

The Herul proclaimed himself king of Italy, ending the twelve centuries of glory and splendor of the Roman Empire. Rome has fallen and with it our civilization, plunging the world into the darkness of ignorance and superstition.

In these last lines, my mind evokes with joy our battle cry, the cry that Salvio Adriano raised when he raised his *spatha* ready to throw himself against the enemies of the Empire: *Roma invicta est! Roma invicta est!* A cry launched into the air with the clamor of glory and truth. The barbarians have plundered our lands, conquered our cities, and robbed our people. It's true. Our enemies have devastated Rome, but they'll never, never ever succeed in defeating the Roman spirit. *Roma invicta est!* I cry out again from the heart, from the corner that houses the noblest and most powerful feelings. *Roma invicta est! Roma invicta est! Roma invicta est!* Unshakable, immortal, because her colossal legacy will be eternal and will last until the end of time.

I've spent the last years of my life writing this work, praying to the good Lord to give me the strength to finish it. With these letters, I've tried to transcribe what my memory has dictated to me: the life of Salvio Adriano, the last legionary of Hispania.

My name is Sextilio Arcadius, old *centenarii* of the extinct Roman legions. I find myself in the year 506 of Our Lord, *ab Urbe condita* 1259, in the remote and arcane lands of Hibernia, the island of the druids.

God save Rome, God save Salvio Adriano.

Alfonso Solis

AUTHOR'S NOTE

This story is a journey through the last twenty-five years of the Western Roman Empire, narrated from the perspective of a Hispanic soldier: Salvio Adriano. Through his experiences, adventures and misadventures, it has been tried to underline the circumstances that favored the progressive decline of Rome and the abandonment, by the latter, of her Provinces, including Hispania. Naturally it's a fiction work and as such it must be read and understood, although it's true that many historical episodes that are related here were real and are well documented. It's the author's duty to differentiate historical events from those that are due exclusively to his imagination, in order not to confuse the reader and to enjoy a vision as truthful and concrete as possible of the events that occurred in the Rome and Hispania of the 5th century AD.

The prophecy of the flight of the twelve eagles is still a legend about the mystical origin of Rome. A rather bloody origin, since Romulus, persuaded to be the one chosen to govern the new city, assassinates his own brother for unclear reasons. Leaving aside the circumstances that led the first king of Rome to commit the alleged fratricide, the fundamental thing is that from its birth, Rome germinates and flourishes watered with the blood of the defeated. The augurs predicted twelve centuries of glory and splendor, and their success is surprising, because if we agree that Rome was founded in 753 BC. and Odoacer deposed the last emperor in 476 AD, the Empire lasted no more and no less than 1,229 years.

In 451 AD a decisive battle for the survival of the Empire was waged between the hosts of Attila, and those of Rome and her federated. The specific place is unknown, but different sources place it in the Catalaunian Plains or *Campus Mauriacus*, some land near the small town of Maurica, about a hundred and fifty kilometers east of the city of Troyes. To describe the battle and its consequences, the author has relied on the work of the Roman historian Priscus, famous for his account of the delegation sent by Constantinople to Attila's court. During the battle the Visigoth King Theodoric dies, and Turismund, his son, is named *Gothorum rex*. Attila is forced by the Romans and his federation to retreat and protect themselves behind his camp. The Hun king, convinced that he would soon be defeated, ordered to light a funeral pyre with the saddles of the horses to rush upon it if his enemies assaulted his camp. But this didn't happen. Aetius persuaded Turismund to rush to Tolosa and be ratified there as king, because if he stayed longer in Maurica he would run the risk that one of his brothers would overtake him. Shortly after the departure of the Visigoth, Aetius removed the Roman camp, freeing the Hun king. Although much has been speculated on the reasons why Aetius allowed Attila, the Empire's greatest enemy to get out of that battle alive, the most plausible is the one that suggests that, once the Huns were exterminated, the Visigoths would fell on the Empire. In addition, Aetius lived as a hostage with the Huns for years and, according to certain writings, he intended to renew good relations with them in order to keep the Visigoths under control.

Once the threat represented by Attila and his horde of Huns had been «temporarily» contained, Aetius sent the *Hispaniarum comes* Mansueto to Gallaecia to negotiate a peace treaty with Requiarius the *Suevorum rex,* the purpose of which was the withdrawal by the Suevian from the lands occupied in the Carthaginian and Tarraconense provinces, territories subjected to looting and depredation since 449 when the Suevian king left for Tolosa to meet his future Visigothic wife. The mission was successful and Requiario agreed to withdraw his troops and respect the rules agreed between his father Rechila and Rome.

Turismund died in 453, assassinated by his brothers Theodoric and Frederic. Possibly the Visigoth princes were instigated by Rome, since Turismund wasn't exactly in favor of renewing the *foedus.* Theodoric was proclaimed his successor by the Visigoth nobles and soon ratified the alliance with Rome. In the year 454 Aetius entrusted the new *Gothorum rex* with the mission of putting down a *Bagaudae* revolt that was devastating the region of Tarraconensis, and Theodoric, «*ex auctoritate Romana* » on behalf of Rome, sent an army commanded by his brother Frederic, exterminating the rebellious peasants.

We are very well informed about Aetius's death thanks to the work of the Eastern Emperor Constantine VII and, again, to that of Priscus. The *magister utriusque militiae* had pressured Valentinian to accept the marriage of Placidia with his son Gaudentius. This marriage would consolidate Aetius's power and make it very likely that Gaudentius would succeed the emperor, since the Augustus had no male child. The proposal harmed the already tense relationship between the general and Valentinian. In addition, after Attila's death, Valentinian understood that Aetius's services weren't so essential for the Empire and his disappearance was even convenient for his own interests. Thus, Valentinian, possibly persuaded by Senator Petronius Maximus, in the course of an audience, killed the *magister utriusque militiae* assisted by Heraclius, a eunuch that was the head of the imperial house.

Aetius's assassination caused a great commotion in the army and after his death a period of instability began. Some of Aetius's officers rebelled in Gaul and Dalmatia, and in order to prevent members of the *magister utriusque militiae's* personal guard stationed in Italy from also rebelling, they were assigned to different units of the army. Petronius Maximus asked the emperor to be appointed consul, but the eunuch Heraclius also aspired to the position and hindered the senator's pretensions, claiming that he intended to become a new Aetius. Petronius Maximus, enraged by Valentinian's refusal, bribed (following Priscus) two high officers of Aetius's personal guard, the Gauls Optila and Traustila. And on March 16, 455 they attacked Valentinian when he, accompanied by Heraclius, was practicing archery in the *Campus Martius*. According to Priscus, Optila killed the emperor and Traustila killed Heraclius, fleeing to meet Senator Petronius Maximus to collect his reward. Naturally, the «theatrical representation» narrated in the book, during which the emperor is killed, is the product of the author's imagination.

Petronius Maximus after getting rid of some opposition was proclaimed emperor, and to strengthen his power he married Licinia Eudoxia, Valentinian's widow. But he wore the purple for a short time, since when he heard that the Vandals had arrived on the shores of Italy, he tried to flee to Ravenna, but the guard abandoned him, leaving him at the mercy of the excited mob that killed and dismembered him, putting an end to his brief reign and his excessive ambition.

Genseric entered a subdued Rome on June 2. Pope Leo I made him promise that he would respect the churches, and that he wouldn't raze the city nor shed innocent blood, in exchange, he gave him part of the Church Treasury. For fourteen days, the *Vandalorum rex* sacked Rome, paying special interest in the Palatine, the Capitol and the residences of aristocrats and landowners, returning to Carthago with a large booty and with the Empress Licinia Eudoxia and her daughters Placidia and Eudoxia.

On the 9th of July, in Arelate, and with the support of the Gaul-Roman senators and the Visigoths, Avitus was proclaimed as the new emperor. The first problem he had to face was the invasion of the Suevian King Requiario to the territories of Carthaginiense in 455, and Tarraconensis in 456. After unsuccessful negotiations, Avitus declared war on the Suevians and sent to Gallaecia the *Gothorum rex* Theodoric "*cum voluntate et ordinatione Aviti imperatoris*" with the emperor's will and order. The Suevian troops are defeated twelve miles from Asturica Augusta and, subsequently, Requiarius is captured and executed. According to Hydatius, Galician-Roman bishop and historian, the defeat of Requiarius meant the end of the *Suevorum regnum* in Hispania. Although the Suevians survived for a few more years, it's true that they ceased to be a problem for Rome, and later, for the Visigoths.

But Avitus' policies weren't to the liking of the Italian senatorial caste and taking advantage of the fact that his Visigoth allies were fighting in the lands of Gallaecia, they persuaded the *magistri militum* Ricimero and Majorian to rebel and depose him. And on October 17, 456, in the vicinity of Placentia, Avitus was defeated by the insurgent generals and forced to be ordained bishop of the city, dying soon after in mysterious circumstances.

Majorian was proclaimed emperor, and in 461 he organized a powerful fleet to exterminate the Vandals of Genseric. The emperor would travel by land with the bulk of the army and would meet with the army, around 300 ships, in Carthago Nova. As planned, the emperor arrived punctually to the appointment but, following Priscus from Panium, he must have been betrayed by the people of Carthago Nova or by some high official and his ships were destroyed by the Vandals. Defeated, the Augustus returned on horseback to Italy, where he was captured and finally executed by order of Ricimero.

The chapter in which Genseric besieges Carthago Nova is completely fictitious. According to the writings of Hydatius, the *Vandalorum rex* left Hispania with all his people in 429, embarking for Africa. But with this episode I have intended to relate the overwhelming situation of the Hispanic cities, always harassed and threatened by the barbarian hordes, and completely forsaken and forgotten by the Empire. Likewise, the chapter in which Salvio Adriano abandons Carthago Nova is fictitious. But I consider that it faithfully reflects the dismemberment of the Hispano-Roman society. The decadence of the Empire was evident and its fall inexorable, and there were not few

Hispanic dignitaries who kissed the hand of the barbarians in exchange for maintaining their privileges and perks. Such was the case of Arvandus, the *praefectus praetorium Galliarum,* Seronatus, the vicar of the sub-Gaul diocese or Vicentius, *the Hispaniarum dux.*

After Majorian's death, Ricimero elected Libius Severus as emperor, but the new Augustus didn't have the favor of the army nor of Leo, the Eastern emperor, and in the year 465 he died suspiciously. After an interregnum of more than a year, Anthemius, *magister militum praesantelis* of the East, was invested with the purple. The arrival of the new Augustus gave new impetus to the Roman aspirations to annihilate the troublesome barbarians of North Africa and, in a new and even more formidable expedition against the Vandals than the one undertaken by Majorian; Anthemius will have the support of the Eastern Empire. In 468 an armada of eleven hundred ships and, according to different sources, between thirty thousand and one hundred thousand soldiers, landed on the African coast about sixty kilometers from Carthago. This fleet was commanded by the Greek general Basiliscus, brother-in-law of the Eastern-Emperor. The objective was to disembark the powerful contingent of troops and march the last miles on foot. Once the armada was anchored, it was attacked by the Vandals and destroyed. According to the Byzantine historian Procopius, the failure of the expedition was due to the treachery of Basiliscus, who granted five days of truce to Genseric in exchange for a huge amount of money, hoping that during that time the wind direction would change, as it did.

Faced with Anthemius's inability to stop the Visigothic advance in Gaul, Ricimero gathered an army of six thousand mercenaries and besieged Rome. On July 11, 472, the city was looted and the emperor assassinated by the Burgundian prince Gundobaldo. Olybrius, Genseric's candidate, was named new emperor, but died that same year, on November 2, shortly after Ricimero's death. And Glycerius, a high official of the imperial guard, was invested with purple.

Euric was proclaimed *Gothorum rex* in 466, after the assassination of King Theodoric, initiating a relentless campaign of harassment against the Empire. He fought in Gaul and his hosts crossed the Pyrenees and conquered Tarragona. The Visigothic *comes* Gauteric took Pompaelo and Caesaraugusta, at the same time that Heldefred and the *Hispaniarum dux* Vicentius conquered Tarraco and the cities of the coast.

Later, they went to Carthaginian, annexing much of the Iberian Peninsula to the Visigothic kingdom of Tolosa.

From these historical facts, «*Roma invicta est*», has been woven together, a fictional novel that has tried to outline the most significant episodes that took place in Rome and Hispania in the second half of the 5th century AD.

HISTORICAL FIGURES

The following list presents a brief review of the historical figures that appear in this work in order to differentiate them from the merely fictional ones.

Aetius
: *Magister utriusque militiae* of the Western Empire. He leaded Rome for 20 years. He was assassinated by the Emperor Valentinian.

Anthemius
: Emperor of Rome crowned by Leo, the Eastern-Emperor.

Arborius
: *Magister militum Hispaniarum.* He replaced Nepotianus.

Ardaric
: Gepid king, Attila's client.

Arvandus
: *Praefectus praetorium Galliarum.* He was accused of preparing the partition of Gaul between Visigoths and Burgundians.

Attila
: King of the Huns. Known as *«flagellum Dei»* or God's scourge, he was the greatest enemy of the Empire.

Avitus
: Emperor of Rome thanks to the support of the Gaul-Roman senators and the Visigoth King Theodoric.

Basilio
: *Bagaudae* chief. He attacked Ilerda and Turiasso, where he killed Leo, the bishop of the city.

Egidius
: *Magister militum Galliarum.* He didn't recognize Libius Severus as emperor and proclaimed the independence of Gaul.

Eudoxia
: Daughter of Emperor Valentinian and Licinia Eudoxia. She married Huneric, Genseric's son.

Euric
: Son of Theodoric I. He was proclaimed king after the death of his brother Theodoric II.

Frederic
: Visigothic prince, son of Theodoric I and brother of Turismund, Theodoric II and Euric.

Gaudentius
: Aetius' son.

Gauteric
: Visigoth comes. He invaded Hispania.

Genseric	King of the Vandals. He sacked Rome and kidnapped empress Licinia Eudoxia and her daughters. He was a fierce enemy of Rome.
Glycerius	Anthemius's *domesticorum comes*. He was invested with the purple thanks to Gundobaldo's support.
Heraclius	*Primicerius sacri cubiculi* (chief of the sacred apartments) of Valentinian. He helped the emperor to assassinate Aetius.
Honoria	Sister of Emperor Valentinian.
Huneric	Genseric's son.
Libius Severus	Emperor of Rome appointed by Ricimero.
Leo from East	Emperor of the East.
Licinia Eudoxia	Wife of Emperor Valentinian. After his assassination, she married his successor Petronius Maximus. She had two daughters Placidia and Eudoxia.
Magnus	Gaul-Roman senator, he was sent to Hispania to ensure the adherence of the Hispanic provincials to Rome.
Mansueto	*Hispaniarum comes.*
Majorian	Emperor of the West.
Meroveo	King of the Franks. He gave his name to the Merovingian dynasty.
Nepotianus	*Magister militum.*
Odoacer	King of the Heruli. He deposed Romulus Augustus, the last emperor, putting an end to the Western Empire. He was appointed dux by Zeno, the Easter-Emperor, later proclaiming himself king of Italy.
Olibrius	Western-Emperor.
Optila	Officer of Aetius's personal guard. Following Priscus, he assassinated Emperor Valentinian encouraged by Petronius Maximus.
Pope Leo	Known as Leo I the Magnus. He was pope of the Catholic Church. According to certain chronicles, he prevented Attila from sacking Rome in a meeting between both personalities in the city of Mantua. Subsequently, he

	negotiated with the Vandal Genseric the surrender of the city in exchange for respecting the lives of its inhabitants and that it wouldn't be burned.
Petronius Maximus	Western-Emperor. According to Priscus, he encouraged the assassination of Valentinian. After the death of Augustus, he married Empress Licinia Eudoxia.
Placidia	Daughter of Valentinian and Licinia Eudoxia, she married Olibrius.
Requiario	King of the Suevian.
Rechila	King of the Suevian and father of Requiario.
Ricimero	Magister militum of barbarian origin. For years, he ruled the destiny of the Empire by investing with the purple the emperors who ruled according to his will.
Romulus Augustus	The last emperor of Rome. He was deposed by Odoacer and interned in Campania.
Sangiban	King of the Alans.
Seronatus	Vicar of the sub-Gaul diocese, he was accused of collusion with Euric and condemned to death.
Theodoric I	King of the Visigoths. He died at the battle of Maurica in front of Attila's host.
Theodoric II	King of the Visigoths and son of Theodoric I.
Traustila	Aetius' personal guard officer. Along with Optila, he killed Valentinian and Heraclius the eunuch.
Turismund	Visigoth king and son of Theodoric I. He reigned after the death of his father in Maurica. He was assassinated by his brothers Theodoric II and Frederic.
Valamir	King of the Ostrogoths.
Valentinian	Emperor of Rome.
Zeno	Emperor of the East.

GLOSSARY

Abdera	Adra (Almería-Spain).
Ad Urbe condita	Latin expression that means «since the foundation of the city», i.e. Rome. This date is traditionally placed in the year 753 BC.
Adiectio sterilium	A tax levied on abandoned land that is returned to cultivation by farmers to whom it has been allocated under compulsory allotment.
Agentes in rebus	Secret police.
Allabone	Alagón (Zaragoza-Spain).
Annona militaris	Tribute paid in kind (grain, oil, fodder, etc.) for the maintenance of the army.
Anticaria	Antequera.
Apodyterium	Changing room in the hot springs, where the citizens kept their clothes.
Araris	River Saona (France).
Asturica Augusta	Astorga (Leon-Spain).
Aurelianum	Orleans (France).
Balteus	Belt where the legionaries hung their sword.
Barcino	Barcelona (Spain)
Barritus	German war cry. It began with a soft murmur and progressively increased until it became a thunderous shout.
Bracara Augusta	Braga (Portugal).
Brigaecium	Benavente (Zamora-Spain).
Bucelarius	Soldier belonging to a private army whose original mission was to protect the haciendas from barbarian looting, but after the disappearance of the legions in Hispania they assumed the protection of the cities.
Caesaraugusta	Zaragoza (Spain)
Calcei senatorii	Footwear dyed red, typical of senators.
Caldarium	Hot bathroom located in the hot springs.
Calends	It was the first day of the month.
Calon	Slave of a soldier.

Campagi	Military footwear.
Caput Mundi	Center of the world, one of the names by which the city of Rome was called.
Carteia	Algeciras (Spain).
Cassis	Helm with plume.
Castigatio	Flogging inflicted on a soldier as punishment.
Castrum	Military camp.
Cataphract	Rider whose horse is protected by scale armor.
Cauca	Coca (Segovia-Spain).
Centenarii	Roman officer commanding one hundred soldiers.
Circitor	Non-commissioned officer on duty.
Clarissimus	Exclusive denomination of senators that was later extended to provincial governors and certain administrative positions such as prefects in charge of taxes.
Clunia	Coruña del Conde (Burgos-Spain).
Civitatis comes	Imperial agent with judicial and military powers. Its concept arose to make up for the limitations of the municipal curias and to complete the centralization process that developed in Rome from the beginning of the 4th century AD.
Comes domesticorum	High officer in command of the emperor's guard.
Comes spathariorum	Captain of the *spatharii*.
Contubernium	Military unit consisting of eight soldiers.
Cornicularius	Administrative Officer, either secretary or scribe.
Cornu	Spiral curved tuba used by the Roman army.
Curator	Senator in charge of tax collection.
Defensor civitatis	Appointed by the *praefectus praetorium*, his mission was to defend the poorest citizens from the abuses of the nobles.
Dertosa	Tortosa (Tarragona-Spain).
Dianium	Denia (Alicante-Spain).

Dignitates	Civilian or military positions appointed by the emperor, which make their holders of special rank.
Dromon	Warship of the Orient Navy.
Ducenarius	Officer in charge of two hundred soldiers.
Dux	Commander of the *limitanei* of a province.
Equites	Horsemen.
Fatum	Destiny.
Foederati	Barbarian tribes linked to Rome through the signature of a *foedus*.
Foedus	Treaty or alliance signed between Rome and the Barbarian tribes.
Frigidarium	Cold water pool in the hot springs.
Gades	Cádiz (Spain).
Garum	Fermented viscera sauce of different fish (tuna, sturgeon ...). It accompanied the main dishes and was highly appreciated by the Romans.
Gothorum Rex	King of the Visigoths.
Hibernia	Ireland.
Idus	It was the thirteenth day of the month, except for the months of March, May, July and October when it was the fifteenth.
Ilerda	Lérida (Spain).
Iliberris	Elvira (Granada-Spain).
Ilici	Elche (Alicante-Spain).
Illustres	They were most of the main positions of the imperial court like the *praefectus praetorium*, *magister militum, magister officiorum*, etc.
Ilorci	Lorca (Murcia-Spain).
Iugatio capitalino	It was the tribute obtained after the valuation given to the units of productive land among the individuals who work them.
Laconium	In the hot springs, steam bath.
Limitanei	Permanent troops whose main mission was to patrol and protect the borders of the Empire.
Lituus	Long cylindrical trumpet with upward curved bell and independent mouthpiece. Used by the

	Roman army. Its sound was sharp and strident.
Lucentum	Alicante (Spain).
Lucus Augusti	Lugo (Spain).
Magister navis	Captain of ship.
Magister officium	Head of the imperial chancellery and commander of the imperial guard (*scholae palatinae*) and of the secret police (*agents in rebus*).
Magister utriusque militiae	Commander in chief of the cavalry and infantry troops.
Malacca	Málaga (Spain)
Miles / milites	Soldier.
Modius	Unit of weight equivalent to 7.6 kilograms.
Nonas	The fifth day of each month except March, May, July and October which was the seventh.
Numerus	Basic term used to designate military units in the late Roman army. It was equivalent to regiment or detachment.
Ordo decuriorum Or Senate	It was the citizen council and was constituted by the dignitates and the landowners. It was in charge of the collection of taxes, the conscription of recruits, the administration of justice, the maintenance of the public services and the games and festivals. Its members were called decurions or curials.
Palestra	In the baths, a central courtyard that connected the rest of the rooms and where physical exercises were practiced.
Palla	A veil or cloak that Roman women used to cover their shoulders or a sort of hood when they went out into the street.
Pallantia	Palencia (Spain).
Paludamentum	A type of cloak worn by Roman officials. A part of it was usually worn over the left arm.
Patagium	It was a not very tight belt that girded the *stola*. It was usually embroidered with gold thread and adorned with precious stones. Its use conferred prestige and distinction.

Pedes	Infantry soldiers.
Perfectissimus	Designation exclusive for *duces* and *comites* and, from Constantine onwards, for officials such as the *magistri census*, and the *primicerii*.
Feet	Unit of length equivalent to 29 centimeters.
Pisoraka	River Pisuerga (Spain).
Pompaelo	Pamplona (Spain).
Praefectus praetorium	Maximum responsible for the prefecture (there were two during the Western High Empire: that of Gaul and that of Italy). They had absolute responsibility over the civil administration and were in charge of levying the levies and supplying the armies.
Palatina legio	Name given to the best legions during the late Empire.
Parcae	According to Roman mythology, they represented the fatum or Fate, and controlled the thread of life from birth to death. There were three Fates: the Nona, the Decima and the Morta. The latter was Death, the one who cut the thread of life. In this work we refer only to the Morta.
Praefectus urbi	Of senatorial rank, he was in charge of the administration of Rome.
Praepositus	Commander of a unit in the late Roman army. Initially it was a temporary rank, but eventually it became a permanent title.
Praetorium	The area of the camp where the legion commander's residence was located.
Primicerius	Commander of a legion in the absence of the tribune. The *primicerius of the scholae palatinae* held the status of *clarissimus*.
Primicerius sacri cubiculi	Head of the sacred rooms.
Pugio / Pugium	Dagger.
Pulpitum	Tribune or box.
Rhodanus	River Rhone (France).
Sagitarii	Archer.
Sagum	Type of cloak used by Roman soldiers.

Saguntum	Sagunto (Spain).
Sardinia	Sardinia.
Scholae palatinae	Imperial guard during the late period.
Scutum	Shield.
Segisamon	Sasamón (Burgos-Spain).
Semissalis	Legionary veteran.
Senator	Roman officer of higher rank than *ducenarius*.
Septimanca	Simancas (Valladolid-Spain).
Spatha	Sword.
Spatharius	Visigothic royal guard.
Spiculum /a	Spear.
Stadium	Unit of length equivalent to 185 meters.
Stola	Tunic that the woman wore immediately after marriage. It used to be worn on top of another inner tunic called subucula.
Subligar	Underpants.
Subucula	Inner tunic of silk or linen, very convenient on cold days. It consisted of a single piece with sleeves.
Tablinum	In the *domus*, office or audience room of the father of the family.
Tepidarium	In the thermal baths, bath of warm water.
Tiro / es	Recruit.
Toga praetexta	Toga reserved for magistrates and minors. It had a purple border at one end.
Toga virilis	Toga worn by all Romans when they reached adulthood. It was white and unadorned.
Turiasso	Tarazona (Zaragoza).
Urbicus	River Órbigo (Spain).
Urbs City.	The word written in capital letters refers to the city of Rome.
Valentia	Valencia (Spain).
Valetudinarium	Hospital.
Vallum	Palisade that surrounded the castrum protecting it from possible attack.
Verutum	Javelin.
Vestibulum	Vestibule.

Printed in Great Britain
by Amazon